Gold Coast

Edmund Gaisie

Edgar K. Gaisie

Collinwood Publishing

Published by

Collinwood Publishing

ISBN: 978-0-9961089-1-1

Sankofa
"Go back to fetch it"
Symbol of the wisdom of learning from the past to build for the future

Prologue
Accra, Colonial Gold Coast
1900

Sir Dennis Hughes, the recently appointed governor of the Gold Coast, was a red-haired, fair-skinned sailor and successful trader turned bureaucrat who repeatedly expressed his displeasure for the African heat. Hughes was meeting with his military advisors at his beachside base camp to discuss the eradication of the Asante rebellion. Hughes sat miserably and shirtless in his chair with a wet rag covering his head while his nurse rubbed ointment on his sunburned face, neck, and chest.

Also present was Colonel Buchanan, leader of the regiment's infantry. Next to Colonel Buchanan stood his subordinate, Lieutenant Drake Richards. The last man present was Jean Nyum, an officer who hailed from the Fante tribe; Nyum was also a tracker who commanded the other indigenous scouts in the regiment. Hughes removed the towel from his head and dropped it into the bucket of cold water sitting next to him. Nodding at his guests, he said, "Gentlemen, thank you for coming. I will make this brief."

His nurse must have rubbed a sensitive part on the Governor's burned neck because in the middle of his introduction, he squealed like a child. He sniped at the nurse and his eyes welled up with rage. The nurse quickly scurried away to avoid bearing the brunt of his anger. Hughes composed himself, sighed, and then continued, "I have received word from London. The crown wants us to put a stop to the Asante uprisings. These constant skirmishes with the Asante have made the Queen quite anxious."

Colonel Buchanan spoke up. "Sir, quite frankly," he said as if he were exhausted, "haven't we been through this enough? It's the same situation over and over again. London can't understand why the Asante won't submit to the crown. This is what always happens: we fight them, barely win, and inevitably lose good men and waste good resources in the process. Just to do it all over again? We've already exiled their Chief Prempeh to the Seychelles islands. Why can't we just bloody leave them alone? I think they've earned it."

Governor Hughes nodded his head in agreement. "I understand, Colonel, however, this time the crown is putting their shillings in place of their tongues. 'We will increase the budget,' they told me. And when we return successful, you and I will get our choice of transfers."

Colonel Buchanan raised his eyebrows in mild approval. He was rapidly warming up to the thought of being given carte blanche for his choice of transfer, which quieted his opposition for the moment.

"We've already proven we can beat the Asante's military because we have the numbers and the weaponry. Yet they keep coming back like forest ants. I, gentlemen, plan to put an end to their arrogance," Hughes said as he grimaced in pain from his sunburn. He then directed his attention to officer Nyum. "Jean!"

"Yes, Governor?" the Fante soldier replied.

"Since you are a native, teach us more about the Asante. According to Asante folklore, what gives them their mystique and their dominance?"

"Their royal throne, Sir," Nyum answered but was reluctant to go into detail. Even as Fante, he knew that the biggest symbol in the Asante culture, and perhaps in all of the land, was the Asante royal throne—also called the Golden Stool. According to legend, Okomfo Anoke (high priest and one of the two founders of the Asante confederacy) conducted a sermon that ejected the Golden Stool from the heavens to land in the lap of the first Asante, Chief sei Tutu. Among the tribes, thrones in West Africa were traditionally symbolic of a chieftain's leadership, but the Golden Stool was also believed to house the spirits of the Asante—those living, dead, and yet to be born.

"Yes, the Golden Stool, as the locals refer to it. Now tell me, Jean, is anyone other than the Asante king allowed to sit on the throne?"

"No, Sir. Not even the Asante king is allowed to sit on the throne. The chief is the only person who can touch or handle the stool, but he is not authorized to sit on it, and the throne is never supposed to touch the ground."

"Well that sounds utterly ridiculous to me," the governor said, raising his voice. "It can't touch the ground? There is only one throne they should acknowledge and it belongs to Great Britain. End of story." Governor Hughes cleared his throat. "We will lead a patrol to march into the Asante village and demand they relinquish that throne. In addition, I want expert verification that it is, in fact, the actual Golden Stool and not some replica. Once I have verification, I will sit on it and pose for a painting. Or perhaps I'll commission that black-magic technology everybody has been using lately." Then he paused and asked, "What is that technology called again?"

"Photography," answered Nyum. "Sir, is it necessary to desecrate something so sacred to them? Is it even ethical?"

Governor Hughes cocked his head and looked at Private Nyum with disgust. "You sit here and lecture me on ethics? Listen, Private Nyum, just because we let you receive a British education and a uniform doesn't mean you can come here and question my authority. You are still my subordinate. You Fantes think you're so fucking smart!" said the appalled governor. "Don't forget that you are not too far removed from the savages we are fighting, like the Asante, just because we have educated many of your tribe. Are we clear?"

Nyum unhinged his neck and cursed the governor in his mind, but in person, he nodded his head in humiliation.

≈

On horses fit for giants, Governor Hughes and his army rode into Kumasi, the capital of the mighty Asante nation. As the representative of a mighty nation himself, Governor Hughes was bestowed traditional courtesies by the Asante. After entering the city, they allowed the governor to ascend the village platform. Once on the platform, he stood above the Asante assembly and talked down to them: "Your King Prempeh is in exile to the Seychelles Islands and he will not return to you. His power will be taken over by the representative of the Queen of England," he paused for effect, "which Shappens to be me. The terms of the 1874 Treaty of Fomena that require you to pay the cost of the 1874 war have not been forgotten. You must still pay an interest of £160,000 a year."

The governor showed no tact in his demands and he was just warming up. "Then there is the issue regarding the Asante royal throne, or as you refer to it—the Golden Stool. The Queen of England has requested possession of the Golden Stool. And as I'm sure you know, the Queen of England is not to be denied."

After the translator explained the governor's message in the local Twi language, there was a mixture of grumbling and laughter. Even after almost being laughed out of the village, the arrogant governor continued his lecture. To add insult to injury, Governor Hughes spoke to the gathered Asante like a pet owner would speak to his dog; he was condescending and patronizing. Instead of learning any common phrases in their dialect to communicate better with them, he unknowingly mocked their accents by emulating the Asante's unnatural use of English, as if they could better understand his lunacy: "I am representative of paramount power. Why you relegate me to such ordinary chair? Where is the Golden Stool for me to sit upon?"

Even though Governor Hughes was not ignorant of the significance of the Golden Stool, he was still dim-witted enough to fail to anticipate the storm his words would produce. The suggestion that a foreigner could sit on the Golden Stool was received with a hostile reaction from the crowd. The governor's irresponsible tone rightfully ignited a fire within the Asante community.

Immediately following the governor's speech, the Asante Queen Mother, the fearless Yaa Asantewaa, assembled a force to attack the British and rescue their exiled Chief Prempeh. When Yaa Asantewaa heard of the dissent among some of the Asante hierarchy to fight the British and rescue Chief Prempeh, she interrupted the all-male tribal council to lecture them in a speech that would cement her admiration among the Asante for generations.

With the irate passion of an injured warrior, Yaa Asantewaa pontificated on rebellion. "Now I see some of you fear to go forward to fight and defend our throne. If it were the brave days of Opoku Ware, chiefs would not sit down to their king being taken away without firing a shot. No European would have dared speak about an Asante king the way the governor spoke to you this morning," lamented the Queen Mother as she pointed to her male counterparts. "And now you tremble," she said in disgust. "Is it true that the bravery of the Asante is no more?" she asked with tears streaming down her face. "I must say this: If you men of Asante are not willing to fight, then we women will. We will fight until the last of us falls on the battlefield!"

Five days before the British were set to invade the Asante villages, a tribal elder man was visited by a Fante, introducing himself as Poku but who was publically known as Private Jean Nyum, a member of Governor Hughes' counterinsurgency team. Nyum explained that he had grown tired of the governor's attempt to turn countrymen against countrymen in the effort to embrace a foreign ruler. For that reason, he decided to arm the rival tribe with valuable information so the Asante could arm themselves against the British Army, which planned to invade their villages soon.

When the Asante elder man relayed Nyum's message to the rest of the royal council, the members not only prepared for battle, they also made arrangements to protect their most valuable possession. As a result, the original Golden Stool still circulates in anonymity around undisclosed locations across the region.

History would prove that the Asante fought valiantly against the British. The tribe was ultimately defeated, but they truly bloodied the noses of their occupiers. In fact, the Asante considered their last installment of the war a victory because their occupiers never captured the royal throne.

To avoid future conflicts, the British called a treaty with the Asante and agreed to let them rule as a semiautonomous state under the protection of the British crown. However, the treaty did not come without severe consequences. As leader of the rebellion, Yaa Asantewaa was sent to the Seychelles islands to join King Prempeh and the other exiled Asante leaders.

Yaa Asantewaa died in exile in 1921. Three years after her death, King Prempeh and the remaining exiled Asante were granted permission to return home. Not only did Prempeh leave behind the living Queen Mother, he also left a legacy of hybrid children with dark skin, Indian-black hair, and green eyes. Prempeh's Ghanaian/Seychellois offspring would later play an integral role in defending the safety of the Golden Stool.

To honor the deceased Queen Mother, King Prempeh insisted her remains return with him for a proper burial on Asante soil. Yaa Asantewaa's dream of an Asante free of British rule was realized on March 6, 1957, when the Asante protectorate gained independence as part as Ghana, the first African nation to achieve this status.

Four months after ending the Asante rebellion, Governor Hughes was granted his transfer back to England. After barely defeating the Asante, it was understood that Governor Hughes was returning to

England with the world at his feet. Unfortunately for Hughes, his victory lap of rubbing elbows with the Queen's men was short lived. Not long after his return, Hughes fell ill to an affliction we now know as skin cancer; he passed away a year later. Ironically, the hate he had for the Ghana sun would follow him all the way back to his homeland of England.

Chapter 1
Accra, Ghana
Two Years Ago

When Clinton Osei stepped outside of Kotoka Airport in the capital city of Accra, the distinct aroma of tropical vegetation and the undertones of open drains permeated the air. The air's pungent bouquet is the first sense of culture shock one encounters as a visitor to Ghana; it is also the first memorable sense one longs for after leaving.

The curbside pickup scene was chaotic and it swarmed with activity. While Clinton was not a large man, he had the build of a young college athlete. However, even he wasn't ready for how easily the crowd could knock him off his step if he was not paying attention. The bulk of the herd was not even travelers: They were mostly noncertified taxi drivers and perhaps the largest congregation of freelance concierges on the planet. He estimated he was solicited for someone's services a dozen times in less than a minute. The mob of concierges yelled over one another. They grabbed and tugged at Clinton as if the person who successfully knocked the shoulder strap off his arm would win the "job."

Momentarily paralyzed by the chaos, Clinton almost surrendered himself to the mob until, through the sea of madness, he noticed a man standing on the curb next to a vintage Rolls Royce. Clinton immediately identified the car as his Uncle Oscar's 1972 Rolls Royce, a car Oscar had owned for as long as Clinton could remember. The man standing next to the car was Oscar's long-time assistant Kwasi. Clinton signaled for Kwasi, whom upon seeing him started to jog over; but Clinton waved and gestured that he remain where he was. Kwasi obliged but immediately grabbed Clinton's baggage and opened the door when he reached the car.

As Kwasi shooed the barrage of solicitors away, Clinton took the time to regain his composure. He sat slightly slouched in the vintage sedan and fully enjoyed its plush interior. If it weren't for the loose stitching in the

1

seams of the seat, the minute scratches on the tan leather, and three small hairline fractures of rust on the exterior, the '72 Rolls would have been considered mint condition. The sedan's imperfections gave the car character, and Clinton viewed them as demarcations of time.

Kwasi drove off and exited the airport. Clinton raised his back one-degree forward and peered out the right rear window to admire the surroundings. Most of the western world's perception of Africa was one-sided, Clinton thought. The notion perpetuated by the western media that all of Africa was famished and war torn aggravated Ghanaian-Americans like Clinton, who knew better. Although Clinton was raised in the United States, he was fortunate to have family still living in Ghana and had visited the country many times. He knew that, like many African countries, Ghana did not get enough credit for its modern advancements. For instance, there were aspects of Ghana's capital city of Accra that were just as contemporary and sophisticated as any city in the western world.

Each time Clinton visited Accra, he was astounded by its growth. The abundance of high-end vehicles and the explosion of suburban neighborhoods were staggering. Although Ghana proved to be a country on the rise, the stark contrast between the "haves" and the "have-nots" was still obvious. While there were many Western-type amenities, poverty still dominated the landscape. This reality was evident as they traveled through the pothole-riddled road that led travelers out of the airport district and into the city.

Accra's inequities were vividly exposed on the pedestrian level. The stereotypical image of rusted corrugated roofs atop unleveled shanties associated with urban Africa was all too prevalent. In all of the optimism surrounding Ghana's narrative, the sobering fact was that the average Ghanaian had a less than 1% chance of experiencing a fraction of what the minority elite enjoyed. Clinton admired the ease with which Kwasi avoided the potholes. Traffic in Accra was starting to resemble a Los

Angeles type of gridlock—not because it was a big city, but because the government had yet to provide sufficient infrastructure to meet the rapidly growing automobile population.

Standstill traffic made roadside vending a popular industry along the airport-district roads. What made this roadside vending so unique was that the consumers didn't even have to leave their cars. The vendors simply showcased their inventories to consumers through their car windows while jogging alongside the vehicles at the same speed. The only inconvenience for a consumer was rolling down his or her window to purchase the desired items.

The mobile-market vendors were mostly women and children, who balanced baskets on their heads. The baskets contained a multitude of merchandise with no common denominator from one to the next. As the Rolls Royce reached the peak of an incline and Clinton looked down onto the mobile market, he noted how it resembled a sea of grocery baskets all bobbing rhythmically along the same current.

For a quarter of a mile in traffic, two adolescent boys pursued Clinton's car. They were scrawny, ashy-legged brothers with round eyes and big smiles. Their baskets were filled to the brim with various items one might find in a New York City bodega. They yelled and tapped on the rolled-up windows, trying to solicit Clinton for their wares. Clinton initially allowed his driver Kwasi to use his own method of handling the brothers, which consisted of abruptly cursing them in Twi and, at one point, threatening to run them over. No matter the harshness of Kwasi's tactics, the brothers were not deterred. They followed the car with twenty pounds of merchandise—each ignoring the other's prospective customers. Clinton couldn't help but be impressed with the brothers' tenacity. Finally, he rolled down one of the windows and entertained the eager salesmen. "I'll give you $10 for all of the cinnamon-roasted peanuts."

The younger brother glanced at his partner. Then the older brother replied to Clinton in the humblest of

3

tones, "Please boss, I beg you—$16 dollars."

Clinton, thinking he had undervalued the merchandise, decided to haggle with the brothers. "Okay, boys, my final offer is $15. Take it or leave it."

"Okay, boss, we'll take it," the brothers replied. They handed Clinton his basket full of cinnamon-roasted peanuts and he handed them the money. He rolled up the window and grinned as he watched the two brothers descend back into the mobile marketplace.

Clinton caught Kwasi's eyes, which were unusually green for a dark-skinned Ghanaian, smiling at him through the rearview mirror. "You're making fun of me, aren't you?"

"That was funny, Mr. Clinton."

"Here's the thing, Kwasi, in the world where I do business, those kids are better served if I bargain tough with them. That might sound harsh but it will serve them better in the future."

Kwasi began to laugh louder than his normal humble chuckle. "Oh, no, no, no, boss! You have it all wrong. In this market, the retail value of what you purchased isn't worth more than five Ghana cedis—the equivalent of three American dollars. I thought you were just being generous because you felt sympathy for those boys." Kwasi continued his hearty laugh while a humbled Clinton kept quiet for the rest of the thirty-minute drive to his hotel.

Clinton was in his hotel room, fixing his collar in the mirror when his phone rang. Kwasi was on the other end informing him that his ride awaited at the entrance of the hotel. Clinton told Kwasi to give him a few minutes as he finished straightening up. He was scheduled to meet with his mother's older brother and undisputed patriarch of the family, Oscar Boateng. His uncle had informed Clinton about the purpose of their meeting in a series of phone calls the previous week. However, like a true salesman, Oscar was not going to make his pitch if the conditions were not ideal, so he requested that Clinton travel to Ghana to talk details.

Clinton gave one last look and noticed his gray hairs were starting to catch up with his thirty-eight year old face, often described as youthful. He smirked at himself in the mirror, not because he was enamored with his looks but to have a laugh. Clinton knew he was an enigma of subtle paradoxes. Upon first meeting him, many people noticed his slightly northeastern-American accent didn't match his West African facial features. Cognizant of this, every once in a while, Clinton would mangle an American phrase in broken English. Or, in the rare occasion he heard an Afrobeat (contemporary West African music) song playing in public, he would stress the accent of the lyrics to expose his ethnicity—similar to how an Italian-American who has never been to Italy will elongate the vowels when pronouncing an Italian dish or designer.

Clinton's paradoxes didn't stop at his cultural conflicts; professionally, he was also an enigma. Recruited by a New York-based consultancy firm (Bradley and Partners) while still a graduate student at George Washington University, he became an analyst at the age of twenty-six. Clinton, however, made short work of the notion of paying his dues. In just one year, he worked his way up from analyst to associate and then Assistant Vice President (AVP). His virtually unheard of 0-60 mph climb from associate to AVP can be attributed to one specific client interaction on a field visit six years into his employment with Bradley and Partners that Clinton masterfully exploited to his benefit.

Chapter 2
Detroit, Michigan
Six Years Ago

One weekend in Detroit on a Bradley and Partner's visit to their large automotive client's headquarters, he accepted an offer from one of the executives to join her for floor seats at a Pistons game. The client's Senior Vice President of North America, Carol Gardner, had an impressive story. She was a fiery forty-one year old, born and raised by second generation Scottish/Irish parents, who were lifelong auto factory workers on Detroit's west side. Carol graduated valedictorian of her high school and earned a full scholarship to the University of Michigan, making her the first woman in her family to attend college. At Michigan, she excelled in economics and was recruited by the Detroit-based automotive manufacturing giant straight out of college. She rose steadily through the ranks to her position as senior vice president. As an executive, she earned a reputation as a sharp-witted, get-your-hands-dirty type of manager.

When Clinton and Carol arrived at the arena, they were immersed into the fast-paced energy surrounding a professional basketball game. Carol easily navigated the arena as if she were the Piston's general manager, whisking them through the aircraft-hangar sized hallways where sharply dressed players were often seen descending in pregame television footage.

When they reached the floor, Clinton followed Carol's lead. For the first time, he took note of her appearance as she casually walked onto the court. She was a fit, attractive woman with mid-length light brown hair that was mostly covered by her Detroit Piston's hat. In addition to her fan cap, she wore a light blue buttoned-down shirt with fitted designer jeans and wedge heels. Carol noticed Clinton was trailing behind and looked back at him, signaling that he needed to pick up his pace. When in step, Clinton realized he'd just crossed by the major network analysts' booth, and two veteran sports announcers he'd watched as a sports fan all his life sat four feet to his right. And that was just in his peripheral vision. Directly in front of him, he watched Carol fraternizing with the players during their pregame shoot as if they were her drinking pals.

She pointed at the Piston's small forward and heckled him, addressing him by his nickname, "Hey Slinky! How about playing some defense tonight, huh?" Slinky received Carol's jab with an uncontrollable grin; he then pump faked the ball he was holding as if to hurl a pass in her direction. Carol didn't even flinch. Clinton noticed her vernacular shift when she spoke on the court, "Nice try, Slink, but everybody knows you never pass the rock anyhow." This made the other players within earshot snicker with ooh's and ahh's. Even Slinky acknowledged the burn.

"Don't worry though, you know you're still my favorite, handsome," Carol soothed before leading Clinton to their floor seats.

"First time to a basketball game, Clinton?"

"Been to several but this is my first time actually being in one."

She laughed, "You mean all this fanfare? Hey somebody's gotta keep these bums in shape." She let Clinton take in the atmosphere awhile longer before she began to pry. "Well, I must say you have the attention from your peers at my office. From what I understand, you stick out like peeling wallpaper on the third floor. You must have an interesting background. Tell me about yourself. Osei? Where is that name from?"

"It's from Ghana in West Africa," Clinton replied. He automatically continued because he knew the next question was always, why don't you have an accent? "I've lived in the States most of my life, so I'm really an American with Ghanaian roots."

Her next question threw Clinton off like a change up from a major league pitcher. "What makes you think that Chris will approve the consulting contract with Bradley and Partners?" Chris was the company's CEO and her boss.

Clinton tried to play dumb. "I'm just an analyst, Carol; that type of conversation is above my pay grade."

Carol smiled and said, "Your tone sounds believable, but the sarcasm is written all in the arches of your eyebrows. I've been doing this for a long time; you're no damn analyst. I can't put my finger on exactly what you do for Bradley, but you really disguise it well. And no offense," she paused for effect, "but your boss, Ron, with his solid white shirts and traditional ties, now he's the real analyst at heart. He's kind of a snore, isn't he?"

Clinton raised his eyebrow at Carol, implying that he would not be complicit in such an insult about a firm partner.

"Are you a sporting man, Clinton?" Carol asked without letting him answer. "Well I'm a sporting gal, and since I was nice enough to make you my guest of honor at this fine sporting event, I ask that you indulge me with one request."

"Sure," Clinton joked, "as long as I won't need an attorney after accepting this request."

Carol protested with a pout and remarked, "Well you're no fun. But seriously, in business scenarios like this, I like to make things interesting. Would I offend you, if I propose we make a medium-stakes wager?

"Sure. On the game? I'll put a few hundred against the Pistons."

"Although, I'd be honored to take your lunch money, Clinton, I'm talking about a wager more valuable than cash. This would be a wager of information. Here are the rules: After this game, we will enter into a series of games I like to call the 'Motor City Triathlon.' You and I will compete in a game of billiards, shot consumption, and back-alley dice. The person who wins the best out of three events is the winner. The victor can ask the loser any question of his or her choosing, and the loser must agree to truthfully answer that question. "

She gave Clinton the time to laugh and let him come to the realization that she was dead serious. Carol noticed one of the referees standing within earshot and finished more loudly with, "Plus Clinton, I'm not dumb enough to bet on this game; I'm pretty sure it's rigged. My friend Benny here gets paid to call the game against us anyway. Ain't that right, Benny? Anytime you're in town you never fail to make a call that screws us, do you?"

Benny shot back at Carol, "With you as a Piston's fan, who could blame me, Carol?"

Carol gestured as if she were going to give him the bird.

While continuing to smile, Benny turned his back to them and walked toward the center of the court to officiate the game. "So are you in?" Carol pressed.

Clinton surrendered with a yes, and complimented her. "You're a live one. I never expected a well-polished executive like you to be into back-alley dice games."

By now, Carol had begun addressing Clinton as Ghana. "Ghana, don't let the pantsuit fool you. I'm a public school-educated girl from West Detroit. My dad used to take me to his bar for his daily happy-hour drink, directly after picking me up from elementary school. I did my homework and studied for tests there. It was also in that environment where I learned to hustle pool and roll dice...it's therapeutic for me. Naturally, my best thinking happens when I'm in places like that."

Clinton nodded his head. "Well I can't argue with that."

After the Pistons won, they commenced their own triathlon at Lambeer's in the working-class neighborhood of West Detroit. Carol obviously had home court advantage since she was a Lambeer's regular. They played a game of pool first; Carol proved to be a shooter, winning two out of the three games with aggressive trick shot type play. After pool, they dug in at the bar and ramped up their drinking by taking eight rounds of Fireball over the course of seventy-five minutes. On the ninth shot of Fireball, Carol suggested they call this round a draw, having seen that Clinton was more than capable of handling his own. She was also concerned that if they continued along that route, they'd be lying in a hospital getting their stomachs pumped for alcohol poisoning.

"Let's have a smoke," Carol proposed.

"Might as well throw them dice, too," he answered.

"I thought you'd never ask."

They loitered near the outside wall facing the alley and decided to play cee-lo with a combined pot of $500. Cee-lo uses three six-sided die and allows three rolls per round, with the winner setting the pace. Rolling a cee-lo means rolling a four, five, and six, and also the highest score in the round.

They bet from $50 to $150 a round. As in pool, Carol seemed to find her luck with the dice. She was winning the rounds at a six-to-one margin. Clinton knew that the binge drinking, gambling, and (not to mention) the subtle yet mutually embraced flirtation they were participating in would be frowned upon by their respective bosses. After another half dozen rounds, Clinton caught up to Carol with a series of high rolls and increased wagers; he now held the majority of the pot.

"It's your turn to roll, Ghana."

"No. You need to slow your roll, Detroit!" Clinton joked, implying that she was getting ahead of herself. "I'll roll but only when I'm ready. Tell you what I'll do so we can finalize this game. How about if we roll for each other's pot? I have more money, but am willing to bet my stack against yours. Winner takes all: the money and most importantly the right to ask a question that the other must answer."

"I'll take your bet. You're going to go down, though."

Clinton handed her the dice. "You roll first."

She rolled a fairly high score of six. Clinton beat her with a triple two. In the second round, Clinton rolled a five, which she beat with another six. In the final round, she rolled the second highest score of a triple six, which inspired her to howl at the moon.

"You can't beat that, Ghana!" she boasted. "You'd have to roll cee-lo, and neither of us has rolled it all night."

10

If Clinton's morale was injured, he didn't show it. Instead, he picked up the three dice, blew on them, and agitated them in his loosely closed fist with a sideways arm movement. Clinton let the dice roll, and before they all landed, he commanded, "Cee-lo!"

When the dice landed, neither yelled. They looked at the dice and then their eyes immediately locked, both had grins on their faces but for entirely different reasons.

Then not being able to take the silence longer, Carol erupted with, "Motherfucker! Are you kidding me? You rolled a fucking cee-lo? How does that happen?"

Clinton just smiled and shrugged as if he'd planned it all along, adding, "I've always had success with games of chance."

Carol picked up the dice and stepped closer to Clinton, close enough so they were chest to chest. Not caring about his personal space, she shoved the dice deep enough into his left trouser pocket that her fingertips were padding his groin. "Well 'Mr. Games of Chance,' these are your lucky dice…better keep them."

Her right hand remained in his pocket, relaxing her fingers a bit and successfully getting a rise out of Clinton. "So what's it going to be?" she purred, while simultaneously firming her grip against Clinton's growing muscle. "What do you possibly want to know about me?"

Undeterred, Clinton grabbed her waist and pulled her closer. Allowing her hand to remain in his pocket, he leaned into her. She closed her eyes anticipating his kiss. However, she was caught off guard when Clinton whispered in her ear, "I want to know why your CEO Chris is torpedoing his own company."

At this, Carol stepped back and looked at Clinton; her look was less surprised and more intrigued. "Where would you get such a creative idea? Chris is getting stellar reviews from the industry. Plus the board is completely satisfied with his performance."

"I'm sure they are, but they don't look at the data the way I do."

"And how exactly do you see the data?"

"I see a man whose last significant initiative has driven the company into a precarious position. Sure, it created the largest fleet of hybrid cars in the industry, but he disguised it as a solution to save the company. Will it? Chris is a smart man, and although he's been a green technology proponent, he's also on record, as of two years ago, saying that taking the industry lead in green technology would be akin to driving the company off a cliff. Why make such a 180-degree pivot? And why do it with absolutely no extensive planning?"

"Come on now, Ghana, he obviously saw the error of his ways. New technology and new resources have been presented to him and he's embraced it."

"We both know that's bullshit. I know you see your company's balance sheet. And also, I know that you know your company is on the brink of being overleveraged. While it's solid in other areas, it doesn't have the resources to afford taking a risk like this one right now—especially, when you don't have to. I've visited your new plants in the Southeast that build these hybrids; they are second rate at best. The level of planning is so abysmal, I realized that it had to be intentional. I just don't see the motivation."

Carol grinned at him. "See, Ghana, I knew you were more than just an analyst."

"What's your boss' angle, Carol?"

"What makes you think I know anything? And even if I did, why would I tell you?"

"For one, Detroit, because you lost the game for which you set the rules. Secondly, it's your job to manage the green initiative, and I've seen memos where you've already expressed your displeasure with the lack of resources allocated to these plants. I think your exact words were, 'We are setting this project up for failure.' Not to mention, you will undoubtedly be the scapegoat for the initiative's failure."

Carol had a rebuttal but ate her words when Clinton suggested she would be scapegoated and let him finish.

"But if given the right information, Bradley and Partners is in a unique position to foil your boss' kamikaze

12

effort and help someone like you benefit after the smoke clears."

Carol did not appear as uncomfortable with Clinton's assertions as he thought she might. After taking several seconds to internally struggle with her decision, she spent the next forty-five seconds sharing the invaluable information she discovered about her boss.

"I've recently learned that Chris is going to leave our company to work for our main German competitor. You know the one I'm talking about. Anyway, I found this out through one of his assistants. I won't bother telling you how I may or may not have 'seduced' the information out of the naïve young buck. But, anyway, according to his account one day during lunch, the assistant overheard a conversation Chris was having with one of our competitor's board members. Chris renders his assistants so insignificant that they appear invisible in his presence; he apparently feels comfortable making incriminating phone calls right in front of them."

Carol pondered for a second and then shook her head. "Now that you mention his idiotic decision about the green automobile initiative, I'm now sure he conspired with that German competitor to sabotage our company; effectively weakening their competition when he takes helm." Then she whispered, "That son of a bitch." After divulging her information, she stepped back and revealed her sleepy eyes, not allowing Clinton a chance to respond to the bombshell.

"It's been a long night, Ghana. This ole lady is taking her ass home. I'll call you a cab. I'm curious to see what you do with this information. You don't strike me as the type of person who would throw me under the bus, so I'll spare you the disclaimer."

Carol turned her back on Clinton and walked toward the door. He stopped her with a question. "So if you had won the game, what would you have asked me?"

Carol laughed. "Honestly?" Then her eyes glanced at where her hands were moments ago, and winked. "I was going to ask you...is that thing as big as I think it is?"

Clinton grinned and was on the verge of telling her he'd allow her to retroactively invoke her question, when Carol's parting words cut him off. "Too late though, handsome, I'm a sore loser. Can't let you have your cake and eat it too." She blew him a kiss. "Good night, Ghana."

A week and a half later, Clinton used the information in a final analysis meeting with the automotive client. In that meeting, he inserted a slide presentation that demanded the room's attention, illustrating how vastly irresponsible Chris' green initiative was to the company and how it would plummet them into financial disarray and perhaps even bankruptcy. There was obvious fallout from the meeting after Clinton dropped this bombshell, with not only Chris but his own superiors, as well.

Behind closed doors, Clinton provided the necessary evidence: phone records Carol convinced Chris' assistant to print out showing the history of Chris' phone calls to their German competitor's corporate office. Luckily, Clinton's information was spot on, and Chris was subsequently ousted as CEO. The SEC also investigated Chris for unlawful practices, although he was never convicted.

As promised by Clinton that night in Detroit, Carol did benefit from the corporate fallout after the smoke cleared. The board, through the recommendation of Bradley and Partners' promoted Carol to CEO, where she continues to reign. The motor company's major investors showed their appreciation for Bradley and Partners by awarding them with the majority of the business in their portfolios, increasing the firm's annual billable hours by 30%. The corporate coup orchestrated by Clinton put him in a position to negotiate a lucrative deal with Bradley and Partners. He was quickly promoted to AVP then senior vice president and made a partner, giving him equity in the firm.

Fast forward to today. When Bradley and Partners was acquired for an undisclosed amount, as a partner, Clinton received a nice percentage of that fortune, immediately transforming him into a very wealthy, unemployed thirty-eight year old with both time and money on his hands. Hence, the reason for Clinton's current visit to Ghana. His uncle Oscar had lured him there to present a unique business proposition; one Clinton would shortly decide whether or not to entertain.

Chapter 3
Tema, Ghana
Two Years Ago

As they pulled up the long, dusty driveway of Oscar's villa in Tema, Clinton was reminded that Oscar wanted as little to do with the 21st century as possible. The grand entry to his villa was meticulously lined with manicured gardens, as well as limestone sculptures of cherubs and lions. Clinton was greeted at the door by Oscar's house staff, who all sported white jackets and white gloves. The dated blatancy of indentured servitude that still existed in the homes of wealthy Africans offended Clinton's modern ideals. But like most westerners who visited the country and were waited on hand and foot, he learned to get used to the pampering. Aside from a desktop computer, cell phone, and flat-screen television, Oscar's Tema villa looked the same as it did in 1977, furnished with antiques and exotic trinkets from his travels. Clinton sat in a plush red-velvet chair with intricately sculpted mahogany arms on a glossy Italian marble surface in the foyer of his uncle's house. He waited alone until he heard voices entering the house. The voices were those of his cousins, George and Jasper Boateng, as they entered the foyer.

George was always a smartly dressed gentleman. He was thirty-nine and already packing on soft pounds, which was uncharacteristic of a Boateng male. After George turned thirty-five, he didn't much care for exercising. Instead of cardio and weights, George opted for saunas and massages. His mother's housemaids secretly nicknamed George "the chubby prince." Despite his recent metabolic struggles, George was still the most charismatic male in the family next to Oscar. Today, George's demeanor helped alleviate some of the anxiety in the room. The meeting hadn't even started yet, and he was already on his second beer.

"I'm a bit disappointed, Jabs," George said to his brother.

"And why do you say that?" laughed Jasper.

16

"At first glance you wouldn't guess that a simply dressed man like him would be chilling with millions in the bank."

Clinton shook his head; he was caught off guard by the greeting. Actually, he was worth just north of $15 million but felt no need to correct his cousin. Especially since George did not find it in poor taste to discuss Clinton's net worth within the first sixty seconds of their reunion.

Jasper was not nearly as talkative as his brother. Unlike George, Jasper was a fit specimen. He was as toned and, at times, could look as intimidating as a pit bull. As a West African who grew up in London, many people mistook Jasper to be a quintessential Brixton rude boy. In reality, Jasper was affiliated with the lesser-known London neighborhood of Hackney. Jasper was the rough-and-tumble family member who embraced his mystique. Jasper was dressed down compared to the rest of the group. He wore a fitted white polo shirt with dark straight-leg jeans; the ensemble was also coordinated with a pair of retro-edition Nike cross-trainers.

George continued, "Clinton, why don't you have one of them blinged-out Rolexes you Americans like to sport?"

Jasper chuckled and said, "Or maybe one of them platinum Jesus medallions you see in them rap videos?"

"Yea, he's got nunna dat," answered George.

Clinton was slightly jet lagged and not up for sparring in a battle of wits with his comedian cousins. He shook his head and said, "You can't be serious. Where is uncle?"

At that moment, Oscar entered the foyer and greeted the three men as he did every other houseguest, usually ten-minutes late and in fashion.

"Yes, yes, my sisters' sons," he bellowed.

In the middle of the floor, the sixty-eight-year-old Oscar cordially embraced his nephews with a hug followed by a traditional prolonged handshake. Today Oscar lived up to the "Dapper Dan" reputation he acquired in his thirties. He had an oak complexion with noble facial features. The subtle silver pin striping on his navy blue suit matched the aging titan's thinning silver hair. In his late sixties, he'd already made several million in various business ventures but primarily as a commodities broker.

Clinton affectionately embraced his uncle. "I see you found the fountain of youth in the waters of Accra. You've aged backwards!" he complimented.

"Hmmm..." Oscar rolled his eyes and sucked his teeth at Clinton. "I hope you select wine better than you flatter the elderly," he joked.

The four of them laughed and then relaxed into their reunion. They ventured into the kitchen where Clinton selected a chardonnay to drink with their entrée of boned guinea fowl sitting on a bed of rice and tomato stew. He finally felt at ease since arriving in Accra. He was closer with his uncle and two cousins than with the other family members who resided in his parents' homeland. But Clinton especially appreciated the fact that his uncle did not try to embarrass him by teasing him about his inability to speak Twi like most of his family members did. Oscar always spoke English with Clinton, making it less of a challenge for Clinton to express himself. Oscar spoke with the cadence of English nobility, and his accent made his already epic stories sound like narration.

"So how is my youngest sister Felicia doing?" Oscar inquired.

"Mom and the family are fine," Clinton assured him. "She and Dad would like to retire in their house here in Accra sometime soon."

Oscar continued to direct the conversation with, "So tell me, Clinton, what are your plans now that you've conquered corporate consulting?"

Clinton politely laughed and downplayed the question with a vague response. "I signed a strict non-compete agreement with Bradley and Partners. I'm not sure I'm even allowed to think about new business opportunities," he joked.

"If I may," Oscar interjected, "I have a golden

18

opportunity for you." Clinton shrugged to acknowledge he was listening as Oscar continued, "This country is in desperate need of young and capable desperados like the three of you to reclaim it."

Although a little uncomfortable, Clinton was relieved his uncle was getting to the purpose of this meeting and proposing a business venture; it was to be expected given his recent financial success. Uncle Oscar wasn't the first family member or friend to pitch a business proposal to him, but he was the only family member Clinton would take seriously.

"I don't know, uncle," Clinton stated, "doing business in Ghana can be tricky. You, of all people, know this firsthand."

Oscar looked his nephews in the eyes and said, "Yes, but these are different times." He then stood up from his chair and asked, "Would you boys humor this old man for a minute?"

Clinton, George, and Jasper followed their uncle's lead. They grabbed their wineglasses and headed upstairs to the balcony overlooking the moonlit Atlantic. Oscar turned to his nephews and gestured them closer, saying, "It is a beautiful night tonight, but the mornings are even more beautiful. When you wake up in the morning, notice how the sun blankets its warm rays over the sandy beaches of this magnificent coastline. You would think that image alone is why this beautiful country was so eloquently named the Gold Coast." He paused to sip his wine and allow his audience to digest the imagery he just laid before them.

"Unfortunately," he continued, "it was labeled the Gold Coast for shrewder reasons that had nothing to do with the picturesque landscape. Many centuries ago, Ghana and our neighbors were called the Gold Coast due to our abundance of natural resources—mainly gold. The Europeans, beginning with the Portuguese in the late 1400s, settled here to trade gold, timber, and slaves. The word spread to the Dutch, the Danish, and eventually the Brits. For centuries, our countries' greatest resources have

19

been negotiated through the hands of European flags. And when these European visitors discovered the abundance of gold on our shores, they couldn't help but name it the Gold Coast. The nickname was its official name until 1957."

Oscar sucked his teeth and continued. "Although Ghana was the first African country to gain its independence from European rule, it is still hard not to be angry when you think how much wealth has been robbed from our country. Can you imagine how rich Ghana would be today if it was allowed to profit from all our gold as the Portuguese, Dutch, and British did?"

All three cousins nodded in agreement.

"Well, believe it or not, the same thing is still happening today as we speak." Oscar continued, "British-owned companies like Kumasi Gold are still dominating the mining industry in the Asante and Volta regions and giving little money back to the communities they mine in, except for the pennies they kick back to greedy politicians. It's deplorable to think that after all these years, we still haven't learned how to control our own assets and use them to improve our conditions. What scares me is that they have recently discovered oil off the coast of Ghana, and now these same foreign interests are flooding our shores like the Portuguese first did in 1472."

Then, with a sharp left turn in the conversation, Oscar asked, "How well do you know our family's history?"

Clinton shrugged his shoulders, took a gulp of his wine, and said, "Mom and Dad always prided themselves on being forward thinkers; they don't dwell on the past too much."

On the other hand, George and Jasper said nothing. Since they had spent more time in Ghana than their American cousin, they were less ignorant about their heritage than Clinton. They knew Uncle Oscar was about to tell Clinton "the Story," as they called it.

Oscar shook his head at Clinton in mild frustration and said, "You are of royal blood, and you don't even know it."

"Well school me Uncle" Clinton urged.

20

Oscar, never declining an opportunity to narrate a story, obliged. "Clinton, are you familiar with the Akan term Sankofa?"

"Yes of course it's my favorite Adinkra symbol with the bird looking back at its tail. I know it translates to 'go back and get it'."

"Very good. Well our family's ancestry is the prime example of Sankofa. As the legend goes—hard to confirm, but later facts seem to support the early part—your great great great grandfather Kwame Ware was son of the Asante king. In a political move, his brother Ata got rid of him by tricking him into the hands of Dutch slave traders; he used a pretty girl to lure Kwame onto a beach where he was taken by slave traders. Kwame's captors sent him to the Caribbean, where most African slaves landed before going to America. Kwame ended up in St. Lucia, Antigua where an owner with the last name of Johnson bought him. Subsequently, Kwame's last name became Johnson, since plantation owners named their slaves using their own last names to indicate ownership. Kwame Johnson married a slave by the name of Aqua (pronounced a-kwee-ya).

"Again, as the legend goes, Aqua just happened to be the very woman who was unknowingly used as the bait to trap Kwame at the beach in Africa. Apparently, they were both sold into slavery to the same family. A generation later, Kwame's son Terrence was moved to Charleston, South Carolina. In Charleston, Terrence had a son Ernest, who was my grandfather and your great grandfather.

After slavery ended, your great grandfather Ernest made a pilgrimage to Freetown in Sierra Leone. He had set his final destination on Kumasi in what is now South Ghana to visit the Asante kingdom and tell them of his grandfather Kwame's journey. Unfortunately, Ernest never made it past Sierra Leone. He lived the rest of his years stranded in Freetown, ever so close to his destination, yet psychologically, he felt further away than he did as a slave in America. While in Freetown, Ernest married a Sierra Leonean woman. Soon after, their son Reginald, my father and your grandfather, was born.

21

"Your grandfather was a remarkable young man. He insisted on carrying his father's torch by visiting Kumasi and appeasing the ghosts of his ancestors. Albeit a seemingly impossible task for a fifteen-year-old boy, your grandfather managed to meet with the Asante king and convince him of the tribulations of his great grandfather, Kwame Ware. The King must have validated some of the story due to the well-documented financial assistance he eventually gifted to Reginald.

"As you well know, your grandfather had a prosperous career. Through his connections with the Asante king at the time, he was appointed to important government positions. At the height of his run in the private sector, he was elected treasurer of Kumasi. In the second act of his career, he returned to the public sector after making money from various properties throughout Ghana. He also started Temateng Agriculture that (as you also know) George and Jasper's mother now owns, which also includes two manufacturing plants.

"Well before that time, your grandfather changed the family name from Johnson to Boateng. He wanted to reclaim his roots and, from what he understood, Boateng was his great grandmother Aqua's maiden name before she was sold into slavery. Reginald learned how to speak fluent Twi within his first three years in Ghana, making him fluent in three languages: English, Creole, and Twi. This unusual mix of languages gave your grandfather an exotic accent the ladies could not resist. I'm sure that's how I came to be. Back then, although polygamy was not legal, the law was certainly not enforced. Like many other affluent Ghanaians, my father had multiple wives and girlfriends. However, my mother and both of your mother's mothers were the only daughters recognized in his will. Reginald Boateng met his first Asante wife, my mother, soon after he moved to Kumasi. They had me and they named me Oscar "Kofi Nana -Yaw," I think after an Asante prince."

What George thought was an internal smile, he soon found out was quite visible to his uncle.

"Why are you smiling?" Oscar asked.

Embarrassed at being caught, George decided to come clean. "Well, you add so much color to stories, uncle, that's all."

Oscar raised one of his eyebrows and said, "You think I am telling tall tales, nephew?"

"I don't know, uncle," George explained. "It's just difficult to verify anything as far back as the 18th century without any documentation. That's all I'm saying."

Oscar shook his head and said, "I don't get this younger generation nowadays. Oh ye of little faith." A slightly ticked off Oscar walked to the door leading to his den and said, "Follow me." Making their way to the bookshelf, Oscar questioned, "Do you know what the earliest form of storytelling is?"

Clinton shook his head and said, "I don't know, I guess some primitive form of sign language? I'm not really sure."

"Well," Oscar said, "that and music. Music is the earliest form of communication. One of the best things about us Africans is, ironically, what we often get criticized for the most. You see we haven't completely lost our 'primitive' ways altogether. When Prince Kwame Ware was sold into slavery, he and the rest of his countrymen carried on their traditions of oral and musical communication. It was customary for slaves to pass their family histories down in musical ceremonies. In our family, this tradition carried through the first generation until Ernest became the first one to learn how to read and write. Your great grandfather Ernest's own words are what validate the history for me."

Oscar then reached in the bookshelf and removed a thin leather-bound book from the neatly arranged collection. He opened the book and said, "This journal is probably my most prized possession. Your grandfather gave it to me on my eleventh birthday. It chronicles the journey of your great grandfather Ernest Johnson on his way to Freetown, Sierra Leone, which at the time was a fairly young colony created by Nova Scotian abolitionist, John Clarkson, for freed American slaves." Oscar handed the journal to George along with a magnifying glass and watched as he read a passage from the journal.

It has been two months since I first set sail to my native West Africa. The waters were rough and food is bad but I know it cannot be worse than the slave ship my grandfather traveled on years ago so I'll be just fine...

George continued to read the journal in awe. The journal looked authentic and elements of the letter confirmed some of what his uncle had told them. When he was finished reading the passage, he sat there and continued to admire the physicality of the book. He came to the conclusion that his uncle was entirely too classy of a man to doctor up something of this magnitude for the sake of boasting. He realized that he was looking at a genuine relic.

Then he passed it to Clinton, who was quietly overcome with inspiration. "Simply amazing," he said before passing it to Jasper, who stroked it with his fingers before returning it to their uncle.

Chapter 4
Tema, Ghana
Two Years Ago

A week had passed since Clinton met with his Uncle Oscar, George, and Jasper. Today they all reconvened in the boardroom of Oscar's Tema office for a meeting. Oscar assembled a larger team that included all of the potential players. Inside the boardroom, a large projection screen hung directly ahead of them and was the focal point of the room. The tables and chairs were set in a horseshoe fashion so every member had a view of the screen.

Clinton was the last to arrive and he immediately made his way to his Aunt Marguerite, who was in a chair with her back turned to the door. Marguerite Boateng, Oscar's younger sister and mother to George and Jasper, was a regal woman, who carried a muscular girth. The Ghanaian elder woman was CEO of one of the largest agricultural importers and exporters in West Africa. Unlike most Ghanaian professionals, she did not care for European and American fashion; instead, she preferred traditional West-African garments. Today she wore a dramatic two-piece, pink-and-yellow-on-green patterned ensemble with a matching head wrap. Her outfit was accented with gold jewelry that was so authentic and unrefined, it looked fake. The Ghanaian baroness valued her time, which was evident this morning by the way she managed her patience. She constantly asked for the time and sharply instructed Oscar's assistants to expedite her requests.

In fact, Marguerite was candid about the nature of the meeting from the moment she caught wind of it. When Oscar sent her the invite several days earlier, she immediately phoned her older brother and said with no sarcasm, "This cannot be a serious meeting if my sons are invited, Oscar." The loving mother clearly had little confidence in her sons' business acumen.

Clinton gave his auntie the customary three-kisses-to-the-cheek Asante greeting. "How is your mother?" she asked.

"She's fine, and says hello, of course." Marguerite, a woman of few words, managed a smile and mustered a head nod.

A thin middle-aged man, who sported a closely trimmed white Afro, sat next to Marguerite. Clinton held his hand out to avoid the awkwardness of the Marguerite's chilly reception. Marguerite spoke again in her soft but authoritative voice. "This is my vice president of imports, Kofi Jackson." He sat quietly and was only in attendance to act as Marguerite's counsel and give his objective advice. He was a man of few words. In fact, the only thing about Jackson that made noise was his loud colorful, kente-patterned bow tie.

Oscar called Clinton to the other side of the table. He was talking to a tall gangly man who did not resemble any of the present company. "This is Kumasi Gold's geologist, Harry Van Bleer." Oscar put his arm around Van Bleer and Clinton shook his hand. "Harry will be conducting our presentation today. He is the reason I did not want to go into too much detail earlier; I would be doing you a disservice if I didn't let you hear from the expert.

Oscar cleared his throat and asked his guests to be seated. "Good afternoon, I know I have kept some of you waiting long enough, so I will just get on with it. My hopes are that all of you present today will represent the managing owners of the new partnership of Boateng-Osei Incorporated (BOI)." Oscar signaled to one of his servants to hand out a copy of the PowerPoint presentation his firm had prepared for the meeting. "I have taken the liberty of researching the approximate net worth of each of you and outlined how I perceive the financial structure of such a business venture might work based on our varied means."

When voices began bombarding Oscar with questions, he held his hand out. "Please allow me to finish presenting my proposal, and I will answer all questions afterwards. Deal?" Oscar did not mind the fact that he had the audacity to make such a bold statement and not entertain one of their immediate questions.

"You leave us with no choice, uncle," George replied.

Oscar ignored his nephew. "Several topics are on the agendas in front of you. One of many, but the most significant, is the acquisition of the Kumasi Gold mining operations in Ghana. I intend to put up all of my assets and cash as collateral toward the acquisition of Kumasi Gold. My investment would represent 25% equity in BOI. If Clinton agrees to my proposal, he would contribute the lion's share of the down payment. Clinton's financial investment and his corporate credit rating would allow us to raise enough capital at a low interest rate. In exchange, Clinton would have the greater equity stake in the corporation. If I may add, this would be a modest percentage even if he decided to contribute more. Harry Van Bleer will act as Kumasi Gold's chief geologist and will work for a nominal monthly stipend to earn a 10% sweat-equity share of the company. The remainder 20% equity would be financed by Marguerite and her sons."

Oscar then glanced at Marguerite and continued, "If we agree to form BOI together, our primary order of business will be to acquire the Kumasi Gold mining operation from the British corporation, Royal Gold. I believe you will discover your sacrifices for this acquisition will not be in vain and, and dare I say, should prove to be wildly lucrative."

Oscar pulled his chair out and eased himself into it. "I will let our friend and current Kumasi Gold geologist Harry Van Bleer explain the particulars."

Harry turned down the lights and began his PowerPoint presentation. "What I am about to share with you does not leave this room. I've worked for Royal Gold more than fourteen years now, and I've lived in Kumasi for twelve years. As Kumasi Gold's head geologist, and a Dutchman, I've fallen in love with this region and its people. Through Oscar, I have cemented good relations with the Asante king and other members of the tribe. Currently, Kumasi Gold is losing a fortune."

27

He paused to correct himself. "They're not losing profit but rather the potential to make a fortune. They've almost maxed out their current gold claims and their future claims are empty." He paused for effect and continued, "What they don't know is that forty miles north of where they mine, there is an untapped wealth of gold outside of Kumasi's borders, which is also on Asante land. Only a few in the Asante hierarchy are aware of this fact. Kumasi Gold's current ownership is not in good favor with the people of Kumasi and, even more importantly, the Asante.

"The tribe believes Royal Gold has been a terrible steward of the land it mines and does not contribute to the community surrounding it. The Asantehene, or current chief, would rather keep that gold a secret for eternity and forgo his significant tribute than let Kumasi Gold's current ownership benefit from it. This is where BOI comes in. If you read the bylaws carefully, you will see that if BOI purchases Kumasi Gold, we have a fiduciary responsibility to the Asante stool. We have a condition with the Asante king that states he must distribute a great percentage of his pay to the Kumasi community for brick–and-mortar projects. To fulfill that condition, we will impose a 15% tax on ourselves for the first two years to pay to the Asantehene—with an annual 10% tax thereafter. In addition to our tribute, we will hold ourselves to the highest environmental and labor standards by hiring third-party environmental and humanitarian watchdogs to oversee our practices."

Van Bleer took a sip of water and with an air of cynicism continued, "Not only is the large endowment to Kumasi and hiring third-party evaluators the right thing to do, make no mistake my friends, it is also our marketing strategy. You see how well the 'Conflict-Free Diamonds' campaign is working for the diamond industry?" Van Bleer skipped to the next slide of a sexy graphic with catchy text. "Well, think of our 'No-Fools Gold' campaign as its baby brother. But the beauty of our campaign is that it's a public-service announcement as much as it is an advertising strategy. With this campaign we will partner with our competitors and proactively address the eyesore of our industry without being asked, all the while still touting the security of investing in gold."

"How do we know for sure all that gold is really up there?" Jasper asked not intimidated by his uncle's instructions.

Harry jumped back in and said, "I understand your skepticism, Jasper. I had my own. Although I'm a humanitarian at heart, I'm a geologist by profession; I'm aware of the geographical symptoms for gold-rich regions—and Kumasi has it. After months of pleading with the Asantehene, he finally granted me permission to explore the hills several months ago. And this is what I found." Harry skipped to the next slide. "As you can see in this slide, there is a picture of what is called 'mean rock' and 'lode,' all of which are strong signs of gold-rich veins existing just below the first shallow layer of earth. A fault line runs horizontally through the northern section of Kumasi. This is where our gold lives."

Van Bleer flipped to the next slide. "I dug eighty sample holes across nearly a football field size of land. At the end of my dig, I had compiled the equivalent of almost a full brick of gold. He then reached into the pocket of his brief case and revealed the gold he'd found. He handed the accumulated gold to them so they could all inspect the three pieces of flat gold squares, each about seven centimeters wide and long. When the gold pieces came to Clinton, he observed how pure gold retained more of a matte finish; he enjoyed its dull brilliance.

While they were being seduced by the gold, Oscar decided to interject, "There are a few challenges our lawyers and investigators have pointed out to me before we decide to go through with such an ambitious purchase. The challenges are quite significant and require sophisticated handling. Royal Gold Corporation owns Kumasi Gold, and Royal Gold is a publicly traded company. In order to acquire the Kumasi Gold mine, the majority of Royal Gold shareholders will have to vote yes for us to do so. This requires the executive committee of

Royal Gold's board of trustees to agree to our offer to buy Kumasi Gold, and then they have to recommend that their shareholders agree to the sale. Subsequently, the Financial Services Authority (FSA) in the U.K. has to approve the deal. I'm certain our accountants and lawyers will put together an application that will satisfy the pockets of Royal Gold's shareholders and appease the legal concerns of the FSA."

Oscar gave them a moment to process his jargon. "Our biggest hurdle will come from Lord Hughes, the chairman of the board for Royal Gold. Hughes is an old-school imperialist who has no love for Britain's former colony of Ghana. Lord Hughes is actually the great grandson of Sir Dennis Hughes, a former governor of the colonial Gold Coast. Hughes runs the board and has no trouble convincing the rest of the members to vote as he pleases. He would rather close the Kumasi Gold mine than acknowledge a Ghanaian corporation is capable of running it. More realistically, they would use our offer as leverage to sell it to another group that wasn't of African descent."

Marguerite broke her silence. "If they're so headstrong, how do we persuade them otherwise?"

Oscar appeased Marguerite by sending her a reassuring, familiar nod, signaling he had something big up his sleeve and would handle it, as he had handled so many problems in the past.

"Now, I will entertain questions, but I urge you to hold them." Marguerite shook her head and actually grunted in protest. Oscar ignored her and continued on, "I ask that all of you take your hard copy of the presentation home to read over carefully. I also had my assistant e-mail you an electronic copy of the presentation so you can click on the links that cite the pertinent data. I really want you to digest the nuances of this proposal so you will be better informed to ask the right questions at our next meeting." Oscar paused to sip his glass of water. "Really this feels more like a family reunion than a board meeting."

He turned to face Clinton. "I want you to get settled before you start wrapping your mind around the complex questions you need to ask to complete your due diligence. Let's continue to drink and enjoy each other's company before we decide to conquer the world."

After dinner, Oscar called Jasper over and asked him to stay behind. He left Jasper in the room as he saw the guests to another room, where he would join them later. Jasper was about look at his watch when a door opened on the other side of the room. A tall, middle-aged, white man walked in from a door at the rear of the conference room. Jasper was confused, as he did not even notice the door it was so well hidden.

As the man was about to introduce himself, Oscar walked through the front door. "Ahh, so I see you have met Mr. Dufrane."

"Not exactly," the man replied.

"Well then, Jasper, let me introduce you to Roland Dufrane."

Jasper nodded at Roland and allowed Oscar to finish his introduction. "Roland is a former intelligence agent for the Israeli Mossad. He has specialized in private security for the last ten years, and is now working with me fulltime as my head of security." Jasper shrugged as if to say so what? "Roland's expertise will be helpful when we try to leverage Lord Hughes into selling Kumasi Gold. Roland, and I believe you, too, may be able to assist in this project." Roland took the seat directly across from Jasper. His skin was a fair with warm undertones; he could pass as a South American, a Pakistani, or even a run-of-the-mill WASP. His hair was a barely comb able layer of salt and pepper strands; and an expressionless face, which added legitimacy.

Dufrane, waisting no time addressed Jasper, "Lord Hughes has a son, Jacob, who is currently vacationing in Thailand for two months. From what we understand, Jacob is addicted to heroin. If caught with heroin, Jacob could face five to ten years in a Bangkok prison. We're hoping we can use these two bits of information to work in concert with one another. Do you understand where I'm going with this?"

31

Jasper smiled and gave his uncle a look of surprise. "You want to blackmail this bloke or sumfin?"

Oscar responded by nodding at Roland, who produced a file from his attaché, opened it, and read aloud to Jasper: "Thailand's senior narcotics inspector, Ahkrat Shiou is as crooked as a cop can get. He's on the payroll of at least three of Thailand's most notorious gangs and is suspected of being a spy for Chinese Intelligence.

"In addition to being a spy and general slime ball, Shiou has also been an asset of mine off and on for the last several years. In a nutshell, Jasper, we'd like you to collaborate with Inspector Shiou to deliver Jacob Hughes to us." Without responding right way, Jasper focused a look at his uncle, and asked "Why me?"

"Well Jasper unlike myself, your brother and cousin, you don't bother yourself with eloquence. You speak plainly, and that's what this assignment needs. I'm not speaking as your uncle right now, I am speaking as your business partner. However, if this is something you don't feel comfortable talking about, I won't mention it again."

Jasper locked eyes with his father-figure uncle to gauge his sincerity. Once satisfied, he turned his attention to Roland Dufrane. Like Oscar and George, Jasper spoke with a prevalent British accent. However, unlike his uncle or his brother, Jasper sprinkled his accent with a healthy dose of Caribbean street slang he picked up in his Hackney stomping grounds.

"Put me in touch with this Inspector Shiou. I'll see to it, that it gets done."

Roland and Oscar nodded their heads. Jasper then stood up, shook their hands, and walked out.
When the door closed, Dufrane said, "This is a very complex maneuver, Mr. Boateng. Are you confident your nephew will come through?"

"Of my three nephews, Jasper I worry about the least. He'll be fine"

Chapter 5
Bangkok, Thailand
Two Years Ago

Poet Paul Theroux once said of Bangkok, "As Calcutta smells of death and Bombay of money, Bangkok smells of sex, but this sexual aroma is mingled with the sharper whiffs of sex and money." It takes most foreigners several days to fully acclimate themselves to the rude awakening of a Bangkok morning. The humidity can be so thick that the fruit flies appear to be moving in slow motion. The endless chatter of street vendors, office workers, and taxicabs can be so intrusive you feel as if the noise is being delivered to your eardrums via ear buds on the highest setting.

On this particular Bangkok morning, British tourist, Jacob Hughes, was immune to the distractions of Bangkok. The night before, Jacob had taken advantage of the darkest vices Bangkok had to offer. The bedroom window to Jacob's downtown hotel room faced east, allowing the rays of the rising sun to bathe its occupants. Jacob sat up in bed while his vision slowly regained its focus, and he took a second to adjust to his surroundings. He surveyed the room and tried to piece together his previous night, gradually discovering visual clues to solve this mystery. Over his right shoulder in the next room, a small tropical bird perched in a cage by the door and sang. It overlooked a middle-aged man slumped in a love seat, tie loosened, and sunglasses resting on his nostrils. Another figure lay in the corridor between the living room and bedroom. As his vision began to focus, he realized it was a young lady, probably in her early twenties.

Jacob untied the rubber tubing from his forearm and rubbed over the scab of the prick hole from his last fix. Lying next to him was a naked boy, who looked no older than ten. It was seeing the Thai boy sleeping next to him that rapidly brought the evening home and he shuddered. Damn it! Once again, my demons have prevailed, he thought.

He rubbed the boy's hair as guilt sweated from his

palms. With his eyes, he promised to make it up to the boy. Somehow believing his promise, Jacob relaxed. He yawned and stretched his arms to the heavens, hoping to expel any other demonic evils that remained within him. Today is a new day, he assured himself. He would make amends by finishing the spiritual portion of his trip by visiting the Wat Benchamabophit temple and pray to the Buddha for forgiveness.

Inspector Shiou did not use elaborate hand signals to direct his team of five armed police officers to break down the door of Jacob Hughes's hotel room. Instead, he casually waived his hand in a dismissive, loose-wrist manner. Behind Inspector Shiou was a camera crew, who appeared to document the arrest of Jacob Hughes. When Inspector Shiou and his squad raided Hughes's room, the $300-a-night luxury suite was flooded with vibrant light from the open-air hallway, exposing all of the bacteria-laden illegalities lying before them. The officers detained the three adults in the room, and Inspector Shiou instructed the sole female officer to rescue the young boy from the smarmy Englishman.

To say Jacob was stunned would be an understatement. Once his mind processed the raid, he could comprehend the police busting into his room, but for the life of him, he couldn't understand, why there was a camera crew filming the arrest. Jacob would shortly learn that the camera crew was with a U.K. television show, To Catch a Pedophile, Bangkok Edition. With Inspector Shiou's permission, the camera crew had followed him on this raid.

An incensed Jacob demanded, "Excuse me? What the hell are you doing? Get that fucking camera out of my face!"

Inspector Shiou said nothing. He walked around the room while tossing furniture, clothing, and linen. It was on top of the cell phone in the drawer of the bedside table, where Inspector Shiou found the ounce of heroin Jacob had carelessly stashed. The inspector picked up Jacob's passport. "Is this you? Are you Jacob Hughes?"

"Yes I am. But the drugs aren't mine," he lied.

Inspector Shiou did not pretend to be a righteous man, but right now, he despised the sight of Jacob Hughes. The inspector walked up to the handcuffed man and lashed him swiftly in the stomach with his baton. Jacob coughed as he caught his breath and looked into the camera. "You caught that, sir, right? You have that on film right? This man just assaulted me for no reason!"

Although painful, it wasn't the agony from being struck in the stomach that made Jacob start sobbing; it was the sobriety of the moment. He cried and babbled like an infant, with a camera lens ten inches from his face. Jacob was fully aware that he had just reached the rockiest of rock bottoms.

≈

Little did Jacob know that his loved ones and lawyers wouldn't learn of his predicament until nearly a week after his arrest. On Monday, Lord Hughes received a cell phone call at his office in Manchester, England. He was greeted by his son who chronicled the nightmare of his last five days in a Thai prison. Jacob told him about the drug charges but failed to mention the pedophilia charge. "You have to get me out of here. The arresting officer said the judge is going to make an example of me, and I could get ten goddamn years."

Lord Hughes, usually a composed man, found himself trembling. "Don't worry, son. Hang in there; I'm calling my lawyers right now and catching the first flight to Bangkok tomorrow to sort this mess out."

Hughes canceled all his meetings for the week and spent the entire day consulting with his lawyers. The news from the lawyers was cold comfort. They informed Lord Hughes that officers of the British courts have no reciprocity with the Thai courts, therefore Hughes's counsel could not represent his son in court. Many of the Thai lawyers appointed by the court were as incompetent as blind racecar drivers, and the private lawyers who have strong relationships with the courts only plea-bargain 10% of the cases they try.

Lord Hughes arrived in Bangkok a day after he received the shattering news from his son. He skipped checking into the hotel and went straight to the police precinct responsible for arresting his son. He waited outside of Inspector Shiou's office in a basement hallway on a wooden bench so worn that the finish was almost completely stripped. It was noon and the precinct was swarming with activity. Lord Hughes could hear handcuffed assailants yelling in Thai at the top of their lungs down the hallway. If the precinct had air conditioning, it wasn't on or it wasn't reaching the basement, because Lord Hughes could already feel the armpits of his shirt flooding with perspiration. Just when a bead of sweat formed at the peak of Hughes's forehead, the door to Inspector Shiou's office opened.

An officer said something in Thai to Hughes and, although Hughes did not speak Thai, he clearly understood the officer was inviting him in. Lord Hughes obliged and walked past the officer into the room. Inspector Shiou was sitting at his desk, smoking a Dunhill in a long cigarette holder, and obviously waiting for Jacob's father. Inspector Shiou physically resembled his colleagues, but unlike those colleagues, he exhibited odd flashes of eccentricity. In addition to smoking Dunhill's in a cigarette holder, Shiou sported a pomade slick hairstyle with a sharply creased part and a razor-thin mustache more fitting for an aristocrat in the Roaring Twenties.

"Please sit, Mr. Hughes."

"Thank you." As he sat in his chair, he noticed Inspector Shiou had a file laid out on his desk titled "Jacob Hughes." This brought some odd sense of relief to Lord Hughes, because he knew he was close to getting some answers. Inspector Shiou instructed the officer who let Hughes in to give them some privacy by waiting outside his office.

"Mr. Hughes. What can I do for you?"

Lord Hughes found that to be the stupidest question he'd ever heard, given the enormity of the situation. But he did not blow a fuse. Instead, he

36

responded cordially, "Thank you for meeting me on such short notice. But the first thing I want to know is when can I see my son?"

Inspector Shiou adjusted the head of his desk lamp to focus its light on the Jacob Hughes file. He put out his cigarette allowing the stench-filled smoke to blow in his guest's face while listing the charges against Lord Hughes's son. "Jacob Hughes has been charged with the following crimes: number one, the possession of a rare animal without proper permits." To this charge, Lord Hughes rolled his eyes. Inspector Shiou continued, "Number two, the possession of an illegal narcotic and number three, the rape of a minor."

To the last charge, Lord Hughes erupted, "Rape of a who?"

"That would be of a ten-year-old boy," Inspector Shiou calmly replied. "Your son, Mr. Hughes, was arrested in a hotel room last Wednesday at 9:00 a.m. in possession of a caged exotic bird called a great barbet, just under an ounce of heroin, and a ten-year-old orphan, who we suspect had sexual relations with your son. These are very serious charges, I assure you, Mr. Hughes."

Lord Hughes was physically sitting in his chair but mentally transported out of his body, as he scrambled for rational excuses as to why the allegations were false. He blurted out, "There were other people in the room, correct? A man and a woman, right?" Inspector Shiou nodded. "So what is your proof that it was my son who had relations with this boy? It could have been the other man or woman in the room. My son is not capable of such things." Lord Hughes genuinely believed what he just said. But Inspector Shiou would not give his glimmer of redemption any legitimacy.

"Mr. Hughes, the man in the room testified that your son solicited him to have sex with two of his clients." Seeing Mr. Hughes looking confused by the term "client," Inspector Shiou clarified it for him: "The man is what you English would call a pimp. The woman and young boy are his prostitutes. She also confirms the man's story. Not to

37

mention that, when we arrested your son, he was found in bed with the young boy…all caught on video. I saw it with my own eyes."

Lord Hughes sighed, devastated by these revelations. He knew about his son's battle with drugs, and he mildly suspected the possibility of him being bisexual or even homosexual, but he'd never have pegged him as a pedophile. Hughes was enraged and had half a mind to let his son rot in prison for the embarrassment that would ensue.

He could see the headline now: "Lord Hughes's Son Arrested for Drug Possession and Child Molestation. All Caught on Video by Film Crew of To Catch a Pedophile." Inspector Shiou also refused to grant Lord Hughes a visit with his son. He would have to wait until the next day, when visiting hours were permitted. After this news, Lord Hughes excused himself from the meeting.

The weight of the situation was too much for Hughes to handle soberly. Directly after checking into his Bangkok hotel, he headed to the bar for some comfort from Johnny Walker. While sipping his scotch on the rocks, he had extensive cell phone conversations with his lawyers. Unrelenting, he pressed them to come up with all possible solutions until Hughes was finally convinced one of them had to be in Bangkok to be of any assistance. The devastated father sat quietly at the bar and finished scotch after scotch before the ice could melt. He was four glasses in before another soul sat next to him at the bar. Lord Hughes had no idea if the bar was empty or packed, he was rightfully distracted by his son's predicament.

His eyes didn't stray from a blank spot on the wall at the other side of the bar, until the man sitting next to him said, "Lord Hughes, correct?

Hughes was caught off guard. He turned to see a recognizable, statuesque black man sitting next to him. However, he could not put a name to the man; all he knew was that the face was in the wrong context. It took only a moment for his brain to associate the name Jasper Boateng with the face. Some weeks ago, Lord Hughes was introduced to Jasper and other BOI executives to discuss purchasing Royal Gold's holding, Kumasi Gold, which was Royal Gold's oldest asset.

This encounter in the bar was not as bizarre as it was annoying. It's not the first time Lord Hughes had coincidentlally run into businessmen from other countries in Bangkok. However, he was not in the mood to chat one up on the eve of what should prove to be the biggest public scandal his family had ever faced. Hughes put on a cordial face with the ease of a thespian and asked, "Bow-a-tang, right?"

The correct pronunciation of the name is actually bwa-tane. However Jasper didn't bother to correct him.

"It's a coincidence seeing you here."

"I suppose it is," Jasper agreed. "What are you drinking? Let me buy you another one."

Lord Hughes wasted no time in declining Jasper's offer. "I can't. Right now's not a good time for me. I'm in town for an urgent family matter, and I have to attend to it right away."

And from out of left field, Jasper responded, "I know about your son, Mr. Hughes; that is why I am here."

By this time, Hughes was seething with rage. He finished the remaining soaked ice cubes of his drink and loudly slammed the empty glass on the table. It took a second for his brain to calm his voice down to a whisper to avoid making even more of a scene. "What did you say to me?"

Although Jasper was highly insulted, he remained calm. "Your son is being charged with possession of an ounce of heroin and molestation of a minor." Jasper paused for comedic timing and added, "And apparently the arrest was documented by a film crew for some wretched reality TV show?"

"All of it is bollocks! I'm sure of it."

"I'm not here to judge your son, Mr. Hughes." Then he leaned in closer. "What if I told you I could make this disappear? The drug charge, the molestation charge, and the embarrassing video." Then Jasper paused for the punch line: "You'll probably have to pay a fine for the bird, though."

Skeptical for good reason, Lord Hughes couldn't resist asking, "And how would you possibly achieve this feat?"

"These are details you need not worry about. But I am confident I can rescue you from these matters."

"Oh yeah? And how much is this extreme generosity going to cost me, Mr. Boateng?"

"Isn't it obvious? You refused BOI's offer to buy the Kumasi Gold operation after we last met. Allow me to use this situation to impress upon you that BOI will extend any resource we have available to you in your moment of crisis. If, in return, we can be assured you will assist us in the purchase of Kumasi Gold."

Hughes looked at Jasper with the intensity of a bull raging the streets of Pamplona. "You take me for a fuckin' idiot; you set this whole thing up, didn't you? You fucking bastard! Here on business? Bollocks! Now you're trying to blackmail me?"

He lunged at Jasper's throat, but the stronger man easily swiped his arm away, grabbed his collar, and pinned him against the bar. Once Hughes was stabilized, Jasper released him from his clutches. He straightened Lord Hughes's jacket and leaned in to whisper, "Now, you're giving me too much credit to think a simple African businessman, could pull off such a stunt. Crazy, right? But even if what you accuse me of is theoretically possible, the truth of the matter is that your perverted son did everything he was accused of, didn't he?" Hughes waited for Jasper to back away before fixing his own clothing and storming out of the bar.

Later that evening, Jasper wasn't surprised to receive a phone call from Hughes, who agreed to take him up on his proposed services. Although unsurprised, Jasper had not expected to hear from him so soon. He immediately phoned his uncle in Accra and summarized their discussion in four words: "He wants a meeting."

Jacob Hughes was released exactly eighteen days

after his arrest. During those eighteen days, Lord Hughes expedited the motion to sell Kumasi Gold to BOI, which took two months to finalize.

Three months after his son was first arrested and a full month after he had signed over Kumasi Gold, Lord Hughes found himself sitting under the painting of his great grandfather, the late Lord Dennis Hughes who was governor during Ghana's colonial era—the same place where he'd first learned the news about Jacob. When his phone rang, he almost didn't want to answer it for fear of déjà vu. The caller ID showed the number of the private detective he'd hired, who was due to give him the final analysis of his son's cover-up case in Bangkok. With great anticipation, he picked up the phone and asked, "So what do you have?"

"Sir, I know this is your secure line, so I will just be blunt. It's my belief that your son's entire Bangkok arrest was a farce—an elaborate scheme set up by Jasper Boateng and his friend, Inspector Shiou."

Hughes shook his head. "What do you have to back that up?"

"Well, I found it hard to believe that your son's serious charges could be dismissed without severe discipline. On a hunch, I paid a number of Bangkok cops to get me the Jacob Hughes file. It turns out there is no Jacob Hughes file. Knowing he could never bring this before a Bangkok court and still have the leverage to cover it up, Inspector Shiou swept the charges under the rug and filed a phony report. Jacob Hughes was never even charged for the drug or molestation counts. The video camera and crew were actually plainclothes police officers on the inspector's payroll. The camera wasn't even rolling the morning they raided your son's hotel room."

The private detective's assessment irritated Hughes to the point where he hung up the phone while the man was still talking. He stood up and looked at his great grandfather's painting; it took much self-restraint to keep from throwing his glass at it. The sense of pride that he once had for that painting now conjured up a sense of

41

embarrassment. "My name must be cursed," he whispered
to himself.

42

Chapter 6
Dubai, United Arab Emirates
Present Day

The high-profile wedding planner, Micelle Florentine, would later tell Wedding Style magazine that the Coufis Zatan wedding was her most fulfilling work to date. The ceremony was held on one of the elaborate Dubai man-made islands, which collectively resembled a map of the world. Later, the guests and the wedding party were shipped off in a series of yachts that replaced the standard dinner-table concept at a reception. The yachts were divided among family, the celebrity guests, and other friends. The attendees enjoyed their cocktail hour, while their respective yachts cruised downtown to continue the party at the Burj Khalifa, also known as the tallest building in the world.

The groom was Egyptian-born, half Ghanaian Coufis Zatan, a professional footballer and once leading scorer in the English Premier League. Several of the bride and groom's celebrity friends carved this day out of their calendars to mingle with their peers. Surprisingly, George Boateng was included on the yacht carrying the more elite guests. Although Boateng had casually met one or two of the celebrities in attendance, he was by no means a celebrity. Boateng and Zatan were best mates since their secondary-school days in England, so Zatan thought it appropriate to give Boateng and his date the exclusive treatment.

George's date for the evening was an aspiring model from Madrid, Maria Renterea, who was particularly eager to mingle with the celebrity guests. She was so impressed by her date's connections that later in the evening, while the sunset over the Indian Ocean, the once-skeptical bachelorette asked George when she could meet his mother. Her question led George to believe the Zatan wedding might be their last date.

The bride was the enchanting Azul Ishmael, most recognizable from her appearance on the U.K. reality series, Wives of Footballers—although she wasn't yet married to Coufis at the time of taping. However, other people who knew a thing or two about the darker ways of the world, recognized Azul Ishmael as the daughter of mysterious businessman, Anwar Ishmael. The bride's father and financier of the evening's extravaganza had a yacht for himself and a handful of his most trusted companions. He'd also hired extra security selected by the ruling sheikh of Dubai, himself, to keep away the celebrities and paparazzi who stalked them.

The way Ishmael saw it, he'd paid for the event and felt no guilt for segregating himself from the rest of the wedding guests; he didn't even find it rude to exclude the groom's parents from his yacht. In fact, Ishmael's yacht was the largest of them all: a fifty-footer lent by the sheikh and equipped with all the latest amenities. The guests on his yacht included his friend and mentor, the international Russian oil tycoon, Sergey Voltransky, who cascaded around the deck with a bottle of champagne and a mistress on each arm. His other guest was the Somali warlord, Idreme, who hounded Ishmael's underboss/chief of staff, Abdul Mulinesbar, for permission to speak with the host in private. Ishmael, though, had elected to unwind in the master suite below deck rather than mingle with his few invited guests.

In his younger days, Ishmael was considered a physically impressive man. Standing at over six feet, his broad shoulders were the last sign of his muscular build. Now his girth gave the fifty-two-year-old tycoon a rounder physique. His dark-brown hair might well have been black, and he sported thick eyebrows connected like clasped fingers. A large dark mustache made him look distinctly dictatorish.

Ishmael stood at the bar and poured himself another Glen Fiddich scotch on ice, unbuttoned his collar, and took a large gulp. He thought about Azul and began to feel a strange sense of anxiety. Unsure how his daughter's marriage to a football star like Zatan would affect his image in the region, he was also curious to know how the rest of

44

the Arab world would react to her secular, over-the-top wedding.

The Lebanese were typically known for being less strict than the rest of their Arab neighbors, but he knew people still talked. He would probably never hear the talk, though, because Ishmael was perhaps the most feared man in the Arab world. The truth was if the average person knew about Anwar Ishmael and his "methods," many would have a hard time sleeping at night.

While his daughter, son-in-law, and guests were enjoying one of the finest weddings in the world, Ishmael remained holed up in his cabin and fixated on an Al Jazeera News special about the overnight success of Ghanaian-owned Kumasi Gold. He had pressing business in Ghana and was intrigued by the fact that when Royal Gold sold Kumasi Gold to a local company called BOI, the precious-metals market had soared for months. Apparently, BOI harvested gold at a remarkable pace and raked in enviable profits. Ishmael leaned in closer when the reporter gave BOI's profile:

"In just two years, BOI took the Kumasi Gold mining operation to a level Royal Gold never reached in nearly one hundred years of ownership. BOI's timing was impeccable, since many nervous investors believe gold to be the safest investment in an unpredictable global economy. BOI quickly expanded, buying half a dozen other companies—most notably, Atlantic Coast Media, the parent of Accra's largest newspaper, the Accra Voice, and WACCR TV station. BOI also acquired a significant commodities brokerage firm in Takoradi and Ghana's fiercest football club, Asante Royals. Many say BOI is now the number-one power broker in West Africa, if not all of Africa."

Just when Ishmael was about to phone his counterparts in Ghana and ask, "Who in the hell is BOI," he heard a knock on the door that reminded him he was still at his daughter's wedding and not at work. He looked at one of the surveillance cameras and saw his trusted underboss, Abdul Mulinesbar.

"Come in, Abdul."

"You have to take this call, sir. It's on the secure line."

Ishmael waved Abdul over and asked, "Who is it?"

Abdul closed the door and walked closer. "The call is from Bombay. It's Detective Patel."

Ishmael put his drink down and grabbed the phone. "Yes?"

The voice on the other line informed Ishmael, "One man was captured and is in our custody at the hospital downtown."

"Well, I'm sure you'll take care of it."

Chapter 7
Bombay, India
Present Day

Around the time Coufis and Azul's guests were attending their wedding, five men armed with M-4 assault rifles invaded the lobby of the Vaj Hotel in downtown Bombay. One man opened fire without warning and prompted screams that were almost as loud as the machine gun itself. Another intruder entered the stairwell and began shooting indiscriminately. Guests and staff scattered in every direction looking for cover. The remaining gunmen headed to the parking garage and opened fire. The terrorists were charged up on enough narcotics and booze to kill a herd of wildebeest.

Bik, the hotel security guard on duty that night, was napping in the security booth when he heard gunfire in the parking deck. He immediately fell off his reclined chair, thumping his head on the ground. Bik moved toward the lamp and shut it off in a frantic hurry. The machine-gun fire continued, and he could see nothing but flashes of light that illuminated the dark garage. Bik reached for his firearm and realized he had yet to fire the weapon since taking his weapons exam in the academy.

He heard terrifying screams, and the gunfire became louder and probably closer. At that very moment, he felt a warm ooze fill his underwear. Unfortunately for Bik, he had evacuated in his trousers; yet, given the circumstances, lying in his own feces was the most comfortable sensation in the world at that point in time. He dropped the gun and began to sob. Putting his knees up against his chest, he rocked back and forth, while listening to the screams of people being slaughtered. While rocking, he noticed the phone receiver swinging back and forth in almost the same rhythm as his movements. He grabbed the phone and dialed emergency.

When the voice answered, he whispered, "Vaj Hotel, hurry up please!" He left the phone off the hook so the dispatcher could hear the carnage in the background.

Bik finally gathered enough courage to grab the firearm beside him; he was still fidgety but slowly gaining composure. He checked the rounds, shut the magazine back into the pistol's handle, cocked his gun, and lifted his head slightly above the desk at eye level with the window.

The gunfire stopped and he heard footsteps jogging at a rapid pace. The parking garage was barely lit, but the guard could see a shadowy figure appear from the down ramp and move toward him. Bik slid the window open just enough to fit the gun's barrel. When he saw the figure emerge from the shadows, he noticed the man was hitting his machine gun as if it were jammed. Bik remembered his training: line up the notches on the top of the barrel, aim slightly lower than the target to adjust for kickback, and pull the trigger.

The target dropped almost instantly after the gun fired. Bik heard the man moaning and cursing and knew he had not killed him. However, he did not plan to leave his post. Instead, he picked up the phone and told the dispatcher to hurry up. Finally, as he heard the police sirens, Bik blacked out.

When the only surviving gunman Essa Mohammed woke up, there was a sharp pain in his right shoulder. Reaching for his shoulder, he felt bandages and gauze wrapped around his arm and chest. The lights were so bright that he eventually kept his eyes squinted after blinking frantically to open them. Mohammed could hear the people chattering around him better than he could see them. From the looks of the bandages and IV, he appeared to be in a hospital; but instead of nurses, he only saw four Bombay police officers. Three of them were in uniform and one was in a half-size shirt and loosely fit tie. He introduced himself as Inspector Patel.

"So it seems your counterparts took their lives before they were captured," Inspector Patel said. "You, on the other hand, were not so lucky; you were taken down by the bumbling night guard at the Vaj Hotel. He actually shat his pants before he shot at you."

One of the uniformed officers said, "You and your

men killed nineteen people and injured over fifty, two of them were police officers. Why the hell did you do it?"

The gunman laughed and said in Arabic, "Go fuck yourself!"

The other officer rushed to the bed and struck Mohammed on his wounded shoulder, causing him to erupt in pain. Patel grabbed the officer and slammed him against the wall. "Stand down, officer!" he yelled and jumped in the other officer's face. "I ask the questions here, do you understand me?" Both men nodded their heads up and down and Patel ordered them out of the room.

When the men closed the door, Patel locked it. The inspector just smiled and pulled a mobile phone out of his pocket. He moved to the window and said quietly into the phone, "Abdul, its Inspector Patel. Let me speak to Anwar." He waited until Anwar picked up and said, "One man was captured and is in our custody at the hospital downtown. The name is Mohammed Essa." He paused and waited for a response. "Very well," he said and hung up the phone.

Patel looked at Essa and pulled a pill from his front pocket. "We found these cyanide capsules on you and your comrades. You didn't get a chance to take yours, did you?" Patel walked over to Essa's bed and handed him a pill. "You deserve eternal paradise."

Essa smiled at Patel. "Allah shall redeem your soul for this. Thank you."

Inspector Patel was ambivalent about the gesture. "Whatever. Just don't take it until I leave," he said while exiting the room.

Among his other responsibilities at BOI, George Boateng's primary role was overseeing the public relations department. Although George was known to attract unwanted attention at times, he was a natural in the position—a well-polished individual who, like his uncle, possessed the gift of gab. Just being the company megaphone did not appease George's appetite, though. Young and ambitious, he wanted to manage a high-profile asset, so it came as no surprise that George lobbied to be head of football operations when BOI bought the Asante Royals Football Club. After unrelentingly pestering like a child, Oscar succumbed to George's whining. Like many young privileged football fanatics with little talent for the game, it was George's childhood dream to own a football team, and he was given the rare opportunity to fulfill it. When George was appointed President of Football Operations, he moved to Kumasi and conducted most of his business from his office in the team's newly built stadium.

While George was still head of BOI's public relations department, he delegated most of those responsibilities and devoted most of his work hours to the football club with little time spent on the rest of his responsibilities. Initially, BOI was to purchase the team and allow the team's general manager to handle all football matters. However, George micromanaged every inch of the club—from the uniforms to the stadium vendors. Ironically, George adopted his mother's brand of business management, which he'd previously considered oppressive. Much to his uncle's surprise, George's meddling in the team proved to have a positive effect. As one local sports writer wrote:

"George Boateng brings a level of panache and celebrity lacking in the African-football landscape. Boateng's unapologetic attitude about spending resources

50

is what many African football clubs need. In the first season of owning the team, he raised the payroll beyond what is normal in Africa. The Asante Royals quickly became the Real Madrid of continental football. Now the best players in Africa are urging their agents to move heaven and earth for them to play football for Asante Royals."

Little did the football community know that George Boateng had bigger game in his sights. He was orchestrating the biggest coup in African-football history by attempting to sign his old friend, Coufis Zatan, the Egyptian born half Ghanaian footballer. To use a football analogy, George was aiming for the "upper ninety" with this deal. No FIFA Player of the Year had ever signed with an African ball club after winning the award. George's only leverage was that at thirty-five, Zatan was considered a declining player. However, the Zatan name still had caché among casual fans. Such an acquisition would send seismic ripples throughout their league. George's pitch to Coufis was simple: he planned to have some drinks and laughs with his old friend, then casually offer him the maximum amount of money the league allowed, which was sizable.

When Zatan entered George's office at the stadium, he was in good spirits. Probably because George had stocked his hotel room with a case of French champagne and an ounce of some of the most pungent marijuana George could find in Ghana. George knew the star footballer, although disciplined during the season, liked to cut loose in the off-season.

Zatan had an athletic physique but was not exceptionally cut. He wore a fitted dark-blue pinstriped suit with a pink button-down shirt and a sea-foam green pocket square. George had to give Coufis credit—he was dressed to the nines, even in the deadly African heat.

"You've put yourself together nicely there," George complimented. "But Jesus, man. God forbid you take off your jacket or something. I'm melting just looking at you. Are you mad?" Zatan doubled over in laughter and remembered how much he missed George's quick wit.

51

George gave Coufis a moment to get his chuckles out before he moved to a more somber matter. "My condolences to your family. I know she meant a lot to you." The loss George referred to was that of Coufis's Aunt Sophia.

Coufis Zatan was the son of the Egyptian football great, Demir Zatan. Although Demir enjoyed only a fraction of his son's success, he was still revered as an Egyptian legend. When Demir had traveled for his team, he and his wife left Coufis with his longtime caretaker, Sophia Rashaan. Aunt Sophie, as Coufis called her, virtually raised him. When Coufis was eighteen, he was shipped off to English professional team's development league, and Sophia moved on to manage the custodial staffs at various upscale hotels and resorts around the world. She remained a devoted fan of Coufis, though; she watched all of his matches and was the first to give him an earful if she suspected he was dogging it. She was a second mother to Coufis and, even though she wasn't consistently around, Coufis kept in contact with her. The last hotel Sophia worked at was the Vaj Hotel in Bombay, India, where she died.

Coufis shook his head. "I can't bring myself to think about it. She shouldn't have even been at that goddamn hotel. She should have been at my wedding, drinking fucking champagne, and passing out with a cigarette in her mouth like she did at all family celebrations."

On the first-floor office of the Vaj Hotel that deadly night, Sophia had been chastising a new maid for not providing timely service to a guest. When she heard the sound of gunfire in the hall, her first reaction was to push the new employee onto the ground behind a desk. One assailant appeared from around the corner and sprayed bullets in Sophia's direction. The employee Sophia pushed down escaped death thanks to the heroics of her perfectionist boss. Unfortunately, Sophia Rashaan died after being struck in the head and chest by the gunman's bullets.

George quickly changed the subject in fear of

creating too somber an atmosphere. "So your wedding was fun, man! Me almost flipped when I found out the cocktails were on private yachts. Nicely played...nicely played."

Coufis was initially put off by the manic change of topic, but he knew George and that he was trying to swiftly veer the conversation away from the tragedy—even though George was the one that had brought it up.

"Yeah, I have to admit it's a pretty hard act to follow," Coufis joked. Then with a hint of disappointment, he admitted, "You can thank my father-in-law for the yacht idea."

"You know, speaking of your father-in-law, I didn't know until somebody mentioned it at the wedding, but did you know he does a lot of business here in Ghana?"

"So I've heard. But then again, what country doesn't he do business in?" Coufis' father in law, Anwar Ishmael was not his favorite topic. Of the handful of times Coufis had encountered his father-in-law, Ishmael always managed to emasculate Coufis without uttering a word. Through his wife and the hints of others, Coufis knew the rumors about her father's exploits. Coufis was genuinely intimidated by his father in law. Ishmael knew this and used it to his advantage to rein in the ego of his son-in-law, the talented footballer.

Coufis changed the subject of his father-in-law as quickly as an NBA guard switched his dribbling hand. "By the way, George, me and the wife are obsessed with the Banksy painting you gave us. It was best in show—of the wedding gifts, that is."

George laughed. "It better have been best in bloody show, you wanka! Considering your other gifts were thoughtless piles of housewares you and your wife's army of homoerotic houseboys couldn't possibly use."

Coufis laughed so hard he accidentally drooled a little bit. He wiped the corner of his mouth with his pocket square and calmed down. "But seriously, George, I mean that Banksy piece? How did you get it?"

"What about it?"

"It had to be pretty fucking expensive, right?"

53

Coufis laughed. "How much did that set you back?"

"Come on, you bugga, even if you don't possess my level of class, you still know that asking the price of a gift is considered rude, right? I won't reveal my methods, but if it makes you feel better, I assure you I did not pay retail for it," George added with a wink.

Coufis had good reason to be curious about George's wedding gift because the Banksy painting was special; it was one of the original paintings Banksy used in his London-museum prank. George was correct when he told Coufis he hadn't paid full price. What he didn't mention was that the piece was obtained by his brother Jasper two years earlier. A dodgy associate of Jasper's from Hackney was a friend of the world-renowned politico prank artist, Banksy. In addition to being friends with the iconic street artist, he had the unique privilege of owning some of the phantom artist's work. Oddly enough, this associate of Jasper's gave the painting to Jasper as payment for a gambling debt.

Fortunately for Coufis and his wife, Jasper's appreciation of art history didn't make him sentimental about the painting. Within ten hours, Jasper sold the Banksy painting to his brother George for a measly £700, which was still next to nothing, considering its actual market value.

George had no problem re-gifting the priceless painting to the celebrity bride and groom. However, in typical George fashion there was a catch. In lieu of the certificate of authenticity, the painting was presented with a letter that read:

"Dear Coufis and Azul,

I hope this painting will bring fond memories of your wedding day. By the request of the artist and dealer, the ownership of the painting is to stay completely confidential. Any publicity of the painting's ownership can result in the repossession of the painting by the artist. Therefore, if the painting is sold or advertised in any way, the artist will consider the action a breach of contract. Enjoy!

54

Best, George"

The wedding gift was working as George had hoped, for he'd preemptively gifted the painting to Coufis for the sole purpose of today's conversation. He handed Coufis a Cuban cigar and a lighter, and as they smoked, George used the time to strike. "Well," he said with an air of jest, "I understand you're a man with taste—and that's the way it will be from here on out if you roll with me, old friend. It's all about high art, fast cars, and fast women."

Coufis laughed, knowing George was only half kidding. George buttoned up his demeanor and continued, "Here's the turkey's giblets, ol' mate. I want you to sign with me and play for Asante Royals." George pulled out a jersey from underneath his desk and unfolded it for Coufis to see the design. It was a mock-up for a slick new away jersey with Coufis's name and number on it.

Coufis smiled and clapped his hands. "George, you slippery fuck! I should've known you 'ad something up your sleeve, that inviting me to Ghana for a 'guy's weekend out' was just lip service." He then wound his laugh down to a respectful smile. "I like the cut of your jib, ol' pal. But I have to tell you straight up, there is no way my agent would let me take this offer."

"And why is that?"

"The drop-off talent wise is too drastic, and my reputation would take a hit."

"Bollocks!" George scoffed, pretending to take offense. "I don't even have a marketing degree, and even I know fifteen ways to spin this into a positive headline." George made a makeshift viewfinder with his fingers forming two Ls, with one inverted. "I can see it now: 'Half Ghanaian Superstar Goes Back to Africa in the Twilight of His Career to Give Back to His Continent.' Plus I'm only asking for a two-year contract. After that, go play in America or whatever it is you washed-up British pros do when you get old."

George gave Coufis a moment to laugh at his insult about playing in America before he hit him with, "Plus, I have to tell you, man—the talent on the pitch for Asante

Royals has gotten so wicked, man. Honestly, if it weren't for your name, I couldn't guarantee you'd even make the starting lineup on skill alone. Most of our starters are picked up in the European leagues after playing only a year or two on their squads. I'm telling you, they're fit, man."

Coufis was genuinely offended by George's statement. "Bullshit! Give me any one of those young'ns and I'll expose them into the amateur footballers that they are. This I promise, you get me?"

George smiled because he knew a slight insult like questioning Coufis's skill would play right into his hand. It was almost too easy. George gently tightened the noose. "Listen, Couf, I know you're right. But you're still in the top 10% of footballers in the world, in my opinion. Many of these younger guys worship the grass your boots touch; given the opportunity, they would go to war for you. You have a chance to play some amazing football with these guys before anybody else does."

By the look in Coufis's eyes, George could tell he was listening, so he marched on. "And I know what you're thinking: no one will see you play in Ghana. But that couldn't be further from the truth. BOI owns the third-largest natively owned media conglomerate on the continent. Twenty games will be aired on Al Jazeera Sports in markets all over Africa, the Middle East, Asia, and Europe. I'm also in negotiations to schedule five high-profile exhibition matches in Europe and the U.S. With your signature, I'm positive the negotiations will close the contracts within days, if not hours. I'll even put a clause in your contract stating if the television deal does not materialize, you can opt out at any given time."

George had made a bold proposal, and Coufis pondered it in silence. He went in to seal the deal with, "What do you say, good friend? Will you take this ride with me?"

Coufis casually glanced at his shoes and asked, "How many pesos are we talking about, George?"

"£7.7 million for two years. Plus a £2.5 million endorsement deal, which is the max our league allows a player to earn." George paused to gauge his friend's expression.

Coufis sighed, reached in his pocket, and grabbed the cone-shaped spliff he rolled on the way over. He handed it to George. "Well, I guess we should celebrate then."

Chapter 9
Accra, Ghana
Present Day

When Clinton Osei arrived in Ghana two years earlier, he understood Twi. However, when it was spoken to him, he always responded in English. Fortunately for Clinton, unlike most West African countries, Ghana was colonized by the British and not the French, therefore a significan percent of the population spoke English—when they wanted to, that is. Clinton's failure to master his native tongue was embarrassing for him. Although his parents spoke Twi fluently, they didn't teach it to him; they feared that being bilingual would hinder their children's ability to thrive in an American educational system.

Clinton was forced to play catch-up. His deficiency in Twi was a hurdle he was determined to overcome. Like many exceptional professionals, Clinton possessed the ability to address his weaknesses until they become strengths. The determination to vanquish his flaws proved a reoccurring theme in his rise to success. Clinton consistently kept his self-imposed afternoon language lessons with a private tutor.

His tutor was the captivating Evelyn Oduri, a linguistics professor at The University of Ghana and runner-up for Miss Ghana two years earlier. It didn't hurt that Evelyn gave her eager pupil an extra incentive to succeed: If he failed, her scant uniform of just panties and bra would be covered up one article of clothing at a time. This carrot-and-stick routine was tailored specifically for Clinton Osei, and it was bearing fruit. Nine months into his lessons, he had mastered about 60% of the language. Now two years later, at the age of forty, he was nearly fluent in Twi. Like many African dialects, Twi is difficult to master for English speakers. Twi requires the use of tonal variations and the enunciation of many silent consonants. Aside from being unable to mask his American accent, one could argue that Clinton no longer needed tutoring. Yet he found it difficult to take Evelyn Oduri off his payroll.

Clinton's tutor was down to her black bra and matching G-string when his assistant Kwasi, who split duties assisting both Oscar and Clinton, had to interrupt them. Clinton would have waived Kwasi away if he hadn't insisted being told when Patricia Young with the Accra Voice arrived. Kwasi knocked on the door to Clinton's office. "Boss, the journalist is here for your interview."

Clinton was less than happy to learn his appointment had arrived. All he wanted to do was continue his studies, but the interview couldn't be rescheduled. His cousin George arranged for the Accra Voice newspaper to publish a fluff piece on BOI, and Clinton was obligated to see it through. Begrudgingly, he responded, "That's fine. We'll meet in my office."

Clinton rolled his eyes. "Miss Evelyn, as always, this was a great lesson, but I have to cut it short."

Evelyn pouted. "Of course, Mr. Osei, I always look forward to our lessons."

Clinton's mind quickly converted to business mode as he walked to his closet. "Kwasi will have a car waiting to take you back home. Please shut the door behind you."

Clinton grabbed random items from his closet and proceeded to get dressed, which took less than thirty seconds. Like most affluent young Ghanaian men, Clinton was a remarkable dresser and had an impressive wardrobe. However, he did not obsess over the process of dressing as other men might. Clinton hastily donned off-white Brooks Brother's pants, tapioca Fred Perry polo, and navy-blue Vans slip-ons with no socks. Despite his hurry, the outfit gave him the appearance of a VIP guest at the Monaco Grand Prix.

When Clinton walked into his office, Patricia Young was already sitting in a couch perpendicular to his chair. Patricia was a junior contributor to the paper and as idealistic as they came. When her editor informed Patricia she was to write a flattering piece on BOI, which also happened to own the Accra Voice, she protested "conflict of interest." Although valiant, her protest did little to dissuade her boss, who thought her idealism charming.

Patricia accepted her defeat and promised her editor she would present BOI in a glowing light. And she intended to but not without lobbing some bombshells their way and getting real answers in return, even if she couldn't use the answers in her piece.

When Clinton caught his first glimpse of Patricia Young, he noted that she was more attractive than he'd remembered. Although Clinton had never met Patricia in person, he'd seen her photograph on the masthead of the Accra Voice dozens of times, and the picture clearly did her no favors. Patricia stood to greet Clinton. Her heels made her about 5'9", an ideal height for a woman with no modeling aspirations. Her skin tone was smooth with a burgundy sheen, and she wore a grey pencil skirt with a fitted white button-down shirt tucked into it. Her hair was a well-organized snake's nest of micro braids wrapped into a bun and held together by a decorative ivory pick. She wore black-framed glasses that reinforced her intellect. Her nerd chic got no complaints from Clinton or his assistant Kwasi, for that matter.

"We're good here, Kwasi. Thank you." Kwasi nodded his head and left Clinton and Patricia to conduct their interview. Clinton stayed silent and directed his eyes to Patricia's tape recorder, as if to say the floor is yours. Once given the signal, she began the interview by turning on the tape recorder and placing it on the table in front of them. Patricia started with half a dozen "softball" questions to put her subject at ease, then became incrementally nosier with each subsequent question. As typed in Patricia's transcript of her interview, it went as follows:

PY: How would you describe the BOI hierarchy? Who's in charge of what?

CO: Well, all of the executives at BOI have their own equitable duties. For instance, Oscar Boateng is our CEO and leader. Below him are myself, and my cousins George and Jasper Boateng, my Aunt Marguerite Boateng, and lead geologist Harry Van Bleer. We are all responsible for various aspects of the business, but I won't bore you with the details.

PY: Some would say you're being humble in your assessment of your role. CEO of Detroit's automobile conglomerate, Carol Gardner, an individual who you've worked closely with told me that you are solely responsible for BOI's success. She said that your instincts in assessing operations, then finding its ailment, while also being able to perscribe the precisely correct remedy is a unique gift. Not to mention that if it weren't for your success in America with Bradley and Partners, BOI would not have received the financing to purchase Kumasi Gold. She also indicated many corporations would not have taken a chance on you, and that the FSA would probably not have approved your acquisition of Kumasi Gold. How would you respond to that?"

CO: It's no secret that my financial success helped our company to purchase Kumasi Gold. I'm sure some lenders thought my track record in America put a more palatable face to our business plan. I don't see anything wrong with that; in my mind, it's simply smart business. Conversely, I evaluated the businesses of my partners, who also happen to be relatives, so I could easily look into their business practices. If I hadn't liked what I saw, I would have abandoned the project at its inception. Much of the personnel who run BOI today came from my partners' preexisting companies. Although my reputation may have allowed us some credit to play with among the international business types, it was my partners' experience and resources that allowed us to perform at a high level.

PY: You just mentioned family, which is interesting, because although BOI is large enough to be a publicly traded company, it is run like a family business. You're not listed on any international stock exchange and your executive staff is mostly comprised of a Boateng, an Osei, or an in-law.

CO: This is true. We're lucky to operate without the red tape of a bloated corporation. We're also lucky to have capable and trustworthy family members to plug into prominent positions. I know they say you shouldn't mix

61

family with business, but knock on wood, we haven't had any problems so far.

PY: Kumasi Gold is reporting higher annual earnings since BOI purchased it than its previous owner, Royal Gold. How do you respond to the allegations that BOI executives colluded with Royal Gold's former employee, Harry Van Bleer, to buy the company under false pretenses? In other words: BOI and Van Bleer withheld information about additional gold deposits from which BOI is currently profiting."

*Clinton cocked his eyebrow and shot a glance at me. This was a curveball he didn't anticipate or appreciate. Especially since he was under the impression this interview was for a fluff piece. To his credit, he didn't dodge the question.

CO: I'm sorry Ms. Young, I have never heard those allegations from the former Royal Gold owners—not in an official statement or even as a rumor. Where are you getting this information?

PY: Well, actually, last week I interviewed one of the former principals of Royal Gold, and this person insinuated (off-the-record) that many of the former ownership team are convinced BOI and Harry Van Bleer colluded to buy the company knowing there were more prospects for gold and that you intentionally withheld that information from them."

*Clinton laughs dismissively.

CO: That's news to me. Personally, it sounds like sour grapes on their part. But I will say that, as you've heard, we've partnered with others in our industry to launch the "No-Fools Gold" initiative. It is our pledge that we will leave the communities in which we mine in better conditions than we found them. Under BOI, Kumasi Gold has drastically improved the mining conditions for our workers, and we have spent millions retrofitting our operation to adhere to stronger environmental and labor standards. Not to mention, we've introduced a tariff on ourselves to be paid to the city of Kumasi and the Asante tribe for our intrusion on their land. These are significant

62

changes that the previous ownership did not adopt. We are better stewards of the land, and I think our good efforts are yielding us a better outcome."

PY: So are you saying Kumasi Gold is doing better than the previous ownership group because of good karma?

*Clinton laughs again.

CO: No, I don't make a habit of using Eastern philosophy to guide my business decisions. I'm simply saying that, in my humble opinion, we're operating from a smarter business model than they were, and it's showing.

PY: You made the majority of your wealth through consulting, which is a lean operation known for low overhead. Why did you decide to get into the cumbersome industry of mining? It seems counterintuitive for a man with your background.

*Clinton laughs at the question.

CO: You know, it's funny. I've heard that question before, but if you think about it corporate consulting, almost by definition is the improvement of large inefficient businesses. Heck, I helped turn around a troubled Detroit car manufacturer. So you see Patricia, I am used to working in inefficient industries."

PY: Ah, I see. But clearly, buying a nearly century-old gold mining company in West Africa has its challenges. Correct?"

*Smirk from Clinton.

CO: My Uncle Oscar Boateng was the architect of the Kumasi Gold operation. He was convinced there was still money to be made in the gold market. My uncle is a student of history and is aware of the sensitive relationship between Ghana and its European interests. He also knew it would send a positive signal to the international community that Ghana's largest gold-mining operation was now owned and controlled by Ghanaians. He believed making Kumasi Gold the flagship business in our portfolio would help us operate from a position of spiritual strength.

*He must have noticed the right side of my lip curl up as I tried to hold back a smile.

CO: What is it?

63

PY: I was just thinking that for a man who "doesn't let Eastern philosophy run his business," your last answer sounded pretty Zen-like to me.

*He smiled and although amused he at this point had had enough of my probing.

CO: I'm sorry, Ms. Young, but I have to meet my uncle in twenty minutes, and I have to leave now to make that meeting. Tonight we are attending a ceremony honoring the participants of BOI's micro-loan program at the Cultural Arts Center. You know our program where we provide financial support for over ninety thousand poverty-level entrepreneurs? Perhaps you can come to the event and talk about our program for your interview?

*He was bragging.

End of Interview

Patricia smiled at Clinton and looked at the door. "Actually, Mr. Osei, I believe I have all I need from you today. So I think we're good. Thank you."

Clinton shrugged. "Okay, well I'll tell George I tried." He waited for his guest to collect her things and follow him to the door. "I look forward to reading the final product, Ms. Young."

She wanted to shout, of course you are, you wanka! You own the fucking paper. Instead, she simply replied, "I'll have a boy from the printers deliver one over fresh off the press."

"Or," Clinton interjected, "you could bring it to me when you join me for lunch next week?"

Patricia almost unsuccessfully smiled at Clinton without laughing. "Thank you for your time, Mr. Osei. As I said one of the boys will drop off the paper to you next week."

Clinton was still grinning after he closed the door behind her. It had been a while since the eligible bachelor had been turned down. The unfamiliarity of Patricia's rejection was so new and foreign to him that he grew a slight erection.

Chapter 10
Cultural Arts Center in Accra, Ghana
Present Day

Oscar Boateng often admitted that out of all of BOI's accomplishments, he was proudest of the micro-loan program, which was also his pet project. He borrowed the idea from the Indian micro-financier and Nobel Prize winner Muhammad Yunnis. The program, by nature, was partly business but mostly philanthropic. BOI raised a generous pool of $10 million dollars to help spur entrepreneurship and business growth among Ghana's working-class poor. In addition to the pool of money, the BOI program reinforced its loans with mandatory workshops and classes.

Oscar started the program because, long ago, he recognized that many in Ghana's poor working class were inherently entrepreneurs. They made their livings as independent fisherman, farmers, bakers, grocers, and craftsmen. The majority of these budding entrepreneurs were hard workers, who were unable to grow their shoestring businesses due to a lack of financing. No financial institution in Ghana makes high-risk loans unless the government demanded it.

From Mohammad Yunnis's micro-loan program, Oscar learned that if an alternative group could relax credit scrutiny and provide financing to this underserved demographic of entrepreneurs, it was a mutually beneficial venture. Oscar also learned this group of entrepreneurs only needed a nominal amount of capital to achieve their goals, since most expenses were in soft costs, such as buying more inventory, materials, and supplies. The goal of the micro-loan program was to award loans to poor, aspiring entrepreneurs in increments between $500 and $5,000 at an extremely low interest rate of .034%.

Ideally, when the loan recipients repaid BOI, it made little money, but it didn't lose money either, and the service to the country was immeasurable. The pool of loan money was designed to stay in flux, and the beauty of

65

doing business in Ghana was that a little money went a long way. Micro-loans were sufficient for the entrepreneurs to grow their businesses and manageable enough for them to repay their loans without defaulting. A participant in BOI's micro-loan program could receive up to three loans before cycling out of the program. By successfully completing the program, the entrepreneurs were now ideal candidates for larger business loans from banks, which, in theory, would allow them to turn their businesses into first-rate operations.

In addition to BOI executives, various political figures, such as the director of Ghana's Chamber of Commerce, attended the ceremony honoring the participants of BOI's micro-loan program. The chamber's director spoke to congratulate the participants and boast about how the chamber of commerce encouraged and fostered such an ambitious program. It was obvious the director was trying to take credit for Oscar's program. However, Oscar ignored petty squabbles and was not in it for the accolades. He believed the micro-loan program was good for business in several ways. His intention was to use a micro solution to help repair Ghana's macro-economic problem of unemployment.

Oscar was acutely aware of how precarious it was to conduct business in a country with no balance of wealth. He often lectured his affluent friends by saying, "If a coup d'état were a recipe for bread, high unemployment would be the yeast, or the ingredient making the bread rise." He'd witnessed it firsthand during the military coup of 1980. The coup's military regime confiscated a significant amount of Oscar's fortune and exiled him for ten years. Oscar had spent his exiled years in France and the handful of Francophile countries that surrounded Ghana, establishing reliable relationships and business opportunities in the commodities trade. Ironically, Oscar's exile actually strengthened his livelihood. He often concluded his lectures by warning his colleagues, "Coups are bad for business. Be careful when rubbing your opulence in the faces of the unfortunate; such careless actions are what

66

fuels murderous revolutions."

Even though BOI was doing well, Ghana's high unemployment made Oscar nervous. He knew the people needed jobs, and he also knew the government had little capacity to create jobs, so he boldly decided to do it for them. He created and funded BOI's micro-loan program, yet he still let the government take credit for it. Oscar knew people needed to have faith in their government; his micro-loan program was an easy assist.

After all of the politicians and private sector bigwigs patted themselves on the backs at the podium, Oscar put in his obligatory hour of schmoozing on the floor of the Cultural Arts Center. Exhausted after the gentle handshakes and polite conversations, he decided to slip behind the stage and head to the green room, but not before inviting his nephew, George. Oscar had saved a case of rare Spanish wine for this occasion, and he insisted George join him to open the first bottle. Clinton shared Oscar's business sense, Jasper shared Oscar's spirit for rebellion, and George shared Oscar's weakness for grandeur. When George was a child, Oscar had noted he didn't play with his toys like his brother and cousins, rather he collected and cataloged them. Watching the young lad who showed promise, Oscar helped refine his nephew's tastes from an early age.

Uncle and nephew sat in the green room, caressing their cramped cheeks from excessive smiling and massaging their sore elbows from excessive rubbing. It took only twenty minutes to finish their first bottle of wine. They had started on the second bottle, when Oscar's assistant Kwasi interrupted them. Oscar pointed a finger at George to signal a pause on their conversation to learn what Kwasi wanted.

"What is it, Kwasi?"

"Sir, you have a visitor." Knowing Oscar was not keen on suspense, Kwasi explained the nature of his visitor's business: "It's a man by the name of Stephen Agyapong. He's member of the loan program and says he desperately needs to talk to you. Should I turn him away?"

Oscar thought about declining the request, but realized it was bad form to refuse a meeting with one of the loan recipients, so he nodded his head and gestured for Kwasi to let the man in. Stephen Agyapong walked into the green room, while clenching his hat and avoiding any eye contact. Oscar gestured for George to greet their visitor; he quickly rose from his chair and made his way to their guest.

"George Boateng. Nice to meet you, Stephen. What can we help you with?" George asked as he led him to a chair closer to where he and his uncle were sitting. Stephen shook Oscar's hand and sat down across from him. It was obvious to both that Agyapong was considerably nervous.

Oscar took it upon himself to break the ice. "Stephen, your name is familiar to me, because I know you operate a small grocery store in the town of Winneba. You are also enrolled in our micro-loan program and have defaulted on your last payment. Am I correct?"

Stephen nodded and was surprised Oscar knew so much about him. The truth was Oscar memorized a running tally of everybody in debt to him, even the hundred or so micro-loan recipients, whose loans were in default. Stephen lifted his head and mustered up the courage to look at Oscar with pleading eyes as he said in Twi, "Mr. Boateng, I am here to humbly apologize for my regrettable performance. I am a passionate participant of your loan program, and it pains me that I have disrespected the program as such."

Oscar grinned and cut Stephen off by saying, "Don't get me wrong, Stephen, there is nothing I enjoy more than an accent from Winneba. However, when discussing business, please use English. Unfortunately, it is the official language of finance and the rest of the world must follow." Stephen again nodded his head eager to express his willingness to Oscar.

In a timid style of village English, he continued, "You see, sir, the last installment of money I received from the loan program went to purchase three goats from a farmer in my neighboring town. My plan was to breed my own goats and sell my own goat's milk and goat meat. My

68

customers tend to enjoy the quality of milk produced from the goats on this man's farm. Although the goats are expensive, they are worth the investment."

The court jester in George had to resist the urge to make a bleating noise after Stephen rattled through his list of goat products. Oscar nodded at Stephen to hurry up with his story. "The farmer I sent the money to did not deliver my goats. When I visited this man and asked about my order of goats, he laughed and told me I have to pay more money now, because I have received big bank loan from the government. He refused to give me the money back and insisted he will not do so until I either give him $300 more, or $100 for each goat. Not only that, when I argued with the man, he smacked me in the face, and pushed me down. He is much stronger than me, so I did not retaliate."

Oscar turned to George and raised his eyebrows. Returning his focus to Stephen, he followed with the obvious line of questioning. "I don't understand. He's keeping your money, and not giving you your merchandise? Is he holding your merchandise in escrow, because you owe him money?"

"No, sir, I am square with the farmer. I have records to prove this."

"Did you contact the police?"

"Yes. The local police will not be bothered with such matters. There is envy in their wicked hearts as well. They, too, ask for compensation in order to fulfill their obligations."

Oscar rose from his chair and poured his guest a glass of wine. Initially Stephen rejected the wine, but Oscar insisted, so he accepted it and drank. Oscar continued to inquire into Stephen's situation, "Have you approached your case manager? How have they counseled you?"

"She wrote letters to the farmer on my behalf, only to be ignored without a response. She is trying to help, but she only has so much time to devote to my case."

Oscar knew this to be true. The biggest problem with the micro-loan program was its ambitious scope. The program took on ten thousand clients but only had one hundred and thirty employees. Fifty of them were case managers, which meant each case manager had a load of two hundred cases and they were completely overwhelmed.

Oscar rose from his chair and thoughtfully walked around the green room. Both George and Stephen's eyes followed his every movement. George was familiar with this demeanor from his uncle; it usually meant he was poised to impart wisdom through one of his many elaborate stories. George was right; not five seconds later, Oscar began to narrate. "When I was a child, maybe eleven years old, my senior stepbrother Richard constantly bullied me. If Richard wasn't stealing my dessert, he was stealing toys and books from my room. Richard coveted my possessions without compensation. He taught me early on that if I made a fuss of the matter, he would beat me senselessly. Moreover, Richard was jealous of the preferential treatment my father showed me, and he responded in very malicious ways.

"One weekend, Richard stole one of my favorite possessions, an autographed picture of the famous American boxer, Joe Lewis. My father gave it to me after meeting Joe Lewis many years earlier in London. Richard threatened to sell my photo to the highest bidder if I didn't give him money from my weekly allowance. He was holding my prized possession for ransom. Naturally, I was quite upset by this, so I went to my father and cried to him about the matter. I knew my father would be upset with Richard. I even believed Dad would give him a whipping for it. However, instead of showing outrage for Richard's devious acts, Dad's response was more ambivalent than I expected.

"He told me, 'Oscar, your older brother has been unjustly terrorizing you for years. And he does it because you have given him permission to do so. You may not have given him written or even vocal permission, but your passive and girl-like demeanor gave him all the permission he needed to take advantage of you. He knows your only power against him would be to come and cry to me. However, Richard also knows I will not always be around,

70

and as long as you cannot personally put a stop to his terrorizing, he will continue to take advantage of you until you force him not to. He has established a dominant and subordinate relationship with you, and he will continue to play it out your whole lives unless you put a stop to it. If you are comfortable with being Richard's victim your entire life, I suggest you pay him the ransom he seeks. However, if you want this unjust trend to stop right now, then maybe you should stand up to him and put an end to this rubbish once and for all.'

"I responded as a victim usually would and cried to my father about how Richard was bigger than me and he would pummel me if I tried to fight him. My father smacked me on my face, pulled me by the shirt collar, and said, 'Bullies don't learn lessons from passive men. There is a solution to your problem. However, you have yet to come to terms with it.' He let go of my shirt and explained, 'My son, I will not intervene in the dispute between you and Richard; if you want to take back your possessions and your manhood from your brother, you will do it on your own accord.'

"My father's message was a rude awakening, to say the least. But what I feared more than my brutish stepbrother was losing favor in my father's eyes. I was determined to accept his challenge and prove my worth to my brother, my father, and myself. The next day, I invited Richard to my room to negotiate the terms of my Joe Lewis photograph. Richard was smug as ever, and he demanded I give him an additional 25 quid, which was 10 quid more than he'd originally asked. He assumed I was caving in, so he was trying to further exploit my weakness. I informed my brother that I would not pay him a penny. He laughed at me, grabbed me by the arm, and pushed me. 'Give me the money, Oscar,' he demanded, 'or I won't even sell the picture. I will rip it up in front of your face and eat it! And if you want what's left of it, I will leave my shit in the houseboy's toilet for you to sift through.'

"I told Richard that he didn't understand. I could not pay him the money for the ransom because I had

71

already spent my weekly allowance to buy myself a present. I asked him if he cared to know what I spent my allowance on. He shrugged while asking, 'Why do I care?'

"I waived him closer and said, 'Because it has everything to do with you.' When Richard leaned in, I pulled out a small but hard baton from my waistband and smacked Richard broadside of the head with it. Richard fell to the ground, knocked out cold. When he awoke, I stepped over him, holding my autographed Joe Lewis picture and pointed the baton at his bloody face while explaining that I'd used the rest of my allowance to buy the baton from one of our father's guards, and that I would not hesitate to use it on him if he tried to rob me again. From the look in my eyes, Richard could tell I was not bluffing—and he would be right, because I wasn't. From that day forward, Richard never bullied me again."

Oscar, not giving Stephen the time to contemplate the moral of the story, inhaled the aroma of his wine and finished it, saying, "Stephen, there are extreme challenges to overcome when doing business in Ghana. Believe me, I know it's frustrating. Your situation is a prime example of how man is often betrayed by his fellow man in this country. It would be fairly easy for me to intervene in your matter and retrieve the money this farmer owes you. However, I ask myself, Is this a service to you? And do I open up the floodgates to have to intervene in each one of our recipients' business dealings?

"Because, surely if I do it for you, wouldn't I have to do it for everyone else? Just as my father did not intervene with me and my brother's skirmish when I was a child, I will not intervene in yours. I want you to find a bold solution to your problem. Consider it your final exam for this course, Stephen. And to give you an incentive…if you return to me next week and you have remedied the problem on your own, I will cover your debt and you can pocket the money you retrieved. If you don't, I still expect you to pay back your loan with interest."

Oscar gestured for George to rise while he did the same, retying his bow tie and finishing his wine with one gulp. Oscar then faced his guest. "That being said, my nephew and I have to go back into the auditorium and give our attention to the members of the program who did accomplish what we asked." Oscar and George walked out of the green room and left Stephen to contemplate his situation.

A week later, Oscar was proud to learn that Stephen Agyapong paid back the remainder of his loan. As promised, Oscar reimbursed Stephen the amount he repaid. However, he was bothered to learn that Stephen was arrested the following week for felonious assault. The victim? The goat farmer who owed Stephen money. Oscar, feeling somewhat responsible for Stephen's problems, anonymously provided him with high-end defense attorneys, and he was acquitted several months later with the aid of his excellent counsel.

Chapter 11
Office of the President of Ghana in Accra, Ghana
Present Day

President Abna Amoako's Armani suit had been delivered fresh from the tailors the previous day, and his Armani shoes had been expedited on a boat from Naples a week earlier. In President Amoako's inaugural year, he had acquired enough designer suits to last him every day of the week for two months. Now a year into his second term, Amoako had gained a considerable amount of weight, which was just the excuse the president needed to expand his wardrobe. It also provided Ghanaian cartoonists plenty of fodder for their weekly comic strips.

President Amoako's assistant, Joseph Nyum, knocked on the door to inform his boss that his afternoon appointment had arrived.

"Thank you, Joseph. Let Mr. Ishmael in." Amoako adjusted his tie and looked in the mirror to make sure his appearance would match the caliber of his guest. As Anwar Ishmael appeared from around the corner, Ishmael instructed his associate Abdul to wait in a chair outside the president's office. Although President Amoako had countless business discussions with Anwar Ishmael, this was only the second time they had met in person.

"Welcome, Mr. Ishmael, and please sit down. I've been anxious to meet with you. I imagine it must be important for you to leave Dubai and come all the way to Accra to meet with me. It's a pleasure to speak with you in person instead of through a third party. Your secretary was vague on the subject of this meeting, so I was unable to have my aides prepare anything for us."

Ishmael ignored Amoako's nervous rambling and instead walked to the presidential chair and admired its plush design. He gently stroked the chair's leather and then, without permission, sat down in President Amoako's official chair. Once he was comfortable, Ishmael gestured for the President of Ghana to sit in the visitor's chair in his own office. President Amoako gave his guest a cross look as if to say, how dare you? But his fear quickly halted his pride. Instead of demanding his seat back, the president smiled and cowered in the chair across from the garish Ishmael.

The Lebanese boss was less physically than psychologically intimidating. Ishmael was a slightly above-average-size man at 6 feet tall and 220 pounds. He was clean-shaven except for a thick mustache. His eyes were a light brownish-green, yet his stare was still murky and penetrating as the Mediterranean. Ishmael spoke Arabic, Farsi, English, and Italian fluently. However, English was his preferred language, even over Arabic. Ishmael showed no desire for small talk; he was in one of his notorious impatient moods and wasted no time attending to his agenda. "So it seems as if Ghana has stumbled across large deposits of oil?"

"Yes, we have discovered 'black gold.' The estimated amount is in the tens of billions of barrels, and that's a conservative estimate according to our consultants."

Ishmael finally smiled at President Amoako, which secretly put the head of state at ease. "This discovery will do great things for you and your country."

"I know this, Mr. Ishmael. The discovery of oil could be the answer to our economic problems. Our minister of finance estimates tens of billions in annual Ghanaian income as a result of this oil."

If Ishmael was impressed by the numbers President Amoako rattled off, he didn't show it. Instead, he probed with another question, "So have you decided which company will be awarded the mining rights?"

"We have many good candidates and are still determining which one would be the best partner."

Ishmael nodded. "How are my friends at PetroCo Oil doing? Are they still in the bidding process?"

"Yes, they are way up the ladder."

"Good to hear, Abna." Ishmael did not even bother referring to Amoako as Mr. President at this point. Such blatant disrespect was intentional. He proceeded to offend.

"You should know, Abna, PetroCo is willing to provide Ghana with a generous offer. The chairman of PetroCo tells me they will offer up to 20% in an annual tribute. This is very competitive with the other offers out there."

President Amoako gathered the courage to ask, "And I suppose you know all this because...?"

"PetroCo agreed to supply the labor through my human-resources company," Ishmael answered with no shame. "PetroCo is also prepared to provide you with a generous compensation package if you are successful in helping us to broker this deal." Amoako's ears perked up, and Ishmael continued, "PetroCo likes to personally reward its friends—and they consider you a friend, Abna. They will act kindly if you use your influence to help them win this contract."

"How kindly?"

Ishmael did not immediately respond to the question. Instead, he studied Amoako's face for eight awkward seconds before answering, "We're thinking an initial deposit of $30 million into an offshore account and an additional $1 million annually for the rest of your life."

One could almost see the dollar signs projecting from Amoako's brain to his pupils. The president put on his best poker face to mask his excitement. "I am humbled that you and PetroCo value my services that much. If I accept such an offer, I will prove that I am worth every penny of your tribute." He paused for a minute and thought about his next statement carefully. "Although my powers of office are strong, they are not as powerful as they would have been in my father's day. Unfortunately, there are some in this government, like Vice President Bonswah, who are plagued with the naive idealism of schoolboys. He has been told that Freestar Oil's offer will help build up the middle class by providing those oil jobs to Ghanaians.

"My vice president and people like him, who lean toward Freestar, are all persuaded by the case made by Oscar Boateng. He is the only other man in this country as influential as I am. Unfortunately, he is rumored to support Freestar Oil. It is his intention to make the bidding process completely transparent. If Freestar loses the bid, there will be serious inquiries to the matter if it appears everything wasn't handled above board. You get me?"

Ishmael pondered as he strummed his fingers along the right arm of the chair. "Well these are issues a masterful politician like yourself can handle, I'm sure. I shouldn't have to hold your hand through the matter. Plus, I shouldn't have to mention the generosity I've shown you in the past—the all-expenses-paid trips to Dubai and India dating back to your time in Parliament. Don't forget about your direct link to my friends at the lab who feed your OxyContin 'habit'." It was a little known fact, but indeed true that President Amoako was addicted to un-presidential vices such as OxyContin, booze and prostitutes. "It would be unfortunate for any of this information to be made public. Should you need an extra incentive, just think about that."

This was vintage Ishmael, the master manipulator, who knew how to motivate his agents of deceit to do his bidding. "Just make it happen, Abna. I get tense when I'm fed excuses. That being said, I can sympathize with your Oscar Boateng dilemma. I've dealt with plenty of wealthy self-appointed saints in my business; they require unique attention. I will handle Oscar Boateng, if you handle the rest. If you feel like this is too much, let me know now, and I will withdraw my offer."

Abna was ware aware of how Ishmael was capable of 'handling' people and his conscious wanted clarification. "How do you plan on handling Oscar Boateng?"

"President, a politician in your position should not bother yourself with such mundane details, but if you must know, I'll tell you. I'm going to speak with Mr. Boateng personally before I leave Ghana. At the end of the day, Mr. Boateng is a businessman, and I'm sure I can persuade him to make the smart business decision. We just have to appeal to his philanthropic weakness and make it worth his while."

Ishmael stood up from the president's chair and stuck his hand out to President Amoako. "So Abna, do we have a deal?"

Amoako stared at Ishmael long and hard before he shook his hand and mumbled, "Deal," as if he obscured the word enough, it wouldn't count. Although the president was energetic about the potential to make tens of millions of dollars, he couldn't shake the feeling that it was a deal with Lucifer, himself.

Chapter 12
Accra, Ghana
Present Day

At the age of seventy-one, Oscar Boateng worked longer hours for BOI than he had during his entire previous career. On average, the chairman worked thirteen-hour days. BOI was now two years old and its interests had rapidly spanned the globe. Whether it was a commodities broker in Stockholm or a Wall Street banker, Oscar had a long-established reputation for making himself available all hours of the day to clients and associates. Although a workaholic, Oscar's age did not allow him to travel much. His nephew, Clinton, conducted most of BOI's overseas business.

At the moment, Oscar was wrapping up business over the phone with Clinton, who had just met with a client in Rome and was briefing his uncle on the outcome. Although Oscar regarded Clinton as the sharpest tool in BOI's box, he was too humble to admit that his own wisdom and experience was probably BOI's most valuable asset; it was Oscar's strategic thinking that gave BOI an unfair advantage against its competition.

Oscar hung up with Clinton and read the memo his assistant Kwasi had left on his desk: "The Chief Executive Officer of Ishmael Ltd., aka owners of Upper Volta Lumber and the Makola Mall, Anwar Ishmael is in town for the evening and would like to invite you to join him for dinner tonight at Brojode."

Oscar thought, yes, the elusive owner of Ishmael Ltd. Oscar prided himself on knowing all of the power brokers in Ghana, and Ishmael was the only one he had yet to meet. It was safe to say the man's mystique intrigued Oscar. He called his assistant into his office.

"Yes boss, what do you need?" Kwasi replied.

"Call Mr. Ishmael's office and let him know I will be delighted to join him for dinner at Brojode at 8:00 p.m."

"Yes, boss."

"Thank you, Kwasi."

Brojode was swanky for Accra standards. Oscar arrived precisely at 8:00 p.m. and noticed the stonewalls gating the property were whiter than normal. Someone must have recently bathed them with a fresh coat of paint. The restaurant's patio emulated the layout of many streetside bistros in France. The patio of Brojode often overflowed with Accra's young and privileged. However, on this night and by the request of its owner, Brojode sat empty when Oscar's driver dropped him off at the entrance. Oscar opened the gate and walked across the cobblestone patio. An extremely bronze-colored man, who introduced himself as, "Abdul Mulinesbar, an associate of Anwar Ishmael", quickly greeted him.

After the introduction, Abdul led his guest upstairs to a table in the center of the empty dining room. The restaurant lighting was dramatic, and the room was dark except for the track lighting directed on the two-top table. Abdul pulled out the chair with its back turned to the front door for Oscar. Most alpha males Oscar's age, which have read the classic novel or watched Shane, preferred to sit in the chair facing the entrance. Being the guest, though, he did not protest the seating arrangement. Not ten seconds after Oscar was seated, a tall figure from the back of the restaurant emerged from the darkness. Like Abdul, he was a sharply dressed bronze-skinned man, except this man was a little thicker and wore a mustache. He paused at the table to acknowledge his guest.

"Good evening, Mr. Boateng, it's a pleasure to finally meet you. I am Anwar Ishmael."

Oscar stood up and shook Ishmael's hand. "Please call me Oscar."

Not allowing Oscar to out-polite him, Ishmael insisted, "And please refer to me as Anwar."
The two titans sat down in their respective chairs. The server arrived to take their drink orders and then disappeared to the bar. Oscar and Ishmael sat quietly at the table taking mental notes of one another while the bartender prepared their drinks. The awkward silence was actually customary when doing business in Ghana. Some

80

people feel it bad luck to discuss business at dinner before drinks are served. The waiter arrived and handed them their drinks.

Ishmael broke the silence. "I hope you don't mind, Oscar, but I took the liberty of having the chef customize our menu for us this evening. I also inquired about your eating preferences with your assistant. I was glad to hear that, like me, you have a diverse palette. I wish I could tell you what the chef is preparing, but it's a surprise to me as well. I only know that it will be delicious."

"Well, I'm eager to taste it; there's not much my tongue won't try. I've eaten akrante and I've eaten termites in Mainland China." An akrante is a gopher-sized rodent found in the bushes of Ghana. To this comment, Anwar responded with the type of chuckle that is two parts sincere and one part polite. Oscar smiled and continued to make small talk with his host. "I'm used to this restaurant being very crowded. What happened tonight?"

"I am not big on crowds, Oscar. And I get to eat here so little that I wanted to enjoy it for myself. But don't worry—by lunchtime tomorrow, I'm sure it will return to its regular state of hysteria."

"Well I give you credit for wielding your power for such a worthy cause," Oscar laughed, "Because as social as I am, I still avoid crowds whenever possible."

Ishmael returned the laugh and agreed with his guest by raising his glass. Over dinner, the two traded stories of boardroom triumphs and business rumors on the international level, which were only privy to true insiders like themselves. Both were experienced enough conversationalists to know that the important subjects were appropriately discussed after dinner.

The two men took little time to finish their dinners. The server cleared their dishes and, as if they'd rehearsed it, both Ishmael and Oscar reached inside their jackets for a post-dinner cigarette. So far, Ishmael impressed Oscar; he reminded Oscar of himself decades ago—an ambitious man who lived a sporting life.

Ishmael briefly apologized about his lack of

presence in Ghana. "For a man who has as many business interests here as I do, I keep forgetting how beautiful Ghana is. Not to mention I feel as if Ghana is part Lebanese with all its residents that live here. Not many people know this but I lived in Ghana for two years as a child, my father worked here as a traveling merchant. I have fond memories of my time here, many of my associates that manage my Ghanaian operations I initially met some forty-five years ago. Eventually we moved back to Lebanon to settle down, I try to make a visit every quarter, but I haven't been here in almost a year; it's a shame."

Oscar dismissed this comment with a wave of his hand. "In this day with so much technology in communication, one does not need to be as hands-on as we used to be." In lieu of saying that being said, Oscar stopped to take a drag off his cigarette and continued, "So what brings you to Ghana today?"

Ishmael nodded his head in anticipation for this question. "I've come to oversee some issues with our lumber yard up north. I wanted to surprise the directors and managers with a visit and make sure they're keeping up the standards I expect from them." Ishmael scooted back into his chair, crossed his legs while speaking. "More importantly, this is a good time for me to catch up with the progress of Ghana, visit old friends, and make new ones."

Ishmael raised his glass and pointed it in Oscar's direction and toasted, "To new friends."

"To new friends."

"From what I understand, BOI is doing a phenomenal job. You are the talk of Africa's business community. It's refreshing to see a home-grown African company like yours become so successful."

"Coming from such an accomplished businessman, this is a compliment."

Sensing that time for small talk was over, Ishmael stubbed his Benson and Hedges in the ashtray, uncrossed his legs, and scooted his chair in closer to the table. He leaned in to his guest and asked, "If I may, I would like to bend your ear with something of real importance."

"By all means," Oscar replied, relieved that they would finally get to the point of the meeting.

"Thank you. Ishmael Ltd. is part of my larger holding company called the Ishmael Group. We have business interests all over the world, more specifically the Middle East, Asia, Europe, and Africa. I feel that our respective organizations have similar interests, especially when it comes to charitable causes. The Ishmael Group is interested in BOI's micro-loan program. I know this model has worked well in India and South America, and BOI has proven it can work in Africa. The Ishmael Group would like to match whatever BOI is putting into its micro-lending program. We would also like to extend the program to Nigeria, Sierra Leone, and Lebanon—all under the BOI banner."

Oscar took a sip of his wine and wiped his mouth gently with his napkin. "You do understand that the micro-loan program is a genuine nonprofit venture? We recoup the money we loan at an almost nonexistent interest rate, and all that money goes right back into the lending pool. There is no profit to be made in this business."

"I understand this, Oscar. You see, the Ishmael Group also wants to be in the business of delivering micro-loans to underserved communities. We feel it gives our organization positive branding opportunities while helping do some good. It makes sense for us."

Oscar smiled. It was obvious Ishmael was lubing him up for a favor. "This is very generous of you, Anwar. Obviously, the Ishmael Group is fortunate to be able to contribute such a generous amount to our program. But if say I said yes to your generous offer, what are the conditions? As you know, my friend, nothing is free in this world."

Ishmael let out a soft laugh and tossed the crumpled dinner napkin from his lap onto the table. "I wouldn't insult your intelligence. I am not offering you a charitable contribution; rather I'd like it to be a partnership or, better yet, a friendship. I help you with a project and you help me with a project—a barter of sorts."

"I've always been taught that you can't buy friendship, Mr. Anwar, so let's call it a partnership for now."

"Fair enough. I'm unofficially consulting with PetroCo Oil on their special operations in Ghana. As you know, PetroCo is in the bidding process for the contract to operate Ghana's newly discovered oil reserves. My people, who pay attention to the selection committee process, tell me PetroCo's application is tied in the lead with Freestar Oil to win the bid. My people also inform me that you, Mr. Boateng, have much influence with the committee, hell— with the whole government, for that matter. I understand your endorsement is as good as gold." Ishmael paused to let Oscar register what he said before saying, "My asking price is for you to endorse PetroCo Oil in this bidding process, and in return, I help you expand the good work you're doing with BOI's micro-loan program."

Oscar lightly scratched his right index knuckle. "Anwar, I have to stop you right there. Full disclosure: I have unofficially put my support behind Freestar Oil. The owners have shown me that they will provide great benefits for Ghana through job creation and environmental responsibility."

"I am aware of this, Oscar. However, I believe if you meet with the PetroCo Oil executives, you will see that they are willing to increase whatever percentage Freestar is proposing to give Ghana, and they will address any environmental and economic concerns you may have."

Oscar shrugged and looked to the ceiling. "I am not on the payroll of Freestar Oil, so I have no benefit to solely support them. If PetroCo truly has the best application, I am sure that will come to light in the process and the committee will vote for the most attractive applicant."

Ishmael gave no time for Oscar's polite excuse to settle into the conversation. "Of course, Oscar. However, the problem is that PetroCo has not met with you personally. Their concern is that as long as there is the perception among the committee that you only support

84

Freestar, the committee will vote for Freestar even if PetroCo's application is the better one. They feel that the selection committee would make this choice in order to stay in your good graces. I know this notion sounds ridiculous, but you know how Ghanaian legislators can be. "Oscar knew this to be the case with many Ghanaian legislators. He had personally expressed to the committee members, in no uncertain terms, that it would be better for Ghana if they voted with their consciences and not deferred to special-interests groups in the oil industry.

And there lie the irony. Oscar Boateng, CEO of arguably one of the largest private special-interest groups on the continent, was lecturing Ghanaian legislators about the dangers of special interests. Even Oscar couldn't be sure they would do what he asked. Oscar thought that politicians were most comfortable when their campaign contributors instructed them how to vote.

Oscar showed he wasn't naive by responding, "Let's drop the spin, my friend. In a roundabout way, you're telling me that the contribution to BOI's micro-loan program would actually be underwritten by PetroCo Oil and not the Ishmael Group?"

"By all means, no. I am telling you that the check will be written by the Ishmael Group, however, an accounting coincidence will occur shortly after the check is written."

"What type of accounting coincidence?"

"Shortly after that check is written, PetroCo will deposit the exact amount of the check I wrote for BOI's micro-lending program into one of my consulting accounts."

Oscar laughed at Ishmael's cynicism and admired his unapologetic and unethical suggestion. "Anwar, as I said, I don't have a horse in the race. All I want is the best set of circumstances for Ghana and its citizens. If you set up a meeting with PetroCo executives, I will meet with them and lend them my ear. I cannot promise you an endorsement, but if PetroCo can convince me they are truly the better corporation for the job, then I will tell this to anyone paying attention."

"And this is all I ask of you, Oscar. Thank you." The two captains of industry stood up, shook hands, and ended their meeting, trusting that one another would fulfill their promises.

Chapter 13
Tema, Ghana
Present Day

Oscar had a full complement of meetings the next morning, but before attending any of them, he made time for a very important phone call. Oscar's nature did not allow him to trust many politicians; in Ghana's current government, he trusted only one man, Vice President Kweku Bonswah. If it were up to Oscar, Vice President Bonswah would be the president of Ghana instead of Abna Amoako. Oscar had known the vice president since Bonswah was a promising young student at the University of Ghana. Oscar always regarded him as a stand-up individual.

Before Bonswah joined the Amoako ticket, Oscar had fully encouraged him to run for president. Despite Oscar's urging and support, Bonswah chose not to run for office due to his loyalty and obligations to Parliament. Much to the surprise of many, Bonswah reluctantly accepted Abna Amoako's invitation to be his vice president—not because he believed in Amoako's politics but because he didn't trust those politics and wanted to keep an eye on the president in case his provocative behavior started affecting his ability to govern.

Vice President Bonswah was in Oscar Boateng's inner circle. However, by design, no one in the government was aware of their close friendship. It was assumed that if the vice president's colleagues were aware of the men's friendship, they would not reveal their true colors to him. Oscar's assistant informed him that Vice President Bonswah was on line one and put him on speakerphone. "How are you Mr. Vice President?" a delighted Oscar asked.

"Doing well, Mr. Boateng. Thank you for asking," Bonswah replied in English. Unlike Oscar, Bonswah's English accent was not accompanied by a highbrow British cadence. When the vice president spoke English, it was clear he hailed from the Fante region. His English carried a heavy Ghanaian accent and was burdened with long pauses in between every fifth word or so. It had charm, nonetheless. "What can I do for you on this fine morning?"

"Not too much. I just needed to get some feedback from you."

"Fire away, captain," Bonswah delightfully instructed.

"Last night, I had an interesting dinner with Anwar Ishmael of Ishmael Ltd."

Bonswah cut in, "This is interesting."

"And why is that?"

"Well, he was at the presidential palace the other day for an unannounced meeting."

"With one of the ministers, I presume?"

"No, no, with President Amoako himself. I found it interesting because Anwar Ishmael is rarely in our country. Most of his Ghanaian affairs are handled by one of his flunkies."

"Mmmm. The subject of our meeting began with Ishmael's interest in matching BOI's contributions to the micro-loan program, which they want to expand to two other African countries under BOI's banner."

Bonswah found that bizarre and immediately asked, "What's the catch?"

"And that was my exact response when he proposed it to me. The sticky part is that Ishmael is an unofficial consultant for PetroCo Oil, and he wants me to endorse PetroCo Oil's bid for Ghana's oil reserves. I don't necessarily have a problem with it, especially if I can leverage my endorsement to grow the micro-loan program."

Oscar left ample opportunity for Bonswah to interject, but since he didn't, Oscar moved along. "Since you're close to the selection committee, is PetroCo Oil a true competitor? Are they prepared to provide Ghana with the best opportunity to benefit from this deal? Because if they are, I will gladly endorse them and accept Ishmael's offer to beef up the micro-loan program. It's a win/win situation." The vice president remained quiet and Oscar, slightly impatient, was forced to ask, "Are you there?"

"Yes, boss, hold on, I'm getting my thoughts together." He deliberated for seven more seconds before saying, "Here is the issue, my friend: The micro-loan program is phenomenal and it helps tens of thousands of Ghanaians on a daily basis. It is a program worth spending political capital on. However, the choice between endorsing PetroCo Oil over Freestar Oil can negatively affect all Ghanaians. By choosing PetroCo, we could potentially lose billions of dollars in revenue and many jobs.

"I truly believe Freestar will bid a 32% commission to Ghana. My sources say PetroCo will not go above a 25% commission. According to a credible source, the CEO of PetroCo Oil is on record telling shareholders at their latest shareholders conference that he would not offer more than 25% in annual commission to Ghana if it acquired the oil-mining rights. The difference between 25% and 32% is billions in revenue.

"In addition, your new friend Anwar Ishmael is rumored to have ties to extremist groups in the region. I once heard the Ishmael Group referred to as 'the most well-known organized crime outfit in the Middle East.' In my opinion, Ishmael is not to be trusted. There is too much collusion between him and PetroCo. The Ishmael Group outsources cheap Lebanese labor to corporations in various industries all over the world including PetroCo Oil.

"So imagine the scenario if PetroCo wins the bid? That means hundreds of Lebanese workers working the oil rigs and taking jobs from Ghanaians." Then Bonswah concluded with the obvious, "Ishmael is correct in his assumption that the weight of your endorsement is critical. For better or worse, the committee will vote for whomever you endorse, Oscar."

Oscar quickly thought through all scenarios and asked, "What if I endorse no one?"

"If you endorse no one, they will vote for the company endorsed by President Amoako. And I suspect, given Anwar Ishmael's recent visit to the president's office, he has already made his play for Amoako."

"Of course he has. This president has the integrity of a lizard. All things being equal, is Freestar the better company to go with?"

"I'm afraid so, Oscar."

Oscar couldn't say he was surprised by the vice president's assessment of Ishmael's proposal, but he was disappointed, nonetheless. Oscar didn't mind doing business with men of ill repute, as long as the negotiations were equitable for all parties. However, if it meant taking food off the tables of the Ghanaian poor, that was an absolute deal breaker. The way Oscar saw it, he was too old to start betraying his values.

"Bonswah, again your political instincts are impeccable."

"As are yours, my friend."

≈

On this particular morning, Oscar had an important noon meeting that he knew would end in a confrontation. By nature he was non-confrontational, but he did not always have the luxury of being amenable in his line of work. Unlike many CEO's, Oscar took no pleasure in being rude or contentious. Years ago, he'd developed a technique to trigger the required prickly behavior before confrontational meetings; he ate only a light breakfast before a late-morning meeting so that his blood sugar was low, which genuinely made him irritable and agitated by the start of the meeting.

Oscar's plan was working. It was 11:45 a.m. and all he'd eaten was a bowl of oatmeal and a small glass of orange juice. He had already achieved being short with Kwasi, his most trusted assistant. Kwasi did not take it personally. After thirty years of working for Oscar, there were maybe a handful of details he didn't know about his boss and friend; Oscar was simply psyching himself up for a showdown.

Noon arrived and Oscar entered the conference room. His guests were two white PetroCo Oil executives and they had already settled in. PetroCo's Vice-President of

90

African affairs was an older Australian man, who sported a well-groomed head of white hair. The person manning the laptop projector was PetroCo's creative director. He was a younger German dressed in a tightly tailored suit jacket, skinny tie, and jeans—perhaps the only art director, who did not own a pair of slick designer glasses.

Oscar greeted each of the men in the room. "Please sit, gentlemen." After the participants took their places, he continued, "I appreciate you allowing me to preview your presentation to the selection committee. Let me warn you that, contrary to what many believe, I do not have a vote on the selection committee. However, men much smarter than me tell me that my stature in this country makes my endorsement influential, so I have decided to consult on the matter. That being said, I would like to know what all parties involved are proposing." Oscar smiled, then gestured to PetroCo Oil's executive, indicating: You're on.

The Australian buttoned his suit jacket and stood up from his chair to narrate the PowerPoint presentation for the next forty-five minutes. Oscar interjected with a few questions here and there, which the VP fielded with great enthusiasm. As far as presentations go, PetroCo's was superb. Oscar would later note that he was more impressed with their presentation than Freestar's.

The art director turned on the lights, Oscar clapped and said, "Well done." The PetroCo delegation smiled and thanked him. It was now time to find out if all their hard work paid off. "I have to say that was an impressive presentation—one of the best pitches I've seen in a while."

The art director handed Oscar an attractively designed folder. "We're glad you think so. That's why we're leaving you with a disk and a hard copy of the presentation for future reference."

Oscar smiled and tapped his fingers on the file. "Gentleman, I think you have a fine organization and it is successful for obvious reasons. I would like to endorse PetroCo Oil for the Ghana contract, but unfortunately I cannot do so."

"Excuse me?" The PetroCo vice president was

floored.

Oscar nodded his head, anticipating this response. "Let me explain. I cannot in good conscience vote for a company that will yank jobs away from Ghanaians. Your dealings with the Ishmael Group's staffing company would award most of the oil jobs to foreigners and not to Ghanaians. Plus, given your CEO's comments at the recent shareholder's meeting, I doubt your commitment to pay Ghana the best annual commission. I know that two months ago PetroCo CEO Gordon Heinrich promised the company would not pay over a 25% commission to acquire the Ghana oil-mining rights, which is far lower that Freestar's commitment. I am still leaning toward endorsing Freestar. But, as I believe in not corrupting the political process, what I expressed today will not leave the room."

"And what does that mean, Mr. Boateng?" asked the Australian.

"Well, it means I will not taint your application in this process, but I will not publicly support PetroCo either. There is really no other way to explain it," Oscar said while standing up from his chair and buttoning his suit jacket.

The Australian shook his head at Oscar. "You had made up your mind before we even booked our plane tickets, didn't you?"

The art director stood up and eased the Australian back because he was steadily venturing too close to Oscar. Watching from the next room, Kwasi darted into the conference room to his boss' defense. Before Kwasi could step in between Oscar and the PetroCo delegation, Oscar raised his hand and commanded him to stand down.

When the Australian realized Oscar was serious, he turned to the art director and said, "There is nothing we can do here. He is wrongfully vilifying us. Admitting he supports Freestar makes him just as corrupt as he's claiming PetroCo to be."

"I wish I could say my decision was 'only business,' but I would be lying. My love for Ghana and the well being of my country supersedes anything business related. Unfortunately I have to run, gentleman; I have a lunch appointment and I'm famished. Feel free to take as much time as you need to collect your belongings. Kwasi will assist you with anything you may need." Oscar shut the door to the conference room and with him went PetroCo's hope of obtaining his endorsement.

Anwar Ishmael's Monday was the busiest he could remember in a long time. He waved for Abdul to open his office door. On the other side of the door stood Detective Patel.

"Mr. Ishmael," said Patel in greeting.

"Have a seat, detective."

"Former detective now," Detective Patel said, taking a seat.

"Yes, former detective. I can't help but ask why you thought it a wise decision to resign so soon after what your newspapers describe as 'the worst terrorist attack in your country's history'?"

"I think it's better than any other time, Mr. Ishmael. The timing made sense to me. I have served over twenty years in the police force, and the terrorist attacks were enough to put me over the edge," he said mockingly.

"Yes, that would make sense if it were only that simple. The fact that you are here today makes things complicated, though."

Patel was confused. "Sorry, I don't follow you, Mr. Ishmael."

"Well, you're the detective—figure it out. Soon you will leave here with access to a bank account that has twice the amount of money you made in twenty years on the police force. If I were your colleagues, I think that might raise some red flags, don't you?"

Intending to set the record straight, Patel said, "Well Mr. Ishmael, since I am a detective, I have taken every step to cover my tracks. I understand your concerns, but I can take care of myself. I'm sure a man in your position knows that a man in my position would not be here if I didn't know how to take care of myself." Patel stood up. "Now I apologize, but I have a plane to catch."

Ishmael was a bit taken aback by Patel's stern, almost disrespectful tone. It was Ishmael's turn to set the record straight: "You don't have to remind me, Mr. Patel; it was my private jet that flew you from Bombay to Dubai, and it will be my private jet that flies you to the Caymans to pick up your cases of money. Now have a seat." Patel sat back down and Ishmael continued, "I'm sure I don't have to tell you why it's important that none of this gets traced back to me?"

"Well you don't have to worry," a humbled Patel replied, "the Arab Liberation Army already took credit for the attacks, which is all the media needs these days; no one follows the money anymore. Besides, even if anyone thought to look, it still wouldn't be traced back to you. There are so many buffers in place, you would have to try very hard to be caught."

Ishmael shook his head. "The surviving owners of the hotel decided to sell the property. My partners and I have already moved to acquire the property and demolish it to build a new complex. I could have used your ear at the Bureau in case anyone started asking questions about the new ownership."

"I understand now. Don't worry Mr. Ishmael, even though I am retired, I will always have my ear to the Bureau."

Ishmael stood to dismiss him. "Very well. Abdul, the door please. My driver will take you to your plane, detective."

Anwar Ishmael, like any businessman, preferred his business dealings to run smoothly, and these issues with the Vaj Hotel were unnecessary. Over a year ago, the Ishmael Group and a commercial development partner made a bid to acquire the Vaj Hotel. The once-thriving hotel was losing money. However, because of the hotel's location, Ishmael and his partner were willing to buy the property for more than what it was actually worth. The owner, Vijay Gupta, who named the hotel after himself, had not considered selling the property until the developer responsible for some of the most eye-catching skyscrapers in Singapore and Dubai made him such an attractive offer.

Gupta had ten other five-star properties in Asia that

were profitable, but the Vaj Hotel was his first and it was his baby. If he was going to sell the Vaj, it had to be for the right price and to the right people. Gupta would have gladly sold his property to the world-renowned developer had he not done more digging. Upon learning the developer would be subcontracting all of the labor to the Ishmael Group, he objected to the purchase. Gupta did not share his reasons with the rest of his investors; at the last minute, he simply said he changed his mind about selling the hotel. The truth of the matter was that he despised Anwar Ishmael and the Ishmael Group. He knew Ishmael was associated with several Islamic-extremist organizations including one operating out of Pakistan, the country he hated the most.

When Ishmael heard Gupta refused to sell the property after being so optimistic just a few weeks earlier, he knew it was due to Gupta's anti-Islamic prejudice. Anticipating this very issue, Ishmael had already put the pieces in place to remedy the problem. The Arab Liberation Army was based in Pakistan; it had been pitching Ishmael to sponsor an attack in India for the past several years. In addition to heroin trafficking and money laundering, one of Ishmael's underworld "services" included financing terrorist attacks for extreme Islamic organizations.

Ishmael didn't finance terrorists because he was a zealot, he only financed and orchestrated acts of terrorism when the outcome benefited his financial interests. His willingness to underwrite terrorist activities gave him leverage to operate a heroin-smuggling operation out of Afghanistan using Taliban and al-Qaeda operatives. After Bin Laden was assassinated, Ishmael realized the terrorism industry was becoming more dangerous and less lucrative, causing him to concentrate more on his legitimate business ventures.

It wasn't until the roadblock with the Vaj Hotel presented itself, that Ishmael considered using his extremist connections again. In addition to financing the Vaj Hotel massacre, he agreed to provide the organization

96

with weapons if the group moved its attention from Calcutta to Bombay. The other caveat was the Arab Liberation Army had to attack the Vaj Hotel on a day when Vijay Gupta was in the building.

Truth be told, Ishmael had lost nearly all of his previous respect for his terrorist connections. Sure, he still hated Israel and everything it stood for, as well as the West for their arrogance and dominance in foreign affairs. But the more legitimate business he did, the more he believed in free trade; Ishmael was a staunch capitalist. He learned the key to victory was to beat your enemies in the global market, not wipe them off the map like many wanted for Israel. Terrorism had become such a convenient smoke screen for Ishmael that he found it hard to detach himself from that world altogether.

Now that his complicated business with the Vaj Hotel was nearly complete, the recent roadblock in the PetroCo oil deal proved to be more of an annoyance in comparison. In all of his dealings with African leaders, they proved totally predictable. From Tanzania to Côte d'Ivoire and Ghana, no leader of an African nation had ever refused him. President Amoako would prove no exception, if not for the interference of that stubborn Oscar Boateng. Ishmael had received the call from the irate PetroCo CEO earlier that Friday and learned the Boateng micro-loan deal fell through.

As he processed the news, Ishmael became disappointed. He'd felt his proposal to match Oscar's micro-loan project was a generous gesture. The five-star criminal was genuinely trying to embrace the business of philanthropy and had considered it a turning point in his life—maybe even an opportunity to pay down a fraction of the interest he owed on his sins. Now Oscar Boateng had taken his moment of redemption and smacked him in the face with it.

Ishmael often relied on his ability to size up a man and learn what makes him tick. He took pride in doing his research and uncovering all there was to know about a subject before pursuing him. When the appeal to Oscar's passion for the micro-loan program didn't bear fruit, he focused his attention on another piece of information about Oscar Boateng that he found quite interesting. Ishmael's research unearthed, among many fascinating facts, that Oscar, like most priceless jewels, had his flaws. After quickly tallying the pros and cons of this knowledge, Ishmael phoned the CEO of PetroCo Oil and said, "Do not bailout on our Ghana venture; it is still in play," and hung up with no explanation.

Ishmael's right hand man Abdul Mulinesbar escorted former detective Patel to the basement-level parking garage, where a black limousine was staged to take him to the Dubai airport. Abdul opened the back passenger door for him. When Patel was in his seat, Abdul joined him in the limo and asked Patel if he would like a glass of champagne. When Patel accepted, he pointed to the bottle of Veuve in a bucket of ice. After the detective poured a glass of champagne, he looked only to see Abdul pointing a pistol with a silencer directly at him. Before Patel could drop his glass and yell No!, a bullet crushed his skull, killing him instantly.

Abdul grabbed his wrist and checked his pulse. He then pulled Patel's cell phone from his pocket and phoned his boss upstairs. When Ishmael answered the phone, the guard said, "The milk has expired."

Ishmael had considered sparing the detective's life even in the moments before he sent him off to the basement. He didn't mind taking a life, but he usually looked for alternative solutions before issuing the death warrant. In the case of the former detective, though, he had no choice—Patel had become a liability. Ishmael received word that Patel's colleagues had been growing suspicious of him.

Over the years, Patel had earned an unsavory reputation. It didn't help that the only surviving terrorist of the Bombay attacks just happened to die under his watch, and he was the only witness. Those facts made it impossible to spare Patel's life. The former detective was Ishmael's only connection to the Bombay attacks. For this,

98

Patel had to go.

Chapter 15
Beirut, Lebanon
1970–Present Day

Abdul had been assigned a critical duty by Ishmael on this day—he was ordered to post bail for an inmate in a northern Ghanaian prison. Although Abdul was aware the parolee had been released from prison just minutes before, he was still taken aback by the man's offensive appearance. He was almost afraid he'd picked up the wrong prisoner, but he had the correct man. When the prisoner was escorted to the car, Abdul instructed the guards to put him in the passenger-side seat, handcuffed to the dash. For some strange reason, Abdul grinned and reflected on his time with his employer Anwar Ishmael and how he had become the man's most trusted associate.

The young Abdul Mulinesbar grew up in West Beirut when Beirut was the most secularist haven in all of the Middle East. In the early 1970s, a disco seemed to be on every corner of West Beirut. It was a city that embraced a liberal lifestyle until the late 1970s when the Islamic revolution ignited in Iran. Lebanon, like many of its neighbors, was affected by the "original Arab spring," when Islamic hardliners began surfacing in Lebanon. The more ambitious Islamic factions in Lebanon showed little concern for the country's domestic issues; they preferred to instigate skirmishes with Israel, the Goliath neighbor to the south.

In 1982 when Abdul was a teenager, Israel invaded Beirut during the Lebanese Civil War. The skirmish between Lebanon and Israel transformed his once suburban-like hometown into a smoldering landfill. Worst of all, it made Abdul Mulinesbar an orphan; both of his parents died in a building bombed that same year.

Like many Lebanese kids who were orphaned by the civil war, Abdul was inspired to adopt extremist views and enrolled in the newly formed political party, Hezbollah. In secondary school, Abdul attended class from 8:00 a.m. until 2:00 p.m. daily, and then headed straight to a

Hezbollah-sponsored recreation center where he polished up on three additional subjects: Quran study, prayer, and weapons training. Like most of Abdul's peers, weapons training were his favorite subjects. Unlike most of his peers, Abdul exhibited signs of excellent marksmanship and athleticism. He easily mastered every weapon, scored high in his martial arts training, and was being groomed as a soldier of fortune for Hezbollah. Around the time Abdul turned twenty, he considered himself a devout Muslim. Although he was no scholar of the Quran, he could make an AK47 sing like a siren out of a holy hymn. Abdul took the teachings of the Quran as law. It wasn't until he met Nassett that he was forced to challenge those laws.

Nassett was a sixteen-year-old neighborhood girl and the daughter of a high-ranking Hezbollah official. After months of flirting and passing notes through their friends, Abdul and Nassett secretly became boyfriend and girlfriend and dated for seven months.

One night, the young couple took their relationship to the next logical plateau when they chose to make love. They exchanged their virginities as awkward teenagers do and fell recklessly in love. When Nassett returned home that evening, she fell asleep in the bed she shared with her sister. Unbeknownst to her, Nassett had ruptured labia and spotted heavily on the bed in her sleep. Nassett's mother Sabina discovered the blood in the morning, and it didn't take long for her to realize the blood was from virginal trauma.

Once Nassett's father Jediah was told, he swore to unleash his full wrath on his daughter. Jediah locked his daughter in their basement; a week went by before she saw daylight. Jediah had consulted the local cleric, who said he wanted severe punishment for his daughter. The cleric appealed to Jediah to make an example of his daughter and seek justice in a warped interpretation of Allah's law.

The cleric recommended Nassett be flogged by members of their congregation in a public forum. As unconscionable as it may sound, Jediah agreed to the barbaric punishment. It should be noted that her father's

101

rage had less to do with his religious zeal than with an embarrassed man trying to redeem himself.

Nassett's flogging got out of hand because the cleric did not restrict any areas of her body from the lashing. As members of the mosque took turns striking her, their inexperience ravished her head, face, throat, torso, legs, and feet. The flogging was not meant to be a death sentence, but Nassett died in the hospital from internal bleeding some seven hours later and only seven weeks from her seventeenth birthday.

The day after Nassett and Abdul made love, he was bound for a Hezbollah-sponsored military operation in Syria and did not learn of his young lover's fate until he returned from his assignment eight days later. There was nothing he could do; she was already gone. Any information he received could not comfort him. For instance, according to Nassett's girlfriend, when Jediah demanded Nassett tell him who took her virginity, she refused. Her refusal to disclose the name only made her father angrier and inspired him to conduct the unfathomable punishment.

One night when Nassett's father pulled into his driveway, Abdul was poised in a dark shadow on the side of the house. When Jediah exited his vehicle and made his way to the door, Abdul tackled the frail man with ease and wrestled his blindsided victim to the ground, where he violently stabbed his lover's father several dozen times in the head neck and torso. Blinded by rage, Abdul would have continued the stabbing had he not been interrupted by Sabina, who released a blood-curdling scream in horror.

Abdul stopped and panted while hovering over his dying victim. He craned his neck to look back at Nassett's mother, whom he believed was just as responsible for her death as the man he was killing. Rising like a mythical beast that had just been spotted feeding on the village dog, his eyes were glowing in the moonlight as he peered at Sabina. Yet it was her mother's vivid eyes that gave Abdul pause, because they looked exactly like Nassett's. Abdul would have killed her with equal hatred as he did her husband, but the grief-stricken man could not bring himself to murder a likeness of his lover. Abdul released his prey and darted off into the Beirut night with phantom-like agility.

In the days following Nassett's demise, he rejected Hezbollah, his religion, and completely denounced Allah. After murdering Nassett's father, Abdul became a fugitive wanted by Hezbollah. Catching him would prove nearly impossible; he was a crafty fugitive. While on the lam, Abdul occupied his lonely rage-filled hours by tacking blasphemous graffiti on the ample amounts of rubble left in the streets of Beirut.

When four young Hezbollah recruits finally found him two months later, he was spotted at a café eating figs and drinking wine in plain sight. The four approached Abdul, insulted him in Arabic, and instructed him to get up from his seat. Abdul remained seated and paid them no mind. The recruit on the end pulled a 45-caliber pistol and demanded Abdul get up, for which he momentarily obliged. The man holding the 45 shifted his eyes away for a second, which was just enough time for Abdul to disarm the gun from the inexperienced gunman, who failed to release its safety.

In possession of the weapon, Abdul held it in his palm like a rock. With a swift forehand swing, he used the gun to pistol-whip its owner. Abdul hit his assailant with the gun so hard that it flew out of his hand. Another Hezbollan approached him with a weak punch. Using the recruit's own momentum, Abdul tossed him through a table breaking two of its legs. With violent velocity, he clutched a fork and swung it at the third man, stabbing him in the ribs.

He quickly scanned the floor for the lost gun, only to see the last member had it pointed at him only a few feet away but out of arm's reach. Abdul froze. The groaning comrades on the floor grunted for him to shoot Abdul, and he would have, if not for an authoritative voice from the back of the café who command the member to put down the gun. Once the Hezbollan saw the man behind the voice, he dropped the gun. Abdul grinned and grabbed for the gun with his back to the voice. Behind him, the authoritative voice also commanded Abdul to stop, but he continued reaching for the gun.

Before Abdul heard the massive eruption of a gun, he felt the sonic vibration of a bullet whiz by his right ear before he stopped. When he turned around with his hands up, he saw three men in secular dress. Two held guns pointed at him, and he suspected the person holding the piece with the smoking barrel had just shot at him. The person belonging to the authoritative voice stood behind the two gunmen; Abdul immediately recognized him as Anwar Ishmael.

At that time, Ishmael was making quite a name for himself as an ambitious thug in the Lebanese underworld. In a mutiny of sorts, he had recently disposed of his previous boss and founded his own outfit called the Ishmael Group. Usually secular gangs and Islamic fundamentalist groups didn't mix. However, gangs like Ishmael's performed niche services for Hezbollah and its ilk, which forced them to coexist whether they liked it or not. This codependence made it possible for ungodly outfits like the Ishmael Group to run the streets of Beirut and remain immune to sharia law.

One of the injured Hezbollans groaned at Ishmael. "This man is wanted by Hezbollah for taking the virginity of a high-ranking official's daughter and killing her father. Please help us detain him."

Abdul did not care to plea for Ishmael's mercy. He was suicidal by this point and would have even denounced Allah in the flesh, given the opportunity. Ishmael told his guards to lower their weapons as he walked slowly toward Abdul, sizing him up and nodded, impressed by this reckless rebel. He addressed the Hezbollah members around him: "Tell your superiors that I know who Mr. Abdul Mulinesbar is, and I demand he remain unharmed from now on."

The Hezbollah member with a gun looked at Ishmael as if he were a mad man. "This is blasphemy! This fugitive will be apprehended immediately and brought to justice under Allah's rule!"

To this, Ishmael brandished his own firearm and shot the Hezbollah member in the throat, allowing everyone in the café to watch him fall and die an agonizing death. The remaining Hezbollans did not challenge Ishmael.

After the café incident, Ishmael took Abdul into his home, giving his fugitive food, clothing, and shelter. After dinner, the two spoke. Ishmael confided to Abdul that he, too, was deeply angered by Nassett's senseless death, because he had two daughters—a four-year-old Azul and Jahline, who was almost Nassett's age.

On a slightly more positive note, Ishmael also admitted he was impressed by the skillful manner in which his guest neutralized the Hezbollah attackers. Abdul spoke little; he mostly sat and replenished his body with the nourishment he lacked while on the lam. Nonetheless, Abdul was keen enough to recognize he had found a new friend. Ishmael invited Abdul to join his outfit, and he gladly obliged.

During the two decades after taking in the suicidal Abdul, Ishmael grew to be one of the most enterprising men in the Middle Eastern underworld. He had transformed his Beirut street gang into a multi-national syndicate. Abdul aided Ishmael in all his illegal and pseudo-legitimate business operations. The Ishmael Group extended its tentacles into Afghanistan and established the largest heroin operation in the region.

As a gift for seven years of loyal service, Ishmael granted Abdul permission to finish avenging Nassett's death. The night before the Ishmael Group made its big move to Dubai, Abdul and several other associates kidnapped Nassett's mother and the cleric who had recommended Nassett's punishment. Proving he was a man who held grudges, Abdul did not hesitate to execute his prisoners in the same manner Nassett was murdered— they were flogged to death. At this point in his life, the executions were less about avenging Nassett and more about punishing them for turning him into what he'd become.

When Ishmael moved his organization to Dubai, he promoted Abdul to underboss, and he has remained Anwar Ishmael's most trusted associate. A talented criminal, Ishmael was able to disguise his criminal operations with pseudo legitimate businesses. To many ignorant of the Middle Eastern underworld, the Ishmael Group appeared to be a legitimate organization. However, even those with the lowest security clearance in law enforcement knew Anwar Ishmael was a high-caliber criminal with a vast organization of lieutenants and foot soldiers. Yet when it came to tasks of a most nefarious nature, he still trusted Abdul the most, who gladly executed those tasks to perfection.

≈

After being handcuffed to the car, the released Ghanaian inmate was baffled. With no idea why he was bailed out so soon, he was convinced the government had decided on a more permanent solution for him. The man looked at Abdul and asked, "Who the fuck are you?"

Abdul did not return the courtesy. He simply handed the foul-mouthed parolee a large manila envelope titled "Max Cotto." Since the package was labeled with his name, he felt obliged to open it. Cotto found a bundle of bills in Ghanaian currency and some written documents but also hygienic products, such as toothpaste, a toothbrush, comb, wet napkins, and gum.

Abdul started the car and drove off the prison property, saying in English, "Chew some of that gum, and go over the information in that envelope. You are being released into my custody as an employee of my organization. I will fill you in on the particulars of your employment later. If you agree to our terms, you are a free man. If not, I will release you back into the custody of the prison. Do you understand?" Max nodded in agreement and started to unwrap the gum in the envelope.

Oscar Boateng kept the hours of a thirty-year-old workaholic and not because he had to. Rather, it was what accomplished men like Oscar did to distract themselves from dwelling on their failed personal lives. In Oscar's case, he was burdened with three marriages, all of which ended in divorce. In addition to his failed marriages. Oscar also boasted four children out of wedlock. His primary interaction with his children was in the form of his signature written on their quarterly checks. What had made Oscar successful in the boardroom also made him a complete failure in the family room. Due to this situation, Oscar's relationships with his nephews were particularly important. It was plain to see that the intimate mentoring of his nephews was directly correlated to his negligence as a father.

Oscar Boateng sat comfortably on his couch in his Tema villa. He'd spent his downtime reflecting on his ancestry this evening. In complete tranquility, Oscar enjoyed his wine buzz. He starred at his prized possession, the fragile leather-bound journal passed down to him by his father Reginald, who received it from his father Ernest, the freed slave who migrated to Sierra Leone from Charleston, South Carolina. Oscar thought about the difficulties his family had experienced to get to where they were now. He thought about his great great grandfather Kwame Ware, the Asante prince next in line to succeed his father's throne, only to be betrayed by his brother Ata and sold into slavery.

Oscar often thought about the plight of his ancestors, and at times, he was so overcome with pride that his eyes welled up. To think that his royal bloodline had been abducted from their homeland, only return as strangers nearly seventy-five years later, was simply incomprehensible to him. It was testament to Prince Kwame's pedigree that his great grandson Reginald would return to the Asante capital of Kumasi and bring closure to the tragic story of Prince Kwame Ware and Aqua Boateng. It was Oscar's intimate knowledge of his ancestry that fueled him to strive for greatness and demand the same from those around him.

Oscar began to nod off around midnight. It wasn't until 1:00 a.m. that he convinced himself to retire upstairs to his bedroom. He used the guardrail to guide him up the staircase, but halfway up, he heard the sound of quick-moving footsteps on the lower level. When Oscar turned around, he saw the silhouette of a figure at the bottom of the stairs, although it was too dark for him to recognize the person. Finally, the shadowy figure came into focus as he approached the stairs. When the light from the stairwell hit the person, Oscar recognized him and said, "It is one o'clock in the morning; what are you doing here? Why didn't the guards inform me of your arrival?"

"You agreed to meet me, remember?"

Oscar shook his head and said, "Oh yes. Well I forgot, but I'm too tired to converse right now. Please wait for me in the morning and I will sort you out, okay?"

"Sorry, this can't wait." With shaky hands, the man drew a weapon from his waist and shot two bullets into Oscar's shoulder and heart. Oscar shrieked and slid down his staircase with his body landing on the marble floor at the feet of his murderer. Oscar Boateng lay dead at his home at the age of seventy-one.

Chapter 17
South Carolina, United States and Freetown, Sierra Leone
1860–1923

Ernest Johnson was born a slave in Charleston, South Carolina on February 12, 1860. His parents were slaves from St. Lucia, and their parents were also slaves who originally hailed from the Gold Coast of West Africa. Since childhood, Ernest had heard the story of his grandfather Kwame Ware, who supposedly was an Asante prince. Each night before Ernest went to bed, he memorized the tragic story of his grandfather as told by father and other slave elders. According to the story, Kwame Ware was tricked into slavery by his brother Ata Ware, in an attempt to remove him as the next heir to the Asante throne, making Ata the heir apparent.

In his St. Lucian dialect, Ernest's father prophesied that Ernest would return to Kumasi one day and restore his grandfather's place among Asante royalty. With the U.S. Civil War over and his parents deceased, Ernest continued working as a sharecropper for the same person, who owned his family as slaves. However, Ernest was convinced he had a higher calling in life. He genuinely believed it was his duty to return his family back to its rightful place among the Asante people.

Thanks to the civil disobedience practiced by his master's daughter, Ernest learned to read and write as a small boy because unbeknownst to her father, she was an abolitionist. While visiting her father's plantation, she learned of Ernest Johnson' family roots and became enamored with the boy's story. With the help of Ernest's father, she offered to help him transcribe the oral story of his grandfather Kwame into English. The journal contained fifteen pages front to back, filled to the margins and scribbled in English. In addition to the story, the journal contained detailed notes about the Asante hierarchy at the time Prince Kwame was kidnapped. It also included maps that detailed the Asante geography in West Africa.

Ernest was emancipated the year he turned nineteen

and, much like an animal guided solely by instinct, his biological compass pointed him northeast to the Atlantic Ocean. Through what seemed an endless journey on foot, horseback, and train, Ernest eventually made it to New York City after years of working random jobs in various cities along the way. On his travels, he heard of a city in West Africa settled earlier by freed slaves and aptly named Freetown. Viewing it as his final destination, Ernest set on a course for Freetown. He believed that in a city founded by freed slaves, someone would be able to instruct him how to reach the Asante village in little time.

Ernest spent over a year in New York City to earn enough for his passage to Africa. He occupied 90% of his week working on the maintenance staff of a midsize Brooklyn hotel. Had Ernest looked up from his grindstone and paid attention to his surroundings, he would have discovered New York City was in the midst of becoming the epicenter of the world. Immigrants were steadily pouring into Ellis Island while, ironically, Ernest worked to earn enough money to leave New York. Ernest was only dedicated to fulfilling his father's prophecy and restoring his name back to Asante royalty.

Ernest finally purchased his ticket out of New York on a boat taking American contractors to Sierra Leone. Upon arriving in Freetown, he was filled with a sense of pride and naive optimism. He was the first person in his family to touch African soil since his grandfather and grandmother a hundred years earlier. Unfortunately, Ernest's optimism was short-lived, since at that time, Freetown was a sparsely developed and lawless pioneer town, much like those in the American Wild West. Jobs were scarce and the settlers were unfriendly. Ernest was bamboozled from the moment he stepped foot on Freetown's shore, leaving him marooned there. Freetown was hardly the emancipated utopia of his dreams.

Ernest also didn't know the land between Freetown and the Asante villages were impassable. No one had carved a trail through the dense West-African forest to travel from Sierra Leone to the Gold Coast yet. All travel between African countries had to be undertaken by boat, which was prohibitively expensive for that precise reason. Only the rich could afford to travel on anything other than their feet. Ernest Johnson was many things but rich was not one of them.

Ten years quickly passed since Ernest had landed in Sierra Leone, and he had yet to fulfill even a fraction of his original agenda. Even though his mission was unsuccessful, he did create a family for himself with his wife Funta and his son Reginald. He managed to occasionally find work on a rickety wooden six-person fishing boat to provide food for his family. Although Ernest was a meager provider, he managed to construct a shoddy lean-to for his family's shelter; it was the bottom of the barrel even by Freetown standards.

Ernest was never accepted as a Sierra Leonean. The West African Creole dialect prominent in Freetown did not jive well with the South-Carolinian accent he was unable to lose. Contrary to what he'd heard in America, most Freetownians were not freed slaves, and they exhibited little empathy for Ernest's exuberance at being in his homeland. Like an albino crocodile in the wild, Ernest was not well received among his species and was viewed as an outsider. Isolation would eventually take its toll on the prodigal son.

By his third year in Freetown, Ernest had developed a taste for palm wine and other spirits. As a result, his alcohol abuse delivered him into a stagnating depression, and Ernest resigned himself as a failure for someone of his pedigree. His alcoholism and depression triggered delusions, and he was known to stroll up and down the central path of his village, lecturing his fellow townsmen about the folklore of his grandfather, the Asante Prince Kwame Ware. Anyone who listened did not believe him and usually cursed and belittled him. When sober, Ernest would admit to himself that the villagers had every reason to disbelieve him; as his bedraggled appearance and drunkenness made him an unreliable source.

Ernest did have one dedicated audience member in

111

his son Reginald, though. Some nights, after returning home from his town foolishness, he continued to ramble about his great grandfather Kwame Ware. Ernest would recite passages from his journal and Reginald intently listened to his father's ramblings. Like Ernest, Reginald had memorized both the oral and written histories of his great grandfather's journey. On Ernest's deathbed, he made Reginald promise to make the pilgrimage to Kumasi and tell the Asante King their family's story. It was a promise the loyal son intended to keep.

Reginald Johnson sat stowaway on a train from Abidjan in the Ivory Coast bound for Accra and then Kumasi in the Gold Coast. At the age of fifteen, Reginald had a wiry frame and an anemic look. He wore off-white, long-sleeve underwear and three-quarter-length trousers held up by a pair of thin red, white, and blue suspenders. Reginald tilted his wicker derby over the bridge of his nose to crop his frame of reference—a wide-open cargo door exposing the dark vegetative landscape chugging along at one hundred miles an hour. It was a soothing view for the young transient. Reginald had spent the past three lonely months on a slow-paced journey that began in Freetown, Sierra Leone.

During the year since his father's death, Reginald had mastered the art of a stowaway. He leeched by land and he barnacled by sea. Unlike his father, Reginald proved quite resourceful in terms of navigating the dense West African infrastructure. On this particular night, Reginald was not the only stowaway onboard; two other hitchhikers had quietly joined him in the empty train car. Through eavesdropping, Reginald gathered they were two Ivorian (from the Ivory Coast) men in their mid-twenties— fugitives, who had escaped from prison more than a year earlier. The two fugitives were not paranoid simply because they suspected no one was looking for them. Reginald got the impression, though, that the authorities' search for the escaped fugitives was so uneventful that the men found it offensive.

Neither said a word to Reginald since they first jumped the train. They had immediately sized each other up, and while the men looked shady, Reginald sensed they lacked the smell of hostility. Although young, Reginald had highly honed street smarts from growing up in an every-man-for-himself home. It was an environment that taught him how to navigate life's brutality at an early age.

West African town life in the early 1920s was less complicated than most westernized cities, but it still presented unique pitfalls Reginald took pride in vanquishing. While failing to acquire his father's South Carolinian twang, he had his grandfather's St. Lucian undertones and his mother's Sierra Leon vernacular. Unlike his father, Reginald grew up learning how to speak a "proper" Sierra Leonean dialect; therefore, he was accepted as a Sierra Leonean and was able to blend in easier.

Reginald broke the silence with his train mates. He spoke in Creole, a mashed-up dialect of English, French, Portuguese, and some African. It was a universal dialect most people of the region understood. "Where are you two heading?"

The two men looked at each other, taken back by the young traveler's bold confidence. The younger one answered, "Accra....we think." His partner hit him with his left hand as if to say, Why are you talking to him? The younger man just shrugged. "What about you, boy? Where are you heading?'"

"I'd rather not say. Let's just say I'm along for the ride."

The older fugitive laughed at his partner. "You see? This is how you should have answered. This boy is half your age and he's already outsmarted you; I should travel with him." The man then turned his attention away from his companion and asked Reginald, "How old are you, boy? And don't tell me you'd rather not say."

He was obviously the most assertive of the fugitive. Reginald decided it did no harm to give his age. If anything, they might underestimate him, and Reginald always fared well when people underestimated him. "I'm fifteen as of two months ago."

"You are too young to be traveling the trains alone, boy. Where are your parents?'"

Reginald shrugged his shoulders and smiled. "I'm fine; my father passed away two years ago, and my mother unsuccessfully gallivants around our village looking for a new husband. If I reach my destination and fulfill my

114

destiny, I will send for her."

The younger-looking man followed up with, "Where did you say you were going again?"

But his reverse psychology didn't work on the young lad. Reginald didn't even turn his head in the fugitive's direction when he replied, "I didn't say."

The fugitive shook his head at his partner.

The three travelers returned to their respective silences. They knew everything they cared to know about each other for the time being. Reginald did not feel threatened by the two men but still clutched the bag holding his few belongings out of instinct. The bag included the leather journal given to him by his father, which told the story of his great grandfather Asante Prince Kwame Ware and details about the Asante kingdom from which his family hailed.

The next morning, Reginald awoke to being violently dragged across the splintered train-car floor by two burly white men with English accents. Looking to his right, he saw his travelling companions were receiving the same treatment. With no regard for how they landed, Reginald and the two men were thrown out of the train car like sacks of soiled linen. Reginald sat up from the fall and spat the dirt out of his mouth. The men who threw them off the train congregated and rummaged through the stowaways' belongings.

The two fugitives argued about the nature of their rude awakening. "I knew it. I knew they're still looking for us. We should have left the Ivory Coast all together," the older fugitive lamented.

"You're telling me?" said the younger one sarcastically. "You were the one who thought it best to stay in familiar territory. 'Hide in plain sight,' you said."

"Well it doesn't matter who said what now, does it? Looks like we're both going back to prison. I knew it was too good to be true; they would never let criminals of our caliber escape justice." The older man turned to Reginald and said, "Don't worry, kid, we'll let them know you aren't with us."

Reginald smiled and had an internal laugh at their expense; the fugitives looked at their impending capture as a compliment—subconsciously wanting to be caught to legitimize their criminal worth. Reginald deduced by the Englishmen's uniforms that they were railroad employees who just happened to catch them trespassing, not bounty hunters. Chances were they knew nothing about the two fugitives' exploits.

One of the Englishmen left the huddle and walked toward Reginald and the other stowaways. Reginald gathered he was the leader of the bunch, because he was the only one who addressed them. He threw their pile of belongings in their general direction and said, "Gentlemen, these are private cargo trains, and you are trespassing on private property. If we ever catch you in here again, we will shoot you. Do you understand me? Now get out of here!"

In disbelief, the bewildered younger fugitive asked, "So you're not going to arrest us? Do you know who we are?"

The Englishman shook his head. "I don't care who you are. If I see you on the train again, I won't arrest you, I'll kill you!"

The insulted fugitive continued, "You mean you're not looking for the two villainous criminals, Bransue and Jokalia?"

"Sorry, boy, never heard of them. But if you're not careful, nobody will ever hear of you again because you'll be dead." The Englishman then pulled his rifle from his shoulder strap and pointed it at the three trespassers. "Now go on before I put a hole in each of you." He returned to his colleagues as they walked up the train line checking inside the other cars to make sure there were no more stowaways.

Reginald and the fugitives dusted themselves off. Reginald caressed his sore shoulder as the fugitives massaged their bruised egos. "How could he not have heard of us?" wondered Jokalia. "We've killed people, for Christ sake."

"Shut up, you stupid fool!" said Bransue. "We still

116

don't know who this boy is and you tell him our crimes?"

Reginald ignored the bickering brothers and inventoried his belongings to make sure his sacred journal was still intact. He internally rebuked himself for not following the most important rule of a train jumper: never be asleep when the train stops. Once Reginald realized his belongings were accounted for, he began walking away from the men.

"Where are you going, boy?" asked Jokalia.

"I'm going east toward my destination. I will catch a train in the next town."

"I don't know where you think you're going, boy, but the next town is after these forests, and these are unfriendly forests. There are vicious tribes and wildlife that can surely bring you death."

"Then death I shall face. I have a destination, and death will be the only thing preventing me from reaching it."

The fugitives stared at the boy as he continued walking. After about seventy paces, Reginald heard the Englishman faintly yelling in the distance, telling the fugitives to move along, and followed by two gunshots into the air. The two men wasted no time catching up with Reginald. Panting, Bransue insisted, "We will escort you through these territories. God would never forgive us for not doing so."

Reginald and the fugitives spent two days trekking and eventually happened on a camp of eight French-Catholic missionaries and their translator from Upper Volta (Now Burkina Faso). The priests were traveling with a mule and seven horses, one of which was hitched to a coach. They informed Reginald and his companions of their plans to teach the word of God to the Baule (pronounced boow-lay) tribe along the Ivory Coast and Gold Coast border.

Acting as the leader, Jokalia negotiated an agreement by which he and his two companions would trade their labor for permission to travel with the missionaries. Feeling it was their Christian duty, the pious

117

caravan agreed to the offer. The new caravan of eleven covered forty-five miles in two days, just long enough for their horses and mule to wear out. For dinner, they sat around a fire and ate the commonly hunted local rodent referred to as a grass cutter along with semisoft bread and wine.

Reginald engaged in conversation with the Upper Volta translator, who was also a man of cloth. Reginald called him Osofo (the regional word for priest). "So what do you plan on doing with the Baule once you find them, Osofo?"

Osofo understood English, French, Italian, Latin, Creole, and most of the native tribal dialects of the region. He replied, "I have been blessed to find the word of God in my life. Several years ago, these same French missionaries rescued me from my primitive ways. The church showed me God and brought me out of the jungle and into the light. Now that my family and I have been blessed by the Lord, I would like to do the same for the Baule, perhaps the most proud indigenous tribe living in this region of the bush."

"What's wrong with the Baule being proud?"

"They are the only tribe we have encountered who refuse to even consider listening to the word of Our Lord Jesus Christ," Osofo lamented.

Reginald had encountered enough zealots in his short time on earth to know that even the most persuasive secular logic would never change their minds. Instead of debating Osofo on the grounds that the Baule already worshiped a god called Alouraua, with whom they were quite content, he simply replied, "Ah, I see."

After supper, they sat around for hours and sloshed their flasks of wine in wicker cozies. It was sunset and they could hear the tree monkeys bellowing in the canopy above. The rain forest was too intimidating a place for a newcomer like Reginald to appreciate its beauty. It was a dense labyrinth of unknowns and imminent death. If it weren't for the wine, Reginald's nerves may not have allowed him to sleep.

When Reginald awoke, the jungle mist and thin lines of smoke streaming from the extinguished campfire obscured his vision, yet his hearing was acute as ever. In the near distance, he heard a soft rustling, which could have been any one of twenty thousand things; nonetheless, the sound was unnerving. He sat up and focused on the tree-lined perimeter of their camp—the dark spaces between the trees, in particular. Peering into the clustered forest, he still didn't see the shadowy, negative space materialize into moving silhouettes. By the time Reginald noticed the movement, it was too late; the figures were upon them before he could yell, Ambush.

Luckily for Reginald, he reacted much quicker than the others, due to his position and attentiveness. Even the other campers who were awake were oblivious to the attack until the final moments. The three sleeping campers did not stand a chance, and they were immediately executed.

Reginald backpedaled into the thicket. He had no gun, no knife, or any other weapon, for that matter. He cowered behind the biggest tree he could find. His cover might as well have been a glass bubble, but it bought him some extra time as he helplessly watched the remaining missionaries unsuccessfully attempt to defend themselves with their rosaries extended by trembling arms. The assailants were of the mighty Baule tribe, the same tribe the missionaries had come to "save."

It didn't take long for the Baule soldiers to discover Reginald crouched in his pathetic refuge. The soldiers pointed and laughed at the overwhelmed babe in the woods. Reginald closed his eyes, waiting for his deathblow but, to his good fortune, it did not come. Two of the Baule raised Reginald up and bound him to the mule. The Baule confiscated the camp's rations and anything of value from the dead. The only other survivor was his stowaway mate, Jokalia. Unfortunately caught sleeping, Bransue's skull was caved in with a blow from a heavy mallet, and he died instantly. Jokalia sobbed bitterly at the sight of his brother as they exited the camp.

For two days, Reginald and Jokalia were tethered to

119

the mule as they hobbled alongside the hijacked caravan. When they reached the Baule camp, women and children greeted their warriors with kisses and praise, while Reginald and Jokalia were greeted with snarls and snipes from the village dogs. The two prisoners were placed in an empty shelter constructed of materials appropriated from the various species of vegetation surrounding the village. They were untied and allowed to roam their ten-by-ten shelter, but if they stepped outside of it, they would have faced brutal consequences at the hands of two Baule guards.

Reginald was a casual student of the different indigenous peoples of the region. He knew something of the Baule because they had a significant relationship with his Asante ancestors. Like the Asante, the Baule belonged to the Akan people of the Gold Coast and Côte d'Ivoire. Two hundred years ago, the Baule had migrated west after the Asante rose to power. Baule oral history says, during the beginning of the Asante's reign, the Baule Queen Aura Poku was in a power struggle with the sitting Asante King. When the Asante prevailed, the Queen rallied her clan and migrated to the land they now occupied.

Reginald stood in the shelter's doorway and observed Baule village life. Like many tribes in West Africa, the Baule's attire modeled a specific color scheme. Their garbs were a limited triad of white-and-black patterns on blue material, a color combination that complemented their onyx-colored skin. The Baule were not flashy like their Asante cousins of the mid-north; they were an agricultural people, who feverishly worked on their crops of maize, manioc, squash, and sweet potatoes. The potato was not native to the region; it was adopted from the Americans during the Atlantic slave-trade era.

Just before nightfall, a Baule elder man came to visit the prisoners. He wore a blue and white on black toga. His traditional tribesman garb clashed with his horn-rimmed glasses, a symbol of modernity rarely seen in such remote parts of the region. What Reginald noticed more than the elder man's glasses were that he held his father's journal.

The elder man sat on a stool in front of the seated prisoners and asked, "Whose book is this?"

Like a child, Jokalia could not keep his thoughts to himself. "You speak English?"

To Reginald's surprise, the elder man did not dismiss Jokalia's unabashed ignorance. "I am an advisor to the Baule chief, and I speak many languages. I have been charged with the duty of negotiating for my people's interests with our neighbors and the European settlers on our land. But again, who does this book belong to?"

Reginald spoke up. "It is my journal."

The elder man turned his attention to the young man and studied him hard. "So is it true what your journal says? Are you a descendent of Kwame Ware?"

If Reginald was intimidated, it wasn't obvious. "I suspect so, and that is why I am on this journey—to find out for myself."

The elder man laughed loudly at Reginald's expense. "And how did you plan to achieve this? Do you know how far it is to Asante land? Two-dozen nights, at least. Between the endless miles of bush and tribal warfare, you will never make it there alive." He then smirked and shook his head. "I'm not sure if you're brave or stupid...I'm leaning toward stupid."

Jokalia, still mourning the death of his brother, was not amused by the elder man's intellectual charm. He asked, "So how are the French going to feel now that you've brutally murdered their missionaries and people of God? Doesn't that betray your agreement with them?"

The elder man diverted his attention back to Jokalia and smiled. "You? You are neither a missionary nor a man of God. Neither is the boy and neither was your brother. The three of you hitched your way with those Catholics." He pointed at Reginald's journal and said, "The boy has chronicled it all here in his journal, up until the morning you were captured." Jokalia rolled his eyes and the elder man continued, "As for the actual men of cloth, they were trespassing. We have a free-trade agreement with the French: If their presence is of a secular nature, we allow

121

them access into our territory. However, we have set strict conditions on the French—the main one is no missionary. The presence of missionaries is considered blasphemous to our faith and our god. The church is aware of this agreement. This group of missionaries was trespassing."

"What do you plan to do with us?" asked Reginald.

"Well we can release you back to the bush with nothing but the clothes on your back—no water, food, or supplies. But it might be more humane to just kill you; we will leave that choice to you. If there is some truth to the claims in your journal, then a third option may be available." He couldn't help but detect a unique strength from the boy. "Do you know anything about my people?" he asked. Reginald nodded. "Then you know the history between the Baule and the Asante?" Reginald nodded again, to which the elder frustratingly responded, "Speak up, boy!"

"Yes, I do," Reginald said in a raised voice.

"Good. There is still some unfinished business between the Asante and the Baule regarding a land dispute. It is a narrow strip of land nine kilometers long. We own it, yet the Asante still make us pay a tribute for it to their chief. If you are who you claim to be, they might be willing to trade you for some land concessions."

"And what if the Asante don't want to compromise?"

Without skipping a beat, the Baule elder man replied, "Then I will banish you and your friend to the bush to die."

Five Baule tribesmen, including the elder man, escorted Reginald and Jokalia to Kumasi to make an appeal to the Asante king. Normally the elder man would not have traveled such a long distance, however, it would take a Baule official of his stature to broker a deal with the Asante king.

When they neared Kumasi, Reginald, Jokalia, and two guards stayed three kilometers outside the town border, while the elder man and two bodyguards entered the Asante royal village to announce their delivery of the descendant of the long-lost Prince Kwame Ware. The Asante King Prempeh I agreed to read Reginald's journal to determine its validity. After reading the journal, the chief found enough circumstantial evidence to stoke his curiosity, and he sent for Reginald.

When Reginald arrived in the village, he became nauseous; the burden of three generations of his ancestors was in his hands. The Asante village was not as grand as one might think for a tribe who was notorious for its flamboyant gold accessories. It resembled many of the well-manicured villages found in Africa at that time. The round huts sat above a nicely raked layer of red dirt. As they walked through the village, a pair of middle-aged female dwarf twins intensely eyeballed Reginald. Their stares made his soul shudder.

Whatever the village lacked in extravagance, the Asante king made up for in fashion. His wrists and forearms were obnoxiously draped with slabs of unrefined gold. He wore an intricate-patterned kente cloth along with gold-buttoned sandals and a sturdy cloth crown weighted with gold disks. The chief sat in a high-back chair bookended by a man holding an umbrella big enough for a family, while another fanned him with a large reinforced palm leaf.

Reginald stood in front of Chief Prempeh I. Earlier in the year Chief Prempeh ceremoniously returned to The Gold Coast from the Seychelles Islands where he was detained in exile for over twenty years under British guard. Although, the conditions of his return demanded that Prempeh return to the Asante's as a civilian his people refused to recognize such conditions. Upon his return Prempeh was still recognized as the Asante king and he still ruled as one. Prempeh stared at Reginald's eyes, nose, face, hands, and feet and he addressed him in English. "What is your purpose here?"

Reginald yielded his response to embarrassingly pass a little bit of gas. Luckily it made no noise and no one was directly behind him to detect the smell. He gave his mind a moment to prepare and focus. He had imagined

123

this very meeting in his head hundreds of times, and it was now time to channel the clarity to which he addressed the Asante King in his fantasies.

Reginald cleared his throat. "Your noble one, fifteen years ago I was born in Freetown, Sierra Leone. My father Ernest Johnson migrated to Freetown from the Americas many years earlier as a freed slave. Through my family's oral history, my father became aware of our lineage to the exiled Asante Prince Kwame Ware. My father was the first person in the family to read and write English; it was he who translated his father's story about his grandfather into the very journal you hold. Now, a year after my father's death, I am fulfilling my promise to him on his deathbed to visit the Asante and tell our family's story. I have also chronicled my own journey in the pages subsequent to my father's translations."

The chief did not acknowledge Reginald's response. Instead he turned to his right and said, "Queen Mother, come here please." A middle-aged woman walked toward the chief; she was the Asante Queen Mother or the Asante matriarch whose authority was only surpassed by the chief. The Queen Mother was not the wife of the King, she was his sister. The Asante are a matrilineal society, meaning the lines of ancestry and land ownership are passed on through the women. The Queen Mother's role is paramount. She is responsible for picking the Asantehene among the litter of potential Asante princes. Her judgment was law and not to be questioned even by the King.

The Queen Mother approached Reginald and circled him while eyeballing him from the neck up. When she finished the examination, she took her place by the chief and whispered something to him in Twi. The Asante king nodded his head and took into account what the Queen Mother said as he continued addressing the young Reginald. "In 1780, a Dutch painter lived here in the Gold Coast to document the life of the Akan people. He painted many portraits of our native ancestors, including King Opoku Ware and his two sons, Ata and Kwame. The painting was passed down through the family of the Queen

124

Mother's husband. After examining you, she is convinced that you look like Kwame and Ata Ware, the sons of former King Opoku Ware." This news intrigued Reginald.

"However, I am not convinced of your story or your likeness to the late Ware family," declared the chief. "I will determine your authenticity through a list of questions. If you answer them correctly, I may let you live." The nausea returned to Reginald's stomach. The chief waved off his fan blowers and gestured for Reginald to come closer. He studied the young man as he said, "The disappearance of Prince Kwame Ware is an almost-forgotten narrative among our people. An outsider's knowledge of the story is what makes yours so appealing. However, I must say the smell of a con artist stenches the air."

Reginald wanted to explain the stench was perhaps the flatulence he expelled due to his nervousness. He began to speak, but the chief quickly cut him off with a swipe of his hand. "You will get a chance to answer shortly." The chief continued, "If this journal is correct, your great, great, grandfather was Asantehene Opoku Ware. Is this correct?"

"Yes."

"Then surely you must know the former British Admiral, who negotiated the terms with the Asante during the Treaty of Fomena during the Anglo-Asante war?"

Reginald began shaking his head before the chief finished asking his question. "Sorry sir, I haven't the vaguest clue."

The chief nodded his head and followed with another question: "Then surely you should know the name of his archrival, the Fante chief who ruled during that dynasty?"

Reginald wore a look of frustration. "Sorry, I don't know that either."

The chief stared at Reginald with skepticism. Reginald's nausea worsened due to his poor performance, and he could already feel the sharp blade on his neck. Prempeh stood up and dismissed everyone else from the shelter. The Queen Mother, her umbrella holder and fan waver, and two bodyguards retired, leaving the chief and Reginald alone. He walked toward Reginald, staring him directly in the eyes. Prempeh circled him and said, "You did not know the answers to easily verifiable questions."

"No, I don't, but I am not a con artist."

The king nodded, and to Reginald's surprise said, "I don't think you are. A con artist would have conveniently provided answers to such questions." He gave Reginald some time to exhale. "When I was a boy about your age, the high priest spoke of the ghost of Prince Kwame Ware returning to Asante land. However, he spoke of it as it would happen at any moment, and it has been thirty-six years since that prophecy. Now here you stand claiming to be this very ghost. As I grow older, I have become skeptical of folklore, although I am obligated to believe it. The Queen Mother, however, wants to believe too much. Her need for Asante prophecy to bear fruit has become an addiction. So it does not surprise me that she thinks you favor Prince Kwame Ware."

Reginald was confused. "But yet you somehow believe me?"

"I'm not sure. I pride myself in being able to detect integrity or the lack thereof from a man's face. You seem to possess such integrity. And truth be told, you do slightly resemble the portrait of Prince Kwame Ware."

Reginald nodded. He knew he had to tread lightly, but he had to know his fate. "So, what do you plan to do with me? If you return us to the Baule, they will leave me and my friend to die in the bush."

The Asante king nodded his head. "Indeed they will. We Asante as well as other natives of this land have lost many loved ones through the Atlantic slave trade. However it is the participation of some of our own members that may have collaborated with these foreign kidnappers, which is an unforgivable blemish that has plagued the Asante people's souls for hundreds of years perhaps eternity. Although I am not as superstitious as the Queen Mother, I do believe in spirits and in redemption. I have to believe your arrival is an opportunity to right a

126

great injustice."

Reginald, as always, stayed truthful. "Your highness, I cannot pretend to tell you that what you suspect is true. I do not feel I come as a representative for the ghosts of slaves. I am only here to keep a promise to my father, a man whose life mission was to tell his grandfather's story to the Asante in Kumasi." Reginald cleared his throat and continued, "However, there seems to be some potency to the words of my father. I feel them to be true."

In a controversial decision, the Asante king ruled that the nine-kilometer strip of land disputed by the Asante and the Baule would be granted to the Baule at no expense—in exchange for Reginald Johnson and his fugitive travel mate Jokalia. The Asante king also bestowed unprecedented rights to Reginald Johnson: He was made an honorary Asante even though Reginald's mother was not an Asante, which disqualifies him from being an Asante, but the chief overlooked that technicality. The chief also bestowed Asante land to Reginald, which he would pay for with the sweat of his brow.

At the age of fifteen, Reginald Johnson successfully restored the legacy of his great grandfather, the late Asante Prince Kwame Ware. He proved to be a productive member of the Asante tribe, as he made a life for himself in Kumasi. He earned a formal education and became a wealthy man in the private sector. Through a series of marriages, Reginald produced two daughters, Margerite, and Felicia and one son, his oldest child Oscar. Reginald also helped to advance the Asante agenda and later that of all Ghanaians in their struggle to gain independence from the British, which finally happened in 1957.

Chapter 19
Accra Ghana
Present Day

It was Oscar Boateng's request to be buried in Kumasi on Asante land and only mourned by close family and friends and the Asante elders. The Boatengs and Oseis complied with most of the deceased man's wishes. However, with such fanfare surrounding the funeral, certain modifications were necessary. When the Accra Voice reported that the funeral would be a private ceremony held in Kumasi, many disappointed readers wrote to express their frustration at not being able to mourn with the family. It was the recommendation of the designated director of Oscar's funeral, Felicia Osei, who was also Oscar's youngest half-sister and Clinton's mother, that the procession starts in Accra and end in Kumasi.

The citizens were grateful to get a last glimpse of their fallen hero, an extraordinary man who championed the common man. Oscar Boateng's funeral procession began in Accra's Nkrumah Square, and his motorcade was met by thousands of animated mourners along the roadside. A trip to Kumasi usually took two hours by car, however, on this special day, Oscar's mourners (many of whom he'd never met) made the trip to his final resting place four hours. The mourners chanted, danced, and cried in the streets. The Boateng family had a Kennedy-like stature in Ghana, so the emotional outreach from the public was overwhelming.

Clinton Osei, Jasper Boateng, George Boateng, and Roland Dufrane sat in the third limousine of the funeral procession. The three cousins mourned in their own ways for their uncle: George severely ramped up his drinking and recreational drug usage; Jasper hit the gym for three to four hours a day to escape the pain; while Clinton moved into his uncle's villa and pored through his uncle's pictures, letters and memorabilia. Doing so for Clinton was bitter sweet because missing from his uncle's prized possession was the archived chronicles of his grandfather and great

128

grandfather. It is suspected that the assailant on that dark night not only took a great man's life, but also stole his family's most precious heirloom. Second only to finding out the identity of his uncle's murderer, finding the journal of Ernest Johnson and Reginald Boateng was the task Clinton impressed upon Dufrane the most. The cousins used the four-hour ride from Accra to Kumasi to discuss Roland Dufrane's internal investigation into Oscar's death.

Dufrane, the former Mossad intelligence officer, now worked fulltime for BOI as head of security. As the consummate professional, Dufrane showed little emotion, however, he took the case personally. To Dufrane's surprise, the family did not hold him responsible for Oscar's death—mainly because they knew Oscar was stubborn and refused Dufrane's recommendation to upgrade his security.

Dufrane handed each of the cousins a copy of his report. "I'll give you all a quick briefing on my findings. It looks like a robbery, but the facts suggest much more than that."

George hastily cut him off and sarcastically replied, "I think we all assume that, Mr. Dufrane. But we need you to provide us with some of that Mossad-type of intelligence you're supposedly known for."

Dufrane glared at George without dignifying the snide remark. "For one, the bodies of the two dead guards were found on their backs, facing the gate in the driveway. Footprints and the bodies' positions show the guards were running toward the front door when they were shot and killed. There was no sign of forced entry anywhere in the house; more than likely, the intruder was let into the gates. The guards either knew the person or he was an expected guest."

Jasper held his hand up, signaling for Dufrane to pause. "So this bastard just walked right through the gate? I know those guards, and they don't let just anybody in. Have we interviewed uncle's personal staff? Drivers, servers, assistants?"

"Of course, we have aggressively interviewed all of

129

the staff. From what I can tell so far, they've all passed with flying colors."

Clinton nodded. "I'm glad to hear that none of uncle's staff are suspects, but I still don't want to take any chances." He turned his attention to Jasper and said, "Tomorrow, please release uncle's entire staff of their duties. Give them the equivalent of two years severance pay and whatever benefits we've supplied them and their families for life. I know they were Oscar's staff, but I still don't want to risk rolling any of them into our other family staffs in case we are wrong. Except for Kwasi, I want him transferred to my staff. He was uncle's right-hand man for years, and Oscar would want him taken care of."

"Sure, man."

"Thanks, Jabs, and please take care of this tomorrow."

"What about uncle's girlfriends?" Jasper asked. "Have we interviewed them yet?"

"We have indeed," answered Dufrane, "and all of the usual suspects' alibis check out. However, the intruder was thorough enough to take the log-in sheets, showing all of Oscar's visitors over the past year."

George took a swig of whisky from the flask concealed in his jacket pocket. It was actually a rare, aged single-malt scotch Oscar had re-gifted to George last Christmas. George had been saving it for a special occasion and couldn't think of a better time to crack it open than his uncle's funeral. He looked at it as a tribute of sorts to the man who schooled him in the good life. After long consecutive pulls from his flask, George proceeded to state the obvious, "We're missing something big here. The problem is that uncle knew people we've never met. Without that day's log-in sheet, it's going to be hard for us to know exactly who all of the suspects really are."

George attempted to replace his flask inside his jacket, but Dufrane quickly intercepted it, took a swig, and then passed it to Jasper. This abrupt, out-of-character action was the first time the cousins had glimpsed Dufrane as a human being with his own personality. It went unmentioned (but not unnoticed) and endeared him to them. Dufrane continued, "Kwasi has already provided me with several leads. Given his intimate knowledge of Oscar's work schedule for years, he can help to fill in some gaps."

Jasper carelessly swallowed a long swig of the scotch and made the face non-scotch drinkers do when they feel the bite. He then passed the flask to Clinton. "So what names has he produced?"

"Too many to name off the top of my head, but I promise you my guys are compiling the list as we speak."

Clinton took a deep sip of George's flask before adding his two cents to the conversation. "Look forward to seeing what you come up with. Keep us updated on any new info the second you find something out, and remember, leak nothing to anyone outside this car....and that means no one."

George retrieved his flask from Clinton and took a sip, then slammed the flask on his thigh. "Bloody cunts—there's nothing left. You bastards finished me fuckin' scotch!"

The gathering after the burial was held at the sprawling ten-bedroom Boateng family compound just outside of downtown Kumasi. The compound was built for Clinton's grandmother Rose by her children as a seventieth birthday present. After Rose passed away five years earlier, the house sat empty, except for the occasional BOI function or Boateng reunion. The family still kept the house staffed with a caretaker to keep it ready for events, such as this one. The funeral attendees had just about exhausted all the tears their bodies could produce, so by the time dinner was over, the once-somber guests were drunk and full of rich foods from the region—giving more credence to the notion that a Ghanaian will never waste an opportunity to throw a party.

The grounds of the Boateng compound were lit up like an airport runway. Bright party canopies lined the lawn of the northwest entrance. Attendees included the likes of Ghana's President Abna Amoako, Vice President Kweku Bonswah, international football sensation Coufis Zatan, a

131

Nobel Prize winner, and a Grammy-nominated recording artist, among others. On the less pretentious side of the spectrum, guests included all of the BOI staff and the lifelong blue-collar employees of Kumasi Gold, as well as some of the better-known graduates of Oscar's micro-loan program. The diverse guest list was a testament to the many lives Oscar Boateng touched.

While the other cousins mingled with the grievers, Clinton granted face time with special guests who requested it. Clinton's last scheduled guest was Vice President Kweku Bonswah. Clinton knew Bonswah was one of the few politicians his uncle fully trusted. In order to keep the integrity of their friendship intact, Oscar kept his backdoor conversations with the vice president secret, even from close BOI executives like Clinton. Bonswah was aware Clinton was not privy to the business he and his uncle were discussing before his passing, so he requested a private meeting with Clinton to remedy that fact.

The two men sat in the office of Clinton's late grandmother. You could tell that when Clinton's grandmother decorated the house that the office was an afterthought. There were two chairs and a rigid desk by the back window with two framed pictures, one of Rose with Asante Royals football team taken two decades before the Boatengs owned the club and a picture of the Asantehene draped in all of his traditional tribal gold. The only other things in the room were duffle bags filled with towels and rags waiting to be washed. Had Clinton not requested to use this room for his private meetings, his mother would have designated it as a coatroom for the guests. Bonswah gestured for his assistant to leave them and shut the door behind him. Clinton's demeanor was neutral. He knew his uncle trusted the vice president, but Clinton also had a natural distrust of politicians. Out of respect to his late uncle, Clinton listened to the man with an unbiased ear.

Kweku Bonswah was a dark-skinned Fante, so dark that the reflection of light on his skin was of a silver-grey hue. He liked to describe himself as "Africa black." Only in his late forties, Bonswah had the presence of a much older and wiser man. "It is a pleasure to finally meet with you personally. Your Uncle Oscar and I were good friends. He was like a mentor to me—even though he was Asante." Bonswah laughed and continued, "I am a Fante from the Cape Coast region. When Bonswah realized Clinton didn't pick up on his tribal rivalry humor, he moved on. "But I know you have other guests to attend to, so I'll make this brief."

"It's a pleasure to meet you as well, Mr. Vice President. My uncle always spoke very highly of you. Please take as much time as you need."

Bonswah was not interested in pretending he wanted to get to know Clinton, so he dispensed with the niceties. "Before your uncle's untimely death, he consulted with me on a matter regarding Ghana's recently discovered oil reserves. Did he discuss any of this with you?"

Clinton immediately jumped to conclusions. "No, not all Mr. Vice President. And I hope I would be consulted before my uncle made a decision about getting into the oil business."

"Actually, your uncle had no interest in BOI getting into that business. He served as a well-regarded counsel to Parliament's oversight committee to choose which company would be allowed to drill Ghana's oil reserve."

"Oh, I see."

"Although oil will provide a great stimulus to Ghana's economy, the cynics, such as myself and your uncle, are more cautious than optimistic. You get me?"

Once Clinton understood the vice president's intentions were sincere, Bonswah received his utmost attention. "Why are you cautious, Mr. Vice President?"

"It is customary in Africa for many oil companies to bribe the abundant amount of spineless politicians to ensure weak laws are created in their favor, such as those that indemnify oil companies from any environmental infractions. You only need to look no further than Nigeria as an example of that corruption. Oil companies have lined the pockets of politicians in oil-rich Nigeria for decades now. Each year Nigeria has the equivalent of an Exxon

Valdes oil spill, with no repercussions to the offending oil companies whatsoever.

You can even look at the 2010 BP oil spill in the Gulf Region of your own country. It turned out BP was paying off state legislators so it could drill under extremely lax regulatory conditions. This situation allowed BP to speed up production and maximize profits. It was also the direct contributor to the worst environmental disaster in U.S. history. If Ghana doesn't prepare for possible corruption on this scale, we don't stand a chance in hell against globalization."

Clinton looked confused. "You are the government, Mr. Bonswah. You are arguably the second most powerful man in Ghanaian politics. I'm sure you can put a stop to this corruption. No?"

Bonswah smiled at Clinton and looked over his left shoulder to ensure no one was eavesdropping on their conversation. "Your uncle expressed how impressed he was with your accomplishments in America and how you've excelled in your BOI position. He said you reminded him a lot of himself. Sitting here and observing you, I am seeing what your uncle saw in you. I am here to extend the special relationship your uncle and I had—to you and only you. This means our discussions remain confidential. Do you understand?"

The vice president paused for confirmation. When Clinton nodded he went on, "There are elements in this government I cannot control. If you think the American vice president has little power, then you will understand my powerless position. Legislators like those on the selection committee are more influenced by private-sector tycoons like your uncle than they are with any of their colleagues. Luckily for Ghana, your uncle was one of those rare titans with integrity who refused to sell his country out. In fear of not being in your uncle's favor, the legislators on the committee were inclined to vote for whomever your uncle recommended." He stopped to see if Clinton was processing this information, because Bonswah knew he had the tendency to speak fast.

134

Once he saw Clinton was with him, he continued, "Your uncle and I used his influence to benefit Ghana as a whole. The two companies in the lead for being awarded the drilling rights in Ghana's oil reserves are British-based PetroCo Oil and Chinese-based Freestar Oil. After doing his homework and consulting with me, your uncle rightly concluded that Freestar would be the best company for Ghanaian interests. If I may add, his conclusion was unpopular among many of our British and American diplomats; making such a large award to a Chinese company does not sit well with them. Several weeks ago, Oscar met with PetroCo executives and realized they weren't committed to hiring a majority of Ghanaians to work the rigs. He also learned they planned to pay much less in annual commission, and they have a less-than-stellar environmental record.

"And now that my uncle has passed, how does this play out?"

"With Oscar out of the picture, the oversight committees will most likely vote for President Amoako's choice. The problem is that I'm afraid Amoako has already been compromised and will convince the committee members to vote for PetroCo Oil."

"Maybe I need to be more direct in my questioning. Is it not obvious that PetroCo has the most to gain from my uncle's death?" Clinton asked.

"It would appear that way, but I highly doubt a major global corporation would deliberately conspire in an assassination for the very reasons you pointed out. While PetroCo may seem to have the most natural motivation to remove Oscar, I doubt its participation," answered Bonswah. "In fact, the CEO of PetroCo called me and other government officials directly after your uncle's death to assure us that although it appeared that PetroCo had some twisted motive, that they were not complicit in Oscar's unfortunate murder. Albeit he was bluffing he even offered to remove their bid, given their tumultuous last meeting with your uncle. I told them that was not necessary. For what it's worth, Clinton, he sounded sincere

135

and believable, but I could just be naïve."

Clinton tried to make sense of the logic. Bonswah knew he was giving Clinton the cliff-notes version of Ghana's oil dilemma, so he tried to be concise. "The Ghanaian politicians would not take such a chance when your uncle was alive. You have to understand that with all the money, influence, and resources BOI has devoted to Ghana, it would be political suicide for a politician to be caught taking a bribe against the wishes of Oscar Boateng. I know it sounds absurd, but believe it or not, your uncle was the only individual who could keep these politicians somewhat honest."

"So how do we change the president's mind? Better yet, how do we have him arrested for corruption and collusion? I mean this is treachery, right?"

"It is, but it will be next to impossible to prove that Amoako is taking bribes, given the money would be funneled into offshore accounts and shell companies. I think our best bet to keep this process transparent is to have you take your late uncle's place. We need you to convince the legislators that you are on the same page as Oscar Boateng, you are devoted to continuing your uncle's good work and you, too, have the country's best interest at heart. But most importantly, if they don't fall in line with your agenda, then you need to impress upon them that you will use all of BOI's resources to put their careers in jeopardy."

Clinton studied Vice President Bonswah long and hard, as if he could detect any impurities in the man's soul by doing so. Then he got up, buttoned his jacket, and reached out to shake Bonswah's hand. "Thank you for bringing this situation to my attention, Mr. Vice President, and I understand the risk to your career. I will have Dufrane set up a secure cell phone strictly for our conversations. Until then, let us drown our sorrows in booze and music. Shall we?"

"I do not indulge in alcohol, but I will certainly celebrate your uncle's life with the rest of the guests."

"That's right, I forgot you're Muslim. My

apologies."

Kweku Bonswah chuckled. "I know people tend to forget I'm one of only a handful practicing Fante Muslims. However, had I accepted, it wouldn't have been the first or the last time a Muslim drank alcohol." Both men laughed as they exited the office and traveled through the foyer into the front yard, where the post-funeral celebration was still underway.

They walked into the sea of canopies where everyone had congregated. Upon entering the largest tent, they were greeted by the sight of a jovial and clearly inebriated President Amoako leading a conga line of female partiers. When Amoako passed, Clinton shot a glance to Bonswah, who responded by subtly shaking his head and raising his glass of water in confirmation.

Jasper Boateng had been running a petite gambling operation long before he joined BOI. It only earned him pocket money, but the gaming gave him pleasure as well as stature in that particular community. In the evenings, Jasper routinely worked out of Eclipse, a small social club in Osu. Eclipse was an enjoyable, low-key place; it reminded him of the dives he used to frequent in Hackney. Like an insecure teenager, Jasper was constantly surrounded by his friends. He roamed with a motley crew of dodgy cocks. They were mostly West African/British men like him—chaps he'd known since his parochial-school days in London.

No one in Jasper's inner circle called each other by their Christian names; they used nicknames received for various reasons. For instance, Jackson was "The Bloke" because he always referred to himself in third person as the bloke, such as, "The bloke needs to take a wicked shit, mate." Atoo got the name "Slappy" after he'd got into a scuffle as a teenager and dismissively slapped his opponent all over the street. Emanuel earned the name "Two Tone" because he was inflicted with vitiligo, the pigment disease in black people that makes their skin gradate from brown to white.

Gregory was generously named "Big Sperm" because he had eight children with seven different women. Then there was Chris, who was absurdly called "Duchess" because his favorite movie was Predator with Arnold Schwarzenegger, in which the governor's name was Dutch. Jasper was simply referred to as "Jabs" for several reasons: It was a condensed form of Jasper Boateng and he had a mean right hook. For the most part, though, the Boateng rude boy simply liked to "take jabs" at his friends by making jokes at their expense.

Friends and family outside the inner circle endearingly referred to Jasper's band of brothers as "The

Guys." When Jasper began earning real money at BOI, he used his gambling-operations earnings to subsidize The Guys' incomes. They were all in charge of taking care of Jasper's personal business. If he needed food, they would fetch it; if he needed dry cleaning, they would pick it up; and if one of Jasper's clients in his low-key gambling operation didn't pay up, they collected with extreme prejudice. The Guys had little work ethic; their real value was intangible. They served as the antithesis to Jasper's buttoned-up life, and they helped keep his ear firmly suctioned to the street.

It was a typical night in Accra during the rainy season; the sun was out for most of the day only to be followed by a downpour lasting for hours. The heavy rain released a sour odor into the air. On this particular evening, Jasper and The Guys were watching English Premier Football highlights and playing billiards, while a handful of groupies entertained them. If you had a gambling debt or needed credit, Eclipse was the best place to get "sorted out." Otherwise, it wasn't the most inviting of clubs for outsiders.

This evening, like every other, The Guys were having a laugh at the expense of one of their own. Jasper held court and lectured Duchess on his incompetence in setting a proper gambling line for a football match. "I don't get it Duchess. You pick Newcastle to win two to one over Man City? This is not 1996, Dutchy. Newcastle can barely manage not to get relegated. If anything, Man City should get the victory two to one! Sometimes I doubt you ever even watch football. London predicted the match would be a draw; did you even consult the papers?"

Duchess shook his head in embarrassment. He'd been dreading this conversation all day, as he knew his blunder was going to make him the subject of mockery. Instead of taking his lumps and keeping his head down, Duchess tried to justify his actions. "Yeah, Jabs. It's just that Newcastle beat Man City last time they played, and people who bet on Newcastle won a bunch of money off us last time. So I figured I'd do the opposite this time. I was

139

working the hunch. You get me?"

"Did ye say a hunch now?" The more Jabs drank, the further his British accent drifted into the cockney range. "First of all, that match was a friendly, so Man City didn't give two shits. Secondly, to 'have a hunch' and take a risk against the odds means you need inside information on the players and what not. So tell me, did you? I mean, did you hear they cloned Alan Shearer and brought him out of retirement or something?" Shearer was a Newcastle and English Premier League legend, and Jasper didn't even give Duchess time to answer the preposterous question. "Of course you fuckin' didn't! Nobody took your bait either, Einstein. Instead of making money on a sure bet, we've got these cunts coming in here tonight and collecting checks like it's their mutha' fucking Christmas bonus. I love you to death, Dutchy. You and me brethren and all, but sometimes I swear you're soft in the fucking head."

Two Tone, trying to collect his composure from laughing so hard, also went in on Duchess. "Chali! And you wonder why we don't give you more responsibility, do you? Duchess, you're better off sticking to what you're good at—like injecting your bum with steroids and beating people up—because Vegas odds makers won't be calling you to run a casino anytime soon."

Only the sound of a running air conditioning unit and crickets filled the air after Two Tone's lame joke, which prompted Jabs to say, "Hey, Tones, do yourself a favor and let me make the jokes 'round here." As if a stagehand cued the audience, the Eclipse patrons erupted in applause and laughter at Jabs' wit.

To Duchess' pleasure, Slappy walked in from the outside rain with a guy called Stix, effectively ending the Duchess' roast. Stix was a low-level hustler, who occasionally took some of Jasper's action on matches. Slappy gestured toward Stix and said, "Jabs, Stix says he'd like a word with you. Says it's important."

"Oh, does he now? Tell me, Stix, did you get a big fucking payday on us tonight for the Newcastle/Man City match?"

Stix laughed. "Naw, Jabs I didn't bet that game. Honestly I thought it was either a joke or you guys had some inside information. Man City won, one–nil, right?"

Jasper shook his head and gave Duchess the most disappointing of looks. "Fucking embarrassment, man." Then he got up from his chair and made his way to the back. "Stix, follow me to my office so we can talk." In half a stride, Jasper pivoted to Slappy and asked, "Tell me before I take this meeting, Stix doesn't need to be sorted out does he? He doesn't owe us money, right? I hope he's not coming to grovel for time to pay up his debts. Because I ain't in the mood for dat tonight. You get me?"

Jasper and Slappy conversed as if Stix was not standing right in front of them. Slappy shook his head. "Naw Jabs, Stix is all good with us. Him have no outstanding debts, just god-awful breath."

Unlike Two Tone, Slappy made everyone within earshot laugh and actually caused Stix to put his hand over his mouth and breathe into it to check his breath. Jasper laughed in an attempt to soften the blow. "Pay him no attention, Stix. Slappy just went to the dentist for the first time in his life a year ago. Have you seen the man's teef?"

Given the opening by Jasper, Stix said, "No worries, Jabs. I can understand why Slappy'd say that."

"You do?"

"Yeah, when you eat as much pussy as I do, it 'as to smell unfamiliar to someone who's never had it."

The whole bar erupted in laughter, including Slappy, who responded by giving Stix the finger and going back outside in defeat to guard the door.

Jasper and Stix walked into Jasper's office and sat in the only two chairs in the room as Jasper got down to business. "So what's on your mind?"

"Not much, Jabs. I just wanted to do my due diligence."

Jasper cocked his right eyebrow slightly bewildered. "Due diligence, you say? You sound like one of me lawyers and not the bloody shotta that you are, don't ya now? Go on wif it, and quit trying to impress me with your slick vocab

141

and what not."

Stix, slightly abashed, recalibrated his diction. "I got a visit from your brethren today. Dat boy looking to buy an ounce of heroin off me."

"Be specific. I have a lot of brethren. Blood brethren?"

"Blood brethren, yeah."

"I find that hard to believe. All me blood brethren are squares and would be too scared to even think of heroin. Trust me. I know me family."

"Well let me rephrase it then. He's brethren you don't associate with."

"Enough with the fucking riddles, Stix. Who is it?"

"Max Cotto, your Uncle Oscar's wayward son."

Jasper looked confused then amused. "What fucking rock did that degenerate crawl out from under? Last time I heard, he was strung out on H and in and out of rehab."

"Well I think he graduated from rehab to a Ghanaian prison in the north."

Jasper stood up and walked around the room. He grabbed a cricket paddle by his desk and practice swung it while he thought. Although Jasper had his ear to the street he did not tangle with drug peddling, and typically he did not associate closely with dealers. However, in some instances he did appreciate the type of intel he could obtain from his sources in that world. "So why you want me help? I don't talk to the guy; he's barely family as far as I'm concerned. Did he stiff you?"

"No he didn't. I told him I'd link up with him later. I just wanted to check with you to see if you'd heard anything lately—like if maybe he's using some inheritance money to buy drugs. And if not, I want to be sure he's not cooperating with the police and conspiring to put me in jail."

Jasper looked at Stix and nodded his head. "He's got a little inheritance money coming to him, but it's part of my uncle's estate, and it hasn't been settled yet. I hope he's being on the up-and-up with you. He knows the rules of the game like anybody else. But I will say you have some legitimate concerns, Stix. I mean, he is an addict and not to be trusted. I wouldn't put it past him, being a snitch."

"What do you think I should do then, Jabs? Not sell it to him? The money'd be nice."

Jasper hesitated before shaking his head and saying, "I wouldn't take the risk, Stix. Plus if he has the money and really wants it, he'll go to someone else. I tell you what—I'll look into it and get back to you. Until you hear otherwise, avoid any communication with him." Jasper then reached into his pocket and pulled out a massive roll of bills. He separated two one hundred pound bills from his roll and handed them to Stix. "Thanks for bringing this information to me. Let me know if you hear anything else. You get me?"

"Of course, Jabs, and thanks for your counsel on the matter," Stix humbly replied. Jasper initiated the customary hug and sent Stix on his way, as he sat back into his chair and meditated on the matter. He had no compassion for his lawless cousin Max; even the thought of him made Jasper uneasy. The last thing he needed was for Max's antics to bring attention to his gambling operation and besmirch BOI's reputation.

Jasper decided to call Roland Dufrane. "I know you're a busy man, but I need you to do something for me."

Dufrane didn't hesitate. "What is it you need, Jabs?"
"I need you to follow Oscar's son...Max Cotto."

Chapter 21
Nima Slum and the Osu District in Accra, Ghana
Present Day

Dufrane was expert at tailing subjects in the field. He mastered the skill nearly twenty years ago as a young agent with the Mossad. Although a bit out of practice, Dufrane wagered he still possessed enough skill to trail a petty drug addict the likes of Max Cotto. Being one of the few pale faces in a sea of dark ones made his task a bit more challenging, therefore Dufrane used extra precautions to keep him from being spotted. For the necessary cover, he brought in Claude Olojay, an agent from the Ivory Coast, to tail Max directly. Although Claude was Ivorian, he still blended in much better than Dufrane would. He equipped Claude with black-rimmed glasses that had a built-in video camera and transmitters in the front and sides. While Claude tailed Cotto, Dufrane could watch Max in real time on his smart phone in his car parked a quarter of a mile away. So far, the plan worked as they designed it: the images transmitted from the video camera were clear, and Max was oblivious to being tailed.

The start of Max's day was uneventful. He woke up around 10:00 a.m. in a shanty in the slum of Nima, a notoriously gritty neighborhood even the police avoided. It sat just below the more-manicured elevation of downtown Accra. A groggy Max strolled through the congested slum while trying to mind the sleeping loiterers and animal feces peppering his path. He walked a mile to the Makola Market to visit with friends. The one-square-kilometer, open-air market was a maze of corridors constructed of canopies and vendor booths. The market's layout created a challenge for Claude to follow Max without being seen. The savvy field agent did manage to keep a respectable distance and still not lose his subject. When Max entered the market, he made his way to a booth, where he disappeared into the back to chat with the person out of clear sight. Unable to keep a visual on Max, Claude wandered around the next aisle over and pretended to

144

shop.

Twenty minutes later, Max exited the booth and headed to the entrance of the market. When Max left the Makola Market, he casually made his way to the closest chop bar for lunch. Claude pretended to read a book at the bus-stop bench adjacent to the chop bar for observational purposes. Max sat down at the middle of the bar and cleaned his hands with the bowl of water and towel provided. The chop bar's owner was an older woman dressed in a blue-and-white adinkra-patterned garb. She seemed particularly happy to see Max by the way she constantly held his hand when they talked. When his meal was served, he tunneled into his mound of kenke and spinach stew with his right hand while the oily juices dripped down his palms.

Five minutes into his meal, the woman handed Max a cell phone. He spoke on it for several minutes, handing it back to the woman and quickly finishing his meal. Max grabbed some money out of his pocket to pay for his meal before she waved her hand and denied his money. Max got up and walked around to the back of the hut to hug the owner and kiss her on the cheek. The woman watched Max walk away until he was completely out of her sight.

Max ventured back toward Osu, where he made a stop at the high-end bistro, Brojode. A man wearing culinary attire and smoking a cigarette on the patio greeted him. The two embraced and Max followed him inside. Claude sat on the wall across the street from Brojode and waited for Max's return. Twenty minutes later, he left the bistro clutching a brown paper bag, and hopped on a crowded trotro. Claude signaled for Dufrane to pick him up across the street from Brojode. Ten seconds later, Dufrane pulled up and Claude jumped in the car. The two followed Max's trotro that eventually dropped him back at the entrance of Nima. He strolled through the slum talking to his neighbors before entering his shanty and putting an end to the day's surveillance.

The next morning, Dufrane and Claude returned to the entrance of Nima for the second round of surveying

Max Cotto. On the previous day, Max began his rounds at 10:00 am. However, today he showed no signs of leaving his shanty. By noon, Dufrane and Claude started to wonder if they'd lost him.

"Claude, did you see him leave at all?" Dufrane asked.

"Nope. I have one of my guys, Peter, staking out his shanty inside Nima since we stopped tailing him last night. According to him, there's been no movement, not even for a bathroom break."

"So Peter's been inside for eighteen hours?" Dufrane asked.

"This is correct."

"Okay, have Peter make contact with Max now." Dufrane had good reason for concern, because the shanties in Nima were tricky. Some have been known to hide underground tunnel entrances so the tenants could evade the police when needed.

"Will do." Claude picked up his phone and dialed Peter inside Nima. "Peter, its Claude. I need you to make contact with the subject to make sure he didn't evade you during the night. Call me back and update me on his status."

Peter hung up his phone and put it in his pocket. He got up from his crouched position and crept over to Max's shanty while minding his surroundings. Knocking on the door several times to no response, he tested the knob to find it unlocked. Opening the door, he neither saw nor heard any movement, so he entered cautiously. Finally inside, he noticed a motionless Max sprawled out on a cot at the far wall of the dark room. He quickly rushed to Max and, with each step, it smelled more and more like a sewer. Checking his vitals, Max had no pulse and his open eyes were dilated to the size of half dollars. On the floor next to his left hand lay a syringe. It was obvious that Max had suffered from a deadly overdose sometime during the night. Peter covered his mouth and nose with his hand and called Claude. "Sir, it looks like our subject appears to be deceased."

"Dead? How?"

"Yes, sir. He's passed out on his cot, with a syringe on the floor, eyes dilated to the size of a silver dollars and no pulse. Not to mention it smells like death. My professional guess is that he's dead, sir."

"Okay. Get the fuck out of there, and we'll call an ambulance. Make sure nobody follows you out of Nima," Claude instructed. He hung up the phone and looked at Dufrane. "It sounds like Max had too good of a time since we saw him. Looks like he had his last fix. He's gone, sir."

Dufrane struck the steering wheel with the palm of his hand out of frustration. "God damn it!"

≈

As the newest foot soldier, Fahim Nechtar was usually given the least desirable duties in the Ishmael Group. These duties usually included feeding the security dogs, picking up lunch for the crew, and washing the cars. However, last week Fahim received a chance to step up, when the underboss Abdul Mulinesbar dispatched him to monitor one of their new Ghanaian "freelancers," Max Cotto.

Fahim had tailed Max for four uneventful days, so he put a loose tail on him due to the man's predictable routine: wake up at 10:00 a.m., hang around the Makola Market for an hour, eat lunch at the same chop bar, and usually take the trolley to Labadi Beach for a few hours. After the beach, he'd take the trolley back to Nima, hang out with friends, and get high, then go to bed. This was Max's clockwork-like schedule.

However, the fifth day was a bit more unusual: Fahim noticed a thin African male with black-framed glasses in Max's general vicinity. Initially he thought nothing of it until Max left the Makola Market and the skinny man with glasses followed Max to the chop bar, waiting across the street to observe him. This was highly suspicious to Fahim, so he called Abdul, who had asked to be alerted of any suspicious behavior.

"Boss, I think Max has another tail. He's an African male, 6'1," 170 pounds, about thirty years old."

147

"Are you sure? What is this man doing?"

"Well he's been behind Max ever since he left Nima, yet they haven't interacted. I calculate he's been around Max for around two and a half hours. That would be one hell of a coincidence, boss."

"One hell of a coincidence, indeed," Abdul agreed.

"What should I do? Do you want me to intervene?"

"No, no don't do that. We don't know who this guy is yet. He could be the police. I want you to call the lady at the chop bar and have her hand the phone to Max."

"How am I supposed to do that? I don't have her number," Fahim lamented.

Abdul sighed, then rattled off, "It's 012359877."

"Why do you have her number?"

"I'll train you how to do your job later," Abdul sarcastically remarked. "But for now give this message to Max when he answers the phone. Tell him to stop by Brojode because we have a package waiting for him. He will know exactly what you mean."

Chapter 22
Accra, Ghana
Present Day

Three weeks before Max overdosed, he had decided to square things with his father. Now a grown man of thirty-two, Max caught a trolley to an intersection two blocks from his father's house shortly after midnight. He wore a baseball cap, dark clothing, and a .38 special stashed in the waistband of his pants. Reaching the security gate, he simply said, "I'm here to see my father."

One of the guards looked at his watch and asked if the boss was expecting him.

"My name should be on the log for a 1:00 a.m."

The guard grabbed the log and flipped it open to the first 1:00 a.m. slot, where he saw Max Cotto's name. That's odd for the boss, thought the guard.

Max cut his eyes at the guard and channeled his anger about the reason his father would only agree to see him at 1:00 a.m. "My father would rather summon me after hours so his friends and associates don't have to be bothered with the likes of me."

The guard moved to the gate and opened it for Max. He then whistled for the other guard to open the front door. When the guard opened the door, Max said he was good from there and walked in the house. At this moment, his blood was pumped with adrenaline, and he had never been more determined in his life. At the bottom of the stairs, Max saw Oscar halfway up them before he noticed his presence.

"It is one o'clock in the morning; what are you doing here? Why didn't the guards inform me of your arrival?"

"You agreed to meet me, remember?" answered Max.

Oscar shook his head and said, "Oh yes. Well I forgot, but I'm too tired to converse right now. Please wait for me in the morning and I will sort you out, okay?"

"Sorry, but this can't wait." Max then reached in his

waistband to produce the .38, fired two shots into Oscar's shoulder and chest, and watched his father tumble down the staircase. When the almost lifeless Oscar lay at Max's feet, their eyes locked by chance. The dying Oscar looked into the eyes of his son, who was also tragically his executioner. Max did not anticipate such an intimate moment and tears immediately began streaming down his face, while snot bubbles popped from his nostrils like lava from a live volcano. If Max hadn't known better, Oscar seemed to grin at him as he mumbled his last words, "I always knew you'd come back to haunt me."

Max ran out of the house sobbing. As he exited the front door, the two security guards were running toward him. He had impeccable aim for a drug addict and shot each of them with a bullet to the face. Dizzy with rage, Max made his way to the security shelter and ransacked it until he found the clipboard hanging on the door with year's login sheets. He grabbed it and ran out of the compound, down the road, and jumped into a waiting black sedan. When he entered the sedan, he punched the inside of his door with his fist while screaming in frustration.

≈

At an early age, Suzanna Cotto exhibited the resolve of an adult. Her parents died in a bus accident when she was only fifteen, leaving Suzanna to tend her younger sister and brother alone. Suzanna managed to take care of her family by working for different vendors at the Makola Market. She worked around the clock and watched after her siblings during her breaks in a nearby shantytown behind the market. Her solid work ethic and strong will allowed her and her siblings to escape the orphanage and the clutches of underworld predators.

Fortunately for many women in Accra, the Makola Market was a matriarchal society. Like many other women, Suzanna took advantage of the market's employment opportunities. She stayed employed at the Makola Market for thirty years. At the age of fifty-three and in the height of her career, she even became a market manager, which meant that in addition to running her own business, she settled vendor disputes and absorbed the hassle from bureaucratic agencies. After seven years as a market manager, Suzanna branched out from the market and opened up her own chop bar in downtown Accra.

Suzanna was a shining example of how fortitude and hard work can help the least fortunate overcome life's unfair hurdles. For all of Suzanna's good deeds, though, not one of them went unpunished, and her days on earth were constantly marred by tragedy. Suzanna's brother Byron was an aspiring boxer, who trained at the camp of former world middleweight boxing champion, Azuma Nelson. After showing much promise, Byron was lamentably killed during an exhibition match in Spain, where he was considered the number-one contender. However, the tragedy of her sister Bessie (and the person closest to her) proved to be the most painful.

Bessie had always been considered one of the prettiest girls around. As she grew older, Bessie aspired to be a singer, and she showed promise. She stumbled on what she hoped would be her big break when The Kitten Club in Accra hired her as a jazz singer. The combination of low pay, Bessie's beauty, and her promiscuous nature created the perfect storm, leading her to moonlight as a high-end escort for wealthy male patrons. Her clients gave her money and gifts in exchange for whatever they wanted from her body.

Bessie's biggest score in those days was Oscar Boateng, part-time Kitten Club investor and full-time playboy. Bessie and Oscar shared a brief affair, yet she still managed to get pregnant by Oscar when he was in his forties, producing a son she named Max. Due to Oscar's political exile, he didn't meet his son until eleven years later.

When Oscar returned to Ghana, he refused to join their lives but he did provide them with monetary support. Unfortunately, Bessie was in a tightly gripped battle with heroin, and instead of using the monthly stipend for food, clothing, and shelter, she squandered it on drugs. Appalled by Bessie's poor parenting, Suzanna took Max away from her sister to preserve his life. Despite Suzanna's good intentions, her sister died from AIDS at the age of forty-five.

To add insult to injury, the same day Suzanna learned of her nephew Max's death was the anniversary of her Brother Byron's death. She was deeply devastated by Max's demise, and wore black to mourn the deaths in her family for the rest of her life. With no children of her own, Max's death felt like that of an only son. The funeral was small, just she and a few friends from the Makola Market. Unsurprisingly, none of Max's mysterious new "friends" showed their faces, but they did send flowers and cards. As Suzanna Cotto buried her nephew, she realized that as the only surviving member of her family, their bloodline would cease to exist when she died.

Two days after Suzanna buried her nephew, she went back to work. When she opened up the chop bar, two suited gentlemen were waiting for her. She thought they looked like policemen, but knew they couldn't be Ghanaian policemen since one was white. Whoever they were, Suzanna wasn't surprised by their presence. Many odd things had happened since her nephew had been released from jail right up until his death. She thought maybe these two men could fill in the gaps. Suzanna initiated the conversation. "I'll be open in a few minutes, gentlemen."

"Actually, Ms. Cotto, we are here to discuss the death of your nephew Max. My name is Roland Dufrane and this is my partner Claude Olojay. We work for Boateng-Osei, Incorporated. BOI's founder is the recently deceased Oscar Boateng, your nephew's father."

Suzanna looked at them without responding. This was Dufrane's signal to continue. "It was Oscar's wish that we keep an eye on all of his children after he died, and this included Max. We would like to ask you a few questions regarding your nephew's relationship with certain people."

Chapter 23
Accra, Ghana
1981–1993

Max Cotto's once-beautiful mother Bessie had turned into a prostitute and drug addict with a bipolar disorder that detrimentally affected him at a young age. Max's mother showed her love in spurts. She was usually her most loving on Sundays and Mondays. Those were usually the days she spent recovering from her weekend zombie-like drug and alcohol binges.

She often took her son to the market on those days and would shower him with sweets. His favorite snack combination was Orange Fanta and toffee, which also caused Max's teeth to decay at an early age. The rest of the week was a reoccurring nightmare. Bessie often left him to fend for himself while she gallivanted around Accra with her Johnny-come-latelies. If Max dared to ask for a Fanta and toffee on her "working" days, she often answered him with a slap across the face and, "Why didn't I go down to the next village and just abort you like I wanted to?"

On the other hand, Max hated his father even more, mostly because he rarely admitted Max even existed. Max did not meet Oscar Boateng until he was eleven. He later found out that his father didn't know about him until he was nine. His father had been his mother's employer and occasional lover at one point. Bessie met Oscar when she auditioned as a singer at his jazz club. Oscar was a local celebrity and usually had any woman of his choosing, so it was inevitable that he and the beautiful young singer needing a job, would seal his offer of employment with sex.

Their affair couldn't have occurred at a worse time: the political atmosphere in 1980s Ghana was shifting like the San Andreas Fault. During the late 1950s, Oscar's father had worked closely with Nkrumah to liberate Ghana from Great Britain, so naturally Oscar was loyal to the old party and supported them. Almost thirty years later, the Ghanaian political landscape changed when General JJ Rawlings initiated several military coups to take over the government and give "power to the people." Although, heralded by some as Ghana's savior, Rawlings' reign was polarizing. His supporters proclaimed Rawlings as a populist who squeezed the rich and diluted the power of the tribal chiefs, while his most vocal opposition dismissed him as a ruthless thug. People either loved Rawlings or hated him, but either way, he became the longest-sitting president in Ghana's history. After Rawlings last term in 2001, Parliament initiated presidential term limits.

The day Oscar was forced into exile, he had almost been tipped off too late. He was actually undoing Bessie Cotto's bra in his office at the jazz club, when Kwasi, his twelve-year-old assistant, hurriedly opened the door to warn him that soldiers were about to move on him. Kwasi was a reliable source because his father was an officer in the current regime's army. Kwasi's father had been tipped off about Oscar only the day before.

Oscar immediately fled to France and was stuck in exile for ten years. During his first year in France, and unbeknownst to him, Bessie Cotto gave birth to his son and named him Max. She gave the child her last name of Cotto because she wasn't certain which of her lovers had fathered him. It wasn't until Max was five years old that Bessie knew he was Oscar's by the boy's his crooked nose and asymmetrical smile, which were exactly like his father's. Four years later, she was able to get word to Oscar about his son.

While living in France, Oscar had reunited with old friends from his university days in the U.K. These same friends helped to firmly insert him in the commodities business. At the time, Oscar became the most prolific broker of African commodities for his firm, NatriSci. His relationship with NatriSci was one of mutual advantage: NatriSci took advantage of Oscar's natural talents for business and his African heritage and connections, which helped turn the firm into the premiere trader of African-based commodities in the world. In return, Oscar negotiated a handsome income for himself.

During his ten-year exile, Ghana experienced a

154

stifling economy while Oscar lived the charmed life of a European businessman. But like all of the white-collar occupations that were prostitution by nature, Oscar's job often left him feeling impure. After accumulating a comfortable nest egg, Oscar bowed out of the commodities racket and orchestrated his return home. After several months of bribing and blackmailing officials in the current administration, the prodigal son returned home to Ghana a wealthy and more refined man, one who simply oozed charisma.

Oscar carried himself with the swagger of a middle-aged Sydney Poitier. It was safe to say he returned to a different Ghana after ten years, and he was a little out of touch. One of the first things he did was set up a meeting with Bessie Cotto to get her and the boy squared away. His first reaction to his son was a comment made to his mother: Without even acknowledging Max, he said, "Ah, what's wrong with the boy's teeth? And Christ, what's happened to you, Bessie?"

Oscar realized his honesty was distasteful by the looks on their faces, so he bent down and ruffled the boy's already ragged hair. "Don't you worry, young lad, we'll find a dentist to fix those teeth. We'll get you some new clothes too, what do you think about that?" The bashful eleven-year old Max nodded his head and said nothing.

Oscar waved over his young protégé, Kwasi. At the time, one hundred cedis equaled one dollar, and traveling with cash was cumbersome, so he had Kwasi carry a tan leather attaché full of cash. Oscar grabbed five stacks of bills from the case, handed them to Kwasi and said, "Take this money and buy groceries for the house. Buy clothes and school supplies for the boy and arrange for a barber to trim his hair." He waived Kwasi off, turned to Bessie and handed her the remaining three stacks of money. "Please don't make me regret this. I will be checking on you from time to time to make sure things are square."

With soft eyes, Bessie leaned in to hug Oscar, attempting to seduce him. Unfortunately, Bessie was already a disaster of epic proportions. Every second Oscar

155

spent in her presence made him cringe to think he'd actually slept with her. Oscar gently pushed Bessie away by her shoulders. "Just take care of your son, okay?" Oscar didn't consider himself heartless when it came to women, however, when he allowed himself to think about that day years later, he would sadly admit he was unnecessarily cruel to the mother of his first son.

Chapter 24
Accra, Ghana
Present Day

After Oscar's death, his duties and the Chairman of BOI title were given to his nephew, Clinton, even though he wasn't the most senior BOI executive; that distinction went to the fifty-nine-year-old Kumasi Gold Chief Geologist and BOI board member Harry Van Bleer. After Harry, his Aunt Marguerite was the second oldest at fifty-seven. The remaining BOI execs were closely clustered in age: George was forty-two, and Clinton and Jasper rounded out the heat at forty.

Clinton's lead investment in BOI had compelled Oscar to request that Clinton be designated the head of BOI in his will in the event of his death. Oscar also believed that Clinton's brief but significant experience doing business in America was critical for BOI's continued success. Oscar knew Clinton's stubborn attitude forced him to conduct business in an aggressive but ethical manner, so he was confident Clinton would avoid the corruption rampant in most Africa-based companies. It was the heart of BOI's mission statement that Oscar authored: "BOI aspires to be the largest and most influential corperation in Ghana. If BOI is guided by a progressive and ethical business model then by the law of physics our influence should be nothing but positive."

Clinton also believed in his uncle's vision of cleaning up the manner in which African corporations conducted business. It was the reason he agreed to take over his uncle's advisory role to the committee that would award Ghana's oil-drilling rights. Today was Clinton's first meeting with the selection committee in Parliament's budget office to hear his recommendation. He arrived fifteen minutes late due to an extended phone conversation with clients in Germany, so he instructed his assistant Kwasi to enter the meeting ahead of him and apologize for his tardiness. Eventually Clinton wrapped up his conversation and walked into the budget office.

To mitigate the embarrassment, Clinton immediately walked to the long table where all seven of the committee members sat. Their faces were devoid of expression and professorial in their demeanor. Clinton introduced himself, and apologized to each member individually. This was necessary because if any of the committee members said they weren't annoyed by Clinton's tardiness, they would be lying; it would be easy to interpret his behavior as disrespect. Clinton took his place at a table next to Kwasi, who had already arranged his notes and talking points.

The committee chairman addressed the group with his obligatory house keeping issues then invited Clinton to present his thoughts at the podium. Clinton thrived at speaking in boardrooms and other meetings. He only needed notes if he was distracted by an off-base question, but even then, it only took a moment for him to get back on track. Like many of the rooms in parliamentary buildings, the budget office had vaulted ceilings that were prone to echo, and the room's lack of a microphone forced Clinton to speak at a louder pitch than he preferred.

Kwasi distributed the outlines and Clinton started his presentation, which only took ten minutes. He addressed the importance of creating responsible legislation so the company awarded the drilling rights would have to adhere to laws already in place. He also urged them to demand the highest annual tribute from each bidder. More importantly, Clinton expressed how accepting personal bribes from corporations in the bidding process took food out of the mouths of Ghana's citizens.

At the end of Clinton's presentation, he concluded that through his independent research, he concurred with his uncle's findings and BOI would endorse Freestar Oil as the best option for the country. Clinton stayed at the podium and asked for questions.

The committee chairman raised his hand and asked the first question. "Mr. Osei, on behalf of Parliament and the selection committee, we would like to thank you for coming here today and giving us your thoughts. As you know, your uncle was a great asset to our committee. His knowledge of commodities trading and his passion for Ghana's well being was unrivaled, therefore, we invited him to guide us in our deliberations. We can only assume you are continuing your uncle's dedicated work, which is the reason we invited you here today."

"And I appreciate the invitation, Mr. Chairman."

The chairman continued, "However, I have to ask—since you were born in America and still do business there, will you keep BOI in Ghana, or are the rumors you have plans to relocate BOI's headquarters to another country true?"

Clinton was confused by the chairman's question. "Mr. Chairman, such rumors are unfounded. I do not foresee any reason to move BOI from our Accra headquarters. Kumasi Gold is our biggest asset with mining operations projected to last at least fifteen to twenty more years. Not to mention, all of my BOI colleagues have lived in Ghana most, if not all, of their lives; they are equally attached to their home as much as my uncle was. BOI is staying here unless some unforeseen cataclysm forced us to leave."

One committee member jumped at Clinton's last sentence. "Hypothetically speaking, what kind of cataclysmic event would trigger you to uproot BOI?"

Clinton smirked at the lawmaker's petty question, but he was still careful not to let it manifest into a sarcastic laugh. "Given Ghana's track record of modernity, I don't foresee any cataclysms. However, hypothetically speaking, a civil war, genocide, or a bloody government coup are the only reasons I can think of off the top of my head. But let me reiterate, I do not see this happening in Ghana."

The committee members were whispering among one another. It didn't take long for a litany of questions and comments to follow, such as, "I'm not sure if you are aware of our history Mr. Osei, but Ghana has never had a civil war or recorded any cases of genocide. So what makes you believe this could happen here?"

Clinton was now caught on his heels as he

159

scrambled, not anticipating this line of questioning. "My apologies, if that is how you interpreted my remarks, but I assure you that is not what I meant. When asked what cataclysmic event might trigger BOI to uproot, I simply acknowledged a few hypothetical but unlikely reasons. And that's not just for Ghana but for any country in which we do business."

Another member chimed in. "I notice your cataclysmic examples were all results of political turmoil and not say…natural disasters. That just makes people like me and my colleagues wonder if you think we're doing a poor job here in Parliament?"

Clinton fought his urge to sigh and roll his eyes but it took significant restraint. "With all due respect, I think some of you may be reading too much into my hypothetical comments. I have been on record in local and international media outlets praising the civic leaders of this great nation. I also boast in private about how Ghana's government is as transparent as most governments in the G8 summit. I have donated and will continue to contribute to the campaigns of politicians I support, many of which sit here today.

"I do not lie when I say I believe Ghana has the most competent government on the continent. However, I would be remiss if I didn't acknowledge the rash of coups that forced my uncle into exile had a profound effect on our family. I do not predict such egregious political actions from this government, and although it is highly unlikely, I will not allow myself the naivety of thinking it can never happen—that would be counterintuitive to my uncle's own experience.

"BOI is proud to support thousands of hard-working Ghanaian entrepreneurs through our micro-loan program. We are financially and emotionally invested in this country, and BOI will continue to do more as the company grows. Hence, the reason I am here today. Like my uncle, I am aware of BOI's unique position in this landscape. Although we have no direct investment in Ghana's oil industry, we are interested in, not only how it affects our own business interests, but also how it affects

160

every working Ghanaian. It is my humble opinion, as well as that of my late uncle and the other BOI executives that Freestar Oil will best serve the needs of Ghana and its people. I pray you will take my recommendation and believe me when I say the research comes from an objective perspective."

After the spirited Q&A, the meeting adjourned, and Clinton left without knowing if he negatively or positively affected the committee's decision. He had perceived a division among the committee members but also sensed they would come to a unanimous decision based on collectively protecting their political livelihoods. Clinton was satisfied that the content of his presentation didn't hurt his uncle's hard work. He knew BOI's influence in Ghana wouldn't disappear anytime soon. If the legislators wanted BOI's money for their future campaigns, they'll do what's right and follow Clinton's recommendation.

Clinton wouldn't get any real feedback about how things went at the meeting until he heard from Vice President Bonswah. Just like his uncle, he and Vice President Bonswah did not disclose their conversations to anyone else. Bonswah's perceived impartiality was integral to getting an honest read from his sources in the selection committee.

Clinton had moved into Oscar's Tema villa two weeks earlier. His move puzzled those close to him because it was a modest home compared to what he could afford. Not to mention that his uncle was recently murdered there. Later that evening, Clinton enjoyed a crisp Gulder beer on the patio as the sun set on the Atlantic Ocean, slowly retracting its shimmering gold veil from the knotty, uncombed shoreline. Usually he was cooped up indoors finishing a meeting, on the phone, or stuck in traffic at this time of day, so he was happy to enjoy life's simple pleasures.

It wouldn't last long when he received a call on his secure line, the one reserved only for Vice President Bonswah. Clinton was anxious to hear what the committee thought of his presentation, but it also meant he had to stop enjoying his sunset.

"Vice President Bonswah, how do you do tonight, sir?"

"Just fine just fine. Do you have a moment for us to talk?"

"Of course. I've been anxious to speak with you regarding our friends in Parliament. How did I do earlier today?"

Bonswah coughed, then took a drink of water. "According to my source on the committee, the meeting did not go as well as we would have liked."

"I suspected that might be the case. What exactly went wrong?"

"Just a bunch of irrelevant bullshit. Ghanaian politicians are notorious for their pettiness, but this might take the cake. My friend on the committee informed me some members were offended by your presentation. They felt as if they were being lectured by an Obruni." Obruni is a Ghanaian term for an American or a white person. It was a loosely used term but nonetheless offensive. "Their words not mine," Bonswah confirmed. "According to my friend, the majority of committee members recognize you have dual citizenship, but they still consider you American first and Ghanaian second. Who knows, maybe your Ghanaian accent isn't strong enough for them. But their biggest concern was they felt you were condescending."

Clinton shook his head and waived his hand in frustration. "So I'm dealing with nine-year olds now? Do I have to hold each of their hands and tell them they are special before we can work together as adults? I don't care about proving my authenticity to them, Mr. Vice President. It isn't even relevant to the debate."

Bonswah tried to put it in perspective. "You don't understand, Clinton. To many old-school Ghanaians, practicality can take a backseat to tradition. Until today, the committee was dealing directly with your uncle, whom as their elder was respected and feared across the board. Many of those same committee members despised Oscar for forcing them to eat crow for many years, though, and

162

they are reluctant to take advice from his boy-faced nephew from America. This is the pettiness I speak of."

Thinking about it, Clinton believed every word. He knew many Ghanaians remained apprehensive of African-Americans. Regardless of his proficiency in Twi, his American accent and look would always remind them he wasn't really one of them. Clinton now realized why his mother warned him that he would always be unfairly branded with the Obruni tag, and it would be his biggest hurdle to overcome.

"So what happens now? Do they ignore my recommendation? Because by doing so, they ignore BOI's influence. Are they aware of how politically uncomfortable I will make it for them? What better choice do they have than voting for my recommendation? It doesn't mean we have to like each other."

"My committee contact informs me that many of the commissioners are now leaning toward voting for PetroCo Oil to align themselves with President Amoako. They feel that as a young American, you will want to move BOI to the U.S. and Europe in due time. They are not concerned about you ruining their political futures. Rather, they believe President Amoako is here to stay and that he can, and will, ruin their careers if they don't vote with him. Plus, I believe they see this as an opportunity to sell their votes to PetroCo Oil. Truthfully, Clinton, they don't believe you have the will to shame them clean, because that's how Oscar did it. Although, many on that committee say they loved your uncle, they also resented his influence over the past three years. These people thought your uncle stopped them from eating as well as they would have liked."

"So you're telling me these so called civil servants are going to handicap what's good for their country so they can make a few more bucks for themselves?"

"This is old-style politics, Clinton. Through his acquired clout over the years, your uncle kept the Parliament as honest as he could. Now that he's gone, they see a large amount of money in an unguarded net, with no goalie in position to keep them from scoring."

"Are you sure Amoako is on the take for PetroCo?"

"I am positive he is. I have a good relationship with his receptionist and she gives me detailed information on his itineraries. Next month the president is traveling to Dubai for vacation. According to her, Blinkman Dealership on his Dubai itinerary is the code name for PetroCo Oil."

"What about having him impeached? I have capable journalists on the payroll who will break a scandal story fast."

"I thought of that already, but the process will take too much time. Plus, what are we going to impeach him for? Bribery? If this goes down the way I think, PetroCo Oil will be bribing half of Parliament. It would be impossible to impeach Amoako when those impeaching him are guilty of the same thing."

Clinton was thirty-five minutes into his conversation with the vice president. The sun had set ten minutes ago and his beer was warm as he paced back and forth in his office on the phone. "Are you suggesting we just allow this vile corruption to keep happening?"

"No, no, Clinton—I'm not suggesting we give up at all. At this juncture, I feel we are somewhat boxed in and will need to try some alternative tactics."

"What do you have in mind?"

"The argument could be made that selecting the lesser of two evils is the committee's better choice."

"There is only one evil and that is PetroCo."

"I understand, but what if we presented our recommendation as the evil that appeals to their consciences? I'm suggesting we approach the members with a monetary package to vote for Freestar. It wouldn't be as much as they'd get from PetroCo, but they wouldn't have to compromise on the lesser amount of annual tribute to Ghana. It should make them feel better about themselves, and they would still have 100% of BOI's support in their future political endeavors."

"But let's call it what it really is, Mr. Vice President—bribery. And who do you suggest will pay these bribes? Freestar? From what I've learned, the organization

164

won't stoop to such tactics. But even say they did? The annual tribute would have to be that much less, so the country's in the same boat."

"Clinton, I'm not suggesting the bribes come from Freestar, I'm suggesting they come from BOI. The only other option is to allow these crooks to take PetroCo bribes without us having the ability to monitor their actions. We have to justify our villainy by remembering that as the lesser of two evils, the best interests of Ghana and its citizens are at stake."

Clinton could not respond to Bonswah's revelation right away. They both stayed quiet on the line for fifteen seconds or so. Clinton was exhausted and he felt a migraine surfacing. "Let me think on this. I will call you in a couple of days with my decision. You have given me much to think about."

"I understand, and I will pray for you."

Anwar Ishmael always said, "Leave nothing to chance."
Whether it meant stuffing the tip jar at the bar to ensure
preferential treatment or stuffing the raffle bowl to increase
his odds of winning the prize, Ishmael pursued all available
options. And if no options were available, he'd been known
to create his own.

Ishmael boasted that 90% of his business affairs
were in order. All of his illegal streams of revenue were
currently running smoothly. His clients, who accessed his
vast network of compromised politicians and legitimate
businesses to launder their dirty money, were all paid in
full. His Taliban-guarded poppy fields in Afghanistan still
netted him several million dollars a week. Even his
legitimate shell companies set up to launder dirty money
were all profitable. But he had yet to capture his single
biggest potential payout—the Ishmael Group and PetroCo
Oil's backdoor negotiations with high-ranking Ghanaian
officials for the country's oil-drilling rights. It was now his
highest priority.

Ishmael had purchased at least one government
official on every continent on earth. So when he learned of
PetroCo's desire to bid for Ghana's oil-drilling contract, he
did not hesitate to present Gordon Heinrich, CEO of
PetroCo Oil a deal guaranteeing PetroCo won the bid.
Heinrich took the bait. PetroCo agreed to Ishmael's
conditions of more than a billion dollars in compensation if
he delivered them the contract. PetroCo and its
stockholders stood to gross tens of billions of dollars if
Ishmael made good on his word, so a billion dollars in
compensation was well worth PetroCo's effort. But as
Ishmael's good Russian friend Sergey Voltransky (a man
who was unknowingly fond of butchering American
clichés) would tell him, "You know what they say about
best lay plans, right? They go in waste."

Initially Ishmael's grand scheme had one significant

hurdle and that was Oscar Boateng, BOI's populist crusader who planned to endorse Freestar. Coincidentally for Ishmael, Oscar had met an untimely death several weeks earlier. The news of Oscar's death brought him enormous relief. To celebrate his imminent victory, Ishmael purchased a seventy-two-foot luxury liner that he unofficially named Oscar. With Abdul in tow, Ishmael perused the deck of his sea-worthy yacht while working the fabric of his burgundy Yves Saint Laurent bathrobe.

"Who is this Clinton Osei?" Ishmael demanded.

"Oscar's most trusted nephew and BOI vice president for three years," replied Abdul.

"I hope you impressed upon President Amoako that failing to fulfill his part of our bargain is unacceptable."

"Believe me, Abna knows what will happen if he fails. But there is some good news in all of this. According to Amoako and the Parliament chatter, Clinton Osei's meeting with the selection committee was a complete failure."

"A complete failure how?"

"They say Osei came across as a brash young American talking down to them and telling them what to do."

"Are Americans capable of coming across any other way?"

"True. From what I could gather, it appears the majority of the committee has shifted to follow President Amoako's endorsement of PetroCo Oil."

Ishmael indulged himself with a smile and a chuckle. "Do we know what we're doing, or do we know what we're doing?"

Abdul couldn't help but unleash a rare smile. "Yes boss, we do."

Ishmael nodded his head in approval. He then remembered the true reason why he summoned Abdul to the new vessel. "Abdul follow me below, I want to show you my latest acquisition." When they reached the back of the hull, Ishmael turned on the lights and gestured to a cage in the middle of the floor, encouraging Abdul to

167

investigate its contents. When Abdul approached the cage, he almost flinched, for there lay a magnificent spotted female jaguar. The jaguar recently purchased from poachers in Paraguay, was unaware of their presence due to the heavy dose of tranquillizers administered by its handlers.

Ishmael stood next to Abdul and whispered, so as to not awaken his new pet, "Since I was a boy, the jaguar has been my favorite animal, and I've tried to emulate its behavior. Jaguars are opportunistic creatures that cloak themselves in their surroundings and strike their prey in a stealthy manner. I would like to think this is how I've trained our organization to pursue its prey. Like a jaguar, quiet yet powerful."

"Indeed, boss. She is a remarkable creature. What will you name her?"

Ishmael smiled. "Her name is Nassett."

Abdul's eyes squinted with confused emotion at the news this beautiful feline was named after his lost love. Ishmael put his arm on Abdul's shoulder; he knew it would strike a chord. "Our organization has enjoyed great success in the past, but none as great as the success we enjoy at this very moment. We are leaders in our industry, and none of this could have happened without you, my friend. You've done a fine job here, Abdul. In fact, I bought her for you," Ishmael admitted. "You've been a loyal friend to me for years. Many people of your ability would have plotted against me years ago. One day soon, you will be the boss. Until that day comes, I figured you have to start learning how to think like one. Study the jaguar and appreciate her movements."

But Ishmael wasn't done. He walked to a table in the corner of the hull and grabbed an oak box big enough for Ishmael to hold with two hands and presented the box to Abdul. When he opened it, he found a white captain's hat, Abdul was confused, but Ishmael gave him no time to figure it out on his own. Instead Ishmael looked up and around admiring the boat and said, "Captain, I hope you find the accommodations of your ship acceptable."

168

Abdul, who was already close to crying, replied, "You're shitting me, right? Boss, you just bought this a week ago." Abdul pulled out the cap from the box and modeled it. Ishmael smiled and felt like a father who had just unveiled his son's first car.

And if the pet jaguar and yacht weren't enough, Ishmael's big gifts came with stocking stuffers. "By the way, there are two female staff in the lounge waiting to take you through your orientation." Abdul snickered at Ishmael as he shook his head. Ishmael didn't give his underboss the time to thank him. Instead, he took advantage of his protégé's speechlessness and walked away.

Before Ishmael left the room, he lobbed one more assignment to Abdul. "One more thing. If what President Amoako says is true and he has control over the committee, this is encouraging news. But let us not take any chances. Let's impress upon those who try to oppose us how serious we are about these matters. Tomorrow I need you to go to Mogadishu."

"Somalia?"

"Yes. I need you to visit our friend Idreme and give him an important assignment."

Abdul nodded and went on with his orders.

Tonight George was supposed to be having a peaceful romantic dinner with his girlfriend, Maria Renterea—or the "Spaniard" as his mother referred to her. They were having dinner in a hotel's beachside bungalow on a temperate (for West Africa) Accra evening. However, George was still mourning his uncle's death, and after the conversation with his girlfriend, he was hardly at peace.

The couple had finished eating and were having an after-dinner smoke via one of the many complimentary hookahs provided by the restaurant. George attended to the hookah's charcoal embers like a Boy Scout would tend a campfire. He stoked it and blew on it to keep it going, but more importantly, he was also trying to offset his uncomfortable conversation with Maria. She continued to speak to him even though he was obviously attempting to ignore her.

"What I don't understand is that you are older than your cousin Clinton, more charismatic, and by anybody's account, more Ghanaian than Clinton. There should have at least been a vote to see who got the chairmanship after your uncle passed. Instead, the board just presumptuously gives it to Clinton? It's just unfair. You deserve it, too!"

George, finally satisfied with the hookah's smoke output, handed the hose and nozzle to Maria as a blatant attempt to silence her. It didn't work, though. She held the hose by the nozzle and continued, "Do you understand what I'm saying?"

George did understand; in fact, he was the one who'd put those ideas in her head. Unfortunately, her views did little to convince him. She was obviously biased and had little interaction with Clinton to have an objective perspective. A frustrated George exclaimed, "Yes, Maria, I understand!" Then he regulated his voice and replied in a sarcastic tone, "But it's not that simple. You know what the media says: 'Clinton has that analytical intellect and rationale that most people don't possess.' Apparently my uncle thinks he's much more capable than me as well, since he requested Clinton be the successor of the company in his will."

Maria, realizing that George was genuinely discouraged, scooted over closer to him and softened her facial expression to exude an air of sympathy. To free her hands, she handed the hose back to George, wrapped her slender arms around his neck, kissed him on the cheek, and said, "Baby, this is not the case at all. Although, I can't speak on behalf of your mother," she mumbled quickly, "because she thinks I'm insignificant and will barely even acknowledge me." She then sighed and got on with the positive part of her comment, "I'm sure your uncle had tremendous confidence in you. Remember the first time I met him?"

George did, in fact, remember that meeting well. He had flown Maria to Ghana for a couple of days to meet his family after the Zatan wedding. That trip was a turn of events in their relationship, since at the beginning of the wedding, George was convinced that would be the last date he had with the young Spaniard. However, as weddings are known to do, the romantic circumstances were enough to charm even a reluctant romantic like George and helped him fall for Maria that night.

"Of course I do." George smiled and continued, "You couldn't stop flirting with the old man!"

Maria laughed. "Hey he flirted with me! And let me tell you, I don't know who could resist your uncle's charm."

While breathing the hookah smoke out his nose, George grinned and nodded; then after exhaling the remainder smoke in his mouth he said, "Nobody could."

"Well, the night we met him at his home, you went to the bathroom and left me to talk with your uncle. I'm not sure if he didn't want to embarrass you or if he didn't want to inflate your ego, but he told me you were his favorite nephew."

George interrupted with, "He says that to all of his nephews' girlfriends."

"No, it was more than that," Maria disagreed. "He told me how you were virtually his son. He went on about how he was a terrible father to his own children and wasn't a part of their lives. He said that with you, he felt he'd instilled the teachings a father would give to his oldest son, and that it was no secret you emulated him the most. But he also said that you were better than him because you were more sincere. He claimed to always have admired you because you were liberated enough to express your feelings, whether it was affection or displeasure. He also said that your sincerity would be the cornerstone of your success."

This was not the first time Maria told George about that conversation with Oscar. She told him that night, way back when they'd left his uncle's house. At that time though, George was more concerned about getting his girlfriend into bed than listening to any sweet things his uncle said about him. It was definitely more significant now, hearing it several months after his uncle had passed.

George didn't respond to Maria's story, but she knew he was affected by it. He just looked off to the moonlit ocean and nodded. Maria took that moment to excuse herself from the bungalow to use the ladies' room. George admired her elegant silhouette as she walked through the sand and up the deck stairs to the hotel's patio until she faded into the distance. Once out of sight, he turned around and sighed.

Reaching into his trouser pocket, he pulled out a small bag containing just under a gram of cocaine, emptied the contents of the drugs on the glass top of their table, and organized it into one line as thick as his thumb and as long as his index finger. Rolling up a 10-cedi bill, he hovered over the narcotic and snorted the entirety of that massive rail, proceeding to cough violently. After coughing, he used his handkerchief to wipe the tears from his eyes and the snot trickling out of his nose. George sat back and enjoyed the view of Labadi Beach. As the narcotic coursed through his veins, he felt that temporary feeling of peace he'd originally sought.

George grinned while left alone with his own thoughts. At times, he recognized a narcissistic amusement with himself. When George got high, he would often imagine a highlights reel of his exploits; tonight was no different. The reel was chronological: It usually began with scenes from his mischievous adolescence, which would feed into scenes of the legendary parties he threw in boarding school, which would then lead into scenes of the legendary parties he threw in college.

However, tonight, George's reel focused on the years after he graduated from college and moved to Ghana to begin his professional career working for his mother's company Temateng Agriculture. George didn't notice it at the time, but those initial years after university were his most challenging. Although, he paid to have 70% of his papers written for him at school, he was still sufficiently bright and legitimately aced most of his exams on his own accord.

Therefore, when George came out of university, he considered himself profoundly educated in international business and finance. The young grad was motivated to begin implementing the sophisticated business models he learned in academia to his mother's agricultural empire. What he didn't know was that his mother's business had little use for a green know-it-all, which he learned in his first meeting with all of the company managers. Before the meeting, it was a foregone conclusion in George's mind that his mother and the managers would be dazzled by his detailed projections report with its dynamic graphs and ample data. However, after his presentation, he couldn't comprehend how insensitively uninterested they appeared. His mother simply chuckled and said, "Okay, professor. Is class over now?" Her comment prompted the rest of the table to laugh, and she instructed her senior executive Kofi Jackson to continue the meeting, making no reference to George's report.

It took George half a dozen failed attempts of trying to modernize the way Temateng conducted its business before he accepted the reality about his position in the

173

family company. Although his title read Vice President of Logistics, he was a glorified, overpaid human resources manager. His days mostly consisted of settling petty disputes between coworkers and creating employee work schedules. After four years, he was finally fed up with being drastically underutilized. George confronted his mother about the situation on a car ride back to Accra from one of the Northern provinces. He remembered interrupting the silence of the car ride.

"Mom, you know I'm capable of being more than a figurehead for the company, correct?"

"Oh, son, you're doing fine. Don't worry; the company is doing well, and we won't fire you or cut your allow…" But before she said the whole word, she caught herself and finished the sentence with "salary."

But it was too late and the damage was done.

"You might as well say it," George protested, "allowance…That's what you see this as, don't you? An allowance that you're obligated to pay your spoiled son. I mean, do you even hold me accountable for the cupcake job I'm doing now? Do you know how embarrassing it is not to be taken seriously?"

Marguerite was slightly taken aback; her son rarely spoke to her in such an aggressive tone towards her. She resisted arguing, though, because she knew she had it coming. In a rare moment of contrition, she absorbed her urge to admonish George and instead attempted an apology. "I didn't know you felt so unfulfilled in your work. I guess I was just trying to protect you from failure."

"Well your 'protection' is ruining me. First, you ignore me in our weekly meetings, but at least I attended them. Now, you don't even invite me to the meetings. It would be different if you were schooling me and imparting wisdom along the way but, instead, you keep Temateng's operational information from me like it's classified intelligence. I'm tired of being a flunky. At this point, I'd take a pay cut to work for a bank or even manage a fast-food restaurant. Anything just to work for a company that appreciates my capabilities."

Marguerite nodded her head in agreement. "I understand. What do you want from me? How can I help you grow?"

George didn't need time to think about his needs; they were already well rehearsed. "For starters, I need to sit in on all of the executive meetings."

"Done," Marguerite replied.

"Let me finish. I no longer want to deal with babysitting the employees. If I am supposed to be the Vice President of Logistics, I want to manage the company's supply chain. I have ideas about how to help grow our distribution that need to be heard. But most importantly of all, I need you to take me seriously—as if I'm a valued partner and not like I'm still in grammar school. Stop giving me imaginary chores just to keep me occupied."

Even though George wasn't smiling, Marguerite was. She knew that was exactly what she'd been doing to him, pacifying him just to keep him out of her hair—just as she treated him when he was a child. "Okay, son, you're right. Here is what I'm willing to do: As of next week, I will delegate at least one item on every meeting agenda to you. Although I cannot let you take over the supply chain of the company right now, I can definitely let you work directly with Kofi to learn the ropes. He will groom you to eventually direct that side of the business. But most importantly, I will be more conscious of valuing your abilities."

George was not expecting all his demands would be met or that he'd get a full apology, so he was pleasantly surprised to get everything he wanted without excessive arguing. After that conversation, George's quality of life at work improved tremendously. He became a contributing executive to Temateng, and his university-trained recommendations were being utilized and were showing optimistic results.

Maria unknowingly interrupted George's internal highlights reel as she returned from the ladies' room. She kissed him on the cheek before noticing the residue of powder on the glass tabletop. She shook her head and rolled her eyes. "You fuckin' asshole! We're supposed to be having a romantic evening. I go pee and the first thing you do is get high as soon as I'm out of sight?"

"I'm sorry, babe. I'm fuckin' stressed, you know?"

She sighed and in a surprising twist of attitude replied, "I know...well do you at least have any more to share?" George looked like a dog just caught eating out of the trashcan. "You snorted all your drugs in five minutes, didn't you? Sneaky and stingy all in the same breath aren't ya?" She then stood up and grabbed her purse. "Please take me home now."

Chapter 27
The Gulf of Aden, Somalia
Present Day

Abdi Sulangi was a fisherman raised on the waters of the Gulf of Aden. He, his father, and grandfather all made their livings as fishermen along the coast of Somalia. It was a trade that would most likely have been passed down to Abdi's son, if not for the shambles Somalia was in due to its bloody civil war. After the war, there was no Navy to help protect the waters for Somalia's fishing trade; its waters were being violated by illegal fishing and toxic waste. A smart man, Abdi realized his family's lives as fishermen would soon become extinct and he felt compelled to do something about it. So at the urging of a colleague, Abdi decided to take action and join a patrol group called the Citizen's Navy.

The Citizen's Navy was mostly comprised of skilled fishermen, who were funded by Somali warlords. Abdi's group controlled their 110-kilometer section of the Gulf of Aden. After a number of international incidents, the Citizen's Navies were now commonly referred to as modern-day pirates. To reinforce their infamy, some crews fashioned themselves in ragged military fatigues often accessorized with scarves, gaudy jewelry, and makeup. Collectively, they were a menacing site. One survivor of a pirate hijacking told a London newspaper that her kidnappers reminded her of a savage gang out of the movie A Clockwork Orange.

Although amusing to the younger crews, the pirate moniker bothered Abdi. When he had originally joined the Citizen's Navy a few years back, Abdi truly believed that he and the organization were doing the noblest of deeds by protecting Somali waters and penalizing trespassers. It was a job he'd felt a functional government should be doing—if Somalia had one. Neo-piracy, as it has become known, was now peaking. Most ships were controlled by the powerful Somali warlord, Idreme, who was commissioned by an anonymous source to hijack vessels of his choosing. The hijacked cargo was to be split among the various crews and Idreme.

In addition to keeping the cargo and receiving compensation from their seizures, Abdi and his men earned bonuses, depending on the number of successful seizures. Idreme's anonymous source supplied the equipment and bribed the Indian Coast Guard to turn a blind eye. Abdi later learned that Idreme was commissioned by an international syndicate that extorted large freight and fishing companies for safe passage through the Gulf of Aden.

On this particular afternoon, Abdi received orders from Idreme to stop a vessel originating from China and carrying two tons of fish bound for Accra, Ghana. This order struck him as strange, because the boat they were to stop was normally considered permissible. Abdi gave it little thought and did not question the order. When the Chinese-based fishing vessel entered Abdi's area, he signaled it to approach for verification. Most other boats would be hesitant for obvious reasons, however, this vessel had no reason for alarm. They recognized the Somali ship and were aware that it was routine to cruise by and flash their credentials.

When the boat pulled up close enough, Abdi waved to the captain and motioned them to drop anchor while he and five crewmembers rode over on a speedboat. When they pulled alongside the Chinese boat, they climbed up the rope ladder minding their weaponry. A few of the Chinese crew even gave the Somali guests a hand getting aboard. The crew was all Chinese with one Ghanaian along for the ride. As Abdi started to speak to the captain, he was abruptly cut off by Idreme's liaison, Victor Asad.

"Abdi, I am instructed to take over from here. Step aside."
A puzzled Abdi quickly dismissed this as a joke. He ignored Asad and continued to address the captain, "Good afternoon captain. We're instructed to check your vessel to make sure everything is good." The next thing Abdi knew, the butt of Asad's rifle was rammed into his stomach.

"I told you to step down, fisherman!" Asad motioned his men to drag Abdi to a corner of the deck to catch his breath. The Chinese crew became alarmed when it dawned on them they were witnessing a mutiny among pirates. However, they were too concerned for their safety to appreciate the irony.

Asad yelled to the Chinese captain, "Do you speak English?"

The Chinese captain didn't understand English, so his Ghanaian passenger spoke up, "He does not, but I do." Asad quickly glanced at the Ghanaian, who continued, "I am Kofi Jackson, Vice President of Imports for Temateng Agricultural. I can assist you with what you need from my colleagues."

"Mr. Jackson," Asad retorted, "we were told to look for you. Do you also speak Chinese?"

"Yes, I speak Mandarin."

"Very well. Instruct your crew to go below deck so we can have a look around."

Kofi turned around and in Mandarin instructed the men to walk below with their hands in the air. Kofi followed with his hands in the air saying, "I don't understand. Temateng Agricultural has paid its monthly tax to the appropriate people. We paid cash too, I assure you."

"Yes, I understand, Mr. Jackson. However, today there is a different arrangement. Apparently, my boss' boss has an important message for your boss in Ghana. Now tell your crew to remain below and nobody will get hurt, okay?"

"Yes, boss man," Kofi said.

"Just get below!" grunted Asad. One-by-one, the Chinese crew and Kofi Jackson filed down the stairs with the Somali crew behind them. Abdi remained on deck after he was through vomiting; still in shock and pain, he sat up in his corner and tried to regain his strength. He tried to run different scenarios for this mutiny, when his train of thought was suddenly disrupted by ten to twelve distinct single-round shots from the pirates' AK47s. Before Abdi could stand, he saw Asad walking up the stairs.

"What the fuck is going on down there, Asad? I want to speak to their captain!"

Asad laughed. "You can try, my friend, but I don't think he or any of his crew will be responsive." When Abdi realized Asad and his men had just executed the crew, he threw up again. Asad handed him a rag to clean up his face and motioned for two of the crew to head back to their ship on the speedboat. The rest stayed on board and guided the Temateng vessel to shore. Asad motioned for another man to assist Abdi to the captain's office.

Abdi was placed in a chair with a gun pointed at him. Ten minutes passed before Asad came to speak to him. While wiping his hands and face free of blood, Asad instructed the man guarding Abdi to leave the room so the two could speak in private. Asad placed a cigarette in Abdi's mouth, lit it, and motioned for him to smoke.

"Abdi, I've always liked you, and I feel bad that I had to deceive you like this. But as a soldier, I am instructed not to ask questions, so I don't. A few days ago, Idreme ordered us to seize this vessel, take the ship back inland, and unload all of its cargo to our headquarters. I was also told that its crew must be dead when the boat touched dock. Despite what people say, I don't enjoy killing; I'm only following orders. Do you understand?"

Abdi grimaced and replied, "Yes."

"Abdi, I honestly have no idea what this is about. And truthfully I don't want to know."

"I don't either, Asad. I just want to go home to my family and get some rest. I beg you, please let me go; they need me!"

By the look in Abdi's eyes, Asad realized he feared for his life. "Do not worry. I'm not going to kill you, silly fisherman." A look of relief came over Abdi's face. "Unfortunately, I regret to tell you that your part of this mission has just begun. This boat was destined for West Africa. In a couple of days, the people in Ghana who were to receive this freight will realize the vessel is missing. Idreme needs you to go there and deliver a message in person. You are not to open or read the message, nor are

180

you to speak to anyone about what happened today or the nature of your trip. When you fulfill your mission, you will find your family safer, happier, and richer than you left them."

It was no surprise that Marguerite anticipated the arrival of cargo from her vendor in China. More importantly, she also awaited the arrival of her longtime companion, Kofi Jackson, who often traveled back to Ghana on their vendor's boat after doing Temateng's business in China. Much to Marguerite's annoyance, the boat in which Kofi was traveling did not arrive on schedule and was not responding to their communication attempts. She missed her companion and wanted nothing more than to enjoy Kofi's company.

Marguerite Boateng was technically the middle child, if you counted her older half-brother Oscar, who was six years her senior. Marguerite and her younger sister Felicia lived a charmed life as daughters of the renowned Ghanaian industrialist and statesman, Reginald Boateng. When the sisters were teens, they were hot commodities due to both their looks and pedigree. Many wealthy Ghanaian fathers made cash offers to marry a son to one of Reginald's daughters.

At one point, it even caused a rift in Reginald's relationship with the Asantehene. Even the Asantehene King wanted Reginald to commit one of his daughters to marry one of the princes and strengthen the royal family bloodline. To the disappointment of the Asantehene and other parental matchmakers, Reginald denied their requests. He believed in freedom of choice. He would not arrange his daughters' marriages because it would contradict everything he'd taught them to be: independent and strong-willed women.

Reginald's attitude about raising daughters contradicted the philosophy of most African men in the 1960s. Marguerite's father was not the only Ghanaian who held this philosophy. He and other free thinkers of his time had a significant role in aiding Kwame Nkrumah and the CPP to help Ghana succeed from the British in 1957. It was

182

only appropriate that the founding fathers of free Ghana would instill an independent spirit to their sons and daughters alike.

Each of Reginald's legitimate children took a different path to success: Oscar joined the British Navy and then went to university in England, later returning to Ghana to take over some of his father's business interests. Felicia, the youngest, received a master's degree in political science from Berkley and became a tenured professor at George Washington University. However, Marguerite's path was indirect. She skipped college and pursued love instead. As a young high school student in Ghana, she fell madly in love with Shallah Ndum, a bright young half Ghanaian, and half Togolese from an all-boys school down the road.

Their teenage romance evolved into much more; after they graduated, Marguerite became pregnant. During her pregnancy, the two moved to Accra to live with her parents, and the young couple had their first son George the following year. Some three years after George, she was pregnant with her second child Jasper. That unexpected pregnancy was the point when their relationship began to strain. The young father eventually finished at The University of Ghana with a degree in Biology. A week after George and Jasper's father graduated from Ghana University, their mother would find "The Letter," as she referred to it as in the future. It read:

"My Dearest Marguerite,
I am not ready to be the father and family man you expect. I will pursue my education in America by myself. When I am settled in my profession, I will send money for you and the children. My sincerest regrets Shallah."

"The Letter" dismantled Marguerite's world, which was further toppled when her father died five months later of a heart attack. After being ruthlessly abandoned by her fiancé and her father taken by the Lord, Marguerite pitied herself. It wasn't until her father's estate was settled a year

183

after his death that she would confront her true calling. Marguerite found that her father positioned her to inherit one of his most successful businesses, Temateng Agricultural.

When the girls were younger, Reginald took Marguerite to the docks to learn Temateng's business as a secretary, where she worked off and on since that time. She maintained their books, paid the invoices, and managed employees. Marguerite was the only possible successor, she just didn't know it. Inadvertently, she came to know the business almost better than Reginald. Within fifteen years of taking over Temateng Agricultural, the operation increased tenfold. Quite the innovator, Marguerite established strategic partnerships with Chinese farmers and fisherman years before it was common practice in the industry. If her father were still alive, he would be proud of his decision to bequeath the business to Marguerite. She turned Temateng Agricultural into the biggest distributor of grains, poultry, fish, and meat in West Africa.

Marguerite's work was truly a labor of love; her once-jilted heart was now gilded. Once she realized George and Jasper's father was never returning, she changed their last names to her maiden name Boateng. As Margeurite's business grew she leveraged her success to give her children the best education she could by sending them to English boarding schools. Although Margeurite missed her children, their absence gave her the freedom to grow Temateng Agricultural into the impressive business it would become.

It wasn't until eight years ago that she lifted her ban on men. It took Kofi Jackson, the recently hired Vice President of Imports, to lure the agricultural tycoon back into the dating pool.

The younger Kofi Jackson successfully courted his older boss by being confident but mostly by being competent. Kofi was an intellectually impressive man; he spoke English, Twi, Mandarin, Italian, and French and held a master's degree in business management. Not to mention, he was unafraid to stand up to Marguerite when

184

he knew she was wrong. Because of Marguerite's success, it had been decades since she met a man with the balls to say no. She slowly became smitten with Kofi Jackson. The two became lovers who understood each other's needs. Even Marguerite's protective sons admitted that Kofi was an ideal match for their mother.

Marguerite sat helplessly wondering about the whereabouts of the Chinese ship and Kofi Jackson. She knew boats arrived late, that was the nature of the business, but they always kept in communication. It took Marguerite two days before she was truly worried. Unfortunately, some of the waterways her vendor's boats traveled were treacherous, laden with bandits, and the "navies" protecting them were equally corrupt. Getting a definitive answer from the authorities was rarely easy. Marguerite was losing faith and decided to consult her nephew Clinton about the problem.

In a phone call, Marguerite explained to her nephew that Temateng Agricultural had expected a large shipment from one of its Chinese vendors three days ago. The vessel lost contact upon entering the Gulf of Aden and had not been heard from since. Clinton insisted she inform the proper authorities until she divulged her own cooperation with a Somali "organization" to protect her boats moving though Somali waters. Marguerite suspected the pirates would request ransom from her, so she felt it unwise to call in the authorities. She insisted Clinton have Roland Dufrane look into the matter discreetly.

Clinton was interrupted by a knock at the door. It was his assistant Kwasi informing him that he had a visitor with an important message involving the missing Temateng ship. Clinton thought it over for a minute before responding, "Who is he?"

"His name is Abdi Sulangi. He claims to be a Somali fisherman with information regarding your Aunt Marguerite's missing vessel. Should I buzz him up?"

"Has he been properly screened?" Clinton asked. "Metal detector, frisked, etc.?" Not prepared to take any chances, Clinton instructed Kwasi, "I don't want him up

185

here until he's been screened by Dufrane. Put him in interview room three, and have Dufrane give him a preliminary security interview for clearance."

"Sure thing."

An hour and a half passed before Dufrane called Clinton. "So who is this man?" Clinton asked.

"Apparently he's a Somali pirate who was on the ship the day it disappeared, and that's all he claims he's allowed to say. He says his message, which is loaded on a jump drive, should answer all of our questions. The catch is that there is an access code, and we won't be given the code unless he is free to go; he will text the code to you after his release. He also added that the message is to be viewed only by us, no other parties, especially the authorities."

"Does he sound believable to you?"

"He actually does." answered Dufrane.

"Very well. Let him leave, give him a secure cell phone number, and have him text the access code to me. Just make sure one of your men tails him after he leaves the building."

"Of course, I will have Claude follow him."

As promised, Abdi texted Clinton the access code. Clinton installed the jump drive to his office laptop while Dufrane watched. Not daring to risk any mishaps by not following orders, Clinton viewed the contents of the jump drive without the police. It was loaded with three photo files and a text document. He opened the photo files first. The first picture was of the Chinese fishing vessel bound for Ghana. The second photo showed the Chinese crew's bodies lying dead on the floor with bullet holes in the backs of their heads. The third and most disturbing picture was that of a beheaded Kofi Jackson.

Momentarily shocked, Clinton and Dufrane sat speechless. The grisly image of their friend Kofi Jackson was not a sight for the faint of heart. Clinton immediately became fearful, an uncommon sensation for him. More importantly, he was concerned for his Aunt Marguerite, as this would devastate her. Eventually he regained his

186

composure and opened up the text document. It was a note addressed to Clinton that simply read: "To avoid such actions happening again, stay out of business that does not concern you."

Clinton was seconds away from instructing Dufrane to retain Abdi Sulangi, when Dufrane received a call. He hung up the phone and gave Clinton the news: "Claude was following Abdi, who was just hit by an unmarked vehicle in the street. The vehicle sped off and we could not catch it. Abdi Sulangi is dead."

Dufrane called a last-minute security meeting for BOI executives at corporate headquarters in downtown Accra. Dufrane was showing rust and he knew it. Oscar Boateng's death could have been avoided had he only ignored Oscar's refusal to reinforce his home's security. Both Oscar and Kofi Jackson died on his watch; it was the worst failure he'd faced in his private-sector career. After the murder of Kofi Jackson, Dufrane offered his resignation to Clinton, who refused it. Instead, Clinton insisted Dufrane double down on his efforts to keep the family secure and find the culprit. Dufrane was determined to make a second-half comeback. While waiting for the BOI executives to arrive, he reflected on his life and how it had led him to this day.

Roland Dufrane had always admired the military while growing up in Annapolis, Maryland. His father was an admiral in the U.S. Navy during most of his adolescence. His mother Darlene was an elegant woman, yet with well-defined almost masculine facial features, which had emigrated from Israel not long after it was officially recognized as a country. Darlene longed to return to Israel and be a part of what she believed was the greatest country on earth. After Admiral Dufrane retired from the Navy, he moved his family to his wife's homeland.

Despite their friends' concerns, the Dufrane's move to Israel was quite successful. Admiral Dufrane was hired as a consultant to the Israeli Navy, and Darlene worked as a grade school teacher, while simultaneously getting involved in Middle East peace campaigns. Even Roland transitioned nicely as an awkward teenager in a new country. Growing up as a Jewish kid of Israeli descent in America, Roland's mother did not let him forget his religion and heritage. She taught him to speak Hebrew at an early age and took him to temple every week. So when Roland moved to Israel, the culture was familiar.

After Roland graduated from high school in

Jerusalem, he requested and was granted full Israeli citizenship and enlisted in the Israeli Army. There he flourished as an elite soldier, showing his bravery in several border skirmishes involving Syria and Palestine. It didn't take long for the Israeli brass to notice the aspiring soldier. Five years into his military career, Dufrane was recruited to join Israel's central intelligence agency, the Mossad. Dufrane's time as a field agent for the Mossad was classified. While he vaguely admitted to being involved in hit squads targeting Hezbollah leaders in the early 1990s, no one outside of the Mossad higher-ups knew anything else.

After eight years as a Mossad field agent, Dufrane's experience and expertise were needed on the international level. During the mid-1990s and after months of ignoring atrocities in Sierra Leone, the United Nations finally intervened. There was bitter fighting between the Sierra Leone government and rebels over control of the diamond mines, which were the country's economic backbone. Slowly but surely, the United Nations Security Council established an international presence in Sierra Leone. Several countries, including Israel, were asked to contribute soldiers to create the UN's presence in the region. Mossad leaders appointed Dufrane as Israel's senior officer.

In Sierra Leone, Dufrane was in charge of organizing commissioned mercenaries to assist the government in eradicating the rebels. Although many innocent lives were lost before the UN's mediation, the mercenaries' presence in Sierra Leone ultimately helped secure the safety of innocent civilians in the war-torn country. Despite his orders to stay out of combat, Dufrane spent the majority of his time helping the mercenaries fight the bloodthirsty rebels. Dufrane saw firsthand the atrocities he'd read about in his United Nation's briefings: He witnessed cases of children with their limbs chopped off by rebel soldiers who were children themselves. He saw captured villagers working as slaves in death-trap diamond mines.

The rebels guarded the mines with every fiber of their beings. They depended on the diamonds yielded by the mines to fund their military operations. Knowledge of the tragedies in Sierra Leone motivated Dufrane to work harder than he ever had in his military career. Dufrane would later say that after his time in Sierra Leone, he vowed never to purchase a diamond because he personally witnessed the human sacrifice that went into each stone.

Relatively speaking, the UN operations in Sierra Leone were successful. Its presence quickly eradicated the rebel offensive from rural strongholds so the ousted government could return. However, peace wouldn't come without being slapped in the face by the international community. Once word got out to the rest of the world that the UN was using mercenaries in Sierra Leone, there was an outcry from international organizations demanding the UN suspend its use of mercenaries. Eventually the UN succumbed to the pressure and pulled the Special Forces out of Sierra Leone prematurely without as much as a thank you for their efforts.

Although the war ended soon after Dufrane's Special Forces were extracted, plenty of civilian lives were caught in the balance. He agonized over how many more lives were lost due to their early departure, and his repeated pleas to his UN superiors to stay the course and finish the job fell on deaf ears. They were forced to pull out of Sierra Leone with the knowledge that the rebels would slaughter hundreds more civilians in retaliation for their defeat.

At this point in Dufrane's career, he was fed up with military bureaucracy. Following his mission in Sierra Leone, he immediately requested a discharge from the Mossad. Now a civilian, Dufrane remained in West Africa. He founded Equator Alliance, a private security group that provided security services for high-profile dignitaries and affluent types throughout West Africa. Equator Alliance quickly gained a reputation for exemplary work by preventing and foiling several kidnapping and extortion attempts for its clients.

It didn't take long for Ghana's Oscar Boateng to

learn of Roland Dufrane and his security company. At the time, Oscar was in the market for a proactive security detail, following a rash of fatal home invasions targeting Accra's affluent residents. A petty-crime syndicate had been paying young men to rob fancy homes. The thieves also took three lives in the process; one of the men killed happened to be a close friend of Oscar's. It's safe to say that Oscar took his friend's death personally.

However, his need to combat this injustice had more to do with Oscar, the businessman. He knew if these fatal robberies were reported to the media and reached the international business community, it would give Ghana a bad reputation and jeopardize outside investment. Oscar had no confidence in the local police, yet he knew someone had to put an end to the terrorizing. Oscar went to many of the affluent Ghanaians and politicians who had a stake in seeing the problem disappear. He offered to end the problem out of his own pocket, with the understanding that these businessmen and politicians owed him significant favors in return. Brokering deals like that was how Oscar amassed much of his political and private-sector influence.

Oscar invited Dufrane, who headquartered his business in Lagos, Nigeria, to his villa in Tema to get to know each other and determine how to identify the culprits and bring them to justice. In a matter of hours, Oscar and Dufrane came to an undisclosed agreement. The next day, Dufrane dispatched five of his special agents to Ghana from Lagos to assist him with Oscar's case.

After a week of reconnaissance work, Dufrane and his men isolated the culprit behind the home invasions— Victor Mensah. A vile, crude excuse for a human being, Victor Mensah was a well-known criminal, whose diabolical deeds included the kidnapping of teenagers to pimp as prostitutes and narcotics peddlers. It was also rumored that Mensah sexually abused many of the teenagers he employed.

It didn't take long for Dufrane's intelligence to conclude Mensah masterminded the recent home invasions and had plans to continue. Unfortunately for Mensah, his greed would lead to his demise. Although Mensah paid off low-level police officers to look the other way, he did not account for their limitations. They may have been able to turn a blind eye to Mensah peddling drugs and promoting prostitution, but when it came to murdering Oscar Boateng's friend, no one could protect Mensah from his fate.

Dufrane had undercover agents tip off Mensah about an unguarded house that was supposedly stocked with jewelry, furniture, and expensive electronics. Mensah was obliged to take the bait, and his amateur crew would be lured into an ambush. That evening, Dufrane and his team looked like professional cat burglars out of a 1970s heist film. Mensah's crew of young boys stood zero chance against the experienced team that greeted them inside the home. The scuffle was executed with finesse. One of agents appeared from the coat closet as soon as the burglars popped the lock on the door and struck the butt of his gun in the head of the first young bandit. The rest of Dufrane's men drew their weapons on the boys, to which they smartly cooperated and dropped their guns. The boys were apprehended and tied up within five minutes. Dufrane later ordered his agents to sedate the thieves with a strong dose of chloroform.

Simultaneously, two of Dufrane's agents easily captured Mensah napping in one of his brothels. Wearing nothing but a robe and gaudy jewelry, Mensah was so drunk from palm wine that he tried to urinate on the men when they drew their guns on him. Mensah believed the men to be local police and naturally assumed he'd be back home after his men paid off the officers. Instead, he was Tasered into unconsciousness and Dufrane's part in the mission was complete.

The next phase was Oscar Boateng's brainchild. He utilized a brand of Akan folklore that was as creative as it was sinister. When the unfortunate bandits came to, they found themselves in a dank, dark, and abandoned unfinished concrete building. Dimly lit torches were mounted in various areas around the room, serving as the

192

only source of light. The young men were gagged and bound to chairs. Their heads covered in paper bags with two eyeholes; they could see but neither move nor talk. They were all seated in a row, except for Mensah, whose robe was now draped off his arms with nothing to cover his naked body but shell jewelry and some odd tribal markings. He was placed eight feet in front of the other captives and positioned on a rustic wooden throne that was surrounded by stones in a ceremonial formation.

By the look of it, Mensah already had a significant amount of head trauma. Both he and his henchmen tried to make contact with each other but could not because they were bound and gagged. They were each more confused and scared as the next. Minutes after they awoke, they heard the faint noise of hand drums, shakers, and low humming transitioning into louder chanting. The vibration became more and more recognizable as it made its way up the stairs of the abandoned building. When Mensah and the other captives finally realized the source of the music, some proceeded to soil themselves.

A line of six Akan tribesmen dressed in traditional Akan war gear entered the room. They looked like exaggerated images of primitive Africans pictured in old books. When the tribesmen entered the room, they created a formation around Mensah with three men on either side of him. Once in formation, the drumming and chanting ceased. Only the muffled screams from the fear-stricken men were heard. Behind the tribesmen, a door slowly creaked open and produced a gangly seven-foot man. The giant's complexion was as black as crude oil, contrasted by contact lenses as orange as the sun. His face and parts of his body were decorated with a chalky white paste. The men held against their will immediately knew him to be the devilish spirit named Boopa.

As children, most Ghanaians have heard the story of Boopa. Folklore says that Boopa was half man, half beast, who came to earth to recruit the wickedest of humans to join his army in hell—but not before he baptized them in a lake of their own blood. The story of Boopa has been used

193

to scare children into behaving themselves for centuries in Ghana. However, just like the boogieman in western households, as children grew older they failed to appreciate the legend of Boopa. So one can only imagine the immense fear Mensah and the other hostages felt when they witnessed Boopa emerge from the shadows.

Boopa stood in front of Mensah and removed his gag. Without delay or shame, Mensah predictably blamed the robberies and murders on the boys and begged for his life. Boopa did not respond. Instead, the demonic creature turned to face the line of his young prisoners while brandishing a large jagged dagger, its handle intricately carved in gold.

Boopa strolled in front of his recruits like a lieutenant inspecting his platoon. He showed them the sharp dagger, while his left index finger pointed at his widely opened left eye, as if to say look. The boys sensed something horrific was about to happen. When Boopa turned around again, Mensah had passed out with fear. Boopa had one of the tribesmen resuscitate Mensah by smacking him so hard in the face that spittle flew from his open mouth.

When Mensah awoke, his torso was slowly being carved like a pumpkin. He screamed louder than a hospital ward of newborn babies. Blood spilled out of his belly like a waterfall. The boys proceeded to watch Mensah being gutted like bush meat. And just as the blood really flowed, a smiling Boopa violently yanked a handful of Mensah's intestines and thrust the slaughterhouse cords into the air, splashing traces of blood, bile, and excrement on everyone in the room. Boopa finalized Mensah's baptism by ringing the toxic juices from the intestines over the dead man's head. Boopa then motioned his tribesmen to remove Mensah's body.

The gangly demon turned to the boys and addressed them in Twi, "And let this be my formal invitation to you. I will collect your souls in due time if you continue on your impressive path of ruin." He smiled at the boys, exposing his fangs, and then descended back into the

194

portal from which he emerged as the Akan entourage followed, but not before inducing their surviving victims with another strong dose of chloroform.

The next morning, the boys found themselves in the abandoned building clothed and untied. If it weren't for Mensah's bloody robe lying in the wooden throne where he once sat alive, they might have thought the previous night's events were a dream. The young bandits quickly scurried out of the abandoned building. After that night, the rash of Accra home invasions ended.

Dufrane and his men were only commissioned to handle the abduction of Mensah and his bandits. They delivered the captives to an abandoned building twenty-three miles outside of Accra's city limit. Dufrane asked no questions about Oscar's plans for his haul. It wasn't until much later when they developed a friendship, that Oscar revealed Mensah's fate to Dufrane. Dufrane learned that Oscar commissioned the men who played Boopa and his cast of Akan tribesman. They were in a secret society of West African vigilantes, who specialized in ritual killings. He did not judge Oscar, rather, he could appreciate the old man's twisted sense of justice.

Chapter 30
Accra, Ghana
Present Day

BOI's headquarters were located in a newly built office building in downtown Accra. BOI's north-wing boardroom usually boasted a panoramic view of the continuing modernization of Accra. However, today the curtains were drawn and the boardroom was dim. All of the top BOI executives were present except for Marguerite Boateng. Although no one wanted to admit it, an air of paranoia permeated the room.

Dufrane requested the meeting, but Clinton opened it up. "Marguerite could not make it today, and personally, I can't imagine anyone who has been through what she has making appearance." He looked at George and Jasper. "I know your mom is a very private woman, but please remind her that we are here for her. Whatever she needs."

Jasper and George both nodded. Clinton continued, "These are troubling times for us. As we mourn two very important family members, I am seriously concerned about the security of each and every person in this room. At this time, I am going to turn the floor over to Roland." Nodding his head, he gestured for Roland to start.

Dufrane poured himself a cup of hot water with a freshly cut lemon slice. "From now on, security must be our top priority. And I don't mean that as some lame 'safety-first' cliché—I mean that BOI is currently at code red. Members of this organization have been targeted and tragically taken from us." Dufrane began to walk around the room. "I've commissioned a round-the-clock security detail for each member in this room along with some of our high-ranking managers. When I say around the clock, I mean 24/7. That means that if you have to leave town, your security detail accompanies you. If you have to slip out of the house to bang your mistress, your security detail will probably be the guy buying you the condoms. We are on lockdown until we find out what is going on and who is responsible."

George Boateng spoke up. "Well, you're head of security, what the hell is going on, Roland? Can you explain how the fuck we pay off these pirates and still have our vessel hijacked and people murdered?"

Dufrane could tell George had been up all night. He'd felt it unnecessary to mention his reports on George, who was drinking more than ever and had turned his rare cocaine use into a daily habit. Although Dufrane did not share that information, he understood why George was behaving like an ass on this particular morning. It was obvious that, out of all of Oscar's nephews, George tried to emulate Oscar the most and had taken his death the hardest.

"I understand your frustration, but as head of security, I beg your patience while we fully investigate the matter. The information is coming in from all directions, and we are trying to put the pieces together."

"Ah, bullocks!" George heckled, but Dufrane did not take his bait.

"Mr. Van Bleer," Dufrane continued, "I'm afraid we'll have to keep you grounded in Ghana for the next few months. Providing the proper security detail for your weekly trips to Holland will be prohibitively expensive. We will at least need to cut them down to once a month or less."

Van Bleer cleared his throat. "You do realize that my children from my first wife live in Holland, correct?"

"Harry," Clinton interrupted, "I'm sorry, but it was my decision. Dufrane gave me an estimate of how much the security detail would cost if everyone went about business as usual. The fact of the matter is that we will all have to travel less. It just so happens that your travel is more frequent than anyone else's."

"Okay, couldn't I just stay in Holland and travel back to Ghana once a month?"

Clinton expected Harry to question the decision, but he didn't have the patience and ended the conversation with, "It won't be forever, Harry, I assure you, but for the meantime you're grounded. Marguerite informed me this

197

morning that she wants to retire. Her Chinese partners have been offering to buy her out for years and she thinks it's time."

George was now out of his seat. "Are you serious, man? Mom never ran this past me!" He looked at his brother. "Jabs, you know about this?"

Jasper shrugged his shoulders. "No, but it's the right thing to do, initit'? Makes sense to me, mate. Mom's been through a lot and she deserves to retire."

"So you don't find it a problem that mom didn't consult us before she made a decision?"

Jasper with no enthusiasm in his voice said, "I trust that she knows what's right for her company."

George looked around the room and shook his head. "You know what? You're right, it's none of me business. Gentlemen, my business is football and right now, our future looks bright."

Clinton looked at Jasper and Dufrane. He said, "Harry, can you excuse us please? This portion of the meeting is adjourned for you."

"Certainly."

Clinton asked Dufrane, "What are the specifics of George's security detail?"

Dufrane cleared his throat. "Well it's not set in stone but George's security detail will be more relaxed due to the fact that he conducts most business locally and is already working within the confines of our security."

"Well all that's about to change, mate," George interrupted. "My business is no longer just in Accra and Kumasi. Not sure if Jabs or Clinton informed you, but I will, since you're practically part of the family. On behalf of the legendary Asante Royals Football Club, I am in the midst of signing Coufis Zatan to play for us." He then clapped his hands and let out an obnoxious laugh. "I already have arrangements to travel to England and negotiate the contract for Coufis's release. Not to mention signing television contracts with our European affiliates. But you don't need to beef up me detail too much. I'm sure Jabs won't mind if I take one or two of his goons with me.

198

They'll work for beer, I imagine." He winked at Jasper.

Jasper looked at Dufrane and asked him to excuse them. Dufrane obliged and left the room.

"There is no easy way to say this, so I am just going to come out with it," Clinton announced. "You cannot follow through with the Coufis Zatan deal."

George looked at them both and laughed. "What is this some kind of joke?"

"No," Clinton replied, "BOI is moving in a different direction, and we are focusing our resources in areas outside of football. Plus, it wasn't a prudent decision on your part George. You didn't consult us before you pursued Zatan. But, as always, the final decision rests with the board, and we will have to revisit it next season after the third fiscal quarter is complete. There is no way Asante Royals brings in enough money to support even one fifth of the salary you propose to pay Zatan. That transaction would require all of BOI's other businesses to cover the balance. With today's ticket sales, there is no strategic model that projects a substantial return on that kind of investment in Coufis Zatan."

"That's bullocks!" George yelled. "The stadiums would sell out for the season. The money off jersey sales alone will skyrocket. Hell, I already know Nigerian oil tycoons who will surely buy out the box suites. Can you imagine how much business this would bring to Kumasi? What the hell is wrong with you, Clinton? BOI is on target to be a billion dollar company in 5 years. Who cares about losing a few mil?"

"I'm sorry, George, but Zatan is out," Clinton said.

"There is more at stake here, George," Jasper said. "There are other forces influencing our decision."

George interrupted his brother, "Give me a second here, Jabs. Clinton, do you really think that making history and getting one of the world's greatest football stars to play for an African club will backfire in any way?"

"The simple answer is yes," Clinton said.

"Ah, you fucking Obruni! What the hell do you know about Africa? I hear you still call football "soccer," and it even makes the houseboys laugh behind your back."

A blindsided Clinton took his cousin's bait and engaged him. "Obruni you say? You should be so lucky for this Obruni. Before I arrived, you were in the minor leagues George....Little did you know early on I recognized your underutilized talents and insisted uncle put you in a position of importance. I'm not saying you have to thank me George, but try not to spit me in the face while doing it.

George got up and screamed, "I am not your charity case, and I've never needed your handouts, cousin. The rest of you can do whatever the hell you want to. I'm done with this meeting." He then unceremoniously walked out.

Clinton looked at Jasper, who joked, "He actually took it better than I thought."
Unlike Jasper, Clinton found no humor in George's rant. This was the second time he had been called an Obruni and he was growing weary of it. Clinton shook his head and called Dufrane back into the room.

Dufrane walked back in with several files in his hand. He opened the files and spread the contents across the table. First, he pulled out a picture of Max Cotto. "I'm sure you all know this fella, Max Cotto, your cousin and also Oscar's bastard son. We have reason to believe he was the gunman who killed Oscar. We tailed him and got in touch with his aunt, who owns a chop bar by the Makola Market. After my associate, Claude, and I interviewed her, she called the next day to tell me that when she went through Max's belongings, she found items that she suspected were stolen from Oscar's home. After examining the items in question, they match up with missing contents from Oscar's home the night of his murder. Most importantly we recovered your uncle's original copy of your grandfather Reginald's journal. Max had his Aunt Susanna keep it with her among his other belongings he wanted kept safe."

Jasper cringed at the news of Max Cotto being the culprit, however, the news of the recovered journal brought comfort to Jasper, and the words soothed Clinton as well even though he was privy to this information beforehand.

Dufrane paused to let this information sink in before continuing, "I guess you can say that Max had a natural motive to kill Oscar. He felt that his father wanted nothing to do with him, and he blamed Oscar for all the problems in his life. After speaking with the police, I'm sure that is how it will be reported. Although I believe a better-connected party put him up to this, it behooves us to let the public buy the police statement."

"And why aren't we buying the story, Dufrane?" Jasper asked.

"The same reason you brought Max to my attention in the first place, Jasper: for an alcoholic drug addict, who had just been released from prison, Max suddenly had money and was spending so much of it people became nervous. So nervous that it was brought to your attention, as I recall. When we followed Max, we tracked him to Brojode restaurant, which is owned by Ishmael Ltd." Dufrane pulled out a picture and placed it on the table. "This is Anwar Ishmael, the head of the Ishmael Group—or as Interpol likes to call them, the Lebanese mafia. Although he was born and raised in Beirut, the outfit's headquarters are in Dubai.

"Ishmael is described as a broker of bad deeds. According to Interpol, he is a drug trafficker and terrorist profiteer among other things. He is suspected of financing such acts of terrorism as the Vaj Hotel slaughter in Bombay and several insurgency campaigns in Afghanistan and Iraq. For the right price, he is a prolific launderer of money for extremist organizations and drug cartels. When I worked for the Mossad, Ishmael was on our radar but back then, he was just a rough-and-tumble gangster. Never did I think he would achieve this level of notoriety."

By this time, Dufrane's water with lemon had cooled, so he was taking more breaks in between sentences. "As you know, West Africa has a significant Lebanese population, especially in Ghana. The Lebanese have been in Ghana for several generations. Many of them are merchants and retailers in the natural-resources industry. The Ishmael Group has been dispatching its own

201

people to operate these businesses in Ghana for over fifteen years. In Ishmael's defense, his Ghanaian operations are technically legitimate. He owns commercial real estate, such as malls and small retail strips that are leased to his Lebanese network of entrepreneurs. He also owns a large logging enterprise in northern Ghana, where lumber is exported to worldwide markets

"These legitimate businesses are used as the vehicles to launder money for his underworld clientele. However, the Ghana market has traditionally been small potatoes for the Ishmael Group. The meat of Ishmael's operations outside of his Dubai headquarters happens in Egypt, India, Pakistan, Afghanistan, Kuwait, and Saudi Arabia. It wasn't until oil was discovered off the coast of Ghana that our country became integral to his business. You see, the Ishmael Group has staffed large corporations with cheap labor all over the Middle East and Africa for years. He has a long history with the German company PetroCo Oil, mostly for staffing oilrigs and bribing politicians for them in Nigeria, Kuwait, and other oil-rich countries with unstable governments. After oil was discovered off Ghana's coast, the government knew they needed outside expertise to drill the oil, so its best option was to subcontract the work to an experienced oil-drilling company. Ghana will lease the wells to that corporation for an annual commission.

"Four large oil companies were asked to bid in the Request-for-Proposal process, and Ghana is poised to select PetroCo Oil. According to my sources, PetroCo Oil Chairman Gordon Heinrich was approached by Anwar Ishmael to help him guarantee that PetroCo would win the contract due to his presence in the region. Ishmael and his associates have been greasing the palms of government officials of the countries they do business in for years, including Ghana. The plus for Ishmael was that, at the time of Ghana's oil discovery, President Abna Amoako had already been in the pocket of the Ishmael Group for several years. PetroCo brokered a deal with Ishmael that he would receive over a billion dollars in compensation plus an exclusive contract to outsource all labor to his organization in all of their African and Middle-East operations including Ghana—if he delivered the Ghana deal."

Clinton then took over because he felt Dufrane's military-style briefing was now anything but brief. "Weeks before uncle's death he had a closed-door meeting with PetroCo executives. It just so happened that Oscar was the most influential person making the recommendation to Ghana's selection committee about which firm should be awarded Ghana's exclusive oil-drilling contract. PetroCo courted his endorsement. However, Oscar refused based on his knowledge of which company would be better for our country and its people, and informed them he would be endorsing Freestar Oil. While I don't believe that PetroCo's CEO and their stock holders were aware of Ishmael's plan to murder our uncle, their agenda is the direct cause of it."

Jasper interrupted, "How do you know all of this?"

Clinton thought before he spoke. He knew he had given his word to the vice president that he would not mention their personal relationship to anyone. That was, of course, before he knew his family's lives were at risk. He decided that Jasper and Dufrane were perhaps the two men he trusted most at this moment. He decided to come clean. "At Oscar's funeral, Vice President Bonswah pulled me aside and told me everything I just told you. He asked me to make a presentation on behalf of Oscar that was supposed to persuade the committee to vote for Freestar."

"So, did you do it?" Jasper asked.

"Yes, I did and it failed horribly," Clinton admitted. "Dufrane and I also discovered that Ishmael taxes freight to travel across the Gulf of Aden, including your mother's Temateng ships. More than likely, it was Ishmael who commissioned the Somali pirates to hijack Marguerite's ship and kill Kofi Jackson and the crew."

Jasper summarized, "So you're saying this Ishmael asshole hired Max to kill uncle and some pirates to kill Kofi Jackson? All for what?"

Clinton answered, "He had Oscar killed because he would block the PetroCo deal. With Oscar gone, President

Amoako can easily deliver the drilling contract to PetroCo, which translates to almost a billion dollars in commission for Ishmael."

Jasper nodded his head. "So what does Kofi Jackson's death have to do with this?"

Clinton explained, "For an extra level of intimidation and as a warning to BOI, Ishmael had Kofi Jackson killed to illustrate just how serious he is and what he's willing to do to get what he wants."

Jasper's well-documented rage began to emerge. "Oh yeah? He wants us to know how serious he is? Well he's got me fuckin' attention now!" Jasper shouted. "I'd rather tongue kiss the grim reaper than hide from this Ishmael pisser. Me and the guys will meet this bitch wherever he's at. You get me?"

Dufrane nodded and put his hands out to gesture for Jasper to calm down. "I understand your anger, Jabs, however, we have to treat the Ishmael situation in a suitable manner. He's too heavy to challenge him head on; you know this, Jabs."

Jasper got up from his seat and rubbed his face with two hands to calm down. "Just tell me we're gonna get Ishmael."

Clinton walked over to his cousin and put his hand on his shoulder as an assurance. "We need your help with this, Jabs; but a cool-headed approach is absolutely necessary. We more than likely have to look into all options...including the possibility of getting the authorities involved."

Jasper didn't look at Clinton. He kept his head directed at the window, accepted the truth, and nodded in agreement.

Vice President Bonswah was no longer irritated when he was forced to wait in the lobby of the presidential headquarters, sometimes for up to an hour, while President Amoako wrapped up his previous meetings. He knew the president could schedule his meetings further apart but suspected Amoako liked making him wait for his own amusement. Presidents of older regimes excluded their vice presidents from military cabinet meetings for fear of a coup d'état. This president was a throwback in that regard. Amoako had no reason to believe that Bonswah would plot against him, rather, he used the old practice of alienation to assert his authority. Bonswah put himself at ease by knowing that the president had every right to feel insecure. If it weren't for Amoako begging Bonswah to run on his ticket at the last minute, he probably would have lost the close election.

President Amoako's saving grace was his charisma, however, no one ever accused him of being an intellectual. At the time of his election, candidate Amoako was the kind of person who distracted people with his self-deprecating sense of humor. He embraced his flaws—at least the ones he could afford to show the public. This was a disarming political strategy that deceived the public into thinking he was one of their own. Political insiders and pundits never took candidate Amoako seriously, though. To this day, you can still find members of the press corps scratching their heads trying to figure out how he was ever elected.

During the debates, Amoako rarely had a command of the important issues necessary for any candidate to be considered legitimate. The equalizer was his opponent's ability to put everyone to sleep. Vice President Bonswah, then Parliamentarian Bonswah, was begged to join the ticket to add some legitimacy and youth to the Amoako ticket. This was proven as Amoako's poll numbers jumped by four points overnight when he announced the moderate and well-liked Bonswah as his running mate.

Now, here he sat waiting on the president as if it were he who'd begged the president to become a part of his own administration. Bonswah was forty-five minutes into his notes when the president's assistant Joseph Nyum said, "Mr. Vice President, the president will see you now."

When Bonswah entered the office, President Amoako was making a drink—a stiff martini on the rocks, to be exact, which was his new thing. For Christmas, Amoako's wife, of all people, had given him a martini kit and a fully stocked bar for his office. Since then, he made a customary martini at 5:00 p.m. on the dot nearly every day.

"Mr. President," Bonswah greeted with a head nod.

"I would fix you one, but unless times have changed and Muslims drink, I will save my gin," the president laughed.

"Thank you for your consideration," Bonswah obliged with a smile.

"Have a seat, Mr. Bonswah."

Bonswah sat down and pulled out his pen. "What's on your mind, sir?"

Amoako wasted time by fiddling with his drink and studying his vice president before saying, "I have informed PetroCo's director that I will make a formal recommendation to award the Ghanaian oil contract to PetroCo Oil. And I want to know what you think."

Bonswah cleared his throat and said, "I think if you really wanted to know what I thought about PetroCo, you should have consulted with me before you officially contacted PetroCo."

The president raised his eyebrow. "So I take it that you are comfortable with BOI being the only organization to make a recommendation to the committee?"

"Never mind that," Bonswah replied. "Tell me, why are you sold on PetroCo, sir?"

"PetroCo is one of the most experienced and successful oil companies in the business. They have done business in West Africa and are offering us an impressive compensation package."

Bonswah laughed. "Freestar is offering us a 32% commission to PetroCo's 25%…and Freestar plans to employ Ghanaian citizens to work on its oil rigs, not Middle Eastern foreigners. With all due respect, it's not even close. How can you think PetroCo offers us a more impressive package?"

Pinky out and all, the president took a sip of his martini and said, "How many times have you met the CEO of Freestar?"

Before Bonswah could respond, the president answered, "Once! Do you know how many times the CEO of PetroCo has been down here? Five times. Bonswah, I know you studied abroad and you are quite the intellectual, but you are no Obruni. You are a proud Fante man who loves his country. So I trust that you still know how we Ghanaians work. Our business culture is such that we believe in personal relationships, and it is those relationships that build a strong foundation."

"Mr. President," Bonswah interjected and proceeded to break down some statistics for Amoako. "With all due respect, that old-school mentality has no place in a debate of this magnitude. Right now, Ghana's GDP is nearly $20 billion and our unemployment rate is still between 22% and 25%. Although our economy has improved, we are still very much a developing country that depends on foreign aid. PetroCo's deal does not address either of those issues as well as Freestar's. You mentioned BOI, and you can say what you want, but BOI has already proven its good faith, and I don't think we should view them as our enemy but rather as our ally." Bonswah was now worked up.

Amoako sighed. "Please, save the campaigning for an election and come back down to reality. Have you ever seen any of our former presidents and vice presidents after they retired? Many of them are still struggling to pay their mortgages even at older ages, they stress themselves over money they need to live a comfortable lifestyle. Ghana has no retirement plans for us. It's unthinkable that after all the hard work public servants like you and I have put in, we may not have enough to retire. This year alone, I traveled to almost every neighborhood in the Volta region when the flood hit. I made sure that the international aid was dispersed in record time. I have been meeting with diplomats all over the globe in efforts to put Ghana in favor with powerful countries."

Bonswah wanted to laugh. He knew the president's trips overseas were hardly productive; they were mostly vacations, where he partied like a sailor on leave. However, he let the president continue with his delusion. "So you see, Bonswah, PetroCo has offered me (and don't forget you, too) the chance to be properly compensated for our hard work so we don't have to stress in our old age. PetroCo knows West Africa; PetroCo knows Ghana."

Bonswah shook his head. "Now who is campaigning? Truth is, PetroCo knows how to cheat West Africa, PetroCo knows how to cheat Ghana."

The president now wore a look of frustration. "I am sorry you feel that way, but I am going to need you to get over it quickly." He then stood up and buttoned up his suit jacket. "Because, on behalf of the administration, I task you with making the formal presentation to recommend PetroCo Oil to the selection committee."

Bonswah felt like someone had swiftly punched him in the gut and knocked the wind out of him. He almost had difficulty breathing and was momentarily rendered speechless. He knew what Amoako was trying to do— make it virtually impossible for Bonswah to distance himself from this oil fiasco in the future. But, most importantly, Bonswah could not imagine being the one to deliver the final blow to Freestar's efforts to win the oil contract. He truly believed Freestar was the right company for the job and that its involvement would help galvanize success instead of hindering it.

The president downed the rest of his martini and said, "You don't have to give me your answer now. You can have the week to think about it. But if your answer is no, I will also be expecting your resignation on this desk." President Amoako then walked out of his office.

Bonswah was speechless and said nothing about the meeting until he got home and picked up his private phone. "Clinton," Vice President Bonswah said, "we have a problem."

Jasper Boateng loved his late-model Audi Coupe. Normally when driving a machine of such caliber, he would turn off the radio just to hear the sound of the engine purr. Jasper parked his car, turned off the radio, and tipped the valet $20 to leave it parked in front of the Asante Royals football stadium. The valet knew Jasper and greeted him enthusiastically. "Wicked whip, Jabs!" Jasper walked over to his security detail's black Range Rover trailing him and asked them to wait in the parking lot while he visited with his brother.

After walking up and down the corridors of the sprawling new stadium, he finally found his brother on the practice field. George Boateng looked out of place in his tailored suit, while footballers in red-and-yellow jerseys darted back and forth going through their drills. From a distance, Jasper could tell by his brother's arm gestures that he was displeased with whomever he was talking to. When Jasper got closer, he saw George was now pointing his finger at the team's head coach. Apparently, he was upset the coach had made a sympathetic decision to rest one of the star players in the weekend's upcoming match.

Jasper decided to intervene before the coach took a swing at George; the man's bulging eyes indicated that he'd had enough of George. Jasper could also tell by the look on George's face that he was on the verge of offering a pink slip to the coach, who many regarded as the best in Asante Royals' history.

"Hey brother," Jasper interrupted as he grabbed his brother's bicep, "the last thing you need is for some reporter putting that exchange in the tabloids."

George gave Jasper a stay-out-of-this look. He then lowered his voice and said to the coach, "Just play the damn kid, okay? Our ticket sales depend on it." George walked away from the coach and past his brother as if to say, If you want to talk, you have to walk with me.

"What do you want, Jabs?" George was clearly annoyed.

Jasper jogged up to catch up with his brother. "I want you to take a ride with me."

"A ride, Jabs? I don't have time now," George said dismissively.

"That's too bad because I just copped that new Audi," Jasper teased.

George stopped walking, "When you say 'new,' you mean the model that doesn't hit the floor for months?"

"That's right," Jasper confirmed.

"So your connection came through?"

"That's right."

George laughed. "You cheeky bastard. You never were one for patience."

Jasper laughed in agreement. It was true that he was usually the more impatient one. Their mother would always call Jasper "the impatient boy." She often said he was born prematurely because he couldn't wait for the world to come to him. However, when it came to the latest business at hand, Jasper had been the more patient and composed of the two brothers. When BOI made the decision to block George's acquisition of Coufis Zatan, Jasper felt he was acting like a spoiled child, who couldn't understand why he didn't get the toy he wanted for Christmas. When the two brothers reached the car, Jasper silently waited for his brother's reaction.

"I thought you wanted the black one. I told you the silver looked better, but you swore up and down the black one looked better." George shook his head and smiled. "Unfucking believable; so what are you waiting for? Take me for a spin, little brother."

Jasper knew his brother all too well. Despite his lackluster reaction, he could tell George was impressed. When he hit the remote to unlock the door, George took the keys and said, "Let me drive. I've seen how you treat your cars, and these roads do not make for a smooth ride in a sports car going drastically over the speed limit." He paused and added, "I can't believe you drove this car from

Accra to Kumasi."

"And why not?"

"Because the ride is terrible on those rough roads."

Jasper was almost embarrassed when he answered, "I didn't make the drive. I flew and made Big Sperm drive the car."

George laughed and said, "Unfucking believable, so you mean you had Sperm make the three-hour drive just so you could roll around in your new toy while you were in town? I've got to say, I thought I had the reputation for being the prima donna, but that is some really arrogant shit, Jabs. And you guys thought buying Coufis was wasteful spending? At least his name would've sold tickets."

Jasper took advantage of the sarcastic remark to get down to business. "George we have to talk."

"Look Jabs, you don't have to feed me Clinton's talking points anymore; I'm over it, really," George said preemptively.

"Really?" Jasper asked unconvincingly. "Because I haven't heard from you or seen you in over two weeks, man. You don't return any phone calls, and when you're in Accra, you stay locked up in your flat. Even mom has made a point of slowly coming out of her hole. I mean, I know this deal means a lot to you, but Kofi was priceless to mom."

"Ah fuck, Jabs, since when do you get to be the voice of reason? Aren't you the hot-tempered one?

Jasper anticipated his brother would play the you-have-no-room-to-preach-morals card. So he'd made an early decision to absorb the insults and get right to point. "Our decision to block Coufis had less to do with money and more to do with his affiliations."

"Our decision?" George mocked. "So you were privy to this before me? Are you fuckin' kidding me, mate? Bloody affiliations? Please tell me you are kidding, Jabs?"

Jasper cleared his throat. "Let me clarify; it's not just his associations, it's his family. We have reason to believe that Coufis's father-in-law Anwar Ishmael is

212

responsible for Uncle Oscar's death, the hijacking of mom's boat, and Kofi's murder."

George slammed on the braks and thrust Jasper's body forward with exceptional force. "What the fuck are you doing, George?"

"How do you know this?" George said in a calibrated tone.

Jasper stretched his neck to adjust from the whiplash. "For a few weeks now, Dufrane has been conducting a detailed investigation into the crimes committed against our family, and he's learned some startling things."

George was now engaged and willing to listen. "Talk to me, Jabs. What the hell is going on?"

"Well, I can't explain it in detail the way Clinton and Dufrane can, but it all boils down to oil." George was both clueless and speechless. Jasper went on, "Coufis's father in law is one devious bloke. Dufrane dug up all kinds of mess on him. Allegedly, Ishmael is associated with many terrorist organizations and has been recruiting martyrs for extremist groups for decades for his own business purposes. They say he's been behind a couple embassy bombings including the Vaj Hotel attack last year. Now it appears he has BOI in his scopes. That is why Dufrane beefed up security and is taking extra precautions, which is why we had to block the acquisition of Coufis."

George still looked lost but was able to ask, "Did you say the Vaj Hotel?"

Jasper was unprepared for George's response. "Out of everything I just told you, the first words you utter are about the Vaj Hotel? Stay focused, man"

George ignored him and asked, "So what's next? What are we going to do? Are the authorities involved, or are we just fucking sitting ducks?"

"Well the first thing I want you to do is come out of hiding and make it to headquarters so Dufrane and Clinton can brief you on the details," Jasper insisted.

"That's fine, but who's keeping an eye on Ishmael? He's picking off our family members left and right. Where is he? And what does he want with us?"

"Like I said, Dufrane and Clinton can explain it better, but I can tell you that no one knows where Ishmael is now; he's off the grid at the moment. All of his businesses are held in his partners' names, while he goes about life in obscurity. He can easily go missing and no one would know how to find him. Dufrane has used all his resources to locate him but has come up with nothing. He's certainly not at his Dubai based headquarters. But, right now, we have to get you to Accra soon."

"That's fine," George said, "I'll catch a flight back with you. I suppose you have to get the keys back to Sperm who will drive your car down for you, so let's go pick him up first."

"Actually," Jasper said, "keep the keys. The car is yours; I don't care much for silver."

George just looked at his brother, smiled, and said, "Unfucking believable."

Chapter 33
Cairo, Egypt
Present Day

On a hunch, George booked a flight to Cairo to meet with his good friend, Coufis Zatan, who also happened to be the son-in-law of the man targeting his family. George thought Coufis might be able to shed some light on Ishmael's whereabouts. He met Coufis at his comfortable villa in a Cairo suburb. The two sat in Coufis's backyard, drank beer, and enjoyed the warm afternoon. It was one of those days in Cairo when the sun was hot enough to extract sweat to the surface of your skin just before a gentle Saharan breeze swept it away.

Coufis looked forward to seeing his old mate. The newlywed had a case of cabin fever and was happy to catch up with his friend. "So what shall it be, old chap? Fly to Ibiza have drinks at the pub or drinks at the titty bar?" Coufis asked. "Because god knows you can't do anything fun in this repressed country of mine."

George attempted to smile but couldn't muster it. He was here to be candid with his good friend. "Unfortunately, I am here to discuss more pressing matters," George admitted. "If you don't mind, I have to burden you with conversation of a very sensitive nature."

"Listen man, if you're worried about me being fit, pull the trigger," Coufis chuckled. "As for the season, don't worry, I'll be ready to play football for Royals when it's time."

"Well, you don't have to worry about it now, my friend. As it turns out, my proposal to sign you was denied by my board of directors."

Coufis paused. "Really? I mean it's no secret I was skeptical about the idea at first. But I'm a bit disappointed, because I was just having my lawyer draft a contract requiring BOI to provide one of its private jets to fly me back and forth to Cairo every two days during the season."

George managed to chuckle and said, "I laugh, but you're probably serious."

"As a heart attack," Coufis retorted. But he soon scaled down his tone to let George know he was ready for serious conversation. "May I ask why?"

"Do you want the official reason or the real reason? But, before you answer, I must advise you that if you choose the real reason, your life may be in danger."

"Get the fuck outta here. Quit yankin' me aroun' and get on wif it, George! What ye meanin'? You're acting weird, man."

"First, I want you to acknowledge that you understand what I mean," George insisted.

"Ah, get the fuck on with it, man; there are no secrets between brethren." Coufis knew this statement couldn't be further from the truth, but he said it anyway.

George looked at his old friend while he poured another beer in his glass. "Officially we're not going to sign you because we can't afford it. That's all bullocks, though. The real reason is a lot more complicated than money. The real reason, believe it or not, has to do with your family."

Coufis looked confused again. "What the hell does my family have to do with Asante Royals football?"

"Actually, it's your father-in-law Mr. Ishmael."

"Really? I've told nobody outside of my agent about our Royals deal. Not even my wife, let alone my father-in-law."

George replied in his dry, almost sarcastic tone, "I hate to break it to you, Coufis, but your father-in-law is a diabolical criminal. Unbeknownst to many of us, he's been crafting a shitload of 'politricks' as of late." George could tell Coufis was still confused so he elaborated. "Apparently your father-in-law is a self-described consultant for PetroCo Oil, which is currently in a bidding war with Freestar Oil to be awarded the drilling rights for Ghana's newly discovered oil reserves. This contract is important to Ghana's economy and our people. Ishmael was hired by PetroCo to deliver them the contract by using his political influence in the country. In return, your father-in-law would get over one billion dollars in backdoor compensation for delivering this project to PetroCo.

216

"However, what they failed to realize at the time was that my Uncle Oscar supported PetroCo's competitor Freestar Oil, because it offered Ghana a much better deal and would create many local jobs. Your father-in-law met with my uncle and kindly proposed he endorse PetroCo Oil, so the selection committee would have no choice but to back his horse. My uncle kindly declined and a week later, he was killed. After Oscar's death, BOI's head of security Dufrane launched an investigation to find his assassin. He easily discovered that his illegitimate son, Max Cotto, a heroin addict with grudge against his father, had killed Oscar. Dufrane also learned that Ishmael hired Max Cotto to murder my uncle in exchange for a small amount of money and heroin. Max was conveniently found dead shortly after Oscar's death; his stash had been sabotaged by Ishmael's men, and he'd 'overdosed' on a hot shot of heroin."

George drank more of his beer and belched, pausing to take a breath. "Now mind you, mate, this is only the first verse of the song; it gets more wretched. After Oscar's death, your father-in-law thought PetroCo would surely win the bid, since the selection committee would take the recommendation of President Amoako, who was bribed by Ishmael. However, my cousin Clinton decided to take on Oscar's mantle of supporting of Freestar Oil to the committee. Not a month later, one of my mother's vendor's boats was hijacked by pirates near Somalia, who killed the crew and beheaded my mother's very close friend. A message later arrived asking us to back off the oil business or expect more family and close friends to disappear. That act of violence is also believed to be sponsored by your father-in-law."

George couldn't blame Coufis for his skepticism. The story sounded unbelievable to George as he repeated it. By now, George was poised to reel Coufis in. "The thing is this, my friend, despite what he's done to my family, the most despicable thing he did was in India on the weekend of your wedding."

If Coufis didn't know his friend better, he might

think George was going mad, because his story was wildly fantastical. Tired of the suspense, Coufis threw his hands up and shouted, "What did he do in India the weekend of my wedding?"

"You're going to find out anyway; I might as well be the one to you. The theory among many is that your father-in-law had plans to buy the declining Vaj Hotel in Bombay. He wanted to level it and build some modern monstrosity. However, the owner refused to sell it to him for his own personal reasons. Allegedly, your father-in-law used his connections with the Arab Liberation Army to conduct a brutal terrorist attack at the Vaj Hotel on a night the owner was there. The thugs completed their mission and brutally murdered the Vaj's owner along with sixteen patrons and four employees, including your Auntie Sophie."

George let Coufis look away as his eyes filled with tears. He reached in his jacket, grabbed an envelope, and handed it to Coufis. "I made you a copy of Dufrane's findings. I think you'll find them extremely thorough. He's former Mossad and a capable man."

Coufis opened the envelope and looked it over as George continued, "We have contacts with an international agency that would like to bring him to justice dead or alive. Since he's your father-in-law, I wanted to give you notice, as well as explain why our football deal fell through."

Coufis read the intelligence on his father-in-law. When he looked up from the report, he sternly said, "Would you quit callin' this prick my father-in-law?"

George smirked and continued with his sobering news. "We're going after him with or without your help. But if Dufrane's intelligence is accurate, you deserve a hand in bringing this piece of shit to justice. Plus the element of surprise will allow us to capture him alive."

Coufis began to pace. He believed George. Tears slowly trickled down his face when he thought about the murder of his helpless Auntie Sophie. Coufis quickly wiped away the tears, guzzled the rest of his beer, and turned to George. "I wish you hadn't told me this, George. What the fuck am I supposed to do?"

George said in a more stern voice, "It's already happened, now let's fix it. Will you help us bring this vile scum to justice? He's gone underground and no one can find him. Have you heard anything from Azul about her father's whereabouts?"

Coufis nodded in agreement and hesitated before he spoke and to George's surprise replied, "I think my wife may have inadvertently tipped me off to his whereabouts."

George's eyes grew large and his head slightly turned to the left so he was looking at Coufis from the corner of his eyes with a look that quietly screamed, Get the fuck outta here!

"Just last night, she took a call from a person I'm sure was her father, since it was on the secure line she uses when he calls. I wasn't paying much attention to the call because she was in the bathroom."

George focused his eyes on Coufis to make sure he was serious. "Did she give you any ideas about his location?"

"Not directly, but I can guess where he could be hiding. Have you ever heard of Geeni Island?" George looked puzzled. "Of course you haven't," Coufis said. "It's a private island. The only people who know about it are Ishmael, his two daughters, wife, special security, and me. I only know about it because it's where we went for our honeymoon. I was blindfolded the whole time I was on the plane. But my wife, bless her soul, isn't the best at keeping secrets. One night, she left her phone out and I happened to check it. She had a Google map of the island's location on the phone, so I'm pretty confident I can pinpoint its general vicinity. The island is ideal for a hideaway. His compound is not visible by air. It was all paid for in cash and the house built by his men; there's no paper trail."

George rubbed his chin. "This is promising information. I have to call Accra now." George got up and held out his hand to Coufis.

"You're leaving already?" Coufis asked.

"We should be seen around each other as little as possible, for now." George then reached in his trouser pocket and handed Coufis a prepaid phone. "Only call me on this phone; my secure number is already loaded. Tell no one about this, not even your wife Azul. Contact me the second you learn more. I know this is hard for you, my friend, but we must make this bastard pay for his crimes." George walked to the door then made sudden stop as he grabbed the handle of the door. He then turned around and said, "Didn't I recall you once joking about how your wife could be worth almost a billion dollars in the untimely death of her father?" He gave Coufis the peace sign and left the residence without giving him an opportunity to answer.

Chapter 34
Accra, Ghana
1956

Thirty-two years earlier the late Asante king Prempeh I had awarded Reginald Johnson with a charmed life as compensation for the injustices done to his family. At a young age, Reginald earned a first-class education and became a wealthy landowner. It was a life that a privileged boy from Zurich could appreciate, let alone a young straggler from Freetown. Reginald took full advantage of Chief Prempeh's embrace. Soon after his reunion with the Asante, he changed his name from Johnson to Boateng, his great grandmother Aqua's maiden name. It was a fine Asante name with the benefit of deep roots.

Shortly after finishing The University of Ghana with a major in business and a minor in philosophy, Reginald was fast-tracked into local Kumasi politics and appointed the city's treasurer. Given his association with Asante royalty, one would be naïve to think Reginald did not keep the Asante interests on the front burner. For the most part, though, his tenure as treasurer was above board. In modern governments, such a conflict of interest would have raised eyebrows, but in less cynical times, it was considered common practice.

In the Gold Coast, it was customary for wealthy men to have multiple wives. Reginald had two wives and three children by them: a son by his first wife and two girls by his second. He also had half a dozen love children, which he didn't catalogue. By 1956, Reginald was an elder statesman with several manufacturing businesses, a budding agricultural operation and equity in commercial property throughout the country. In the years leading up to Ghana's independence, he enjoyed life as a wealthy entrepreneur. However, Reginald would be asked to serve his country as a civil servant one last time in the most important juncture of the country's development.

The Gold Coast was on the verge of being the first sub-Saharan African country to gain independence from colonial rule. For good reason, history credits Ghana's first Prime Minister and President Kwame Nkrumah for its victory. But as in most revolutions, there were many behind-the-scenes players integral to its success, and Reginald Boateng was one of them. At the time, Kwame Nkrumah was leader of the Convention's People Party (CPP). He was feverishly pressing for the Gold Coast to be completely free from British rule. Although many moderates gave the British credit for relinquishing significant control of the government and allowing the Gold Coast to function as a semi-autonomous state, there was no question that virtually every native Ghanaian believed the British had overstayed their welcome.

Kwame Nkrumah, who had studied at Lincoln University in Pennsylvania, had a unique relationship with the United States. The Nkrumah administration tasked Reginald Boateng with courting the appropriate American allies to support their cause. He functioned as the Gold Coast's first U.S. ambassador before the position even existed. Reginald usually took meetings in his government offices; his guests could include those from the U.S. delegation, including America's ambassador to Great Britain or high-ranking senators. On this particular day, Reginald hosted a more inconspicuous individual, Chester Caldwell, who was a CIA field agent planted in Ghana. You couldn't tell by Caldwell's average middle aged Caucasian American with male pattern baldness appearance, but he was a slick CIA operative, effective in gaining access in the least penetrable of circles. The two made small talk for all of seven minutes before Agent Caldwell began to expose his hand. "So what are your thoughts of Kwame Nkrumah?" asked Caldwell.

Reginald, a man always cautious with his words, responded to Agent Caldwell with a smile, "Well considering I serve at Nkrumah's privilege, I think it's safe to say I am a supporter."

Caldwell nodded his head and leaned back in his chair. "Let me ask you this. You are a very successful entrepreneur, correct?"

"By African standards, I suppose so," Reginald chuckled.

"Yes, and trust me, even by American standards you're successful, Mr. Boateng. So far, your businesses have been able to flourish under a free-market economy. Given your success with capitalism, does it bother you that your party's leader is cozy with certain socialist factions in Moscow?" Agent Caldwell then leaned forward to reinforce his statement. "The reason I ask is this: It is no surprise that the geo-communist movement has its eye on what's happening here in the Gold Coast. They want nothing more than to utilize your country as a breeding ground for their godless, antibusiness ideals. There's no question that the Gold Coast will soon become a sovereign nation free of British rule. What happens then? Do you feel comfortable with Nkrumah as your elected president? A man who will more than likely allow the Soviets to dictate his financial policies?"

Reginald smiled to himself and noted the American fear of communism ran much deeper than the Senate's McCarthy hearings that he'd followed a few years earlier on BBC. He wasn't foolish enough to fall for such American naiveté, but he also wasn't foolish enough to dismiss their concerns and squander necessary American aid.

"With all due respect, Agent Caldwell, I can appreciate your concern with the Communist party's agenda permeating our politics. However, I assure you, I will not be involved with a party that intends to reduce free-market policies; we have always been a free-market people and always will be."

"I understand this, Mr. Boateng. However, as influential as you think you are, you are not as influential as the Kremlin."

Reginald was slightly offended by Agent Caldwell's suggestion that he had delusions of grandeur. Instead of objecting, he decided to educate his guest about African politics. "Agent Caldwell, I don't care if Nkrumah is a card-carrying Communist as we speak. Communism will never take hold in Africa for one reason alone—tribal

223

politics. As in most African countries, the Gold Coast's natural resources are found in the lands owned by tribal chiefs. Any political movement in this country needs the support of those tribal chiefs, and no one is more against nationalizing industry than the chiefs.

"If they don't want to share their natural resources with their own people, they surely won't hand them over to the government. I myself am an Asante. We are perhaps the most powerful tribe in Africa in terms of economic strength. You can believe me when I say that the CPP has no power without the Asante, and the Asante will pull the rug out from under any party trying to establish a communist doctrine." Reginald paused before adding his "but" clause: "That being said, Agent Caldwell, as a CPP member and an Asante, I'm aware of some important elements of socialism that it would behoove the people of my country to embrace. Basic safety nets, if you will. In fact, the same types of safety nets your own country utilizes."

Reginald let that sink in before closing with, "Although I and other tribal landowners have done well under a free-market system, the average citizen has not. Policies to help create economic opportunity for average Gold Coast citizens must be put in place, while government and the private sector feed off what is rightfully theirs, too. But I can almost guarantee you that no communist government can be sustainable in this country."

Agent Caldwell was still skeptical, but he we was convinced Reginald believed what he said to be true, so he dropped the subject.

Today was the eleventh birthday of Reginald's son, Oscar. By the time his father, who regularly worked twelve-hour days, arrived home, Oscar was in bed pretending to sleep. Reginald walked into his son's room while he lay in bed. Reginald, like many African fathers of his generation, was not a sappy or overly sensitive father. However callous, he did show occasional flashes of sentiment, and tonight was one of those times.

Reginald carried a wooden chair next to his son's

224

bed. Without announcing his presence, he sat in the chair and studied Oscar as he lay in bed. Reginald reached in his attaché case and pulled out the journal his father Ernest Johnson gave him before he died. His fingers strummed through the pages of the journal until he found the passage he was looking for. It was dark in his son's room, with little to no visibility except for the candlelight creeping through the cracked door from the hallway. But darkness didn't matter since he'd committed the passage, like every other passage in this journal, to memory.

Reginald read his father's words softly:

"The majority of my time on earth has been filled with optimism and hope. Even as a child before I was a free man, I still was optimistic. And for a Negro of my generation, that was rare. Even after the Civil War, many Negroes managed their expectations. Collectively we never lost site of the fact that we weren't much better off than when we were slaves. The white man could strip us of our dignity at any given time without appropriate justice.

"But even given this dismal outlook, I was given the gift of awareness and self-importance at an early age. The true story of my grandfather Asante Prince Kwame Ware's tragic fall from the heavens gave me purpose. It was infused in my blood that a descendent of the Ware clan would return to the Gold Coast and restore our family's branch to its rightful place on the royal tree.

"Through the grace of God, the wishes of my grandfather began to take shape. In the United States, the Negro was no longer enslaved, and through God's will and the fortitude of my ancestors, I was able to return back to the continent of our beginnings.

"The irony that I now find myself in a pathetic state of poverty and despair can be soul crushing. I have concluded that I do not have much time left here on this earth, and I will not fulfill the purpose of my life's long journey.

"However, I don't confuse the sour tone of my present predicament with failure. Despite what many in this hellhole of a town may believe, this grim realization does not deter my journey. The magic of my ancestry still dances in my blood. Today is my son's birthday and I see an intense light in his eyes—the same light my father possessed (and me too, as I was always told). The only difference is that the light carried in the eyes of my son is brighter and even more intense. That intensity is as humbling as it is reassuring. It is through him that I live and through him that I pass along the invaluable gift of optimism."

Reginald closed the journal and tucked it under Oscar's pillow. He walked out of his son's room and closed the door behind him. It did not bother Oscar, who was awake the whole time that his father neglected to wish him a happy birthday. He coveted the clandestine affection his father had exhibited on that night. Of all the grandiose gifts Oscar received throughout his childhood, none matched the simple gift he received from his father that quiet night of his eleventh birthday.

Chapter 35
Accra, Ghana
Present Day

President Amoako's personal assistant, Joseph Nyum, had been instructed to wake him up at 6:00 a.m. sharp to begin his day. Amoako, Joseph, and four of the president's security detail were on a business trip in Mozambique for the African Nations Summit. Joseph had the hotel kitchen prepare President Amoako's favorite breakfast, which consisted of a cup of tea, a sweet roll, a bowl of oatmeal, and two eggs over easy. It was a simple but substantial breakfast, the type of meal the president needed to get him through the morning. Joseph chatted with the security detail about the day's itinerary before making his way to the president's suite. Joseph knocked on the door and waited for permission to enter. After waiting several seconds without an answer, he knocked on the door again and used his copy of the key to open the door.

Joseph suspected the president had tucked himself into bed with a bottle of gin and had slept through the alarm. When he walked into Amoako's room, all was peaceful: no naked women or bottles of booze on the floor, just the president lying in his bed with his sleep mask on. Joseph walked over to the side of the bed to nudge him awake. He hated doing it because the president always yelled at him, but if he didn't and President Amoako was late for his meeting as a result, he would be fired.

Joseph nudged the president and noticed he was unusually cool to the touch. After the second nudge, it took Joseph exactly two seconds to come to the realization that the man was dead; he wasn't breathing and was nonresponsive. Joseph yelled at the top of his lungs for President Amoako to wake up. When Joseph lifted up his sleep mask, it revealed lifeless, dilated eyes. Joseph cried out for security and then picked up the phone and called an ambulance. With no strength in his legs, he dropped to his knees and began sobbing uncontrollably.

When the paramedics arrived, all attempts to

resuscitate President Amoako were futile, and the man was pronounced dead at 7:26 am. The cause of death, stroke, he was sixty-five years old.

Clinton Osei had just returned from his morning run when one of his security guards handed him his secure phone. Vice President Bonswah was on the line, which seemed odd to Clinton since he never called so early. "Vice President—good morning. This is an early surprise. What can I do for you?"

"Unfortunately, I have some bad news."

Clinton filled the gap in conversation. "What is it, Mr. Vice President?"

"President Amoako passed away earlier this morning from a stroke." Clinton stood speechless, with his phone still in hand. "Are you still there?" Bonswah asked.

"Yes, sorry, Mr. Vice President," Clinton answered. "I'm just at a loss of words, Mr...What happened, sir?"

"He was in Mozambique for the African Nations Summit. Apparently his staff found him lying still and nonresponsive in his bed this morning. When the paramedics arrived, he was pronounced dead."

Taken by surprise, Clinton replied, "This is disappointing news."

"There are rumors floating around Mozambique that he died of a drug overdose. Between you and me, it is true he was dependent on OxyContin, however, he legitimately passed away from a stroke. These ugly rumors surrounding his death lead me to the reason I am calling you now. Since BOI's subsidiary owns Accra's leading news station and newspaper, I beg for your assistance."

"Of course, whatever you need," Clinton offered without hesitation.

"Is it possible to put one of your reporters in direct contact with the doctor on the scene in Mozambique to report the facts and refute the rumors? I don't have to tell you that the false report of an African president dying from a drug overdose would be bad for business."

"I agree. I'll have George dispatch Patricia Young to Mozambique immediately."

Bonswah knew of her and was concerned about her inexperience. "You don't think she's a little green for this?"

Clinton quelled his concerns. "Perhaps, but she is more than a competent journalist. Trust me, I know this personally." Then Clinton admitted his cynical motivations as well. "But also, I have my company's own selfish interests in mind. We want to win the ratings battle on this story, and I would prefer to have her attractive face in front of the camera."

Bonswah managed not to be offended by Clinton's selfish interests and agreed. "Fine. Actually I will do you one better. I am heading to the airport in an hour to fly to Mozambique to speak with our people there on the ground. Have Ms. Young meet us there immediately and she can fly in the presidential plane, so my press agent can explain the facts as we know them. Plus I will let her ask the first question at the press conference."

"Of course, Mr. Vice President," Clinton thankfully replied.

Bonswah breathed deeply. Then his conversation took on a reflective tone. "The irony in all of this is that just last month Amoako was bragging about his annual checkup in a cabinet meeting, saying he'd received a clean bill of health."

The vice president paused and Clinton could sense he was choking back tears. Clinton gave him a second, then decided to direct the discussion to a less emotional realm. "So this makes you what, sir?"

Bonswah took a second to compose himself before answering, "Yes, I am now the acting president. I was sworn in an hour ago by a Supreme Court Justice."

Acting President Bonswah paused, sniffled, and chuckled after sucking his teeth. "Clinton, I never really enjoyed the executive branch of government. Truth be told, I've disliked the VP job and I never in a million years desired to be president. Ironically, a few days ago I informed my wife that I would resign as vice president. I was going to give President Amoako the news when he returned from Mozambique, and now this happens.

Apparently, God has a twisted sense of humor."

Clinton laughed in agreement. Then in an attempt of reassurance, he said, "Mr. President, let me know if there is anything I or BOI can do to help you with your transition."

"Actually, Clinton, there is," Bonswah said clearing his throat. "In order to govern in an unbiased fashion, I think our backdoor conversations should cease—at least for the time being. Especially with all this oil business going on, it's probably safer if we don't give my colleagues the perception that we are in collusion."

"I understand. But my offer still stands, Mr. President," Clinton reiterated.

President Bonswah let out a faint chuckle. "You know, Clinton, other than the chief justice who swore me in, you're the only other person to call me that. Those are two words that will take some getting used to. But thank you and good bye."

When Patricia Young returned to Accra from Mozambique, she'd already penned two thousand words for The Accra Voice and logged an additional seventy minutes of camera time. Patricia was credited as the first journalist to break the story. News outlets all over the globe accessed her as the point person for the story. Even given the somber subject matter of the president's death, Patricia Young understood that as a journalist, she had arrived.

As a young, single, and ambitious professional, Patricia had little social life and no close family. When she arrived home from the assignment, she was exhausted. Within three minutes, she was undressed with a glass of wine in one hand while drawing a bath with the other. As the water filled the tub, Patricia examined herself in the mirror. She appreciated how her body had developed over the years. When younger, she was tall, scrawny, and flat chested, but had filled out nicely in her early twenties. She was genuinely attractive with a valedictorian-caliber IQ. Young credited her looks to her father, who was a dark-brown, baby-faced man with cool grey eyes. As a younger man, he was often referred to as a "pretty boy." Her reputation as a top-rate journalist, however, she credited to her tenacious mother, who was an advocate for resident's rights and unsuccessfully ran for her town's city council twice.

Patricia was inquisitive; she knew the right questions to ask and how to ask them. Patricia also enjoyed the paradox of having brains and beauty, but she also realized it came with a price. Always working, she rarely had time to fulfill her own romantic needs. Contrary to what her male colleagues whispered, Patricia was not frigid. She was actually quite the opposite—a woman who was immensely sexual but burdened with the good sense to rarely indulge it.

While enjoying her bath, she was interrupted by her cell phone. Patricia intended to drop the call until she glanced at the screen and noticed it was a London number. For the sake of not shooting her career in the foot, she decided to answer the phone. A representative for Quills Publishing was on the line, making her glad she answered.

For the past six months, Patricia had been shopping a manuscript around to publishers. During her years as a journalist, she archived every story and event she had covered in Ghana and had assembled it into a book format, which also included her notes and background information for the pieces. Young had covered everything from football matches to West African state dinners. It didn't take long for her to realize that her journalistic notes made for interesting reading, so she began compiling and organizing them. The narrative took a sensational tabloid-like perspective into the region's most provocative headlines; she dished on political leaders, celebrities, and business titans alike. Ironically, her subjects also included powerful members of BOI, her employer's parent company. Young did so in the attempt to wash her conscious clean from contractually having to bury negative stories about them.

She answered the phone with, "Patricia speaking."

"Hello Patricia, this is Jordan Blake with Quills Publishing. Several months ago you submitted a manuscript proposal to us, correct?"

She laughed. "So much has happened over the last month, I almost forgot I approached Quills with the proposal."

Blake laughed along with her. "I'm sure that's true. Well, Quills has been watching you closely on the news via several different media outlets and we're quite impressed with your work."

"Thank you," Patricia graciously replied.

"Since then, we've revisited your manuscript proposal with fresh eyes. And I have to say, we are very interested in optioning your manuscript."

If Patricia was jubilated by Jordan Blake's words, she didn't show it. "Let me ask you something, Mr. Blake."

"Sure, anything."

"Why the interest now?"

"Quite frankly, Ms. Young, I'm sure you already know the answer. Your recent celebrity from the Amoako story breathes new life into your manuscript. Now, it's anchored to a trusted source, making it a much more marketable book." Patricia agreed. "Let me get down to the bottom of the matter for you," Blake insisted. "We would like to option your story and offer you an advance of £100,000."

"Mr. Blake, this is great news, however, I'm not prepared to commit to a book deal over the phone. When is the soonest we can meet in person to discuss negotiations?"

"I'm sorry. Of course, you're right. Let's say Monday of next week, we fly you to London?"

"How about this Wednesday's red eye?" Patricia suggested.

"Ms. Young, I'm sure that can be arranged," Blake agreed.

"Good. E-mail me tomorrow with details." Before Blake could say goodbye, Patricia hung up the phone and threw it on top of her bathrobe. As far as she was concerned, she was the only person on earth who mattered at the moment.

Chapter 36
Off the Coast of Somalia
Present Day

Victor Asad had worked for Idreme, the Mogadishu warlord, all of his life. His father, Sujai, was Idreme's fiercest soldier during the Somali civil war in the 1990s. Sujai lost his life during the historic battle against the Americans in downtown Mogadishu, where Idreme's insurgency defeated U.S. Marines and shot down one of their Black Hawk helicopters. It was a rare defeat and a black eye for the Marines. The Marines would later pull out of the war-ravished land in embarrassment.

The victory over the United States emboldened Idreme's syndicate. Victor Asad's father was credited with the strategy leading to that victory, and it could be argued that Sujai's death was not in vain. After he died, Idreme adopted the young Victor and raised the boy as his own. Asad was fast-tracked through the ranks of the cartel. Raised in the cartel, he witnessed (and was taught to administer) the harshest of crimes against his fellow Somali. That is why he did not flinch when given orders several weeks earlier to capture a Temateng Agricultural cargo boat, kill the crew, and specifically behead one, Kofi Jackson.

One breezy night on the Gulf of Aden, Asad and his band of pirates enjoyed another idle night at sea. They drank rum like nineteenth-century buccaneers and smoked cigars like Cuban rebels. Unexpectedly, Asad received a call on their patrol boat's radio, tipping him off to an unprotected speedboat traveling into their waters. The news injected a feeling of optimism in Asad. His crew had not been active since they hijacked the Temateng vessel and they were getting anxious. Although a speedboat was usually small game, it still gave the misfits of the sea something to do during the boring patrol. Speedboat loot tended to be small, but every single penny he brought home helped Idreme. Asad hoped to impress Idreme enough to be taken off the boats altogether and promoted to one of the warlord's land operations. Being on the sea five days a week was taking its toll, and he desperately wanted out.

Motivated by the news, Asad briefed the crew on their mission: hijack the boat, blindfold the crew, tow the boat to landing, unload the contents before daylight, and then release the crew to sail their boat back home. The plan sounded perfect to Asad—hopefully they'd easily score thousands of dollars of merchandise without having to kill anyone. Asad and his crew had around an hour before they would encounter the vessel, so he halted their rum drinking, hoping for a somewhat sober heist.

They waited nearly an hour and a half for the boat before Asad began to get anxious. He was only minutes away from calling his contact about the ship's arrival when the small light of a speedboat headed their way. Asad ordered his men to aim their guns at it but hold fire; the speedboat slowed down as it neared the patrol boat. The pirates turned on their lights and signaled the boat to stop while they approached it.

The speedboat, showing no movement or sound, complied and remained seventy yards from the pirates. It had already occurred to Asad that it was odd for a speedboat to be in unfriendly waters this late at night. He shined his handheld torch on the boat's cockpit, and when drifting closer, they were perplexed to find it apparently empty. Asad panicked. He scanned the perimeter to ensure no one had outflanked them, but nothing was in sight. The night-filled waters were calm all around them. Asad's anxiety was gradually creeping into fear.

One of the pirates loudly whispered, "Ghost ship."

The calm evening supported that statement, but Asad would not succumb to juvenile superstition and believe ghosts existed on land, let alone the water. Asad waved his handheld torch and instructed one of his men to board the boat and search it; his point man volunteered for the job. The man climbed onto the edge of their boat closest to the speedboat. Handing his rifle to the person behind him, he jumped onto the speedboat.

234

Asad and his men never expected that the slightest pressure of his body would detonate hidden explosives on the boat. The explosion was strong enough to blow up both boats and violently transform the pirates from living beings into shredded human projectiles thrust into the Gulf of Aden like bits of shark chum.

On a higher elevation of land less than a kilometer across the cove from the explosion's ground zero, Felix Grucier focused his binoculars on the scene. The explosion lit up the night sky, and Felix admired the view from his vantage point. The sight was bittersweet. Bitter, because Felix had restored the exterior of a 29-foot Baja 247 Performance down to the pin striping. He'd also fabricated from scratch the boat's interior mechanics, explosive lining, and even the handheld remote control that maneuvered the speedboat and detonated the explosives. The Improvised Explosive Device (IED) sinking into the murky waters had been one of Felix' craftiest designs. But he considered the sight of the explosion sweet, because his elaborate IED managed to destroy his targets with greater accuracy than anticipated.

Felix hurled the remote control over the cliff where he perched, crashing it onto the jagged rocks and watching its broken pieces fall into the waters below. Felix focused his binoculars on the water's surface surrounding the explosion to detect any dog-paddling survivors, whom he would have to put out of their misery. Anyone surviving that blast would be miraculous. Yet out of the top right corner of his lens, he spotted a survivor, desperately flailing on a plank of smoldering driftwood. Felix reached for his sniper rifle leaning against the large rock next to him and directed its scope on the bobbing target. Felix aimed at the mark, locked in on the temple of the survivor, and pulled the trigger. He saw a mass come off the mark's head. The mark sunk from Felix's efficient shot nearly a kilometer away.

Felix would be on a plane flying over the Mediterranean Sea before Idreme would find out Asad and his fellow pirates were minced shark fodder in the waters they proclaimed to "protect." In his cabin, Felix documented the job for his memoirs. He noted: "Although this job took a seemingly endless three hundred hours of meticulous planning and execution, it only took less than two seconds for the explosion to destroy all evidence of my labor."

Today would mark President Bonswah's fifth press conference to date since the untimely death of President Abna Amoako. In Bonswah's first four press conferences, he only answered questions about the specifics of Amoako's death and his funeral arrangements. Ghana's new de facto president would not answer any questions about policy until today's press conference. He was now prepared to answer those questions because he finally felt he, his staff, and cabinet members were all on the same page. President Bonswah's strategy for this press conference was simple: give few specifics but promise to divulge more in the future after he became better adjusted in his new role. Given the unprecedented circumstances, he intended to take full advantage of the situation and hoped the press corps would cut him a little slack.

Bonswah put his strategy into play when fielding the first question from Patricia Young of the Accra Voice. She asked, "It's no secret that before the primaries a couple of years ago, you and President Amoako had differences of opinion about many issues before he added you to his ticket. How does your administration plan to reconcile those differences now?"

President Bonswah anticipated this question. It was true that Parliamentarian Bonswah was on record criticizing then-candidate Amoako's inability to improve the country's infrastructure after chairing the transportation committee for twelve years while in Parliament.

He took a drink of water before answering, "Patricia, I've thought very hard about my role as an appointed president in this tough time for our country. The last thing I want to do as an unelected president is to drastically change the course of our nation. Currently, Ghana's economy is in fair condition, so you shouldn't notice much difference in terms of policy change. I want to respect the agenda President Amoako had already set before his untimely demise."

Patricia Young anticipated the political doublespeak from the new president. Unsatisfied with his answer, she quickly followed up with a question before any of her colleagues could chime in. "Many people are concerned about the bidding war going on between PetroCo Oil and Freestar Oil. The worst kept secret in the country was that President Amoako planned to endorse PetroCo Oil to the selection committee. As you know, the selection committee's decision will be heavily influenced by the president's endorsement. So I ask you, President Bonswah, which company do you plan to endorse? PetroCo or Freestar?"

The other senior reporters in the room basted Patricia Young with unkind looks. It was bad enough that she was first to get the scoop on President Amoako's death, but now she was the first to ask President Bonswah the one question every reporter wanted to ask. The honeymoon period between the budding reporter and her colleagues had officially ended; she would receive nothing but spite from them from then on

Bonswah grinned at Young. On the one hand, he admired the young journalist's tenacity. On the other, he felt betrayed by her inability to return his favor. Here he stood—the man who had gift-wrapped the exclusive story of President Amoako's death for her, and instead of being grateful and sticking to a softball question, she hurled a fierce curve ball at him. But the newly appointed president tried to answer her question as directly as possible.

"Patricia, as I'm sure as you know, President Amoako was personally involved in our country's entrance into the oil industry," Bonswah soothed. "So much so, that as vice president, I was not given access to the selection committee proceedings. His dedication to the oil issue freed me to attend to other important matters on Ghana's agenda. Although I'm privy to a little more information on the oil-drilling contract process than you, I still have to play catch up. I beg to differ with you on one point, however. Contrary to popular belief, President Amoako did not

238

express to me that he favored one oil company over another; he appeared neutral on the matter. And even if he wasn't, the decision ultimately lay in the hands of our bipartisan selection committee, and I trust their integrity to come to a consensus and make the best decision for their country."

President Bonswah was surprised at how seamless his litany of lies, half-truths, and generalities came together in his answer. He didn't expect the seasoned reporters to buy all of what he'd just said, but he did expect the majority of home viewers to believe him. At that point, Bonswah felt comfortable at the podium. And for the first time since he was sworn in as president, he thought he might have the stomach for the job.

≈

After Bonswah answered Patricia Young's question, Anwar Ishmael powered off his laptop. He'd been streaming the press conference via satellite at his private home on an undisclosed island somewhere in the southeastern hemisphere. Ishmael heard all he needed from the newly appointed president of Ghana. That irritating tingle of anxiety originating from the pit of his stomach, which turns into frustration and elevates to rage, was beginning to build. However, Ishmael willed himself to deny his rage. At this point in his life, he was well aware that decisions he made in rage were not his smartest. He lit a cigar and walked out onto the room's balcony, then waved for Abdul, who was standing on the other side of the room, to join him. The two sat across from each other and discussed strategy.

"What are your thoughts on President Bonswah's press conference?" Ishmael asked.

Abdul shrugged and said, "It's hard to say; he didn't give us much information. Our local contacts say Bonswah is known to be a man of his word. There is a part of me that wants to take him at his word, when he says he wants to keep on the course Amoako already set forth. Because, why would anyone in his position want to put such unnecessary stress on himself?" Ishmael gestured for Abdul to continue.

239

"Out of all the things he could change, the biggest decision would be to interfere with the oil-contract process already in the final stage."

Ishmael decided to chime in. "As you stated, we do not know President Bonswah that well, do we? He's in our blind spot; therefore, we have no idea how to predict his play. Smart money says he would honor the existing backdoor agreements in place, assuming he knows about them, before being appointed president—especially since the decision is only a month away. That is very little time for a prudent man such as Bonswah to justify reversing the direction of a huge issue. However, who knows if he shares the same philosophy as Clinton Boateng and BOI?"

Abdul nodded his head in agreement. "So what do you suggest we do?"

Ishmael looked through Abdul, while he went over a series of possible plays. Within mere moments, he had intellectualized his plan and recited it to Abdul: "The way I see it, we have three options: Option A—we roll the dice and hope the natural course will play out in our favor. Option B—we approach Bonswah with the same offer we made Amoako and hope he takes it. Or option C—we remove Bonswah from the equation and take our chances with his successor, Eddie Mankwah, the Speaker of Parliament. Reminding you that our relationship with Mankwah has already relaxed zoning restrictions for our timber company in northern Ghana."

Abdul rubbed his chin and briefly meditated on the pros and cons of the three options. "Option A is definitely the least messy of the three choices. However, it leaves us in the vulnerable position of not being able to predict the outcome. Option B would appear to be the best decision, because most politicians we've dealt with in that region are easily manipulated. However, what if Bonswah's reputation is true, and he is the antithesis of the typical African politician? A bribe could backfire and expose us so close to the vote.

Amoako was our ace in the hole, but now that he's gone, we have no direct connections to many other

Ghanaian politicians. It was much easier to administer bribes through Amoako's channels than our own. Option C is the riskiest for the obvious reason: we'd be assassinating a head of state so close to the death of the previous president, and it would draw a lot of unwanted attention. A job of this magnitude does not need that kind of attention. However, if option C were executed properly and we were able to position Speaker Eddie Mankwah as president, I would have to believe the probability of winning this thing increases exponentially."

Ishmael rose from his chair and exhaled a long smoke trail from his cigar, while looking over the balcony and processing Abdul's assessment. With the deliberation of a high judge, Ishmael gave Abdul his ruling. "That was a very astute analysis on the matter, Abdul. And it has helped me reach a decision. While I want to believe every politician in that country has a price, I also have to account for the rare case in which I am wrong. This would require a backup plan. Let us start with option B. I want you to have Amoako's former assistant Joseph deliver a cash offer to President Bonswah in person. If Bonswah's answer is no, I want you to immediately activate option C."

"How do you propose I implement option C?"

"I want you to instruct the Arab Liberation Army to dispatch a splinter cell to Ghana and have one of their soldiers martyr himself while taking the life of President Bonswah at Amoako's public funeral service. In exchange for Arab Liberation Army taking credit for the assassination, we will increase our donation of weapons and money to their cause. We will draft a message for the head of Arab Liberation Army and the media stating that the reason they assassinated President Bonswah was to protest Ghana's lack of interest and concern about its Muslim citizens and neighboring Muslim countries. The Arab Liberation Army will accuse Ghana's politicians of being agents for a Western agenda in Africa and President Bonswah as a self-loathing Muslim. I believe this is a plausible motive, and most importantly, it will throw them off our scent. What do you think?"

Abdul grinned at Ishmael in approval. He was in awe of his boss's ability to calmly trivialize the enormity of a problem and recommend such an ambitiously violent alternative with such ease. Inspired by his boss, Abdul took the leap of faith with him. "This plan can work; I will make arrangements immediately."

Chapter 38
Accra Ghana
Present Day

Joseph Nyum was one of the brightest minds to graduate from his class at Ghana University. He was accepted into an English university to study law but could not afford the cost to attend. After graduating from The University of Ghana in search of an employer who could appreciate his talents, Joseph accepted an offer to work for the ambitious fifty-six year old Parliamentarian, Abna Amoako. Joseph soon proved invaluable to Amoako and rose to become Amoako's top aide, handling all aspects of the enterprising politician's life. Joseph was a policy wonk, who dictated the talking points to Amoako and his staff. He knew Amoako's schedule as well as he knew the origin of every scar on his body.

Joseph knew all the intimate details of his boss's life, such as his mistress's birthdays and the phone number of Amoako's doctor, who fed his OxyContin addiction. Joseph also knew the bank account numbers of Amoako's offshore accounts he used for depositing his bribes. It was easy for Amoako to transition him into the administration when he became president. Joseph was valuable, so Amoako paid him six times what any top political aide made in Ghana (or anywhere else in Africa, for that matter), mostly under the table. Joseph understood his salary was more hush money than a reflection of his performance. Amoako could not afford to pay him as much as he did if not for Anwar Ishmael's substantial bribes; Joseph was complicit in Amoako's wrongdoings, and he knew it.

As Joseph's personal finances grew, the opportunity to attend law school in England dwindled. He was now thirty-three, corrupt, and becoming content with selling out his dreams. This caused Joseph plenty of internal conflict. It wasn't until he ran into his old college friend, Patricia Young, at one of President Amoako's press conferences that he found someone to confide in. Patricia had just been hired as a political reporter for the Accra Voice. Shortly after the friends reunited, Joseph began throwing Patricia tidbits to help her budding career. It didn't take long before they became drinking buddies. Although Joseph and Patricia awkwardly managed to find themselves in the same bed a handful of times, for the most part, their friendship was more platonic. However, their platonic status was a unilateral regulation invoked only by Patricia.

By habit of trade, the friends often swapped stories and information. Given his position, Joseph usually divulged more than Patricia. He had more guilt to unload, and she inadvertently became his therapist. It didn't take long for her to convince Joseph to become her "deep-throat" source for the exposé she was writing on Ghana's political and business elite. At this point, Joseph felt it was the only way he could repent for enabling the despicable corruption rampant in the Amoako administration. While Joseph fed Patricia juicy tidbits for her book, President Amoako was none the wiser, and she promised to keep it that way—unless Joseph gave her permission to reveal him as a source.

Joseph wanted out of politics soon after Amoako died, despite the many job offers he received from Ghanaian politicians. By saving enough money from his high salary, Joseph thought it was time to start over and pursue his dream of living in England, so he began making arrangements to leave the country. It was beginning to look like a reality until the night he was visited by Abdul Mulinesbar. When Joseph saw Abdul at his door, anxiety set in; his palms were sweaty and laser-sharp pains of nausea ravished his stomach. However, he also knew better than to keep Ishmael's man waiting. Joseph let Abdul in and calmly led him to the living room and played host.

"Would you like something to drink? I have water, beer, wine, and soda."

Abdul waved Joseph off, sat on the couch, and invited Joseph to join him, so he pulled a chair closer to Abdul.

"Are you the only one at home?" Abdul asked.

If Joseph weren't already about to piss his pants, he

244

might have chuckled at the question. "Yes, I live alone. Working for Amoako all these years gave me little time to date, let alone start a family."

Abdul slightly nodded and looked around the living room, taking notice of the packed boxes and suitcases. "What are your plans now that you're no longer working for Amoako?"

"Well, honestly, I've been thinking about leaving the country and applying to law school. Maybe in England. I don't know yet."

Abdul nodded again, took a cigarette from his jacket, and began to smoke. Joseph didn't allow smoking in his house, but he wasn't about to enforce that rule with Abdul Mulinesbar. Abdul took a few drags of his Turkish cigarette before saying, "You know, this is a very nice house for a political assistant."

"Thank you, sir. It took me two years to make all of the improvements it needed..."

Abdul quickly cut off Joseph midsentence. "Please don't interrupt and let me finish."

Joseph nodded and kept quiet until it was his turn to speak.

Abdul continued, "For years, Anwar Ishmael paid Abna Amoako generous amounts of money to attend to his interests in Ghana. As I'm sure you know, President Amoako was working with the Ishmael Group to help deliver Ghana's oil-drilling contract to PetroCo Oil. In Amoako's defense, he was doing a good job up until he recently passed away. Our deepest condolences go out to his family of course. However, his sudden death does not end our investment with him. He is still responsible for fulfilling his contract—even in death."

Joseph nodded his head and began digesting the large lump in his throat that developed the moment his houseguest arrived. Abdul continued, "From where I sit, you live a charmed life for a man in your profession. Due to the kindness of the Ishmael Group, President Amoako was able to compensate you more generously than you deserved. As far as we're concerned, Amoako's debt extends to you as his right-hand man. All these things you possess are not free. Do you understand me, Joseph?"

Joseph softly said, "Yes, sir. I will gladly repay whatever Mr. Ishmael feels I owe him."

Abdul smiled. "You could not possibly repay such a debt monetarily. We need you to continue working for us and, in return, we will absolve your debt and give you enough money to retire early or pursue any other career goals."

Joseph nodded his head aggressively. "Mr. Abdul, I am so honored to be recruited to work for your organization. Unfortunately, I have to decline. All I want is to leave Ghana and travel for a while."

Abdul sighed. "You obviously misunderstand me, Joseph. This is not a request; it is a confirmation of booking. You are in debt to Mr. Ishmael and he insists you pay him in full."

Joseph nodded his head again, except this time he stopped trying to wiggle out of it. Abdul continued, "I don't know why I am about to tell you this—perhaps it's to motivate you or to instill some sort of appreciation in you for Mr. Ishmael. You should know that several months before his death, your beloved mentor President Amoako asked us to kill you."

Although Abdul was completely capable of fabricating such a story for motivational purposes, this story was true. Amoako did, indeed, approach Ishmael with the request to murder his assistant, because he feared Joseph would expose his corruption. Joseph's face was almost expressionless, but the why me? Was evident, nonetheless.

Abdul explained, "Amoako realized you knew where all of his skeletons were buried, and keeping you alive was too great a risk. Luckily for you, Ishmael rejected his request on the grounds of disloyalty." The last part of Abdul's story was a fabrication; Ishmael had promised Amoako he would grant his request to kill Joseph when the PetroCo oil deal went through. Abdul continued, "He also instructed Amoako that if you were to 'accidentally' perish, he would face worse consequences than death. Your father

246

figure tried to have you killed, Joseph. Right now, you should be thanking Mr. Ishmael for your life."

Joseph, still speechless and eyes to the ground, just nodded his head, while battling his mounting tears.

"Since President Amoako is no longer with us, we do not have an in with the new administration. Amoako's endorsement of PetroCo was a lock, but with Bonswah in power, we're not sure if he favors PetroCo or Freestar. It is in all of our best interests to make sure he endorses PetroCo. Do you understand me?"

"Yes, I do," Joseph agreed.

"Good. Since you still have connections in the new administration, we need you to extend our offer to President Bonswah in person. You are to deliver a package to President Bonswah that contains a small down payment for his cooperation. We need you to express in clear terms that it is to his advantage to continue the path of President Amoako and endorse PetroCo. Do you understand?"

Joseph nodded. "I completely understand, Mr. Mulinesbar. However, I have to add that President Bonswah is quite different from President Amoako. He may not accept your terms."

"At this point in the game, I doubt President Bonswah has the energy to fight the daunting battle ahead of him. We're confident he will accept our terms. And if he doesn't accept, we have a contingency in place—to make sure our plans succeed."

Joseph looked at Abdul with curiosity. "What sort of contingency?"

Abdul pulled an envelope from his jacket pocket and handed it to Joseph. "In that envelope is the name Mohammed Salaam, a member of the Arab Liberation Army. He is an agent planted in Accra. The Arab Liberation Army has agreed to perform a service for us in the event President Bonswah does not cooperate with our wishes. If he dies in office, we have assurances that his successor Speaker Eddie Mankwah will cooperate with us. First, I need you to deliver these instructions to Salaam before you deliver the package to President Bonswah, so he

247

knows what to do in case Bonswah rejects our offer."

The news of the contingency plan sent chills down Joseph's spine. This new information made him complicit in an assassination plot against the president. If he weren't so afraid to turn his back on Abdul, he would have run to the bathroom and thrown up. Instead, he gulped down the bile creeping up his esophagus and stared at Abdul in a daze.

Recapturing Joseph's attention, Abdul said, "Don't be alarmed, my boy, I'm sure Bonswah will accept our generous offer. I've learned that everybody in this god-forsaken country of yours has their price, and I doubt Bonswah is any different. Get some rest, Joseph. I will be sending you daily instructions through our associates. And, by the way, please don't be stupid and attempt to alert the authorities on this matter. I'm sure it insults your intelligence to tell you this, but your every move is monitored. You have a Siamese twin attached to your cock and you don't even know it."

Joseph didn't debate this assertion. "I understand."

"Good, Joseph. You'll receive the first $1 million installment of your payment after you deliver the package to President Bonswah. After the deal with PetroCo is completed, you will receive an additional $2 million. I think you'll find these terms more than fair." Abdul rose from his seat and walked toward the door. Before departing, he left Joseph with, "Until then, may Allah be with you."

Joseph had no way of knowing, but Abdul's parting statement was completely disingenuous because he was an atheist. He let himself out the door and left Joseph to process the colossal news.

≈

If President Bonswah did not have a lunch meeting, he worked through his lunch break. On today's lunch break, he picked at his plate of kenkey (a cornmeal-based dish served in slices) with gravy and sardines, while simultaneously unpacking boxes in his new office. One of President Bonswah's aides, Sandy, came to the door and informed him that he had an unexpected visitor.

"Who is it?" the president asked.

"Joseph Nyum," Sandy replied.

"Who's Joseph Nyum?"

If Sandy could have gotten away with sighing and rolling her eyes at the president, she gladly would have done so. Despite Bonswah's many gifts, he was notorious for forgetting the names of rank-and-file staff members. Sandy reminded him, "He was President Amoako's personal assistant for ten years, sir. You know Joseph— 'Amoako's side kick'?"

"Oh right! Joseph, the young man who discovered Amoako's body. Please let him in."

When Joseph entered the president's office, he walked directly to Bonswah and firmly shook his hand, saying, "Hello, Mr. President."

"Welcome, Joseph," Bonswah returned.

Joseph gave the transitional office a once over. "I see you're in the process of settling in?"

"Yes, I am; it's odd to be taking over this office. It doesn't feel like it belongs to me. You must know what I mean."

Joseph eagerly nodded his head in agreement and responded, "If these walls could only talk, Mr. President."

"I'll bet." Bonswah smirked.

"You know, Mr. President, there are many memories in this office for me, both good and bad. For instance, I met Barack Obama himself right underneath this chandelier. I can also remember sleeping in that chaise longue in the corner many a night, because it made no sense to leave the office when I had to be back here in three hours. And at that desk behind you, I've been privy to overhearing the most fascinating phone conversations between President Amoako and other world leaders. Conversations, I may add, that a young man my age had no business hearing. I have to admit I've led a charmed life all these years."

"Yes you have. I was in a similar position when I was your age."

"And how was that, sir?" Joseph asked with a tone

of skepticism.

President Bonswah stared at Joseph for a second longer than necessary before answering, "I, too, know how it is to work for a powerful man. Very few people know this about me, but I'll tell you, because I think you can relate. When I graduated from university, I spent a few years as Oscar Boateng's assistant; he was in his mid-forties at the time and had recently just returned from exile. Boateng ended up playing a combination of roles in my life: a boss, mentor, father figure, and friend. I witnessed this man achieve such success in humanitarian work that he should have been nominated for a Nobel Peace Prize. I've also seen him reach into the darkest corners of his soul and behave in ways that contradicted his humanitarian efforts. What I'm trying to say is that I can only imagine what a young man in your position is going through right now. I'm sure had President Amoako lived, you would have found him to be that person in your life."

Joseph gave a confused smile to Bonswah as he continued. "Oscar always joked that my career as a politician should not be tainted by being associated with men of class and integrity, such as himself. He said doing so would be unbecoming of a politician. As my political career bloomed, my friendship with Oscar faded, and now I miss him dearly." Although it was not true that their relationship faded, Bonswah felt it better to remain consistent.

"I feel privileged that you would tell me this story in confidence, Mr. President. It means a lot to me. With all due respect, sir, the comparison between Oscar Boateng and Abna Amoako is much appreciated, but, trust me, they were completely different monsters. God bless his soul, but Abna Amoako doesn't deserve to be mentioned in such a generous comparison."

Now it was Bonswah's turn to give Joseph a confused smile. Then he glanced away and changed the subject. "So what brings you here today? What can I do for you?"

"I wanted to officially say good bye. I'm not sure if
250

you know this, but I am resigning from the public sector for the time being."

"Oh really? What are you going to do?" President Bonswah asked with genuine interest.

"I'm going to travel and see the world. But I know you're busy. So like I said, I just wanted to wish you luck in this difficult job."

"Thank you, Joseph. I wish you luck in your endeavors as well, and when you return from traveling, please get in contact with me. This government still needs good young men like you."

Joseph gave the president a polite smile. "In all honesty, sir, I've had my fill of this occupation."

President Bonswah responded with a hearty laugh. "I knew you were a smart kid."

Joseph shook President Bonswah's hand and turning to leave, he grabbed a thick gift-wrapped manila envelope from his suit jacket. "Oh, and Mr. President, I almost forgot your welcoming gift."

"What's this, Joseph?"

"Nothing much, just a present that a few of your favorite supporters put together for you. It's a gushing love letter of sorts. I just ask you don't embarrass me by opening it in front of me."

President Bonswah laughed. "Are you sure? I'd like to show my appreciation."

"No, thank you, Mr. President. Either way, I'm positive you'll appreciate its content."

Bonswah put the present on his desk and continued to unpack his boxes for the next few minutes. After twenty minutes, his curiosity got the best of him, so he stopped unpacking and unwrapped Joseph's package.

What he read startled him. Subsequently, he dropped the package on the floor and ran to the phone and called his aide. "Sandy, don't let Joseph leave the building. Stop him and bring him back to my office."

"Sir, he left the building not a minute after he left your office. What's the matter...?"

Before Sandy could finish, President Bonswah hung up the

251

phone and looked out the window in astonishment.

Chapter 39
Accra, Ghana
Present Day

In typical Ghanaian fashion, the national funeral service for President Abna Amoako was held several weeks after he passed in Accra's Nkrumah Square. Most businesses and all schools were closed for the day so the public could pay their respects to the late president. The ceremony was an impressive undertaking. To hold the almost endless list of world leaders and celebrities scheduled to eulogize Amoako, ceremony organizers set up a 100-foot stage from the arch of Nkrumah Square jetting into the center of the plaza. President Bonswah was scheduled to speak last. In the meantime, he relaxed behind the scenes in a trailer doubling as a green room not far from the stage.

While the ceremony was building up momentum, Mohammed Salaam was preparing himself in a rented flophouse, paid for in cash and close to Nkrumah Square. A Senegalese-born Muslim and member of the Arab Liberation Army's West African cell, Mohammed was preparing for his destiny and to meet his maker. Mohammed conducted his daily ritual of cleaning his body and praying in the direction of Mecca with Zen-like focus. After prayer, he looked at his watch and knew it was time to dress for the day and get into position. He put on his uniform for Nkrumah Plaza security, a job he acquired two weeks earlier. Before Mohammed buttoned his shirt and knotted his tie, he strapped a relatively light vest of explosives to his body. He grabbed the dummy cell phone that was rigged as his detonator from his dresser. Mohammed turned it on to make sure it was working, then turned it off, and placed it in his trouser pocket. Mohammed exited the flophouse and headed to Nkrumah Square.

President Bonswah went over his speech in the trailer. He was fairly anxious about this particular speech, as he knew the whole world would be watching him give the closing eulogy, his biggest forum ever. Bonswah looked

253

at the clock in his trailer and realized he only had ten minutes before walking onto the stage. The keynote speakers would be walking from their respective trailers to the back of the stage on a 100-foot carpet much like those at red-carpet events, except this one was green and red with a border of black stars. Security guards were lined up along the edges of the carpet, forming a perimeter to block onlookers. When it was time for President Bonswah to ascend the stage, two of his private security guards flanked him on either side, shielding him from any obvious threats.

Mohammed Salaam reported early to his duty as a security guard for the funeral service. Despite his difficult task of assassinating President Bonswah and also becoming a martyr for his cause, Mohammed was quite calm. Since his older brother died in Afghanistan fighting with al Qaeda, he dreamed of the day he would avenge his brother's death.

After his brother's death, Mohammed dedicated himself to his cause. Through years of working all over West Africa with small groups of Arab Liberation Army sympathizers, Salaam was finally getting this opportunity to avenge his brother and enter the kingdom of Allah. It was safe to say Mohammed was excited, nearly giddy with anticipation to complete his short life's mission.

President Bonswah stood outside of his trailer, waiting for his security detail to get organized. It was a beautiful summer afternoon with a slight breeze from the Gulf of Guinea rolling past the shore onto the mainland, nicely complementing the dry heat. Each savory breath President Bonswah inhaled from the Accra air seemed to energize him more than the last. The president took this time to reflect before ascending the stage. He found it interesting that for several months now, he would admit to being jaded by his career as a politician. Much of his frustration and cynicism originated from his relationship with the very man he was to eulogize.

Today, however, he was struck with a sense of patriotism and national responsibility on a level he hadn't felt in years. It must have been seeing tens of thousands of his countrymen flooding the streets, all mourning as one nation. They mourned President Amoako's death the way Ghanaians knew best—by celebrating his life. Men, women, and children all gathered in the streets in the most rambunctious of moods. President Bonswah was aware that, due to the circumstances, this event would be the closest thing to an inauguration he would enjoy as an appointed president.

Eventually, his security detail was in place and they began their journey down the green carpet. President Bonswah shook as many hands and waved to as many people as possible, while walking down the aisle. Meanwhile, Mohammed Salaam was focused on the president's every move. He pushed back the crowds and performed his security duties without distraction from his main target.

Bonswah was fifty feet from Mohammed, who was positioned such that when the president eventually walked by him, he could detonate his vest's explosives. As the president walked down the aisle, Salaam locked eyes with his target. Although the president was looking past him, for some strange reason his potential killer felt Bonswah was also preparing himself to meet his destiny. He was now fifteen feet away, and Mohammed's left hand lay poised to reach into his trouser pocket and set off the cell-phone detonator. He planned to wait for Bonswah to be directly in front of him before stepping onto the rug and yelling, Allah Akbar! (God is great) and setting off the explosives.

When the president was five feet away, Mohammed started to reach in his pocket to unleash his holy destruction, but the terrorist was a hand movement too slow. An anonymous person aggressively wrestled his left wrist behind his back, while another hand reached into his left pocket and grabbed the cell-phone detonator. Mohammed was Tasered in the neck and quickly scurried off the premises before no more than twenty people even recognized any commotion. President Bonswah picked up his pace on the carpet with a light jog and galloped to the stage with the swagger of a prizefighter before a championship match.

Mohammed was quickly escorted into the back of a conversion van and taken to a remote location twenty miles away. Two bomb specialists attended to him in the van; it didn't take him long to realize his mission had been thwarted. He protested to his captures in Arabic and informed them their souls would be punished for interfering with Allah's will.

Although the detonator was removed, the job of defusing the explosives on Mohammed was still complicated. Removing the barnyard-style explosives from his body was too risky and not a chance they were willing to take. Instead of attempting to deactivate the bomb manually, the specialists exited the conversion van, leaving Mohammed tightly shackled in it. They entered another vehicle waiting for them and drove off to a safe distance.

When Mohammed's capturers reached a safe distance, they used his own detonator to set off the lining of explosives under his clothing, destroying, Mohammed, the van, and all proof of the assassination attempt. Although he had failed in his mission, Mohammed Salaam martyred himself at the age of twenty with the help of the Ghanaian Secret Service and BOI's special security. Salaam's seventy-two virgins and eternal life awaited him in heaven, or so he believed.

When President Bonswah reached the stage, he was greeted with a roar of applause and adulation from the sea of thousands. The first ten minutes of his speech eulogized the late president and sang his praises, albeit begrudgingly. However, the last twenty minutes of his speech were the most honest and genuine sentiments he'd ever given, and he'd not cleared it with his advisers or speechwriters. After discovering the plot on his life and the subversive elements surrounding Ghana's oil, President Bonswah decided to amend his speech by making it a call to action.

"My fellow Ghanaians," Bonswah roared, "as I stand here today and look over your radiant faces, you inspire me like a pious man in a house of God. You are a people whose patriotism, honor, and dedication should never be taken advantage of." After a measured pause, he continued, "However, I am here to regretfully inform you that has not always been the case. Historically, Africa has been exploited for its rich natural resources by foreign interests, both pre- and post-colonialism. These special interests have used our political and tribal leaders to facilitate their bidding. Well, my fellow Ghanaians, I regret to tell you that even to this day, the cynical courtship between special interests and government is still happening in the vilest of ways."

He pushed through his message, not letting the awkward confusion from the crowd disturb him. "Ghana's newest natural resource is the oil recently discovered off our coast. Regardless of the many conflicts it has caused across the globe, oil is still a resource that if harnessed correctly can catapult Ghana into a global economic leadership. However, my fellow Ghanaians, there are crocodiles perched deep in the lake waiting to sabotage our prosperity and growth as a nation. These crocodiles do not care about creating jobs or building your country's infrastructure. No, they are only concerned with one thing—lining their already stuffed pockets with your inheritance!"

The crowd booed and hissed after Bonswah dropped the sobering news. He then motioned for them to calm down and let him finish. "But I bring you good news today, my friends! I am here to announce my first significant decision as president of Ghana. Through careful investigation, I have learned about the many corrupt actions on the part of PetroCo Oil, one of the two leading contenders for drilling our newly found oil. As a result, I gave the executive order to disqualify the company from bidding on the drilling contract for our oil reserves. This means that the remaining company, Freestar Oil, will undergo a thorough and transparent investigation. And if its affairs are in order, Freestar will be granted the contract, which will be a big win for our nation." President Bonswah took a moment to let the crowd sort out its cheers from its hisses and boos.

"I am also insisting that if Freestar Oil wins the contract, it will pay a mandatory tribute of 40% of the annual earnings to Ghana. In addition, Freestar will ensure that two out of three of its trainable jobs must be given to Ghanaian citizens. These terms are nonnegotiable. I've already spoken with Freestar's chairman, and he has agreed to comply. This should net Ghana an annual infusion of $30 billion, which is $11 billion more than we would have received from PetroCo. This deal will also create fifty thousand new jobs—or thirty-four thousand more jobs than PetroCo would have created."

With an air of confidence, he concluded, "My fellow Ghanaians, the terms of our own assets will no longer be dictated by others; we will do the dictating. If the West accuses us of socialism, let them do so. We still know who we truly are. Because the days of unregulated global trade have left us with nothing but a sore bottom!" Then with a surge of adrenaline, he yelled, "Nyame nhyria Ghana! God bless Ghana!"

One would have thought the Black Stars had won the World Cup the way the crowd repeated, "Nyame nhyria Ghana!" louder and louder. Villagers ten miles north of the rally could hear the vibrations from the crowd.

President Bonswah had more to say, but was smart enough not to interrupt Ghanaians buzzing with patriotism. Instead of trying to quiet the crowd, he joined them and continued to lead the chant on the microphone, "Nyame nhyria Ghana!"

≈

The morning after Joseph was visited by Abdul, he stood at the sink and shaved with heightened focus. After shaving, Joseph washed the excess shaving cream off his face and studied himself in the mirror. He was successfully building up the courage to go through with his plan. After Joseph finished, he drafted a handwritten letter to insert into the package from Abdul he had to deliver to President Bonswah. He also made a copy of the letter for his journal. Since his early days as Amoako's top aide, he'd been documenting his years with the administration. Joseph had

258

just put the finishing touches on his final journal entry. He packaged it up and addressed it to Patricia Young; the journal was his last installment of source material for his friend Patricia to use in her book.

Joseph's meeting with President Bonswah was brief but served its purpose. After small conversation, he handed the package off to the president, insisting it not be opened until he left. After leaving Bonswah's office, he called Abdul Mulinesbar and said, "I have delivered the gift to President Bonswah."

Abdul's reply was simple. "Good, now stop by Brojode and pick up your money and instructions. Don't be late, don't even stop to use the bathroom. Do you understand?"

"Yes, I do," Joseph remarked, although he was lying. Joseph knew if he went to Brojode, he was as good as dead; he was smart enough to know Ishmael considered him a liability. He'd already delivered the "bribe" to Bonswah and had informed ALA of the mission to assassinate President Bonswah if he refused Ishmael's bribe. Joseph knew they would rather kill him than pay him. As afraid as Joseph was to cross the Ishmael Group, he was more disgusted with the idea of blatantly betraying his country by helping them assassinate President Bonswah. Since the night Abdul visited Joseph, something Abdul said shamed him: "I've learned that everybody in this god-forsaken country of yours has their price, and I doubt Bonswah is any different."

If Joseph had been asked a month ago whether such a comment offended him to the point of risking his life by attempting to do the right thing, he would have seen death facing him down and disagreed. But, somehow the Ishmael Group morally offended him. The next morning, and unbeknownst to Abdul, Joseph made other plans. Before he delivered the package to Bonswah, he removed the $250,000 worth of diamonds, which were the down payment on President Bonswah's bribe, and replaced them with a personal letter. He then put the diamonds in his backpack along with his journal for Patricia Young. In his last journal entry, he gave Patricia instructions to hold on to the journal until she heard from him again.

Joseph was on his way to Kotoka airport, not the Brojode restaurant as instructed. Through an anonymous cell phone Ishmael was not aware of Joseph used e-mail a few days earlier, he'd bribed airport officials and a pilot he knew to have a private plane waiting to take him to his desired destination. Joseph even had the foresight to bribe airport police to intercept Abdul's men following him, before they reached the parking lot. When Joseph entered the airport, he was rushed through the checkpoints with the help of his paid accomplices. He comfortably walked on the plane with only the clothes on his back and a backpack containing his journal and the diamonds meant for President Bonswah. Joseph now had enough money to begin a new life, and he was more than determined to do so.

Joseph had worked for Abna Amoako for six years and quickly learned how to negotiate the world of unscrupulous individuals. So well, in fact, that he'd managed to outmaneuver Anwar Ishmael, perhaps the world's most diabolical mind. Joseph boarded an undisclosed plane that day. Abdul Mulinesbar and Anwar Ishmael would never hear from him again.

Joseph had no way of knowing that his courageous and patriotic service was consistent with his bloodline. It was Joseph's great great grandfather, Private Jean Nyum, who had saved the Asante royal throne in 1900. The brave Fante had leaked the fact that Governor Hughes' British forces were planning to raid the Asante village to steal and desecrate the Golden Stool. With that knowledge, the rival Asante were able to prevent the British plans and save the royal throne.

≈

On the day of Joseph Nyum's visit, President Bonswah quickly becomes bored with unpacking his boxes. He looked at his desk and saw the present he left for him almost half an hour ago. The president smiled and thought now would be a good time to take a break and open his gift, so he unwrapped the present, which was a large manila folder, empty except for a letter. He thought it an odd gift. After reading the first paragraph of the letter, he dropped the package and ran to the window overlooking the parking lot, where Joseph would have parked.

He immediately asked his assistant Sandy to locate Joseph. When she informed him that Joseph had left much earlier, Bonswah hung up the phone, with no idea how to process the information he'd just read. His first inclination was to contact the Secret Service, but he didn't know if he could trust even them now. President Bonswah grabbed his jacket and his secure cell phone and walked outside on the back lawn of the presidential estate to call the only person he knew he could trust.

"Hello, Clinton."

"Mr. President, what can I do for you?"

Although panicked, Bonswah hid his anxiety. "Clinton, are you by yourself right now? Because I have some very sensitive news I need to talk to you about."

"I am, Mr. President."

President Bonswah took a deep breath and continued, "Almost thirty minutes ago, I received a visit from Joseph Nyum, who was President Abna Amoako's top aide for years. Before he said good-bye, he left me a gift that I was to open after he left. Inside I only found a letter, and its contents were shocking. I feel you are the only person I can trust with this information and who could possibly help."

"What was in the letter?" Clinton asked.

"Can I read it to you verbatim?"

"Please do."

Bonswah proceeded to read:

"Dear President Bonswah,

By now, you are opening your present and realizing it is nothing but this letter. I hope after you read it, you will appreciate its value more than what was originally in its place. This envelope was previously filled with $250,000 worth of diamonds, which was a down payment from the Ishmael Group to you in exchange for your endorsement of

261

PetroCo Oil for the drilling contract. The $250K was a small down payment of an overall compensation/bribe of $6 million. Before you were sworn in as president, Anwar Ishmael had been working with President Amoako to award the drilling contract to PetroCo Oil. Until President Amoako's untimely death, it looked as if they would get what they wanted.

You have no way of knowing this, but I've always had tremendous respect for your honest style of politics—more than for the late Amoako, my own boss and mentor. I know you are the type of leader Ghanaians deserve. I like your stark contrast to Amoako and the other politicians like him. Plus you are a fellow Fante. Although betraying the Ishmael Group by writing this letter will undoubtedly put my life in danger, I would rather risk my life than know I assisted in continuing to help corrupt our great country to serve outside interests, such as the Ishmael Group.

You should know, however, that my life is not the only one in danger. If you do not accept Ishmael's bribe, he will have you assassinated on the day you are to give the eulogy at President Amoako's public funeral service. With you dead, the Ishmael Group has already corrupted your successor, Speaker Eddie Mankwah, who would be happy to do their bidding.

They plan to use a member of the Arab Liberation Army. His name is Mohammed Salaam, but this is an alias; I do not know what he looks like. I had to deliver the assassination instructions to his address of Post Office Box #39081. However, I do know that the man will be dressed as a security guard for Nkrumah Plaza and will be posted on the green carpet while you walk to the stage.

I have aided President Amoako in undermining this country for years, however, I draw the line here. I know I cannot fully redeem myself, but for me this is where redemption begins.

Truly Yours,
Joseph Nyum"

Clinton sighed and said, "There are no limits for Ishmael to close this deal." With great hesitation, Clinton decided to divulge more sensitive information to the president. "Mr. President, there is something else you should know."

"Tell me!" the president insisted.

"I recently learned that Anwar Ishmael was behind the assassination of my Uncle Oscar. He used Oscar's son Max as the tool to murder him, because Oscar refused to help deliver the drilling contract to PetroCo. After Oscar died and Ishmael learned BOI would still be endorsing PetroCo, he hijacked one of my Aunt Marguerite's vendor's boats and killed the entire crew including her VP of Imports and close family friend Kofi Jackson. Now you are his final hurdle, and he can't afford to leave you alive."

"What do you propose we do now?"

"Did you tell anyone else of this?" Clinton asked.

"You are my first call, Clinton," Bonswah insisted.

"Good. Let me be your only call; you never know who is on Ishmael's payroll. It could be your own security, for all you know."

"So what's our plan of action?"

"Can you trust me with this matter?"

President Bonswah paused before he spoke. "I think I can. But let me hear exactly what you're proposing before I commit to your plan."

"Of course. What you don't know is I have already set plans in motion to help international authorities neutralize Anwar Ishmael. These plans can't be disturbed. If he discovers them, he will slink into a dark hole and disappear like a lizard. If you don't respond to his bribe, he will assume you are refusing his offer, and the plot to assassinate you will go into effect. I want you to let that happen. However, a team from international agencies will abduct the assassin before he can complete his mission."

Clinton told President Bonswah his plan to use him as bait to capture the assassin Mohammed Salaam. He then gave Bonswah time to process the information before asking, "What do you think?"

"I think it's crazy, but I'm foolish enough to go with it." The president let Clinton hang for a bit before he added, "I want a complete briefing on every detail of the plan. I want to personally vet each and every one of the men and agencies involved in the operation. And most importantly, I want to make sure I won't die."

Chapter 40
Geeni Island
Present Day

On the same day as President Amoako's funeral service, a hit squad of highly trained men were assembled on an unmarked naval raft heading toward a small island two miles away. They were in a different part of the world, a time zone six hours ahead of Ghana. The squad was equipped with a small but powerful arsenal of assault rifles, handguns, grenades, and night-vision goggles. The men sat quietly in their boat throughout the ride to their destination. They were focused on their plan; each man on the raft knew how complicated and dangerous the task ahead of them was.

The squad arrived at the rendezvous point just before midnight. They left one man on the raft to guard it, while the rest trekked up the rocky northern bank of the obscure island. The 8,000 square-foot island hideaway was deserted except for its sole resident and a dozen or so of his entourage, who only appeared several times a year to take refuge. Compared with the owner's other properties, the island compound was modest, but it was still the most expensive property the owner posessed. It sat on a densely vegetated private island for which he paid over $20 million. The owner considered it money well spent, because no one knew the island's location except its most trusted security and his immediate family. He felt safest when at this location, or so he thought.

The hit squad reached the horizontal plain of the island and huddled in a semicircle behind a sand dune as their team leader whispered his final instructions. Each member was assigned a letter and never used their real names in case of capture. On this mission, agent A was the team leader. Agent A signaled for group one (consisting of agents G, H, and I) to splinter off to the western-most checkpoint. He signaled for group two's agents (D, E, and F) to take the central checkpoint, while group three (himself and agents B and C) infiltrated the eastern-most checkpoint.

Group three perched in the bushes on the lower elevation of the eastern checkpoint of the sprawling compound. Only 100 yards of island thicket separated group three from the closest guards. The agents' rifles were equipped with silencers and pointed in front of them, as they slowly moved forward in a linear front until only 30 yards remained between them and the target.

All seemed quiet to agent A, until twenty paces in, when he heard swift yet quiet steps behind him. Not four seconds later, agent C screeched in horrific pain. Agents A and B pivoted to investigate the situation. When they reached agent C, he was being violently mauled by a spotted jaguar, which growled ferociously as it feasted on their comrade. Both agents flinched at the sight of the awesome beast.

"Shoot it!" commanded agent A. Agent B shot the cat in the head and in the heart. As the big beast lunged toward them, it collapsed to the ground. Agent A noted the jaguar wore a collar with the word "Nassett" engraved on it, and he quickly deduced the beast was the resident's exotic pet.

By the time agents A and B killed the jaguar, it was too late to rescue their comrade. The big cat, through a violent combination of claws and jaws, had already fatally gashed agent C's jugular and torso. The sight profoundly shook them both. If their scouting report had indicated a jaguar roamed the premises, they probably wouldn't have believed it anyway. The veteran agents shook their heads in disbelief; this was truly a first, even for them. The two agents awakened from their shock when they heard faint gunfire in the distance; agent A realized groups one and two had engaged the compound's security. Agent A instructed Agent B follow him, but this time they guarded their flank to avoid any further ambush by nocturnal predators.

In the distance, Agent A saw the closest security guard run away from them and toward the gunfire. This followed the plan, which called for the compound guards to

266

move toward the gunfire and expose the least-secured entrance to the compound for group three. They double-timed it to the compound gates, and in an athletic step and hop, they hurled the gate with ease. Upon reaching the compound's rear courtyard, they scurried to the screen door. Agent A worked on the door, while agent B turned guarded their flank. To agent A's surprise the screen door was unlocked, and they quietly crept through the room.

Upon reaching the room's second doorway, they heard footsteps above, running down the stairs and right toward them. The agents took cover in the shadows of two walls bookending the stairway landing. When the guard stepped off the stairs, agent B grabbed him by the throat and covered his mouth, while agent A repeatedly stabbed him with his knife. Agent B threw the guard to the ground, zip tied his wrists, and gagged his mouth—so no one upstairs could hear him dying on the floor while twitching inhumanely.

The agents charged up the stairs to the second level of the compound, since they were assigned to advance upstairs and capture the target. Groups one and two were assigned to keep all of the compound guards occupied on the central perimeter of the compound in a firefight. Agent B led the way as they both tiptoed upstairs. When they reached the next floor, they heard a man running and yelling in Arabic.

At the end of the hallway, agent B confirmed a visual through a cracked bedroom door. He signaled to agent A that the target was spotted. They both tiptoed toward the door. When they reached the door, agent B charged in first, only to be shot in the belly by a man hiding behind the door. Agent B fell to the ground clutching his stomach. Agent A pivoted behind the door for cover, then quickly pivoted around it and let two rounds off into the room.

The shooter on the other side of the door retreated further into the room toward the man he was protecting. Agent A kicked the door open and peeked the nozzle of his rifle into the doorway. The man inside saw the rifle head and shot at the doorway. The bullet hit the door jam, which subsequently ricocheted wood shrapnel into agent A's right eye. The shrapnel infliction wasn't enough to seriously wound agent A, yet it was enough to make him take a knee and emit a loud grunt.

Hearing the grunt, the shooter grinned and moved to finish off his target. When the guard got to the door, he found agent A, kneeling by the door and favoring his right eye. He pointed his gun at agent A and positioned his index finger to pull the trigger. A fraction of a second before pulling the trigger, the guard was hit by a bullet to the scapula; turning around, he saw agent B lying on the floor and clutching his stomach, with smoke pouring out of the barrel of his pistol. The guard, although shot, had a good position on agent B and shot him in the head, instantly killing him. However, he also exposed himself to agent A, who utilized the opportunity to shoot the man in the back of the head without hesitation. The guard fell down in front of agent A, who stood up, stepped over the dead man, and strode into the room. He glanced down at agent B, lying motionless on the floor, already expired.

When agent A looked up, his target Anwar Ishmael was standing in the middle of the room in a bathrobe with his hands in the air. The fierce Lebanese crime boss had stashed himself away on his private island several weeks ago. Given his recent nefarious activity, it had become clear to Ishmael that he and Abdul needed to lie low in the shadows. Ishmael thought there was no better place to hide than his island; however, he now felt a rare moment of helplessness.

Staring at his slain protector on the floor, Ishmael's face now expressed enormous anguish. "You've killed Abdul! You've killed Abdul!" he cried.

Agent A had just killed Abdul Mulinesbar, Anwar Ishmael's most trusted lieutenant and friend. His face trembled with grief, and the magnitude of the situation began to hit Ishmael. He thought Abdul was invincible, ever since the day he rescued him in that Beirut café many years earlier.

Agent A said nothing while scanning the room for any more surprises. Finding none, he gestured to Ishmael and demanded, "Kneel! Kneel on the ground now!"

A defiant Ishmael refused by saying, "I kneel to no one, not even Allah."

"I was hoping you would say that." Agent A rammed Ishmael's face with the side of his weapon.

Ishmael spat blood from his mouth and began to tremble with anger. "Who are you and what do you want from me?" Agent A removed his mask to breathe easier. Ishmael began to speak faster. "Who are you? But it doesn't matter. What is it you need? Money? I can provide for you, but I'll be no good to you dead."

Agent A received a buzz on his radio. It was agent F informing him they had secured the perimeter and all of the island guards had been neutralized. "Very good, F. Have a man sweep the interior and link up with me in the master bedroom."

"Yes sir," agent F replied.

Agent A looked at Ishmael and grinned. "I'm afraid you're all alone in this…"

It took Agent F several minutes to sweep the interior of the compound. As agent F approached the master bedroom, he heard two gunshots and entered to find Agent A standing over his mark. Anwar Ishmael died as soon as his body hit the floor; he was fifty-five years old.

Chapter 41
London, England
Present Day

Patricia Young had been looking forward to her contract negotiations with Quills Publishing. Wisely, she kept her book a secret and made anyone who read it sign a nondisclosure agreement. Not because she didn't want the buzz, but because her book contained sensitive information, and she didn't want to be sued for libel before the book was even published. Patricia's manuscript described how government officials, tribal leaders, and heads of corporations have corrupted Ghana through their policies. In the book, she portrays a negative image of Ghana's wealthy elite and power brokers. The dirt included chapters on the late President Amoako, some of Ghana's influential leaders, professional footballers, members of Parliament, and Osei and Boateng family members.

An unbiased critic would probably deem the book tabloid drivel, but Patricia's integrity as a journalist helped her sleep at night. What most people couldn't know was that Patricia Young had an intimate source, Joseph Nyum, who had worked behind-the-scenes in Ghana's executive branch for years. She vetted the information Joseph gave her to the best of her ability, and for the most part, it all panned out.

Most of her usual contacts refused to go on record to corroborate her findings, though, so the authenticity of her book took an unexpected turn when Joseph decided to give Patricia permission to use his name. Although Quills had already agreed to publish her book, this turn of events gave Patricia the leverage she needed to negotiate the original £100,000 advance from Quills Publishing to £200,000.

Patricia put the finishing touches on her book after President Amoako's funeral. Some of the juiciest tidbits were about Amoako, making the rumors about his abuses in office even more relevant after his death. Patricia knew she would have to resign from the Accra Voice immediately after she inked her book deal. The paper was owned by BOI, which also happened to be her favorite whipping post in the book.

She was well aware the paper would fire her after the book was published anyway. Her £200,000 advance was more than she could make at the Accra Voice over the next ten years. In addition to the substantial royalties she'd earn from book sales, she was comfortable with her decision and felt no need to justify it. Plus, by the time the book hit the press, Patricia would be somewhere other than Ghana; she was leaning toward the Amalfi Coast of Italy, where she'd treat herself to the decadence she'd been deprived of all these years. Daydreaming of designer clothes, wine, and the occasional lover, at the age of thirty-three, she was determined to stop and smell the bouquet.

Jordan Blake and Patricia Young sat in a well-known London restaurant, drinking its finest wine while putting the finishing touches on her book deal. He handed her the pen and presented one last opportunity to decline the deal: "Remember, Patricia, after you accept this advance, your book belongs to us. We own the rights to market it and release it whenever and however the company chooses. You cannot publish a word about anything relating to the book without our permission. Do you understand?"

Patricia Young smiled, nodded, and waved for Blake to pass the papers over to her to sign. "You worry too much, Jordan. I've been waiting for the day I could sign these papers. You don't understand—this isn't just a book deal to me, I'm signing my contract for freedom."

Jordan Blake laughed and raised his glass. "To freedom!" he pronounced.

"To freedom." Patricia giggled.

The two sat at the table and finished their wine, while winding down the conversation. "Well this was a splendid time, Patricia. Unfortunately, this old man must get some sleep. Should I have a car drive you to your hotel?"

"That won't be necessary, Jordan. I'm going to stay

here and enjoy another glass of wine. It's a nice night out, and I'd prefer walking to my hotel. It's only several blocks down the street."

"Very well. Don't worry about your bill; the restaurant will send it to the office. Congratulations. I will see you tomorrow. Good night," Blake said, then he politely kissed her on both cheeks and left the restaurant.

Patricia started on a new bottle of wine after Jordan Blake left, feeling proud of what she had just accomplished. She took great pleasure in every sip of wine. After two glasses, she had to relieve herself. She scanned the restaurant for the ladies' room and made a beeline for it.

Returning from the ladies' room, she would find Clinton Osei waiting for her at the table. Patricia wasn't sure if she'd had too much wine or if her vision was failing her, but the last person she expected to see was Clinton Osei. "May I help you?" she barked. Clinton smiled, prompting her to bark again, "What are you doing at my table?" Patricia sternly demanded as her hands clinched in frustration.

Clinton stepped out of the booth and gestured for her to sit down. "Please don't be alarmed. Let me explain." Patricia reluctantly sat down. Clinton sat back down across from her and waited for her to relax so she would listen. Although far from relaxed, she had calmed down, so Clinton took his chances. "Like you, I too am here on business. BOI is acquiring a London-based company, so I'm in town to sign the papers and button up the deal."

Patricia clarified, "No, what are you doing here at my table?"

Clinton grabbed the bottle of wine and gestured to fill her glass while asking, "Do you mind?" She nodded and Clinton proceeded to fill both their glasses. "As I was saying, BOI is acquiring Quills Publishing. And, yes, that would be the same Quills Publishing you just signed your book deal with."

As if Clinton had blindsided her with an overhand right hook, Patricia was dazed by that news.

Somehow she managed, "That's impossible, Mr. Blake mentioned none of this to me in our discussions."

Clinton laughed. "With all due respect, Patricia, Mr. Blake helped me devise the strategy." She reached in her purse for her phone. "What are you doing?"

"I'm calling Mr. Blake," she replied.

"Believe me, you're wasting your time. Please put down the phone and just listen to me for five minutes, would you?"

Patricia stared at him for almost ten seconds before putting the phone back in her purse. Her head was spinning. How was this happening to her? She thought.

What Patricia didn't know was that her friend and primary source of information, Joseph Nyum, had betrayed her. Three months earlier, Joseph had contacted BOI's public relations director George Boateng and tipped him off to her tell-all book. Joseph was hedging his bets by investing in both camps, a trick he learned from the late President Amoako: play both sides to your own advantage.

Joseph wasn't completely sure why he decided to cut his friend Patricia off at the knees. Some nights, alone in bed, Joseph would shamefully admit to himself it was because Patricia lured him into the "friend zone." Although he'd had the pleasure of an occasional fuck, she would never love him. More importantly, Joseph took delight in sabotaging Patricia's project because he despised the fact she'd pitied and underestimated him. It insulted him, and with this move, he intended to checkmate her.

When George learned of her project, he wanted to sack Patricia on the spot and blacklist her from the continent. However, Clinton insisted he wanted to handle it personally, and indeed, he had. To George's surprise, Clinton let the nosy journalist keep her job, making her oblivious to the fact they knew what she was doing.

Quills Publishing were not a particularly profitable company. Clinton viewed the money he spent to purchase it as hush money. The investment was well worth containing the potential nuisance of the book's publication.

He used the opportunity to press on after Patricia took a generous gulp of wine. "Let's talk about your book, shall we? I actually had the pleasure of reading your manuscript, and I have to admit it made for good reading. There's some very juicy stuff in there..."

"But, let me guess," she interrupted, "you're not pleased with the treatment of you and your family." Patricia was becoming increasingly aggravated by the second.

"I think we both know exactly what your book is: some factual evidence peppered into a heaping bowl of fabrication. Frankly, I find it irresponsible. You haphazardly implicate many people who have a lot at stake."

"You mean people like yourself, Mr. Osei?"

"Precisely, Ms. Young," Clinton snapped back. "However, your false allegations about me and my family are the least of my concerns, which are primarily about the negative perceptions your book would create. Ghana is still a young country with great potential. Outsiders besmirch Africa's image enough; I don't see the point of an insider like you jumping on the bandwagon of the unfair African stereotypes already out there.

Ghana is trying to change those unfair perceptions, and in my humble opinion, I'd like to think BOI is helping the cause. We're invested in Ghana's image, Ms. Young, as superficial as that may sound to someone like you. Debunking the negative myths about doing business in Africa is critical for our continent's success. The problem with your book is that it threatens to deflate the momentous strides this country has made in improving its credibility in foreign markets."

Patricia attempted to defend her book. "I don't see it that way..."

Clinton cut her off with extreme prejudice. "Our first order of business with Quills Publishing is to bury your book; it will never see the light of day."

Patricia's eyes widened and her hands began to tremble. "You can't get away with this. My lawyer will fuck you for this!"

"Patricia," Clinton replied in a calm, smug voice, "my team of lawyers will have your drastically under-resourced lawyer tied up in injunctions for years. As a journalist, you should know the reality of suing a man with my resources; it's not worth it."

Patricia's nerves now reached a fever pitch. "You are a devious man, Mr. Osei. More than I could ever have imagined. On the one hand, you try to put on your 'African-American knight-in-shining-armor' nonsense with that smug air of integrity. But you're just as disingenuous and selfish as the politicians you and your family conveniently lecture to about ethics and morality. Your only concern is protecting your own self-interests."

Patricia's swift combination of insults stung Clinton. A small part of him wanted to congratulate her on the candor, but the majority of him just wanted to smack the audacity out of her.

Clinton eagerly vocalized his thoughts on her hypocrisy. "You claim I'm looking out for my own self-interests? This is true, but who isn't? You? Hardly. At least my self-interests include the prosperity of working-class Ghanaians. You sit here in all your self-righteousness and lecture me on protecting my self-serving interests? Do you know how many men and women's jobs BOI are directly and indirectly responsible for, Ms. Young? It's in the tens of thousands.

"You speak of self-interest when you just signed a ridiculously high-priced book deal? A book I might add, that sabotages the advancement of the very country for which you claim empathy. And from what I understand, you're planning to move to London or Rome when the book is published—so you can leave the country you just shat on and never have to face the backlash?" Clinton's admonishment of Patricia was effective because he genuinely disapproved of her agenda. He finished with, "You belong in London, because you're a tabloid hack masquerading as a legitimate journalist."

A livid Patricia spat in her wineglass and pushed it

toward Clinton's side of the table. "I couldn't care less about your assessment of me on any level," Patricia retorted. "There is no way you bury this book and leave me high and dry without me kicking and screaming the entire way! Are you fucking mental?"

Clinton, realizing he might have increased the negative rhetoric, calmed down so he could present a productive resolution. "Nobody said we were going to leave you high and dry. I'm a fierce competitor, but I'm not heartless. We are prepared to pay your original advance of £100,000 along with an additional £1 million for what you might have received in royalties. I believe this is a generous offer. If you take it to court, I guarantee you will end up with substantially less than what I'm offering you right now."

"Do you think I'm going to stand for this, Mr. Osei? You throw a little bit of money at me and I'll give up?"

Truly concerned that she was making an unwise business decision, Clinton took off his competitor hat and put on his empathic-counselor hat. "Patricia, firstly one point one million pounds is not a little bit of money. Believe me when I say this is your best deal. You signed the contract, and we can do whatever we want with your book. You won't be able to win in a court of law, and even if you could, it would bankrupt you in the process. Not to mention my cousin George will dedicate himself to making sure you don't work in any journalist capacity in any country whatsoever; you won't even be able to deliver papers when he's done with you. You're trying to make it about you versus me. Don't let your pride get in the way of your brain," he said as he winked at her. "You'll get the best of me sometime in the future anyway, I'm sure of it."

Patricia tapped her middle and ring fingers on the table while focusing all of her attention on him. She prided herself in her ability to detect when someone was bluffing, and he showed no signs of it. It took her over a minute before she stopped staring at him and could speak again with some additional clarity. Unclenching her muscles and trying to relax her nerves, her normally unwavering psyche

276

needed to become amenable to compromise. Despite her idealistic persona, Patricia Young was a pragmatist to the core. This side of her took over. "So you're telling me you'll pay me £1.1 million to settle this matter with you?"

"That is correct," Clinton confessed. He pulled out his billfold and said, "I already have the check made out to you, Ms. Young." He handed Patricia the check. She opened and read it, while feeling tears begin to seep onto her pupils. They were not tears of joy, sadness, or anger—rather a mixture of all three. She lifted her chin into the air in an attempt to force the tears back into their ducts. When her chin came back down, she wiped her cheeks and in her pathetic attempt at deadpan humor proclaimed, "Well, I think champagne is in order."

Clinton smiled, as he was relieved to see her transition. He gestured the waiter over and ordered a bottle of Krug Clos du Mesnil. Halfway through the first bottle, she loosened up. By the end of it, they agreed another was in order. Patricia studied Clinton while he ordered the champagne. She was ashamed to find herself enamored with him after what he had just pulled. The man had the looks of a character actor and the confidence of a leading man. Strangely enough, her vulnerability was transitioning into attraction. Later in her journal, she would liken the feeling to that of a lioness unwillingly dominated by a male lion crowned king of the pride. With each sip of champagne and each passing minute, Patricia grew friendlier toward Clinton.

Since the negotiation ended, Clinton allowed himself to rediscover the attraction to Patricia he'd noticed the first time they met. As if he'd changed contact lenses, Clinton's eyes softened toward her, and she once again intrigued him. "How about more food...and while we're at it, more champagne?" Clinton proposed.

Feeling a little embarrassed, Patricia said, "I should get going."

Clinton detected that he may have humbled his opponent more than he'd hoped. He tried to reassure her with, "If it makes no difference to you, I'm going to order some food anyway—more than enough for two people. I recommend you join me. I can actually be enjoyable company, given the right circumstances. Let me prove it to you."

Patricia stayed at the table and replied shyly, "Okay, a little bit of food and another glass of champagne, then I need to sleep."

Clinton softy clapped his hands once and quickly separated them saying, "That's all I ask."

The next two and a half hours passed quickly. They forged through two bowls of mussels, a plate of Carpaccio, two entrees and another bottle of champagne; he was impressed with her consumption abilities. The two of them were now champagne drunk and enjoying each other's company. Their intense skirmish hours earlier seemed like it occurred months ago. One of the servers approached their table to inform them the restaurant would be closing shortly.

"Where the hell did the time go?" he asked.

"Apparently with the bottles of champagne and bowls of mussels."

He handed the server his card, and while waiting for the bill, scrambled to find an excuse to leverage more time with her. "Would you like to take a ride with me around central London? It's captivating at night," was all he could come up with.

She smiled and since knowing him, this was the first time he'd shown any insecurity. She agreed to Clinton's request but first acknowledged, "Why does this sound like a poor decision?"

They were in the limo for less than two minutes before their mouths met. He clutched her face with both hands to maximize every movement of their lips and tongues. Like an inexperienced high school couple, they clumsily smooched for a while before synchronizing their mechanics into an acceptable rhythm. They moved onto sensual heavy petting that quickly transitioned into crass pornographic groping. Patricia eased into her seat, slipped off her sandals, and let her skirt hike up her thighs.

278

She raised her bare leg over his lowered shoulder. He grabbed her ankle on his shoulder and held it there while his lips glided down her beautifully dark slender leg and thigh until he reached her lace panties. Before he made any assumptions and went for the gold, his eyes locked onto hers. She smiled because his pause exposed an unfamiliar innocence about him. It was this nuance, out of all of the other physical activity that aroused her the most. She sat up to kiss him one more time on the lips. Then while still looking him in the eye, she arched her back to make it easier for him to remove her underwear—effectively giving him permission to do as he liked.

Chapter 42
Various Worldwide Locations
Earlier in the Year

Felix Grucier's portfolio of hits included heads of state, religious leaders, CEOs of blue-chip companies, and garden-variety nobodies. He killed without prejudice and had many methods for disposing of his targets. An employer once described him as "the carpenter of assassins" for his ingenuity and craftsmanship when fabricating elaborate mechanisms to gain unfair advantage over his marks.

One night in Mozambique, Felix found himself confined to a 10' long by 6' high and 4' wide crawl space hidden between two walls of a hotel hallway. It was what he referred to as his "hunter's blind." The previous week, Felix posed as a guest and rented the same hotel room his mark was scheduled to occupy. As a guest in room 783, Grucier fashioned his hunter's blind from the outside in. Once the blind was constructed, he returned to it a week later to hole up there until he deemed his mark defenseless. Essentially, Felix turned the hotel room into a glorified spider's web.

The crafty hit man set up this particular blind in the southwestern corner of the hotel room. That vantage point gave him a view of 65% of the room, minus the bathroom. Felix waited for his subject for what seemed a fortnight, and he was losing patience. His goal was to have no use for his adult disposable diaper, and he vowed not to leave the blind until his mission was accomplished. Felix practiced his breathing exercises to take the edge off the claustrophobic-like conditions.

Maybe the breathing exercises worked too well, because Felix managed to fall asleep. When he awoke, he was briefly startled that he had forgotten exactly where he was. It was one of the rare times in his prolific career the assassin for hire was starting to doubt his game plan. He took pride in his discipline, and dozing off on the job was the antithesis of discipline. Felix turned on his scope's night vision and quickly inserted it through the peephole into the dark room. The mark was alone and asleep in bed. Looking at his watch, Felix estimated the man had been asleep for an hour; this was his moment.

He squatted on the floor of his blind until his butt touched the ground. The custom-built door was fabricated to be seamless and undetectable from inside the mark's room. He quietly pushed it open with his feet and scooted into the room using his heels, butt, back, and elbows. Once fully inside the room, he rolled onto his stomach and army-crawled farther to the subject's bedside. Quietly, Felix rose from the floor and stood over his subject, making sure it was the right man. Indeed, it was his target, Ghana's President Abna Amoako, who rested quietly in his bed fit for a king.

Felix unsheathed the syringe from his kit; it held a deadly cocktail that would cause several of the president's organs to go into shock and fail. Felix pulled down President Amoako's shirt collar to expose his skin for injection. With care, he slowly pricked the needle and emptied the contents into Amoako's vein. Subsequently, the president's body jerked violently and then twitched until he lay lifeless.

Grucier placed his finger on the man's neck to check for a pulse; there was none. Knowing his job was complete, Grucier knelt next to Amoako's bed and coiled himself much like a serpent. He then lay on his belly and slowly uncoiled his body, as he carefully slithered back into the dark hole from which he'd emerged. When fully retracted into his blind, Felix secured the cover. He crawled backwards into a narrow hallway leading to a vertical gap, the floor's laundry shoot and his escape exit. Felix exited the hotel, leaving virtually no trace of his presence. It wouldn't be until years later, when the hotel commissioned an exterminator to address its rodent problem, that anyone would discover Felix's hunter's blind in room 783.

Several hours after Felix's visit, President Amoako's assistant Joseph Nyum tried to wake him for his breakfast, only to find his lifeless body in the bed. Unsurprisingly, the doctor on the scene pronounced a stroke as the cause of death, and the unmotivated coroner failed to detect the tiny prick mark on Amoako's neck. The virtually unknown assassination of President Abna Amoako would go down as Felix Grucier's crowning achievement and one of the best-kept conspiracies in history.

≈

Unbeknownst to the newly appointed President Kweku Bonswah, he was not the first person to inform Clinton Osei of President Abna Amoako's death. Two hours earlier, Roland Dufrane had visited Clinton in his home. While washing his face, Dufrane gave him the news. "The broker just phoned me."

Clinton's belly tightened with anxiety. "And?"

"President Amoako passed on schedule and, so far, with no missteps."

Clinton's stomach relaxed. He grabbed a hand towel and wiped the water from his face. Not turning his body, he spoke to Dufrane's reflection in the mirror. "And our asset, Grucier? He's paid in full?"

Dufrane nodded and explained, "I anonymously deposited the money at the drop location specified by the broker. Our asset has no idea we were the contractors."

That was the riskiest $10 million I ever spent, Clinton thought. He thanked Dufrane and sent him on his way. Clinton remained in front of the mirror examining himself; he recognized his face but not the person behind his eyes. The BOI executive had sailed into uncharted territory. No one ever asked Clinton if he were a vengeful man, so he hadn't contemplated the thought, until that moment. As he took stock of himself in the mirror, he realized he was beyond vengeful. He was, in fact, wrathful.

Clinton could not pinpoint the exact moment he found it necessary to start imitating God. The decision to assassinate President Amoako was shrewd. He only consulted Roland Dufrane to ensure that, if discovered, his other associates could claim plausible deniability. From Clinton's perspective, Amoako was an intestine-dwelling

282

disease in Ghana, a parasite lodged in the bowels of government, gorging until it caused debilitating damage to the host. By Clinton's estimation, the best way to cure the illness was to surgically remove Amoako, the parasite.

With Amoako gone, Ghana stood to reap the immediate benefits, the biggest of which was Kweku Bonswah sworn in as the new president. Bonswah was a unique politician for the region and a complete contrast to Abna Amoako. Through a newly appointed President Bonswah, Clinton could put a positive end to the oil-drilling issues. As he'd predicted, Bonswah eventually removed PetroCo Oil from the selection process and awarded the contract to Chinese-based Freestar Oil a deal that could potentially propel Ghana into the upper echelons of the global economy.

≈

President Amoako's death wasn't the first time Dufrane outsourced the services of Felix Grucier for BOI affairs. Several months earlier, he'd requested Felix's services through their broker to execute the Somali pirates who'd killed the Temateng Agricultural cargo-boat crew and Kofi Jackson. It was a special request from Clinton's Aunt Marguerite, and he gladly obliged. In terms of logistics, the pirate job was minimal for a man of Felix's talents—he only charged $1.4 million for the job, paling in comparison to the $10 million price tag for the Amoako hit.

Felix enjoyed the pirate project. Through contacts with one of his American weapons dealers, he utilized U.S.-engineered drone technology to build his remote-controlled IED, a speedboat designed with enough explosives to obliterate everything within a 20-yard radius. The pirate job nearly cost Felix more than it earned, but he was less interested in the money. It was about the craft, a statement to his colleagues: "I am stepping up the game. Follow me if you can." When Clinton heard about Felix's ingenuity in disposing of the Somali pirates, he instructed Dufrane to offer him the Amoako hit, an offer Felix's brain told him to decline but his ego demanded he accept.

≈

Then there was the demise of Anwar Ishmael. While orchestrating the killing of Ishmael was personal to Clinton, he also considered taking out the Lebanese crime boss an act of self-defense. Ishmael had clearly proven he had no problem killing everyone Clinton cared for—simply to sustain his greed. Fortunately for Clinton, Ishmael dismissed him as a naïve civilian with no resolve. Not to mention, Ishmael was ignorant about the tools Clinton had at his at his disposal.

Clinton's most effective tool was Roland Dufrane and his contracted Special Forces, who were some of the most elite private soldiers on the planet. It also didn't hurt that Dufrane had become obsessed with avenging the death of his friend and client, Oscar Boateng. Ishmael's biggest vulnerability was closer than he could have imagined via his son-in-law Coufis Zatan. It never occurred to him that Coufis, whom he constantly rejected as a serious man outside of world-class football, would have the opportunity to ruin him. It was through Coufis that BOI learned of Ishmael's possible whereabouts. When Dufrane was given Ishmael's location, he insisted to be allowed to contract the combat unit that would handle the maneuver. Clinton easily agreed to Dufrane's request.

Anwar Ishmael's body was found twenty-four hours after Dufrane's tactical hit squad assassinated him, Abdul Mulinesbar, and their goons on Ishmael's private Geeni Island. Through an anonymous broker, Dufrane bribed a crooked Interpol officer to take credit for the raid and death of Anwar Ishmael. It was a topic of international news, and the beauty was that no one suspected the clandestine BOI committee of having anything to do with it.

Although Ishmael's men were brutal thugs, they were no match for highly trained mercenaries of Dufrane's caliber. Collectively, Dufrane and his men (whom he had labeled agent's A through I) had over a hundred years of combat experience among them, and they displayed their lethal expertise on that triumphant night on Geeni Island. However, victory did not come unscathed as Dufrane, still mourned the casualties of his victory: one of his agents was shot in the neck by Abdul Mulinesbar and another was violently mauled to death by Nassett, Abdul's pet jaguar.

Dufrane, aka Agent A that night, took comfort in knowing Ishmael died an unflattering death. Before executing Ishmael, he imparted the fact that his execution was ordered by Clinton Osei for the deaths of Oscar Boateng, Kofi Jackson, and Sophia Rashaan. This news came as a complete insult to Ishmael, since his demise would come from Clinton Osei, who was a criminal by no one's estimation.

Clinton's Machiavellian behavior didn't stop at murder; his involvement in Ghana's new oil industry was also unscrupulous. After agreeing to advise the selection committee after Oscar's death, BOI could not enter the oil business or it would be a conflict of interest. However, Clinton was too shrewd a businessman to miss capitalizing on the country's oil agenda. Without telling a soul other than his accountant in New York, Clinton bet on himself and his belief that he could deliver a successful contract. Anonymously, Clinton bought $20 million worth of Freestar Oil stock.

Fast-forward to many fiscal quarters later, when Freestar was awarded permission to drill Ghana's oil reserves; its stock skyrocketed and so did Clinton's investment. Never one to let his good-guy image cloud his business judgment, Clinton's anonymous $20 million Freestar stock purchase would gross him nearly $70 million after taxes. He treated the $70 million like Vegas winnings, but more responsibly, and shared the wealth by awarding across-the-board bonuses to all essential and nonessential BOI staff.

Clinton was also determined to dedicate his rogue investment earnings to a constructive cause. In remembrance of his late Uncle Oscar, he gifted the majority of his Freestar profits to the newly branded "Oscar Boateng Initiative for Scholarship and Investment." The nonprofit's agenda had already been authored by Oscar before his death, just not in the framework of a formal foundation. Clinton and the trustees of the foundation saw to it that they fulfilled each of Oscar's philanthropic interventions to the best of their abilities. For instance, in its infancy, the well-endowed foundation had already allocated tens of millions of dollars to academic scholarships for poverty-stricken students with college aspirations.

Additionally, the foundation contributed $50 million to spur industry and economic opportunities for underemployed Ghanaians. By expanding opportunities like the BOI micro-loan program, the foundation sought to cultivate a more savvy class of native entrepreneurs. Clinton also planned to implement one of Oscar's more ambitious interventions: to dramatically change the landscape of the country's textile industry by subsidizing the construction of regional garment-manufacturing facilities, which would be owned and operated by locals. Oscar believed that by utilizing Ghana's affordable, skilled labor, they could offer competitive textile pricing and attract business in the global marketplace. Through this foundation, his name was now immortalized and attached to a cause that represented the kind of man Oscar Boateng was and his values.

The barbarians were past the gate; in fact, they were in the building. On February 24, 1966, while President Nkrumah was on a state visit to North Vietnam and China, his government was overthrown in a military coup led by Emmanuel Kwasi Kotoka and the National Liberation Council. The coup of 1966 (code named "Operation Cold Chop") began a tradition of bloody military coups that took place over the following fourteen years. The series of coups would claim the lives of some of the newly formed republic's founding fathers. For instance, only a year later on April 17, 1967, a failed coup attempt (code named "Operation Guitar Boy") involved junior officers of the reconnaissance regiment based at Ho in the Volta Region. After heavy fighting, Lt. Moses Yeboah killed Emmanuel Kotoka, father of the 1966 coup. Yeboah would later be tried and executed by a military tribunal.

Although the military contingent in charge of "Operation Cold Chop" wasn't very experienced, it received tactical support from the CIA, thereby ensuring its success. Reginald Johnson was personally assured by Chester Caldwell, the lead CIA agent in Ghana he'd met nine years earlier, of his safety during the transition of power. But Reginald wasn't taking any chances; he'd already made arrangements for his two daughters and son Oscar to take refuge in Sierra Leone until things settled down in Accra.

After stopping by his office to retrieve travel money stashed in his hidden wall safe, Reginald jogged down the stairs leading to the parking garage, where Agent Caldwell waited for him in a black Mercedes sedan. Caldwell promised Reginald he would personally escort him to the clear port to safely catch a flight to Freetown, a city he hadn't visited since he'd left at the age of fifteen.

With no additional security detail, Reginald and Agent Caldwell drove through the chaotic streets of the capital city. The diplomatic tags on Caldwell's Mercedes gave them immunity as they drove through the dumpster-burning corridors of downtown Accra. From an outsider's perspective, the mobs roaming the streets on the eve of the coup were terrifying; however, as an insider, Reginald was not worried. He knew they were in no danger because Accra's residents viewed the coup as an excuse for the hooligans to party with reckless abandonment. Reginald was confident they would not be bothered as long as they kept their heads low and kept moving.

When Reginald and Caldwell pulled into the grounds of the clear port, the commuter plane on the runway was gassed up and its propellers were spinning. Their car pulled 25 yards away from the plane, while another sedan waited closer to it.

"Good," Caldwell said, "our liaisons are here." As the men got out of the car and walked toward the plane, the other car turned on its high beams, effectively blinding them. Caldwell was highly annoyed by this amateurish behavior. "What the hell are you doing? Turn off those goddamn lights!" he yelled.

The agent became more irritated when the two men ignored his irate request. The man from the passenger's side walked to Caldwell, while the other walked to Reginald. Caldwell squinted to make out their faces, but the lights were too bright. Agent Caldwell never identified the man walking toward him because two bullets were emptied into the side of his head. A startled Reginald dropped his bag and put his hands in the air. The second man pointed a gun at him, while the man who killed Caldwell walked behind Reginald and handcuffed him.

The assailants were two African men dressed like British intelligence officers in their tan, tailored suits. Their chiseled faces featured brownish-green eyes that seemed to light up against their dark, almost navy-blue, skin. Reginald gathered that they weren't Europeans or Americans or even pure Ghanaian, for that matter. Rather, they were a Ghanaian hybrid with their dark skin, green eyes, skinny noses, and tribal scarification marks.

Reginald was seated in the sixth row from the cockpit. The assailants put their guns away and unlocked Reginald's handcuffs. The kidnappers handled him with kid gloves; he was not bumped once during his transport through the small plane, which took off shortly. Once in the air, the man who killed Caldwell walked from the back of the plane and handed Reginald a cocktail. He looked at the glass and then at the man, who smiled because he knew what Reginald was thinking. "Don't be alarmed. It's a gimlet: three parts martini and one part tranquilizer," assured the man, who spoke English with an almost East African accent. "It won't kill you; it will just put you to sleep long enough for the plane ride."

"Where are we going?" Reginald asked.

"You will know in due time," said the man, Reginald, "but for now, just drink."

When Reginald awoke, he found himself in a comfortable king-size bed draped with mosquito netting. The wide panoramic frame windows in his room were open, overlooking a marvelous cliff-side view of a tropical beach and crystal-blue water. One look at the vegetation and coastline, Reginald knew he was no longer in West Africa, but he couldn't tell if he was dreaming or possibly even dead.

Before he could get out of bed, the two kidnappers walked in the room. One instructed Reginald, "Get dressed and meet us downstairs at the car."

When Reginald got into the car, he was instructed to put on a blindfold, which he did cautiously. The car ride took eight minutes. After parking, he was escorted into a room, seated in a chair, and the blindfold removed. His two kidnappers stood next to him, while a woman perhaps in her mid-forties sat in front of them.

The woman smiled at Reginald as she said, "Welcome to the Seychelles islands, Mr. Boateng."

"Seychelles?" Reginald asked. This was confusing because the Seychelles was off the coast of East Africa, just north of Madagascar in the Indian Ocean. He was thousands of miles away from home. The woman continued, "My name is Ama Asamu. I am granddaughter to your late Asante king Prempeh I."

"Impossible," Reginald replied without flinching.

Asamu maintained her smile. "At the turn of the century, the British authorities invaded Kumasi and arrested Prempeh, his parents, his younger brother (the heir apparent Prempeh II), and several Asante elders. Women, children, and attendants were also taken captive by the British. As you know, Prempeh and his entourage were then exiled to the Seychelles, where he lived until his return to the Gold Coast after his pardon in 1924. However, people tend to forget that Prempeh left a legacy in the Seychelles. If you listen to the dialect in this part of our island, many of its residents speak Twi. That is because some children of the exiled Asante were left behind to maintain the colony here. Children like me, Mr. Boateng."

Reginald had many questions but, not knowing where to begin, he just sat quietly and let her continue. "Our existence is kept secret from most Asante; King Prempeh wanted it that way. When Prempeh returned to Kumasi, he was mortified by the careless manner in which the Golden Stool was being cared for. Although it was in secrecy, the guardian was less precautious than the chief expected. Prempeh stripped the guardian of the stool and instructed the royal throne be secretly transported here to the Seychelles, where it still remains in a sacred hiding place.

"My small group of siblings and cousins are secretly referred to as the Abohyen Klan. Whenever the stool is needed for a rare mainland appearance, as its commissioned guardians, we handle the transportation and guarantee its safety. In return, we are supported by revenues from the Asantehene for our livelihood and training. Currently only eleven living souls know of this; you make twelve."

Reginald did not know how to process this information, so he asked the first question that came to mind, "I thought the Golden Stool had to stay on Asante's soil?"

"It is," Asamu assured. "During Prempeh's exile, he deemed his village in the Seychelles as official Asante territory. The seat you now sit in, Prempeh once sat in over fifty years ago."

"What does this have to do with me?"

Still maintaining her smile, Asamu continued. "Before Prempeh's death, he made plans to reinitiate the guardianship program back to the mainland Asante. The guardian must oversee the stool's upkeep and its safety during transportation. He believed that you, Reginald, should be the next guardian of the Golden Stool. Prempeh wished for the stool to remain in the Seychelles. Next to the Asante king and the Queen Mother, the guardian is the highest title among our people. The guardian tells no one else of his knowledge of the stool. And if the guardian mismanages his duty in any way, he can be punished by death."

Asamu allowed Reginald to let that sink in before she continued, "Although Prempeh gave us instructions to appoint you the new guardian, he insisted that it not happen until you were in the twilight of your years. Right before his death, Chief Prempeh assigned two men from the Abohyen Klan to watch over your every move, although you were unaware of them. Over the years, those people have quietly shadowed your daily movements. Today your guardian angels are my twin cousins, Kwaku and Oyoku— the men who stand beside you now."

"Guardian angels?" a cross Reginald lamented while pointing to Oyoku. "That one killed my CIA contact Chester Caldwell last night on the runway!"

She nodded. "Ah yes. CIA Agent Chester Caldwell. Your friend Mr. Caldwell had plans to deliver you to the plane safely, all right. However, once your plane reached 40,000 feet, he had arranged to have it shot down by a mercenary fighter jet. Your knowledge of the CIA's involvement in "Operation Cold Chop" could not be risked. He was going to eliminate you that very night."

"And how do you know this?" Reginald asked.

"Easy. While Caldwell watched you, Kwaku and

291

Oyoku watched Caldwell. Believe me, Mr. Boateng, you were as good as dead."

Reginald was surprised but not naïve. Deep down, he knew Caldwell was untrustworthy. He tried not to dwell on his brush with death and stayed focused on the present. "So what am I doing here?"

"We didn't plan to contact you about your duties to maintain the royal throne for several months. But since your life was in danger now, we were forced to intervene and reveal ourselves."

Reginald looked at Kwaku and Oyoku and nodded his head in appreciation. The men nodded back. At a prompt from Asamu, they grabbed a large case covered in a black drape and set it on the floor in front of Asamu and Reginald. She gestured for Kwaku and Oyoku to remove the cloak. In the case and lying on its side was the authentic Golden Stool in all its glory.

When the royal throne was unveiled, Asamu looked at Reginald with all seriousness. "Do you accept your requested duty as guardian of the Asante throne?"

With an equal amount of sincerity, Reginald looked at her directly and replied, "Yes. If this is what Prempeh wanted, then I accept."

Asamu then proceeded to place a wooden Osudum Chief Priest mask on Reginald's face. "This mask, among other relics were left here by our Asante parents as a reminder of our homeland. Let this mask act as a portal, which will connect our kinship. We are bound with an obligation from our ancestors to protect the Royal Throne. The throne is the lifeblood of our heritage. By the directive of his majesty King Prempeh, I induct the Reginald Boateng as protector of the Royal Throne...The Golden Stool."

A week later, Reginald left the Seychelles and reunited with his family in Sierra Leone. When he returned to Ghana, he did so as the official guardian of the Asante Golden Stool. As guardian, Reginald provided financial security to the Abohyen Klan, who provided the stool's day-to-day security, and kept his knowledge of the stool's whereabouts confidential. Reginald would hold this honorary title until his death fifteen years later. Years after his death, the same honor would be passed on to his first-born Oscar.

Chapter 44
Plane Bound for Kumasi, Ghana
Present Day

The morning after her confrontational turned romantic evening with Clinton, Patricia woke up in his hotel room. Her champagne buzz was wearing off and the guilt was starting to seep in. She was well aware of her compromises from the night before. But given the financial rewards, compromise trumped guilt for once in her life. For the first time in a long time, Patricia felt liberated. She also felt spontaneous. So spontaneous that she agreed to take Clinton on his offer to fly back with him to Kumasi to attend Asante Royals' opening match against the Accra Capitals.

When Clinton and Patricia's plane arrived in Kumasi, a car awaited to take them to the stadium to watch the game. Usually Clinton didn't get excited for sporting events like his cousins George and Jasper, but today he was in a rare celebratory mood. Today's game was significant for several reasons: It was the season's home opener, in which Asante Royals would debut their new, high-profile acquisition, Coufis Zatan. In addition to Coufis' debut, the team's owners were announcing the stadium's new name—the Oscar K. Boateng Stadium, in memory of the late local philanthropist and former team investor, their uncle.

When Clinton and Patricia arrived at the stadium, a handful of security guards escorted them to their box suite. Awaiting them were his cousins George and Jasper, his Aunt Marguerite, Roland Dufrane, Harry Van Bleer, and George's girlfriend, Maria Renterea. The suite's occupants erupted with excitement at their arrival. Like Clinton, they were also high from today's events. Clinton introduced Patricia to the room. Five minutes into the introductions, he left Patricia with Maria so he could have a private moment with George, Jasper, and Dufrane.

As the three men stood at the front of the suite, looking out onto the crowded stadium, they paused their conversation and anticipated Clinton's approach. Clinton smiled at his cousins and gave them each a handshake and a hug. When he reached Dufrane, he went for a handshake, to which Dufrane pulled him in for a hug as well. George gestured towards Patricia, smiled and mentioned, "It looks like Ms. Young took the bad news quite well."

Clinton grinned, shook his head and changed the subject, "Gentlemen it's been one hell of a year."

Jasper piggybacked off the statement with, "Of epic proportions."

Dufrane, raised his cocktail glass to and added, "Epic, indeed."

George, feeling contrite focused on Clinton. "You should know, cousin. I have nothing but respect and admiration for you. I know I've said some things in the past which may have imp…"

Clinton couldn't let him finish. "George, you are the vocal leader of this family; no need to apologize for that. I have thick skin, as do you and Jasper. We'll continue to break each other's balls once and awhile. It's no secret that you took Uncle Oscar's death the hardest, which makes the most sense because of everyone in this family, you embody his spirit the most. But at the end of the day, your ability prevailed and your Intel got us through this thing."

"Believe it or not, George," Jasper chuckled, "BOI is at its strongest when you are fully engaged and not having one of your bratty tirades."

George surrendered a laugh to his brother and followed it with, "Hey, bro what can I say? I wear my fucking heart on my sleeve."

Clinton winked at George and added, "You wear your heart on the barrel of a megaphone."

They all laughed and turned around to observe the good will that filled the room. Marguerite and Harry Van Bleer appeared to be in their own world, as they engaged in a serious conversation highlighted by laughter. Patricia and Maria sat on the suite's comfortable sectional and got acquainted. It was as peaceful a social gathering as Clinton could remember in the last year.

Then as if the god of irony generated a gust of guilt

in the form of the suite's new guest, Azul Ishmael-Zatan entered the room. While Patricia, Maria, Marguerite, Harry, and Azul, for that matter, were oblivious to the significance of Azul's presence, George, Jasper, Dufrane, and Clinton were all too aware of it: Here stood the daughter of the very man the four of them successfully conspired to murder some seven weeks earlier.

Not only was Azul oblivious to the fact that people in her present company were responsible for her father's death, she also had no idea that her own husband had gift wrapped the coordinates (she'd inadvertently gave him) of her father's secret whereabouts, ultimately leading to his demise. She would never know of her husband's connection to her father's death, as Coufis had no problem going to his grave with that information.

To Azul's credit, she was a stoic, almost unaffected mourner. She was genuinely saddened by her father's death, but when she was honest with herself, there was also a sense of relief. Her father's passing was inevitable. She felt that the dark cloud looming over her family's head could finally be lifted. It also didn't hurt that a sizeable sum of her father's accounts were protected enough to serve as her inheritance.

Clinton, George, Jasper, and Dufrane did not succumb to awkwardness; they were expecting this encounter and acted accordingly. George dashed over to warmly greet Azul. He gave her a hug, kissed her on the cheek, and integrated her into the environment. Then, just when the god of irony would seem to be out of tricks, the game's announcer (the game they'd been barely watching) erupted with excitement and declared, "Zatan has trapped the ball on the eighteen....he steams past one defender, two def....he's alone! Strike to the far post....He scores! Gooooal! Coufis Zatan just scores his first goal for Asante Royals....and it's a beauty!" Everyone in the room hugged each other with no regard to their beverages spilling all over their clothes and the floor.

After the victory, Clinton set Patricia up in his late grandmother's estate to get ready for the victory party later that evening. In the meantime, Clinton had to fly back to Accra to tie up some loose ends. Accra was a short plane ride, and he assured Patricia that he'd be back in time to help her with the zipper on her dress.

With his assistant Kwasi, Clinton drove back to the clear port, where they boarded the corporate plane. He made his way back to the sofa, where he and Patricia had made love earlier on their flight from London, and smiled at it endearingly. He thought about his new romantic interest and was embarrassed to admit that in such a short period of time, he may be falling for the trouble-making journalist.

After the plane took off, Kwasi asked Clinton if he could make him a drink; Clinton obliged. When Kwasi returned with the drink, he handed it to Clinton and sat in the adjacent seat. Clinton enjoyed his drink while he conversed with Kwasi. Kwasi's demeanor was always a mystery to Clinton, because although Kwasi was a loyal employee and friend of the family, he'd always kept his distance and observed not only the people in present company, but their surroundings as well. It was almost as if he knew something they didn't.

Clinton marveled at Kwasi's brownish green eyes against his dark skin. As he studied Kwasi's unusual eyes, his own eyes grew heavy, as if he were being hypnotized by Kwasi's. Clinton shook his head and thought, Man, that drink's got a bite. Then he said, "Kwasi! How much liquor did you put in this drink?"

Kwasi smiled and replied, "It is a gimlet, sir. Three parts martini and one part tranquilizer."

An increasingly disoriented Clinton looked around and mumbled, "Tranquilizer?"

"Yes, sir," Kwasi confirmed. "I'm sorry, sir, but it will not hurt you. This is for your safety; all will be explained later."

"Where are you taking me?" Clinton slurred.

The last words he could remember Kwasi saying before he drifted into sleep were, "You are going to the Seychelles islands."